UNEARTHED

FRACTURED BOOK 2

UNEARTHED

FRACTURED BOOK 2

by Keith Robinson and Brian Clopper

Printed in the United States of America
First Edition: February 2016
ISBN-13 978-1530271269

Cover by Keith Robinson

Visit www.WorldofApparatum.com

UNEARTHED

FRACTURED BOOK 2

CO-AUTHORED BY

KEITH ROBINSON

unearthlytales.com

AND

BRIAN CLOPPER

brianclopper.com

PREVIOUSLY . . .

In the eastern city of Apparati, Kyle Jaxx looked forward to receiving a tech implant on his fourteenth birthday. What would the system determine his strength to be? His father was a Grade-A Diagnostics Technician, so Kyle figured he had good genes and would get a reasonable score in Cybernetics. If so, he could finally upgrade his younger brother Byron, whose entirely mechanical body was wearing down.

Unfortunately, Kyle's implant procedure failed—a pitiful 2% score in Robotics and a flat zero in everything else. He had virtually no tech-wielding abilities at all, and with no way to manage even the most basic technology with the power of his mind, he was destined to become what Mayor Baynor called a *deadbeat*, unable to contribute to society in any useful capacity.

The city of Apparati had no room for deadbeats. Kyle's parents were forced to choose his fate: exile to the wastelands known as the Ruins, or an honorable death where his body parts would be preserved for a long list of needy transplant patients.

Naturally, Kyle preferred exile. However, his parents considered that to be a slow, torturous way to die and instead chose *repurposing* on his behalf.

With the aide of his robotic brother and a strange old man, Kyle escaped from the Repurposing Factory at the very last minute. He found the crowds outside willing to help, and with new clothes and a pocketful of cash, he made his way across the city to the Wall at its perimeter. With police cruisers whining through the air, he dropped down into the Ruins and fled to safety among the ancient, deserted alleyways.

But he wasn't safe for long. Gangs roamed the Ruins, and Kyle was soon accosted, losing everything but his pants. He thought it would be less risky beyond the tech ridge where machines and computerized weapons did not work, but he ran into a man named Archie who sought to cut his throat and eat him for dinner! Kyle escaped, stole some replacement clothes, and blundered onward.

All he could do was head east toward the distant Tower and beyond. Maybe the tales were true and there was some sort of civilization out there somewhere. But first he had to rest, and he collapsed in the back of an old, abandoned wagon.

When he woke, the wagon was in motion, driven by that strange old man who had helped him back in the city. After introducing himself as Abe Torren and suggesting that Kyle head directly to the Tower without delay, the man promptly vanished into thin air.

Kyle had no reason to trust Abe. But he had nothing to lose, either. He arrived at the Tower many hours later, and Abe was waiting at the top as promised . . . along with a ghost.

* * *

In Apparata to the west, Logan Orm knew long before Tethering Day that none of the seven spirits would bond with him. He'd faced them numerous times on risky solo expeditions into the Broken Lands, the home of untethered phantoms. Time and time again, they had deemed him untouchable.

Upon turning fourteen, Logan went absent on his Tethering Day. Why bother if it would just publicly expose what he already knew—that no spirits would have him, effectively branding him useless in his rigid society. Determined to forge his own path, he marched out to the Broken Lands on that day of celebration for everyone else his age. His younger brother Kiff followed him and was soon besieged by a Breaker spirit. Being too young to tether and master the volatile spirit, Kiff was locked in an inner battle to best the overwhelming Breaker. Fearing for his little brother's sanity, Logan took him back to the Fixer Enclave.

There he faced a hearing to determine his own fate. Untethered, he was a burden. Only two options existed for rare citizens such as himself: exile to the Broken Lands or death. The sovereign and chancellor, along with Logan's own father, advocated for his demise. They also ruled on Kiff's fate. Those so young risked losing themselves to the stronger-willed spirits, and Kiff posed a danger in his present condition. Logan and his mother pleaded for Kiff's fate and managed to buy him a little more time to fight off the Breaker. However, Logan was imprisoned and scheduled for execution the next morning.

Logan's mother came to him that night and released him from the Pens, handing over a few meager supplies to aid him in the Broken Lands. At least there he'd have a chance at life.

Completely alone, Logan stepped foot into the wastelands, drawn to the one landmark in the deadly ruins that offered any hope: the Tower.

To get there, he outwitted hungry kalibacks with help from sources unknown and fled a swarm of orb scavengers. He trekked through a desolate, ruined city whose history eluded him, then stumbled across a large gathering of untethered spirits huddled along a river, barred from heading westward by some unseen barrier that he easily passed.

A mysterious stranger who called himself Abe Torren directed Logan to continue to the Tower, promising answers to his true place in the world.

After a further kaliback attack at the base of the Tower, Logan raced to the top to find Abe Torren waiting as promised.

Along with a strange, phantom guest.

* * *

Though both Logan and Kyle were physically present at the top of the Tower with Abe, the boys were 'out of sync' and appeared to each other as ghosts.

The old man told the boys of two worlds: the enclaves to the East, and the city to the West. They, too, were out of sync, effectively invisible to each other. Abe explained that Kyle was born in the enclaves and Logan in the city, that their powers were in fact very great indeed, and that they were swapped at birth for their own protection. Now it was time to switch them back and reunite them with their birthplaces.

Abe's specially designed Tower worked its magic on them, slowly phasing them into their opposite realities. Kyle's smog-filled city in the west faded out, and sprawling clusters of houses appeared in the forests and hills to the east. Meanwhile, as everything Logan knew vanished behind him, gleaming buildings rose ahead, tiny machines moving across the hazy sky.

The old man explained that Logan had advanced control over tech while Kyle was adept at tethering to spirits. The magnitude of their abilities would have made them puppets to the corrupt governments if Abe had not acted to safeguard them from an early age. Switched to their new havens, they were ignored throughout childhood simply because they were unremarkable. *Too* unremarkable, as it turned out, for their lack of prowess as they'd turned fourteen had nearly gotten them executed!

Now, because of their actions, both their younger brothers were in serious trouble back home—only there was no going back for Logan and Kyle. They would have to trust each other to save their siblings, for their newfound abilities were needed to bring about a new order and take the first step in repairing the fracture to the World of Apparatum.

* * *

Logan made his way across the Ruins to rescue Byron, Kyle's robot brother. Along the way, he saved a family from a kaliback and discovered he could work tech with extreme control. Meanwhile, Kyle set off to the east, narrowly escaping canyon clackers and nearly drowning in his attempt to cross a raging river. There he found masses of spirits and successfully tethered to all seven types at once.

Just outside of the city, Logan was taken in by the authorities. He took an instant dislike to the corrupt Mayor Baynor, who had slotted Byron for execution for aiding in Kyle's escape. The mayor discovered Logan's versatility with tech and sought to exploit him.

Kyle, gliding into the enclaves from the sky, entered a packed Sovereign Hall to find young Kiff Orm strapped to a chair trying to control an aggressive, overbearing Breaker. With seven spirits of his own, Kyle was soon drawn into a battle of wills with the evil Sovereign Lambost and Chancellor Gretin.

Abe Torren had explained about wink-outs. The two fractured worlds were inextricably linked, and most 'pure' citizens had a twin they never knew existed. The death of one caused the mysterious 'wink-out' of his counterpart. Kyle and Logan were linked—and so were the members of the government.

Logan thwarted Byron's public execution and caused a cybernetic enhancement to explode in General Mortimer's chest. But it was Mayor Baynor's careless use of an Assault Grinder that got the chancellor killed. The mayor himself mysteriously winked out.

At the other end of Apparatum, Kyle's simultaneous struggle in the Hall prompted the half-crazed Chancellor Gretin to stab Sovereign Lambost to death in an effort to protect their dark secrets. And then he vanished into thin air.

After that, exorcising Kiff's unwelcome Breaker was a simple matter.

With the corruption of the two city leaders exposed to the public, the seeds of change were planted in the citizens of Apparati. Logan Orm from the Wild became a hero to all. In the enclaves, Kyle Jaxx of the City was revered for his unheard-of control over all seven spirits, and his ability to recall and channel the memories of the defeated government sparked a wave of unrest and demand for a new, brighter future.

Logan upgraded Byron's old robotic housing to a sleek, modern design. Kyle used his Fixer spirit to mend Kiff's scarred leg. All was well.

Nearly a week later, at opposite ends of the land, Logan and Kyle discovered tunnels under the ground, sparking a new adventure destined to reveal more of the old world of Apparatum . . .

Chapter 1
Logan

As Logan Orm leaned farther into the massive underground chamber for a better look, he felt his brother's grip tighten around his wrist, tugging him back. "It's time to go," Byron whispered in his electronic voice.

Byron's new robotic housing was larger and stronger than the old one, plenty strong enough to yank Logan back.

Below, another world opened up before him. He scanned the large chamber, easily fifty feet deep and twice as wide. It had to be more than a hidden storage space. Not that he could see any of its contents. The doors he had managed to open with his tech prowess had been ceiling mounted and had dropped tons of dirt into the area, swallowing up whatever might have been contained in the underground space.

They stood in an empty lot in a run-down district of the city of Apparati, Logan's new home. It was a strange land. He had apparently lived here for the briefest of times as a toddler before a renegade old man, Abe Torren, had whisked him away to the mythical Tower at the center of the Ruins and switched him with Kyle.

He had very little time before the authorities arrived. While the evil Mayor Baynor and General Mortimer were no more, Mayor Trilmott seemed like a powerless stand-in. That much was clear from the last six days Logan had spent in this city in the midst of upheaval. The mayor took his orders from the Hub and only seemed to have the nerve to speak up when he was out for himself. Logan didn't like him, but he was an improvement on the previous mayor.

He returned to the cold reality before him, ignoring Byron and the sirens for the moment.

Logan reached his mind out and switched on a bank of lights along the wall opposite him. He saw a large shuttered door at the end of the room to his left. The mounds of dirt barely touched it. He delved into the control panel next to the large door, seeking to awaken the ancient tech and open it as well. He noted the door led in the direction of the Ruins, eastward. While he futzed with the unlocking protocols, his mind probed deeper. There was more. Momentarily, he nudged his mind to the east, detecting another door access panel spaced about seventy feet in, still powered up and ready to be used. Could this be an indication of an underground manmade passage?

Logan thought back to the secret file on Abe Torren he had accessed while imprisoned by Baynor. There was a world underneath the two fractured worlds, that mending the two realms above could only happen if something was done with the hidden region below as well. The file had not been complete in all respects so Logan was unclear what needed to be done. He just knew to be mindful of a Guardian and someplace called the Well. If only Abe would pay him a visit and fill him in more, but the cryptic traveler had been a no-show since their encounter at the Tower.

He focused again on the door and its control panel. The sirens of the approaching patrol were much louder now. He cast his mind upward, sensing several squads of soldiers converging on him. They were less than two minutes away.

He briefly fixated on Byron's helm plate, a darker part of the exterior atop his head that was a perfect imitation of an area of hair, but Logan knew its function was of protection and not vanity. Made of a dense molyvillbrite meld, it could withstand extreme pressure.

Byron said, "We have to go. If you do a blind sweep of the neighborhood spy pylons, you can erase us from record. I only detect six. Easy work for someone with your abilities, but you have to do it now before any soldiers show up."

This stirred Logan into action. He wrestled free from his brother's cold metallic grip and sprinted into the middle of the street. Far from the center of the bustling city, this district was a blight. Most traveled on foot or in ancient vehicles belching out foul exhausts. He reached out again and detected the six pylons. He swatted them into submission with a feedback algorithm and looked at Byron. "Done. Let's go."

Byron sprinted past Logan and into a narrow alley, his heavy-duty hydraulics clicking and whirring at a frenetic pace. Logan caught up, and together they veered left into another.

Byron waved Logan under a metal overhang just in time. Above, the thrumming sound of several flying platforms, each a clunky rectangle of hulking metal with a control pedestal mounted at the front and manned by a single soldier, disturbed the relative quiet of this neighborhood on the outskirts.

"You cut it close," said Byron.

He scoffed. "What are they going to do? We're heroes! We liberated the city from two nasty guys."

"It's not that simple," Byron said, his almond-shaped photoreceptors much more human in his new body than the ones in his old.

Even though Byron was eight and Logan fourteen, his little brother looked down on him by about four inches. His upgraded body was built to last well into young adulthood and its larger stature reflected that.

"The Hub gave me a commendation. You were there for the ceremony. What are they going to do to me? I just dug around in an empty lot."

"You unearthed secrets."

"Exactly. They should be used to that." Logan knew he was being a little arrogant, but he was bored, having spent the last three days in a mind-numbing routine of waking up, going to Kyle's old academy, and learning about the history and culture of Apparati when he had already gleaned so much more of it with his frequent dips into the data screen.

"Just be careful," Byron chirped and directed his sensors skyward. He cocked his head slightly. Logan knew he was using his hearing arrays. They were top notch. Logan had done the upgrade himself, so he knew all of his brother's capabilities.

Logan said, "They've landed. I bet they'll be concerned with cordoning off the area before they start searching for the perpetrators."

It amazed him how much cityspeak he had grown accustomed to in the last week. Perpetrators? Cordons? Nothing like that would have come out of his mouth back at the enclaves. There, he might have spoken of plucking clean a durgle for dinner or of building pens using stout twindle branches.

Byron moved out. "We have to be careful."

"I can't wait to get the expedition to Apparata started. Trilmott promised it would happen soon, maybe even next week." The Hub had approved an exploratory trek through the Ruins to reach out to the people of the enclaves, and Logan was in the running to be a key figure in that effort. His experience with the wildly different culture was essential to their success.

Byron took a sharp right and crossed an open street, looking up in case any soldiers hovered overhead. "Use the data stream and figure out when they're really leaving."

Byron pointed to a spy pylon, and Logan quickly wiped it, erasing their presence in its recorded digital memory. They ducked back into another alley, this one filled with far more debris. In some places they climbed over large dunes of trash and discarded old tech.

Logan marveled at what these people threw away. His mind flitted from item to item, engaging with each only briefly. *Even their old stuff is so advanced.* He tinkered with an obsolete skip pack, a device one strapped to their back, allowing the wearer to make giant leaps of thirty feet or so. The one he linked with was damaged, its impact regulator out of sync. Anyone who used it would receive broken bones for sure.

Byron sensed what he was doing. “Stop mucking around and get moving. We need to get back into the flow of people. These streets are too empty. We need to blend in.”

Logan abandoned his tech rummaging and sprinted over two mounds of junk. The Weavers at his enclave could never hope to match the refined metalwork of even the simplest tools and devices found in the city.

They crossed an overgrown greenspace. The parks closer to the center of the city were well maintained. This was practically a jungle. Logan took out two more spy pylons, ensuring their progress would not be noted.

They passed through a small play area, the different structures showing obvious signs of neglect. He was unhappy that so much of the city looked like this. Why did those in the center have so much and the many on the fringe so little? While the Fixer Enclave he called home wasn’t as sleek as much of Apparati, it was well maintained. Of the seven enclaves, only the capitol, the Hunter Enclave, was extravagant, and even that was marginally so. Why was there such disparity here?

“Do you think it will be good for our two worlds to reach out to each other?” Byron asked.

“I do. Things need to be shaken up in both places.” Logan knew that was what Abe wanted. The old man desired the two worlds to realign. Having been out of phase with each other for hundreds of years was a bad thing. Not that the old man had been specific about what would happen if the worlds kept drifting farther out of alignment, but Logan was certain something bad would result.

“And maybe it would stop the wink-outs.”

“Maybe.” Logan didn’t know how it would all work but certainly eliminating the wink-outs would be a good thing.

Ahead, he spied a busy street. They were emerging in a better part of town. Many people walked about, heading out for their morning errands.

"You can probably stop disabling the spy pylons now. We can just mix in with everyone else. I think we're safe now." Byron sped up and stepped into the flow of sidewalk traffic. A few people looked at him, but none recognized him. He had been in his former, rundown robot housing on the day of the execution. It had been broadcast on stream screens throughout the city.

Drastically altering his appearance was of course a necessary part of Byron's complete mechanical overhaul, but he had changed in other ways, too. With faster processing speeds and upgraded software, it had been like discovering a whole new world of previously unattainable data waiting to be plucked out of the air—especially since Logan had quietly lifted the usual built-in security restrictions. With a voracious appetite for knowledge, Byron had been downloading technical manuals almost nonstop since the first day, and his vocabulary, indeed his entire manner, had matured. As a result, it was now very easy to forget he was only eight years old.

But while Byron was almost unrecognizable in his entirely new body, Logan was more likely to be identified. He pulled his collar up and slumped back. Almost everyone had heard of Logan Orm from the Wild, the boy who came from a land beyond the Tower.

Suddenly, a flying platform swept overhead and dropped to the ground in front of them. Two others followed suit. All three soldiers hopped off their transports and pointed their guns at Logan and Byron.

The lead soldier, a man with extra body shielding, said, "Mayor Trilmott wants to see you."

Logan absorbed the crowd's reaction. Everyone retreated. Soldiers were the supreme authority. Those whose implants aligned with this warrior class were not to be trifled with, much like the men and women who tethered with Hunter spirits back at the enclaves.

Logan knew he could override their weapons, but he didn't want to. Already, he heard onlookers syncing their wrist tablets, recording the event. He might be able to block a few of them, but dozens would be hard while trying to evade the soldiers.

"This is concerning what matter, sir?" Byron inquired, keeping his volume low and not at all threatening.

The soldier gave Byron a dismissive look. "Tampering with access to restricted areas."

The tunnels. They must've been caught on at least one of the spy pylons before he had swiped it. And Logan thought he had been thorough.

The soldier glowed a faint yellow. Intrigued, Logan sorted through the tech on his person and found the glow's source. A simple device worn around his collar was creating the low-yield force field. Why did the man have his contagion barrier activated? He quickly saw the other soldiers wore theirs as well. What was going on?

The soldier motioned for them to step onto his platform. "Come with us now. You pose a potential hazard to the citizens around you."

Many in the crowd took a step back and the curious chatter died down. In the silence, Logan became keenly aware of how many eyes were on them.

Logan knew they were better off complying at this point. He stepped onto the vehicle first, immediately detecting the restraint field latch onto him. It wasn't meant to hold him prisoner. It was merely a safety feature of all hovering platforms. The small invisible field would hold them secure as they flew at dizzying speeds, aiding their upright bodies in any changes in momentum and direction. Logan knew it played havoc with Byron's external sensors. He'd be sure to give his little brother a tune-up as soon as they finished their meeting with the mayor. Hopefully, there wouldn't be any surprises.

The citizens caught the police action with their wrist tablets, each sending it on to their network of stream teams, their various social networks. The incident would be public record, something the previous mayor would've tried to suppress. At least Trilmott wasn't trying to hide his actions. If their capture had been covert, then Logan would have something to worry about.

The soldier mounted his platform and took his place in front of the control pedestal. They were high in the sky and zipping toward the city center in seconds.

Logan whispered to Byron, "Let me handle this."

Byron said nothing.

Chapter 2
Kyle

Kyle Jaxx tried to contain his grin as Leet Orm, looking as dazed as the rest of the men and women at the temporary loss of their tethered spirits, raised his flickering torch to the hole. After a moment, the man turned to face the crowd. "There's a tunnel."

"I knew it!" a woman said. "Didn't I say so?"

"But a tunnel to where?" someone else asked.

As voices rose to an excited babble, Mr. Orm patted Kyle firmly on the shoulder, causing a multitude of Breaker spirits to snap ineffectually at him. "Good work, son. Good work."

Kyle felt a thrill of pride. This man was both his biological dad and a complete stranger—and yet he was oddly familiar as well, a doppelganger of the dad he'd grown up with. The two men were wildly different on the surface but exactly the same on the inside. Or maybe it was the other way around.

In any case, Kyle felt the same thrill as when his own dad complimented him back home in the city. He glanced at him and allowed a half-smile to creep across his lips. "No problem, Mr. Orm. I'll be through this wall in no time."

Feeling like he could tear down the manmade structure in a matter of minutes, he flexed his fingers and allowed the Breakers to muster their strength. With fifteen 'borrowed' spirits merged with his own, all somehow contained in his body, grunting and fidgeting restlessly, he knew nothing could stop him now. The surrounding natural rock of the cavern had felt like butter when he'd raked his fingers across it. Breaker spirits had that effect on anything inanimate—it just broke apart, crumbled away. But the smooth, manmade surface behind the natural rock was built of much tougher stuff, somehow able to withstand the pummeling of the strongest Breaker in the enclave. Even so, he'd knocked loose a bowl-shaped chunk and revealed a four-inch hole to the blackness on the other side.

The crowd edged backward as he reached out to widen the hole. The teeming mass of Breakers were unified as he lifted his fist, and he marveled at the combined auras of all those spirits as—

"Stop!"

The voice echoed through the cavern, and everyone swiveled around.

Kyle couldn't see the source of the voice over the heads and shoulders of the adults crowded into the cavern. He did see Kiff, though, and he blinked in surprise. What was he doing here? The eight-year-old boy must have snuck in and weaved his way through.

"What do you mean, 'stop'?" one of the men demanded.

The crowd parted slightly, and the newcomer moved into view. He was one of the sovereign's red-cloaked guards, his hand on the hilt of his sword. Two others followed close behind, their shiny armored chest plates and helmets reflecting the flickering glows from several torches and lanterns.

"Acting Sovereign Durant has ordered that activities in this cavern cease immediately and the place closed down," the guard said loudly.

A murmur spread throughout the chamber. A woman spoke up. "It's okay, we've done it. We've broken through. There'll be no more time wasted. From now on, it's—"

"The sovereign said to clear out immediately," the guard told her. "He specifically said *not* to try and break down any walls."

Mr. Orm puffed up and strode forward. "Now wait a minute. What's going on here? We just made an important breakthrough! We need to explore beyond that wall. Who knows what we might find? The general consensus is that there are tunnels behind that wall, maybe endless miles of them, and if that's true, there might be resources down there that could—"

"None of that matters right now," the guard said, drawing his sword a few inches. The action was noted by all, and a silence fell. The guard stared, his jaw tight and anxiety etched into his forehead. His spirit, a pale-green translucence outlining a creature with narrow eyes and a long snout, rose a few inches from the man's head and shoulders, snarling with jagged teeth. For a moment, the horn on top of its muzzle looked like it projected from the guard's forehead, an odd effect that Kyle had noticed before with these types of spirits. Hunters were fierce predators commonly tethered to armored, red-cloaked guards.

The tension eased a little as the guard pushed his sword back into its scabbard. "Let's not make a fuss, people. I'm just the messenger. Take it up with the sovereign."

"*Acting* sovereign," someone snarled.

There didn't seem to be anything more to say. After a muted exchange of words, the men and women agreed to take a break while a spokesperson—Leet Orm—and a few others went to meet with Acting Sovereign Durant. "You'll find him over at Sovereign Hall," the guard told him.

However, nobody would leave until Kyle had returned their spirits. Somewhat disappointed, Kyle urged his borrowed Breaker creatures to return to their hosts. Some of them went willingly enough, but others lingered, and Kyle had to eject them. The cavern was momentarily filled with a ghostly glow while the spirits soared around trying to find their hosts, and then the light faded. Everybody seemed relieved, some of them patting themselves for assurance that they were once more complete.

When the borrowed Breakers were gone, only his own remained. Kyle felt strangely empty—but not for long. Six other spirits came out of nowhere and shot back into him, apparently grateful at being home again. With a familiar brief, ice-cold feeling in his chest, Kyle was complete with a Weaver, Hunter, Skimmer, Fixer, Glider, and Creeper joining his already-resident

Breaker. They rummaged around deep within as if inspecting the mess left behind by the unruly Breakers.

"Shall I come with you?" Kyle asked Mr. Orm as everybody started shuffling out of the cavern.

The man glanced back at him. "Perhaps not. You make people nervous, son. Go home and have lunch. I'll see you this afternoon when we've cleared up this confusion."

It was true that Kyle had everyone on edge. In Sovereign Hall itself he'd publicly demonstrated the ability to host all seven spirits at once, something previously deemed impossible. Most people were lucky enough to tether to *one* spirit without succumbing to its overbearing presence. How could anyone safely host all seven within one fragile, human body? Then he'd spent the last six days using those different powers to heal the sick, helping to build houses, and much more—and now this, breaking down an impenetrable wall by borrowing other people's spirits and channeling their combined energy! He could imagine the uproar when the rest of the enclave found out. What else was this boy from a faraway place capable of?

Mr. Orm spotted Kiff in the crowd. He frowned, opened his mouth to say something, then shook his head and left without another word.

Kyle and Kiff were the last to leave except for the three guards that remained behind. Outside in the dazzling sunshine, more guards were posted. Acting Sovereign Durant meant business!

"What do you think all this is about?" Kiff asked in a whisper as they followed the line of workers out of the rock quarry.

"No idea," Kyle said. "With this many guards around, there's obviously something in those tunnels the sovereign doesn't want us to see."

"Nobody could stop you, though," Kiff said, looking up at him. "You broke down that wall when nobody else could. You're tougher than everyone put together!"

Kyle smiled. "Something like that. But it's not about being tougher. I can't just fight my way in there. We'll have to wait and see what the sovereign says. Maybe he's just being cautious."

Still, he had to wonder about the change of heart. Durant had seemed utterly uninterested in the newly discovered tunnels under the ground, and the Breaker community had been left alone to do what they wanted, enlisting Kyle to help with his unheard-of powers. And now that they'd broken through, suddenly Durant was desperate to stop them going any farther?

"He changed his mind long before I broke through," he mused as they climbed the path to the top of the quarry. "He sent out guards, who got here just as I was making headway. So it's not the fact that I broke through that has him spooked—it's that he'd already guessed I might. But what's the big deal?"

The men and women headed off in different directions, clearly going home for lunch the way Mr. Orm had suggested. Breaking was the sort of job that worked up a ravenous appetite. Kyle, though, was hungry for something else: information.

"You go on," he said to Kiff, giving him a gentle shove. "Go eat. I'll be home soon. I'm going to, uh . . ."

"Going to what?" Kiff asked, frowning.

"I'm just going to find out what's happening. I'll see you later."

Parting ways with a disgruntled Kiff, he headed into the heart of the Fixer Enclave. The dusty streets were busy as men and women went about their business and children played. What day was it? Was it the weekend, or did kids get out of school early in this quaint place? He'd lost track of the time. It was weird having no stream screen playing in the background while he ate breakfast. He was used to a news team constantly reminding citizens of the exact time and what the weather was like right outside the window.

It couldn't be much later than midday, though. At home in his city, school lasted well into the afternoon. Here . . . well, there seemed to be more attention to learning practical skills than stuffing heads with history and math.

People stared at him as he walked. They all knew him as Kyle Jaxx of the City, the one who had ended the reign of a thoroughly corrupt sovereign. Kyle had been the talk of the town since his dramatic arrival in the enclave six days ago. Thinking he was the fugitive Logan, guards had arrested him on sight and marched him into Sovereign Hall where Kiff had been dealing with an unwanted tethering. The proceedings had erupted into chaos, and both Sovereign Lambost and his nasty Chancellor Gretin had perished on stage after Kyle had dragged their dark secrets out into the open. Exorcising Kiff's spirit had been a simple matter, at least for Kyle.

The very same Sovereign Hall loomed ahead, a structure three times the height of the neighboring buildings, with a steep, pitched roof. People milled in the street outside the front, and red-cloaked, armored guards lined the wide stone steps. Kyle half expected the guards to pounce on him as he approached.

Only a small audience had been witness to his otherworldly display of power at Sovereign Hall. All that had changed the day after when he'd formed a massive circle of linked hands with everyone in the enclave and used his Skimmer to impart detailed, dreamlike visions. What he'd shown them about the late Sovereign Lambost's evil reign had sickened all. However, they'd been entranced by images of Kyle's world: high-rise apartment towers, silvery snakelike maglev trains, and vehicles that flew through the air. The fabled city in the far west, Kyle's home, was a setting of breathtaking wonder to the people of these enclaves.

He paused at a safe distance, wondering why there was so much activity at the Hall. Granted, the acting sovereign was still here. In fact, he'd spent more time in the Fixer Enclave than at the Hunter Capitol. Still, it didn't explain the heightened excitement in the air today. Something else was afoot.

A couple of the Breaker workers from the quarry stood outside, looking fed up. Kyle had to assume Logan's father, Mr. Orm, had alone gained audience with Durant. They were probably talking right now, and Kyle wished he could hear the conversation.

The moment he thought about it, his Creeper spirit rose up from within, and he had to suppress the urge to go sneaking around the place. Knowing the way Creepers operated, it would probably lead him to an open window or underground access panel . . .

He forced the Creeper back down inside. It wouldn't do to get into trouble with the new sovereign. The man was on edge enough as it was. Kyle resigned himself to waiting. Leet Orm would emerge from his meeting soon enough, and the reason for the quarry closure would spread quickly. There had to be a simple, logical reason.

Still, Kyle couldn't shake the feeling something was amiss.

Chapter 3
Logan

Mayor Trilmott met them at the rooftop landing pad. Their three-soldier escort handed Logan and Byron over to the mayor's pair of personal bodyguards. The threesome was dismissed by Trilmott and left on their respective platforms.

Like the soldiers, the mayor and the bodyguards had their contagion barriers turned on.

Within the large bodyguard to the mayor's left, Logan detected cybernetic enhancements, a battlebuster hammer arm, and lift braces embedded deep in his calves. The man was built to handle a pretty comprehensive assault. The other had various scanning devices wired into his ghost helm. Logan probed very little into the specialized tech. The helmeted bodyguard was already radiating a hands-off vibe.

The mayor didn't invite them into his apartment, a top-floor suite that Logan knew well. He had retrieved its blueprints from deep within the data stream, illegally of course. He knew of all the dwelling's features, including a panic room that the previous mayor had used twice according to the log record Logan had hacked yesterday. He hadn't delved deep enough to determine the events that had driven the mayor to sequester himself away.

Trilmott sighed and nodded first at Logan and then at Byron, not offering up a handshake. He scratched at his well-manicured dark beard then fiddled with his ear-com. His nose was bulbous and excessively protruded. He arched an eyebrow and said, "You like to pry."

Logan didn't say anything.

Trilmott kept his tone friendly. "But that's been a boon to our city. You have forced us to rethink our motives. You proved our previous leadership was lacking."

Logan saw Byron was slightly dazed from the restraint field. His mind slipped into the robot's equilibrium matrix, and he swiftly corrected the minor havoc their platform ride had caused. His brother's eyes flashed slightly brighter, and Byron nodded a simple thanks.

Trilmott said, "I want to work with you. The public sees you as a force for good. It will not benefit either of us to look like we are at odds with each other." It sounded like Trilmott was trying to convince himself of this sticking point.

"I wasn't trying to hurt anyone."

"No, of course not. You detected something hidden away, and your curiosity got the best of you."

"I think the tunnels are important." He wanted to ask about the contagion barriers, but also knew Trilmott was aware of his curiosity and was, perhaps, letting him wonder and worry more than was necessary. *He's toying with me. If I say something, he keeps the upper hand.* Logan moved closer to the mayor.

Trilmott's larger bodyguard shifted his weight toward Logan.

"There are boundaries and limitations in place for a reason, Logan. Not all areas are open to everyone, even those lauded by our fair city as do-gooders."

Logan glanced at Byron. The robot boy's impassive face revealed nothing. Did Byron know something was off about the mayor? Surely he had detected the contagion barriers with his refined sensors sooner than Logan had.

"I want to safeguard you and every citizen." The mayor folded his arms behind his back. "More importantly, I want to safeguard the future. You can see the value in that, can't you?"

Logan nodded.

Trilmott said, "Tell me, are you feeling well today?"

Logan shrugged. "I'm fine."

"No headaches? No discomfort in your joints?" The mayor laced every word with polished concern. "No issues with your vision or balance?"

"None." Logan hated holding his tongue, letting the mayor dart around what he obviously wanted to bring to light. *I get it. You think I'm sick.*

"I can't tolerate the idea that our city's hero would be coming down with something."

Logan exhaled sharply. "What are you getting at?" He didn't like being played. He didn't care if he lost the upper hand by asking questions. "Why are you and the soldiers that brought us in wearing contagion barriers?"

The mayor didn't react to his outburst. "There are no tunnels. You found only a classified lab space, abandoned for a reason."

The mayor had to be lying. He knew Logan had detected tunnels extending out under the Ruins. Why the contagion charade?

"I get it," Logan said. "You don't want me down in those tunnels. But why are you making up a medical crisis? I feel fine."

"Because you were exposed. You unearthed a medical lab's dropload bay, one that my records show dealt with hazardous materials. I have dispatched a clean-up crew to seal it back up and assess any negative environmental impact you've caused." He nodded at Byron. "Your brother won't need to be seen by a doctor, but you will. Can't have the city's hero exposed to anything lethal, can we?" The mayor held his gaze with Logan for a long time.

Wasn't this mayor supposed to be better than his predecessor? Something was off about his story, but Logan couldn't put a finger on it. Trilmott could very well be lying, manufacturing the contagion story to get Logan to fall in line. Logan badly wanted to call him out on it. A part of him was uncertain, though. What if he had been exposed to something?

He hadn't done a sweep of the room to determine its purpose. It could've been a lab. It had been closed off and sealed away, so there was a possibility the mayor was being truthful.

Byron inserted himself into their conversation. "Logan should get checked. If he got exposed to something, then walking into the nearest readi-med facility wouldn't be smart. You should call in a doctor immediately."

Logan sighed, relieved his brother had defused the tension. Had the robot boy sensed Logan was about to throw out an accusation? It was entirely possible. The boy had such an array of sophisticated sensors, he could probably deduce when Logan was about to break based on his pulse rate, carbon dioxide output or something.

Trilmott shrugged at Byron and fussed with his wrist tablet. "Not a problem. We can have one here in no time."

"Is this really necessary?" Logan asked. Byron's directness and desire to expedite their situation seemed to have deflated the mayor's bluster a bit.

Trilmott finished his requisition message. The mayor crossed his arms and addressed Logan. "Would you want to jeopardize your participation in the expedition back to your enclave? Imagine if you brought a nasty strain of some sort to your quaint home. I doubt your Fixers—that is what you call your medical experts there, isn't it?—would be able to contain such a foreign outbreak. Would you want that to happen?"

Logan shook his head. "No."

"Good. It's probably nothing. Cooperate and we'll have you heading home in no time. I'd hate to hear a grim diagnosis, one that leads to an extended quarantine." He smiled. "You'll find I hold sensibleness in high regard. An appreciation to duty and upholding public safety are key points in my platform. My appointment to interim mayor isn't permanent unless I actually run in the next election, which I plan on doing."

Logan did not want to hear more about the mayor's political ambitions. He had endured enough of that when

Trilmott had paid him a visit two days ago, asking for Logan's endorsement. Something he had discreetly refused.

He opted to change the subject. "How did the soldiers find us so easily?"

Trilmott laughed and lifted an iced drink from a hover server that had zipped to his side only seconds earlier. It whisked back into the suite, its task accomplished. He took several long sips of the bright blue drink. "We scanned for where there was nothing."

"What do you mean?" Logan was surprised the mayor was being so forthcoming. Then again, the man liked to boast.

"You thought you covered your trail, but all you created were blind spots. We looked for gaps in the data streaming in from the spy pylons, and it drew us an obvious map of your flight. I'm surprised you weren't aware of what you were doing."

I'll have to rethink how I handle spy pylons. Just blinding them isn't enough.

Durant patted the cybernetic arm of his larger bodyguard. "Captain Twimmer and Lieutenant Mendelson will wait with you for Dr. Hajill. He can conduct his exam out here. I don't want you inside, infecting my quarters."

"And should I be given a contagion scrubbing? Could I be carrying anything on my exterior that would endanger others?" Byron grabbed the mayor by the wrist and held tight.

Trilmott snorted and said, "Not required. You don't pose any risk to others like your brother." He wrenched his hand free of the robot boy's grip. He fiddled with his wrist tablet and turned away from them. He marched toward his home. "I expect you to steer clear of any underground exploration, Logan. That is not your concern."

Logan said nothing. He and Byron walked back to the landing pad, putting a good twenty yards between them and the guards.

Byron spoke low but with slight urgency. "He's lying. His pulse was all over the place."

"Well you did grab him pretty tightly."

Byron responded, "He didn't look away, but he was blinking a lot. A normal adult blinks ten times a minute. He blinked on average twenty-three times a minute during the nine-minute conversation. He's lying about the contagion."

"I know." Logan eyed the sky, searching for Durant's on-call medical help approaching transport.

"A doctor won't find anything. My sensors may be crude, but I know nothing got on us from that lab or whatever it was."

"It was more than a lab," Logan said. "There are answers down there, and I'm going to find them."

Dr. Hajill arrived, riding in a deluxe transport. He exited the vehicle and walked stiffly toward Logan and Byron, glowing yellow thanks to his containment barrier.

He pulled out several devices and began his exam. Logan synced up with each and saw that none of them were taking actual readings. He slipped into the doctor's wrist tablet and intercepted a bulletin being sent out about his exposure to a contaminant. The report indicated that the best medical care was being provided, and the outlook was good for the city hero's full recovery.

"Did you find anything?" Logan asked.

Hajill coolly said, "No. You check out fine."

His tests concluded, he stowed away his tools in his bag and glared at Logan. "There are many places where trouble can find you, young man. Do yourself a favor and don't be so bold."

Logan said nothing. He grinned and thanked the doctor.

Hajill boarded his vehicle and left with little fanfare.

A few minutes later, the three soldiers who had escorted them to the mayor's rooftop returned on their platforms, no longer glowing yellow. News traveled fast, Logan thought. They escorted Logan and Byron back to their home.

Logan went to his room and busied himself with combing through the data stream for any incidents of citizens stumbling across underground chambers or tunnels. He found none. He thought again about the mayor's explanation of how his soldiers had found Logan. They had looked for blind spots. He knew finding no mention of any tunnels was a red flag.

There had to be others who had come across the city's underside. Logan's determination swelled. He would find another way below.

And this time, I won't trip any alarms.

Chapter 4
Kyle

Kyle lingered by the corner of a store. The sign out front read ANKWAR'S AILMENTS, and in smaller lettering underneath, *Unruly spirit? Our ancient talismans are guaranteed to put them in their place.* He spotted all manner of sinister-looking artifacts as well as dusty tomes on the shelves. The whole place looked depressing.

Still, it made him realize that some people might not always get along well with the spirit they tethered to at the tender age of fourteen. Logan's mother, Prima, was a good example with her decidedly cranky Fixer. The small, furry healers were very rare, only five in the local area despite this being the Fixer Enclave. A girl called Nomi, someone Logan had a crush on, was the most recent to tether to one. She seemed to have gotten lucky; hers was fairly well behaved.

And now there was Kyle, who had picked up a Fixer of his own out in the Broken Lands at the spirit barrier, where dozens of varying spirits clustered. He'd readily joined Mrs. Orm in her daily routine of healing, jumping straight in to tackle broken bones, burns, and other physical disfigurements around the enclave. Soon he would gravitate to unseen ailments, which were notoriously difficult and beyond the capabilities of most Fixers.

Peering through the grimy window, Kyle spotted a twenty-something man strapped to a chair. A woman, presumably his wife, gripped his hand tightly as the small, thin store owner dangled one of his advertised talismans before the man's face and recited a strange incantation, the flickering light of a dozen candles lighting up the trio in an eerie orange glow.

Despite everything, the customer's grimace suggested his Breaker spirit was fighting the so-called talisman magic and refused to be cowed.

"There he is!" someone whispered, and Kyle jumped and spun around. Passersby were nudging each other and gossiping about him. His seven spirits squirmed deep down inside, and one of them, the Skimmer, seemed intent on reading minds as he hurried away from the corner of the store, brushing shoulders with men and women as he went.

He caught snippets. *So skinny and pale . . . Weak in body but incredibly strong-willed . . . How is he still alive while tethered to so many spirits?* But these were standard comments he'd come to expect. The only voice that caused him to falter was a woman's: *Is he going to heal my father's cancer or not?*

Stopping dead, he twisted around to see who he'd come into contact with. Several faces peered back at him, but his Skimmer guided him to a small, serious woman wrapped in a shawl. She stood perfectly still in the middle of the street while others kept moving. When she noticed he was looking at her, her frown dissipated in an instant, and her mouth dropped open. Then she turned and hurried away, obviously flustered.

Eavesdropping had that effect on people. He wanted to go after her and tell he was sorry for the delay, that he would get to her as soon as he felt confident using his Fixer.

Cancerous masses were one of the many unseen ailments Fixers had trouble with. Hospitals back home in the city could eradicate tumors in minutes, but Kyle wasn't sure his Fixer would be as effective. And getting it wrong spelled disaster.

He realized he was standing there in the street with everyone gawking at him like he was a prize exhibit in the City Zoo. Nobody was brushing shoulders with him now though, and even his Skimmer found it impossible to read minds without direct contact.

Should he go after that woman? He'd healed Kiff's leg without much effort at all, and that had been a real mess of lumpy scars and a badly healed bone thanks to a kaliback attack. How much more difficult could a single, cancerous mass be, unseen though it was?

But as he searched for the woman, his gaze fell instead on another figure that had appeared on the steps of Sovereign Hall. Something about that figure caused his spirits to fall silent. Suspicion and dread filled his soul as he stared at the black-robed man. Though slight in stature, he had a presence that caused the surrounding guards to twitch nervously. His face was hooded and heavily shadowed, his hands tucked inside folds of material.

And he didn't have a spirit.

This struck Kyle as very odd. As far as he understood it, everyone over the age of fourteen was either tethered to a spirit or exiled to the Broken Lands.

The man—if indeed it was a man—seemed to be staring straight at Kyle as he stood there in the street. Everyone else appeared to have noticed, too. An uncomfortable hush had fallen, and people began to hurry on with their eyes averted as the ominous man stood silently on the steps, surrounded by a team of red-cloaked guards.

Kyle felt something stir within him as one of his spirits battled for a chance to help. While he could house all seven at once, only one could be in his head, physically driving his body. Standing absolutely still, Kyle imagined them jostling one another deep down inside as though vying to climb up his neck. His mental image extended to a vision of wriggling tentacles as the Creeper spirit climbed into his skull. At the exact same moment, Kyle felt its presence for real as it eased into place and took control of his limbs.

Suddenly he was moving. Before he knew it, he'd managed to lose himself among the passersby in a series of graceful ducks and weaves that left everyone around him blinking with confusion. He darted into an alley a hundred yards from Sovereign Hall. He guessed the black-clad stranger was still standing on its steps, scanning the street, trying to figure out what had just happened.

Kyle had no time to marvel at his own stealth and agility because he was already on the move again down the alley. He turned left at the end and sidled along the rear of a sturdy building with a lower wall of stone, then left again when he arrived back at the monstrous Sovereign Hall.

Where are you taking me? he asked his spirit. His curiosity allowed it some leeway, though. He could rein it in anytime and take back control, but right now the Creeper was doing what it did best: creeping about.

A shoulder-wide passage ran between the Hall and the neighboring building Kyle stood at the rear corner of. His Creeper spirit urged him into that passage, and less than ten seconds later he reached the other end and looked back onto the main street. The black-clad stranger moved down the steps and ordered the guards to search in both directions.

Kyle hunkered low, peering around the corner, suddenly feeling like a fugitive. Would he be arrested if the guards caught him here? On what grounds, exactly?

I wonder why— he thought, but again he was interrupted by the Creeper's astonishing speed. Before Kyle could stop himself, he darted around the corner and, staying low and moving fast, sprang up the steps of the Hall to where the hooded figure stood looking the other way.

The timing was perfect. A split second earlier or later and the stranger would have seen him coming. By the time the stranger had turned his head, Kyle was flinging himself forward. At this point, his Hunter spirit shoved the Creeper aside and took over, forcing Kyle to grapple with his quarry. With the ease of a seasoned fighter, he knocked the man flat on his back on the stone steps.

"What—?" the hooded man grunted.

Kyle pressed his weight down on him. *What am I doing?* he thought frantically.

His spirits worked fast. The Skimmer slipped back into his head just as the stranger lifted his arm and his sleeve fell back. As the sovereign's guards shouted and came running, Kyle gripped the bare, skinny wrist and received a flood of dark, twisted thoughts:

—An enormous chamber with dull metal shielding on the walls, the inner reaches of three spires high above, the entire place cluttered with huge piles of tech and even several partially dismantled vehicles, all of it ancient. Kyle's view seemed to be from the perspective of the stranger as he edged into the chamber and waited for someone to turn and face him—a figure shrouded in darkness, curiously bulky and twisted with what looked like an array of tech attachments—

Something clobbered Kyle on the back of the head. He lost his grip on the hooded man's wrist and tumbled sideways. Guards were suddenly all over him, pinning him down as the stranger in black struggled to his feet and adjusted his robes. His hood had peeled back a little to reveal a beak-nosed man, but the sighting was brief.

"Sorry," Kyle gasped as the guards yanked him to his feet, three of the four gripping him tightly by the arms. He jerked his head toward the stranger. "I . . . I thought he was an assassin or something."

"Him?" a guard squawked, his eyebrows shooting up. "Are you serious?"

"Take him inside!" the hooded man snapped.

Kyle's head throbbed, and his feet barely touched the steps as he was frog-marched through the grand entrance doors of Sovereign Hall. All he could think about was the very last thing he'd seen in that all-too-brief vision when he'd grasped the hooded man's wrist: that room full of metal and the frightening figure shrouded in darkness.

Something that had once been human.

Chapter 5
Logan

Logan hated having to take the maglev train to meet up with Rissa. Today was not a school day, but it was still expected he work on his research project with his partner. Byron had indicated that getting Rissa as a partner would've made Kyle's year. Apparently, he had a crush on her. Logan was not so impressed. His few encounters with the girl at the academy had left him cold. She was pretty but not at all pleasant. She walked around with a bit too much conceit.

And now he had to spend the better part of the afternoon with her, researching the tradition of implanting. All the info was easy for him to acquire from any mobile media device, just dip into the data stream and pluck out some choice details. He already knew plenty about the ritual that was a perfect parallel to the tethering that happened in the enclaves. It was downright creepy how both cultures had selected the age of fourteen to be the exact time for the deeds.

Logan was positive Rissa would arrive by pod. Her family was well off, and she didn't mix with the rabble—her words when he had suggested they take a maglev together to the city archives located near the convening hall of the Hub, the city's ruling body.

He exited the train alongside a steady stream of commuters. Several gave him knowing looks, recognizing him from recent news bulletins. He rode a lift to the upper level of the station, then walked down a long aerial concourse and through a glass tunnel that offered a breathtaking 360-degree view of Apparati's sprawling legislative center. Was Trilmott down there scurrying to report on his recent actions? Logan imagined the politician standing before the seventy-nine representatives, spouting off about Logan's impulsive and inquisitive nature. Trilmott would prefer to be there face to face in lieu of simply checking in by stream screen.

Logan refocused himself and continued down a course of wide steps. *Get in and get out unscathed. Less time with Rissa, the better.* He'd much rather be meeting up with Nomi, the girl he worshipped from afar back at the Fixer Enclave. *I'm really afar now.* Was Kyle spending time with Nomi? Logan doubted Kiff would let such a thing happen. His little brother knew just how badly Logan had it for her.

Now at street level, he spryly moved through a crosswalk, marveling at how pristine the city was here at its center—a big difference from the outskirts where he and Byron had been this morning.

A street vendor had his food cart set up at the corner, and Logan was surprised to see Rissa there arguing with the cart's merchant. Why wasn't she at the entrance to the archives as agreed?

"I don't care if it takes longer. I want it to look like what it shows on your data board." She pointed at a large hovering screen above the man's head. Two-thirds of it featured the cart's small menu, while the lower section showcased an image of a wrap filled with mora fish. Logan's mouth watered. While the city didn't have the tastiest durgle meat, their seafood was a treat. Because his father didn't like fish, the rest of the family didn't see it at the dinner table often. He could count on one hand how many times he had eaten something from the Great Sea.

The man scratched at his thick beard and shook his head. "No, I can't do that right now. Have to prep for the commuter rush. Mora fish will be back on the menu this evening. Come back then or pick something less involved, a savory meat bun perhaps." He raised his hand and swiped the screen. The image of a meat bun filled with morribie meat and topped with fresh greens dominated the screen.

“Don’t advertise something you can’t provide.” Rissa stuck out her bottom lip and wrinkled her tiny nose. Her long blond hair was eye-catching, and she was as equally dark-skinned as Logan, but he knew her skin pigment was by artificial means and not from a life spent outdoors. She wore a loose-fitting yellow blouse with gauzy sleeves. Her neckline was low, giving all a glimpse of her smooth, unblemished skin. While she was very attractive, he still didn’t understand Kyle’s fixation. Logan found her treatment of this merchant off-putting.

Two men slipped behind Logan and craned their necks to look at the menu, which the merchant had reinstated on the floating screen. He also tapped on the screen and blacked out the listing of the mora fish wrap.

“Oh no you don’t. Make it active again.” Rissa’s face reddened. “Who do you think you are, excluding it right in front of me? I’m tempted to tell my daddy about your business practices.”

“And who is your father, Miss?”

Logan could tell the man strained at keeping his tongue in check. What he really wanted to do was lash out at his boisterous customer.

“A high-ranking soldier. In fact, he’s the prime candidate to replace General Mortimer if the Hub can ever get his nomination out of committee.”

The merchant’s eyes widened. He gave Rissa several placating hand gestures and then whisked over to his grill. Logan watched him prepare a mora fish wrap with an air of subservience.

Rissa smirked and looked over at Logan, finally deeming him worth acknowledging. “You want anything?”

Logan’s appetite shriveled up. He shook his head. “We can’t bring food into the Archives.”

Rissa synced her wrist tablet with the food cart’s pay port and finalized her payment. Logan peeked into the encrypted transaction and noticed she left no tip.

"Watch me," she replied and turned away from him to glare at the merchant with impatience. The man apologized to the growing line of customers for their wait and offered each a free side of twee toast to appease them.

Logan stepped out of line and moved to stand next to a nearby tree.

A few minutes later, Rissa approached him. She unwrapped her meal and gave it a dismissive look. "He put on far too much sauce. I should make him redo it."

She made to spin around, but Logan grabbed her shoulder and held her in place. "No, leave him to his customers and his livelihood."

Rissa's entire face twitched, and she inhaled slowly. Logan did not let go of her.

She sighed and delivered him a sweet smile. "You're right. He's not worth wasting any more of my precious time. Let's get this research done. I'm meeting friends later. Please don't make this take more than an hour."

Gladly, Logan thought as they marched up the steps and into the archive. Rissa made a show of carting food into the building despite receiving several judgmental looks from the staff manning the main lobby desk.

I miss you, Nomi.

Chapter 6
Kyle

Kyle found himself dragged before Acting Sovereign Durant, who sat on a large, thronelike chair on the raised stage of the grand hall. A similar chair stood alongside him, empty. A new chancellor could only be appointed by an incumbent sovereign, and Durant had not yet been officially sworn in.

Leet Orm stood before the stage, twisting around at the commotion as Kyle and his guards marched up one of the aisles. The hall had seating capacity for hundreds, but its current emptiness caused their footsteps to echo loudly.

"What the—?" Mr. Orm started to say, glaring at Kyle. His face darkened through anger or embarrassment, perhaps both. "Kyle, what have you done now?" he hissed.

The guards shoved Kyle forward to stand before the stage next to Mr. Orm. The man on the throne looked puzzled and a little wary, and he glanced over Kyle's head at the black-clad, hooded man at the rear of the group.

"Nailor?" he said softly.

The stranger slipped past the guards and, careful to give Kyle a wide berth, approached the stage. Rather than stopping there and addressing the acting sovereign as most lowly citizens of the enclave would, he shuffled to the nearest steps and climbed them, then seemed to glide across the polished floor to where Durant sat. As if that wasn't disrespectful enough, the man had the audacity to flop down in the empty chair intended only for the next chancellor.

Kyle blinked with amazement.

Durant showed none of Kyle's surprise. He simply waited. Only when the stranger was seated comfortably did he slide his hood back. He was in his early thirties, his face white, hair black and oily. He leaned a little to one side and said loudly, "The boy attacked me."

Durant closed his eyes briefly. He was a small, wiry man, middle-aged with neatly cropped light-brown hair streaked with grey. His tiny chin sported a pointed beard. When he opened his eyes again, his drooping eyelids suggested he was perpetually tired. He spoke with a croaky voice as though he'd been talking far more than normal lately—which was probably the case. "Please explain yourself, young Kyle."

Kyle felt everyone's eyes on him, and he swallowed. He wasn't scared by any of these people—not the sovereign, not Nailor, not even the four guards—but he wilted under the weight of Leet Orm's stare. "I was just passing by and saw this hooded man," he said, nodding toward Nailor. "He looked suspicious. I thought he was an assassin."

This impromptu excuse had popped into his head outside on the steps, and he'd mentally patted himself on the back. Whether the sovereign bought it or not was another matter.

Oddly, Durant pursed his lips and nodded. "I suppose I should commend you on acting so selflessly to protect me."

Kyle and Mr. Orm each did a double take.

Nailor scowled in disgust. Durant swallowed and smiled weakly. "Come now, Nailor, give him some leeway."

Feeling a little more emboldened now, Kyle pointed at the stranger lounging in the chancellor's chair. "So who *is* he?"

"Kyle!" Mr. Orm snapped. "Show some respect!"

A guard prodded Kyle on the back with his sword, and it dug in painfully. "Shut your mouth," a voice hissed in his ear.

Durant held up a hand. "It's all right. He has a right to know. He's not from around here, after all. Indeed, he's something of a celebrity. We should all be grateful to him for what he's done for our people. For revealing the previous sovereign's sordid past."

He glanced sideways at Nailor as if seeking approval. After a pause, Nailor nodded.

"This gentleman seated next to me," Durant continued, returning his attention to Kyle, "is a revered servant of the Hallowed Spires. His name is Nailor, and he is one of seven spokespersons for the Guardian, one at each enclave. We are honored by his presence here today."

"We are indeed," a guard blurted, sounding nervous.

"I've . . . I've never heard of the Hallowed Spires," Kyle lied. A chill ran through him as he recalled what Abe Torren had said about the Guardian who lived there.

"And you may be excused for your ignorance," Durant said, forcing a smile. He stared at Kyle for a moment. "It's surprising, though, that you didn't, uh, *see* the Hallowed Spires in your spectacular vision earlier this week. When you, um, looked into the late Sovereign Lambost's mind and had the misfortune to witness his entire life."

Kyle honestly couldn't remember seeing anything about the Hallowed Spires other than perhaps a flash of an image, a striking building with three towers rising above the Capitol. "There was a lot to see," he said. "I might have missed that detail."

Or maybe Lambost and his chancellor just didn't have much to do with the Guardian, he thought. There was some logic to that. Maybe the mysterious Guardian had been quiet for many, many years, only rearing his head now that Kyle had shown up. It would explain why nobody had mentioned these hooded servants before. Still, the Hallowed Spires was located in the Hunter Capitol, the home of Lambost and all his predecessors, and indeed Durant when he wasn't out visiting other enclaves. Lambost *must* have knocked heads with the Guardian over the years. And one or two of these black-clad servants, too. They weren't exactly inconspicuous, nor respectful of sovereignty.

"It makes me wonder what else you missed," Durant said softly. He licked his lips. "Me, for instance. We all shared your collective vision when the entire Fixer Enclave linked hands.

We all saw the depravities that Sovereign Lambost and Chancellor Gretin built their reign around. But nobody recalls me in your vision." He leaned forward, his chair creaking slightly. "I'm ashamed to say I knew Lambost and his many wives over the years. I met with him frequently. Is there something you saw about me that perhaps you didn't share? Something perhaps you wrongly interpreted as . . . corrupt?"

The focus of the conversation had shifted. Kyle frowned as he realized that Durant was nervous, perhaps even scared as if he had something to hide. "Like I said," Kyle said carefully, "there was a lot to see. I don't remember anything special. I didn't even know you at the time, so maybe I saw something but didn't pay attention. Everyone saw something different in my vision depending on what they were interested in seeing. I showed them the whole movie, but certain parts meant different things to different people."

A silence fell as everyone in the room digested his words. They wouldn't understand the word "movie," but perhaps they got the gist.

Durant eased back in his chair and nodded slowly. "I ask because certain naysayers are unsure of my eligibility to be the next sovereign, hence the irritating delay in swearing me in. I suppose there are always some who like to cast doubt, no?" He grinned humorlessly and raised his eyebrows.

Kyle nodded. What would he have seen in this man's history if he'd been paying attention? He'd been hearing whispers all week that Durant had always been "in Lambost's pocket," but he had no recollection of anything specific from the previous sovereign's mind. Perhaps if he could get close enough for his Skimmer to find out a few little tidbits . . . but that seemed out of the question without sparking anger and getting himself thrown in jail.

"Off you go, then," Durant said with a dismissive wave of his hand. "No harm done. Eh, Nailor?"

"None at all," Nailor growled, glaring at Kyle.

Kyle forced a respectful bow. As the guards began to usher him and Mr. Orm from the hall, he couldn't help twisting around and asking, "So why is the tunnel off-limits now?"

"Kyle," Mr. Orm growled, reaching out to grip Kyle's arm.

In that moment, Kyle felt his Skimmer locking on. It didn't seem to matter that his sleeve got in the way of skin-to-skin contact. It hadn't mattered when he'd thrown himself on the previous sovereign's back, either. Physical contact was good enough even through clothing.

In a second, the entire conversation between Mr. Orm and Durant played through his mind:

"—The order came directly from the Guardian of the Hallowed Spires," Durant told Mr. Orm in a low, nervous voice. "I'm afraid there's nothing I can do about it. As you know, the Guardian was here long before all of us and will be here long after we're dead and buried, and his infinite wisdom is not to be questioned. The tunnel is forbidden. Not only that, the cavern will be filled in and the rock quarry abandoned." He looked toward the rear of the hall. "Now, please don't make trouble, Mr. Orm. Nailor graciously stepped outside to allow me this private, friendly word in your ear. If he has cause to speak with you himself about this matter, I'm afraid things will be altogether more serious—"

The vision ended as Mr. Orm let go of his arm, but Kyle had seen enough.

Meanwhile, Durant flushed with sudden anger. "Learn to hold your tongue, young Kyle Jaxx of the City. Don't press your luck."

Moments later, Kyle and Mr. Orm were shoved quite roughly from the hall. They stumbled down the steps and into the street.

"And don't come back," one of the guards warned, drawing his sword a few inches. "Do as you're told." In a lower voice, he whispered, "Think of your family."

Chapter 7
Logan

Glad to be done with Rissa, Logan exited the Archives building as the sun drifted below the horizon. She had left over an hour ago. He had stayed, preferring not to exit by her side. Their research had gone fine. She had spent most of the time complaining about the limited information on implanting.

For a while, she had heaped attention on him, asking if he had spent time with any of the rich and elevated. When he had been sparse with the details of his limited encounters with the city's elite, she had retreated to her wrist tablet and repeatedly checked in on what she kept calling 'stream teams.' This resulted in him having to listen to an exhaustive accounting of her many friends and their ties to various important people and families.

Using the data stream, he had fleshed out their report even more in the hour after she had fled. He was grateful for the quiet time. Once he was home, he would send her the report through the stream and knew she'd offer a bounty of revisions whether the paper needed them or not. Hopefully, he could wade through them tomorrow in class and have the project ready for their presentation the next day. Even if she asked to meet up to practice, he'd steer her into doing it through their respective devices. He doubted he could survive another face-to-face with Rissa. Poor Kyle. What was he thinking, pining over someone so lacking?

Foot traffic was minimal as most commuters had already headed home. He passed the food cart operator and almost stopped to order the mora fish wrap but then thought better of it. What if the man had seen him leave with Rissa? He didn't want the merchant to associate him with her little scene.

Instead of heading directly to the maglev station and home, he turned right and stalked up the broad avenue of Garramint, named after the regal bird of prey that was all but extinct. The stream screen had clued Logan into the City Zoo, an artificial refuge that penned in species so the citizens could visit without mounting a trip to the wilds of the Ruins. They had three of the four-clawed birds in a large aviary. Byron kept threatening to take Logan, but they had not mounted a trip thus far. Maybe in two days when they had another day off school. Even with the frequent breaks, he was spending too much time at Kyle's academy.

Back at the enclaves, schooling only ran to the age of twelve. Logan, as curious as he was about this new world, didn't want to learn about it in a cramped classroom.

He had seen a good deal of the city in the last seven days but had not explored much of the area around the Hub. One place in particular held his interest. It was a building they had flown over just days ago when Trilmott had ferried him and Byron to some sort of fundraising event. That night had been uneventful except for the ride home. Logan had reached out, delving into the different buildings and their tech systems as they whisked by. Most were governmental in nature, and he had only given them a cursory exam. But one building intrigued him. While he could only scan the few floors closest to him, he could get some impression of the tech in the buildings. Not a deep scan though. For that, he'd have to be inside.

He now reached out with his mind, knowing exactly what to look for: a place in the city absent of any tech. How the mayor and his soldiers had found Logan—by looking at where the spy pylons had shown nothing—crept back into his thoughts. He was using the same tactic here.

He crossed through a small park and jogged down Clacker Street. None of the large burrowing beasts, the street's namesake, had emerged in the city, but the citizens of Apparati had taken to canyon clacker sighting parties along the Wall with growing frequency, even more so since Logan had emerged from the Ruins. They searched for the clackers on rainy days, the most likely time for the large creatures to surface thanks to the loosened terrain. Some sold alleged recordings of the worm's sonic screams, but Logan knew they were fakes as no devices he had catalogued in the city could receive the clacker's unique frequency from such a distance. Maybe if one of the worms broke through the thick pavement within the city limits, then the devices might stand a chance of recording something legit, but that had never happened before.

He slowed his pace as his mind encountered the large dimensions of a building devoid of any tech.

Logan had not gotten a good look from the flyer that night prior, but maps he had pulled up of the area indicated the structure was a bland rectangular building no more than two stories tall.

It stared back at him, windowless. He approached the only entrance he could spot on the structure's long north side.

Luckily, no one was about. He detected a nearby spy pylon and almost disabled it but thought better of it. It would only record his back as he approached. He pulled his hood up to better shield his identity. It was a cool evening, so such an action would not rouse suspicion with Peepers sorting through all the images collected by the pylons.

A long rectangular sign mounted above the door announced the building's purpose. He moved closer to read the faded lettering. The doorway was not lit, but the light from a nearby street pole helped immensely. He read the out-of-place words with no trouble—*Primary Housing of Guardian Designate. No Trespassing.*

There was that mention of a Guardian. Abe had told them the inhibitors were watched over by Guardians, one using magic to keep spirits out of the city, and the other using tech to deactivate machines long before they reached the enclaves.

But if the city's inhibitor involved some form of magic, Logan's tech abilities would be useless. There was no tech to manipulate! Likewise, Kyle's spirit talents would be equally ineffective against a tech-wielding Guardian in the enclaves. Abe had only been half right about this. Dealing with corrupt leaders had required the boys to switch places, but it seemed the opposite was true where the Guardians were concerned.

Abe had not contacted him. Logan was operating without any clear guidance, and he suddenly felt such guidance was needed. *Should I return to the Tower and try to summon Abe, or will the old man pay me a visit soon?*

Motion by the corner of the odd building farthest from Logan prompted him to dart back into the shadows of an alcove.

Someone approached the Guardian building's entrance with great speed. Logan pressed himself deeper into the shadows, placing a stack of empty dorium barrels between him and the new arrival.

The man emerged into the light, and Logan was taken aback by his pale skin. His clothing was slightly tattered and a collection of muted browns. He wore boots that looked like they had been reinforced at the soles many times over. He stopped, but not before Logan assessed that the man had a slight limp. He moved pretty fast despite the handicap.

Something was off about this person. Logan reached out to read the individual's implant. He could at least find out his profession.

Logan's mouth gaped open. The man didn't have an implant.

The stranger dropped to his knees and retrieved an item from a worn satchel at his side. It was a canvas bundle. He placed it on the ground, whispered something unintelligible, and then sprinted back to the corner from where he had come. He disappeared around it.

How was this possible? Logan was the only one in the city without an implant. At least as far as he knew.

Logan stepped out of his hiding place. The door glowed, casting a yellowish light. He didn't wait to see what happened next. It was clear someone was coming out to snatch up the strange delivery.

He suddenly didn't want to meet the person within. He'd rather take his chances with the man fleeing the scene. Logan sped up and soon found himself at the corner. He peered around it, quickly, eager to get out of sight before the Guardian or whoever was within the building stepped out.

He spied the pale stranger darting into a narrow alley to the left a hundred feet up. Without risking a look back, Logan took off in pursuit. Far too many mysteries were presenting themselves tonight, and he needed to get to the bottom of at least one of them.

* * *

It didn't surprise Logan to see that the man he chased never took any city transportation. Having shadowed him for more than half an hour, it was clear he was keeping to the back ways, out of sight of the citizens of the city.

He doesn't know I'm following him or doesn't care. Not once had the man looked back or given any sign that he knew he was being trailed.

They were now wading through an overgrown park. Logan was amazed how much ground they had covered. They were officially in the outskirts. Several times in the last five minutes, Logan had spotted the distinctive upright presence of the Wall around the city. They were close to the Ruins.

Logan crouched behind a large rock and caught his breath as quietly as he could manage.

The man directly ahead of him ducked down into a ditch. Logan counted to thirty before following. With the high grasses thick in the ditch, it was a perfect place for an ambush. Maybe the man would double back and pounce on him. *If he were a kaliback, that's what he would do,* thought Logan. *Of course, if he were a kaliback, he'd have the rest of his pack descend on him.* He scanned the area, suddenly aware of the numerous hiding places all around. If the man's associates also lacked implants, they would be undetectable to Logan.

He heard the sharp wrenching of metal on metal and froze. His foot slipped slightly down the incline. The sound had come from his left, probably no more than twenty feet away.

He heard the man grunt as more sounds of protesting metalwork rang through the park.

Logan stepped closer and pushed aside the shoulder-high grasses. Ahead, he spied the stranger opening a large reinforced grate. The man heaved it the rest of the way open and sagged against his hinged opponent, catching his breath. He muttered something and stepped into the passage. Logan ducked down as the man turned to face him. *Did he see me?*

Logan registered the sound of the grate slamming shut and what sounded like chains being hoisted in place. Several grunts followed by the percussive patter of retreating footfalls told him the man had fled underground.

He waited several minutes before stepping out of his hiding place. He approached the closed grate and eyed the crude lock and chains secured to the rusted metalwork. The entrance was out of place even for the outskirts. It looked old, like it belonged in the Ruins. Or led to them.

Logan peered into the dark passage and instinctively knew where the stranger had gone.

He had found his way into the tunnels. An ingress that was absent of any tech, of any alarms Logan would trigger by entering.

Chapter 8
Kyle

Kyle suffered a stern lecture from Mr. Orm as they hurried away from Sovereign Hall. Some things never changed. Even traveling to the far reaches of the land wasn't enough to escape the sharp end of a father's tongue.

He escaped eventually, saying he was going to see Nomi about healing a terminally ill patient. Mr. Orm could hardly argue with that, though he tried. "What about your lunch? Come home and eat with us."

So you can keep an eye on me? Kyle thought. "I'll grab something," he said vaguely, and darted away.

Gazes followed him as he made his way through the streets. He soon got himself lost, and he turned in a circle, wondering how he'd managed to wind up in a dead end. Trees towered ahead, forming a barrier between the enclave and the Broken Lands. Kyle knew it was only a short walk through the strip of forest to where kalibacks and other dangers roamed. Anyone could find their way into the Broken Lands if they wanted to, even children, though not many dared until they were of age and ready to tether.

He returned to the dusty street and looked left and right. He'd never get used to this place. The entire enclave was as alien to him as his city must be to these quaint people. Most of the streets here were unpaved and extremely muddy in rainy weather. Timber houses with stone bases stood close but *separate* from one another, a luxury Kyle knew would cost an absolute fortune back home in the city. It was hard to believe ordinary people owned so much space. Yet despite their apparent wealth, life was simple here—no electricity, no basic communication beyond word of mouth, no stream screens reporting the day's news . . . It seemed impossible that anyone could go from day to day without reports from the Hub.

But maybe that was why they were so happy. No distractions from reality, no wrist tablets bleeping updates and news, no stream teams taking up huge chunks of people's lives. Maybe Kyle could be happy here in the enclave if he stuck around long enough. But he doubted it.

He sighed. This place wasn't for him. He had no friends here. Flesh and blood though they were, Mr. and Mrs. Orm were nothing more than temporary parents to him. His equally temporary younger brother Kiff was a good kid but not a replacement for Byron. It was almost disturbing and a little sad to see how Byron probably would have looked today had he not suffered such a catastrophic accident four years ago. Kyle almost felt resentment toward Kiff in that respect, and though he knew his feelings were unjust, they gave him an even stronger desire to go home. Despite a lingering anger over his dad's decision to repurpose rather than exile him, he still missed his family and wished he could see them again, not to mention his friends from school. And Rissa, the girl of his dreams.

Nobody compared to Rissa. Certainly not Nomi, a nice enough girl but somehow a little too quiet for him. She knew Logan well, and by some twisted logic, this meant she also knew Kyle. The two boys were, after all, cast from the same mold. Kyle had avoided her for that reason, in case she somehow assumed he liked her as much as Logan did.

She's Logan's girl, he thought. *Or will be if he ever plucks up the courage to ask her out on a date. He's too—what was it Kiff had said?—too much of a durgle to approach her.*

He shook his head. He couldn't stand around dreaming all day long. He needed to do something useful.

Calling on his Glider spirit, he waited while the elegant birdlike creature shifted into what he thought of as the driver's seat of his brain and spread its incorporeal wings. He could see the pale-green appendages behind his shoulders; they stuck out like webbing in a spindly frame. He had only flown once, and it had been the single most thrilling experience of his life.

Once again, he lifted into the air before realizing it was happening. Stifling a gasp, he rose above the rooftops. The logic still failed him. He understood how a phantom creature could float through the air, but how could one lift its host's physical body off the ground? It made no sense, and yet here he was, soaring high, leaving wispy contrails in his wake.

He left the Fixer Enclave behind. Though he was tempted to fly out over the Broken Lands and head for home, he knew he would only get so far—to the raging river that spanned the land. There, an invisible barrier prevented spirits from traveling any farther west. While Kyle was confident of his powers, not even he could break through that magical wall with his spirits intact.

Instead, he headed south, following the vaguely defined boundary of the Broken Lands. There was no sense maintaining a physical barrier over such a great distance, but a barrier of sorts existed in the form of three-foot-high posts with blue ribbons tied to them. These had been marked by the Banisher, a spell cast to keep the spirits away from the enclaves.

Kyle flew fast and came upon the Hunter Capitol, which spread out along the southern coast. The enclave was big, the buildings more substantial, somehow grander. Surrounded by forest on three sides and coast on the other, its log homes sturdy and sprawling, city folk would consider this a rich district indeed, unattainable by the vast majority of citizens. It certainly beat high-rises poking up into the smog.

His thoughts and emotions kept getting mixed up. One minute he envied the people of the enclaves, the next he wished he were back home among familiar tech.

He spotted an impressive building with three towers, the tallest in the center. The structure stood high above the rest of the enclave, though a few notably large homes nearby looked like they might belong to the sovereign and his highest-ranking cohorts. Could this be the Hallowed Spires? Nothing else fit the bill, and it seemed logical that this mysterious Guardian, who apparently lorded over the sovereignty, would live in such a grand palace.

On closer inspection, the place was far from majestic. Its stone walls were dark and grey with one slender bank of windows too grubby to see through. As Kyle flew around, he decided the place was more like a prison than a palace, with only one entrance that he could see. He felt a shiver as he recalled his vision of a chamber strewn with tech and the inner reaches of three towers high above.

His Breaker might be able to punch a hole through the wall, but he doubted entry would be that easy. And the metal shielding he'd seen in Nailor's memory would certainly keep Kyle at bay even if he penetrated the outer shell.

The Guardian would be well protected. He'd been there for generations, perhaps hundreds of years if Abe's story held water. Surely not the *same* Guardian though, not unless he was immortal! Then again, perhaps he kept himself alive with tech, although that would suggest tech worked inside the Hallowed Spires, which seemed impossible considering it was the source of the inhibitor.

Kyle flew around and around, seeking another way in. There just seemed to be the one entrance, a very grand one, no doubt well secured. The windows might be a possibility . . .

Disgruntled, Kyle landed in the nearby streets and nudged shoulders with the first person he came to, a pudgy lady loaded down with a filled basket of fruit.

"Sorry," he said with an exaggerated look of dismay. "I was busy looking at the Hallowed Spires." He made sure to point up at the monstrous building looming over them as he gripped the lady's arm longer than necessary and allowed his Skimmer to leap into action.

"Hey!" the woman said, yanking free and turning white. "Stay out of my head!" Her spirit, a Weaver, snapped furiously at the intrusion.

Kyle nodded and hurried away. He'd gleaned some of what he needed to know. Mentioning the Hallowed Spires out loud and pointing at it had invited the woman's mind to dump out the relevant information whether she liked it or not.

Absolutely no entry for anyone, ever, his Skimmer relayed. It was more like a hiss in his head, but the meaning was clear. *Servants visit from time to time, fetching and carrying supplies as needed, passing messages across the seven enclaves, doing their master's bidding. The people of the Hunter Enclave look upon the Hallowed Spires with a sense of awe and foreboding.*

"Is there another way in?" he muttered.

He caught the briefest flash of a tunnel deep below the ground, a fleeting scrap of information based more on legend than common knowledge. Then the image faded.

What about his Creeper? They were unnervingly good at finding hiding places. He allowed the spirit to take control and waited in the middle of the street for it to guide him. People glanced at him as they passed, and he realized he must look like he'd lost his mind as he stood there staring into space with phantom tentacles projecting from his midriff.

The Creeper was absolutely no help. Disgruntled, it sank deep into his body as if ashamed of its inability to seek out any hidden tunnels.

Guards suddenly appeared. Six of them came running around the corner, and when they saw him, they picked up their speed and drew their swords. Kyle frowned. What had he done to upset them now?

"You!" one shouted. "Stay where you are!"

"Why?" he yelled back.

Behind them, peering around the corner, Kyle spotted the pudgy woman he'd skimmed earlier. Surely she hadn't complained about him? But even so, six guards seemed like overkill. And they'd come so quickly. A passing squad? Or had they been sent by someone else? Perhaps the Guardian of the Hallowed Spires?

Sighing, Kyle quelled the urge to use his Breaker to pummel the guards into the ground. As always, most of them were tethered to Hunter spirits, and they bobbed eerily, rising up from the shoulders of the guards as they ran.

Quietly, the Glider slipped into Kyle's head. He waved goodbye and slowly rose into the air as the guards skidded to a halt below.

* * *

When he walked into his temporary home later that afternoon, Prima Orm was bustling about preparing a meal while Kiff carefully set the table. "I'm glad you're home," she said, looking a little flustered. "Sorry to rush, but I have to go back out. A swarm of orb scavengers flew into the enclave in the north sector! Can you believe it? Twelve people injured, mostly minor bites but a couple of quite severe lacerations and burns."

"I'll come with you," Kyle said.

"No, stay here." Prima paused and pushed her long, flowing blond hair back over her shoulder, absently causing her Fixer spirit to flinch. The small, furry creature with stalk legs and three tails spent a lot of time perched there in a partially corporeal state, about as solid as a spirit could get.

Kyle tilted his head. "You don't need my help?"

"They're minor injuries. The five of us can take care of them."

Kyle knew she referred to all five Fixers of the enclave. "So Nomi's there?" he asked, then felt his face reddening as Kiff grinned broadly in his periphery. "I mean—"

Mrs. Orm placed a tureen of soup in the middle of the table and gestured for Kyle and Kiff to sit. She remained standing, her Fixer appearing to chew on her earlobe. "I want you to save your strength for Grelda."

"Ah."

"I think it's time you pushed yourself," she said, at last sliding into her chair. As Kiff noisily spooned soup into his bowl and began slurping at it, she reached across the table and grasped Kyle's hand. "She's asking for you again. I said you'd see her."

"Tonight?" Kyle said, quailing. What if he messed up? How did anyone know for sure there was a cancerous mass inside her body? What if he tried to fix it and ended up hurting her worse, turning her organs to mush?

"Tomorrow," Mrs. Orm said. "In the morning. Just do what you can. It's either that or she'll die. We think it'll be soon." She patted his hand. "I'll be with you. So will Nomi, if you like. We'll be there to support you and help wherever possible. You can . . ." She pursed her lips. "You can borrow our Fixers, if that will help."

"It might," he agreed thoughtfully, staring at his empty bowl.

Mrs. Orm scooped a ladle of soup into it for him. "So rest tonight. Eat well, then go relax. Healing is tiring work, and I want you to be at full strength in the morning."

He did eat well. The durgle soup was delicious, and he ate three bowls before realizing he should have stopped at two. He retired to his—Logan's—room while the sun was only just setting. He didn't plan on sleeping, just reading for a while. As it happened, he only read eight pages before he let the book fall onto his chest.

Sometime in the night he dreamed of tunnels, a lost underground city, weird and wonderful fungi smothering the rocky ceilings, creatures lurking in the darkness, vast caverns and gurgling streams, curious vapors of light and dense mists.

And the old man Abe Torren, who beckoned him.

Chapter 9
Logan

Logan sat up in bed and sucked in an exaggerated breath. Checking with his wrist tablet on the nightstand, he saw that it was early, just minutes before sunrise.

He pushed the thick covers off and shuffled to the bathroom, clutching his forehead. Abe had sent him a vision, and he had awakened before it had ended. Splashing water on his face, he tried to recall the events from the dream.

While Abe had not made an appearance in the dream, Logan was certain it had been his doing. The last time he had received a vision had been in the Broken Lands. Then, Abe had sent him a glimpse of the city of Apparati. This time, it had not been any part of Kyle's world. This vision had revealed the world below.

Logan trekked through a dark tunnel, its walls rounded yet rough in spots. Had it been a clacker tunnel?

He carried a lantern, but the environment itself lent him illumination as well. In fact, the very air he breathed seemed to glow with each exhale. He wound up in a large chamber filled with crude, crumbling buildings almost overtaken by a jungle of fungal growths, some reaching easily over a hundred feet in the air. A flurry of activity near the center of the cavern drew his attention. While he was certain he was seeing living things scurrying about, the vagueness of their shape and purpose had him stymied. No matter how hard he tried, getting a precise look at the entities was simply not possible. The sense that they were intelligent and working together to accomplish a set task flooded his mind. The scene dissolved, and he felt himself moving through the darkness. Seconds later, a tunnel came into focus.

He walked for a time, until the tunnel ended at a shaft that extended both up and down, disappearing into darkness in either direction. His breath was much brighter here.

One second he was absorbed in examining his glowing breath, the next someone shoved him from behind.

He dropped into the shaft and plummeted.

As he plunged into the darkness, no amount of huffing and puffing provided him with the breathing light. Somehow, his lantern had not fallen in with him despite having had a firm grip on it. How that was the case evaded reason.

And that was when he had awakened, before he had hit bottom.

Logan looked at his reflection in the mirror, pleased to see color returning to his complexion. He dabbed at his face with a towel and stood up straight.

What was the point of Abe sending him such a frightening vision? Did the old man want him to go underground or not? Of course, while the gist of the vision had been Abe's doing, Logan was willing to bet that the more terrifying aspects had simply been his own frazzled subconscious taking hold. Even Abe had admitted the staff he used to send the visions wasn't the most reliable tech.

With his wits returning, the panic and fear the vision had elicited faded more and more. He took in a measured breath and returned to his room to see the early signs of dawn arriving over the city.

He slipped on a fresh pair of pants and a long-sleeved shirt and walked out to the common area to wish Byron good morning. Byron, thanks to his robotic body, really had no need for sleep. Although he suspected the boy required some time for his human brain to recharge, Logan had never caught him unawares. Maybe this morning he would.

He slipped out of his room, kaliback-quiet, and padded down the hall, determined to catch his prey unawares.

* * *

Foiled again, Logan thought.

Byron was already on the move in the kitchen, preparing breakfast for the family. Logan stalked in, doing his best to hide his frustration at not being able to get the drop on his robotic brother.

"Doesn't your brain need any rest at all?" Logan said as he retrieved a plate from an upper cabinet.

"Minimal amounts. I tend to snatch downtime in increments of seconds and minutes, not hours like you and the rest of the family. Plus, I don't snore. I only wish the same could be said of you." Byron danced his head to the left and right slightly, his gesture to indicate a humorous jab.

Loreena and Josef, Kyle's adoptive parents and Logan's biological ones, walked in. Mr. Jaxx fiddled with a large wall panel and muttered to himself about recalibrating the steam drink intake before placing a mug into the small port that seemed to slide open in response to his haranguing. Even though Josef was top of his game in Appliance Diagnostics and Repairs, some things were beyond him. Logan had been careful not to outperform the man in his specialty in front of him. Going over and offering to enhance the steam drink apparatus would not sit well with Josef, even if Logan could do it in half the time. Respect trumped expediency, he knew that much.

Josef sat down as Byron served him a plate of eggs and toast. Loreena took her seat and poured juice into Logan's empty glass. He thanked her and dug into his own plate of eggs.

Loreena said, "Glad to see your appetite is finally back."

Logan knew she fretted over him. Thanks to his side trip last night, he'd returned late from his research with Rissa. Loreena hadn't questioned where he had been but had voiced her concern at his willingness to skip dinner.

"Probably couldn't think straight after spending time with Talios' daughter last night," Mr. Jaxx said. "Watch that girl. She does more than turn heads. Ambitious like her father." He flicked on the stream screen. "News of his appointment as Mortimer's replacement should be coming out today if the Hub's got its act together."

Logan didn't respond.

Byron placed the dirty pan in the washer and took his place at the table, his plate conspicuously absent.

"Thanks for breakfast, Byron," he said with a mouthful.

"What's on your schedule today, Logan?" Loreena asked.

"School all day and then back to the Archives. Rissa wants to meet up and practice our presentation. I shouldn't be as late as last night." He felt bad lying but didn't want to tell them what he was really planning to do.

Byron gave him a look, but he ignored it. *With his advanced sensor array, he can suss out when I'm lying.*

Josef rose, placed his plate in the washer, and took a long swig of his steam drink. He smacked his lips and gave a harsh look to the wall unit he had hovered in front of minutes earlier. "Still don't have it perfect, but I'm close. I bet I'll tweak it just right tomorrow." He shot an imaginary gun at the device as he left the kitchen. "Watch yourself around Rissa."

Logan finished his meal and politely excused himself. As he retrieved his satchel from his room, Byron entered and blocked the door. "What's going on?"

"What?"

"Where are you really going after school?"

Logan held up his hands, offering a weak gesture of surrender. "I knew you had me."

"Where?"

"Just running around."

"And does this running around involve going underground?" Byron put his hands on his hips.

Logan knew he couldn't throw another lie out there. "Maybe."

He expected Byron to scold him, tell him not to go. Instead, the boy surprised him. Byron looked pleading, his green photoreceptors projecting convincing appeal. "Then I'm going, too."

Logan squeezed by his not-so-little brother, thankful he didn't have to move the heavy robotic body out of the way. "No. I'm just scouting some place out. Don't worry, I won't trip any alarms this time." He added, "Stay here and cover for me, please. I'll be back safe and sound, and Josef and Loreena'll be none the wiser."

He didn't wait for a response. He just fled out the front door, his thoughts on the supplies he would need to mount his foray into the world below.

He recalled his vision. *For one, I'm going to need a lantern.*

Chapter 10
Kyle

Kyle woke with the sunlight streaming through the window. For a moment he felt blissfully happy and content, but then he remembered he was supposed to go with Prima this morning to see the terminally ill patient, Grelda, and try to heal her.

He dressed slowly, deep in thought. He had to make an attempt sometime. But if he botched his effort and killed her . . .

To his surprise, Prima wasn't around. Instead, Mr. Orm had made breakfast: fried durgle eggs, a slice of thick morribie hide ladled with honey, and chunks of bread toasted over the fire. It all looked a little rough and ready, but Kyle pulled up a chair next to Kiff and filled his plate.

"Where's your mom?" he asked Kiff.

Kiff started talking with his mouth full, but Mr. Orm broke in. "Prima got called out again early this morning. It's those orb scavenger victims. Two of them had a delayed reaction to the bites, and now she's scared the fire-plague is setting in."

"The—the what?"

"Poison. A nasty side effect of orb scavenger attacks. They're just filled with disease." Mr. Orm stopped eating and pointed his fork at Kyle. "But never mind that. You took off before I was finished talking to you yesterday. What in Apparata possessed you to attack one of the Guardian's servants?"

Not this again, Kyle thought with dismay. He felt like saying it was a Hunter spirit that had possessed him, but he refrained, knowing Mr. Orm wouldn't appreciate the joke. Besides, the man was suddenly so fired up about the whole thing that Kyle couldn't get a word in edgewise.

"Ordinarily, people don't throw themselves on servants of the Guardian and expect to get away with it," Mr. Orm said.

"You were lucky that Durant fellow didn't slap you in irons and throw you in the Pens. He had every right to."

"That wasn't luck. He's scared of me," Kyle muttered, his gaze on the table.

Next to him, Kiff sat silent, his plate already empty.

"Nobody in their right mind tackles one of those servants," Mr. Orm said, still brandishing his fork. "I understand life in the enclaves is new to you, Kyle, but you must know that assaulting a loyal subject of the Guardian—assaulting anyone for that matter—and stealing their thoughts without due cause is intolerable behavior by any standard. I was ashamed of you yesterday. I still am."

Kyle felt guilty. He'd do anything to be in his own kitchen back home in the city. If he was going to suffer an ear-bashing like this, it should be from his own dad, not Logan's. It felt wrong. Mr. Orm looked familiar and had the same intense glare, yet he was tanned and weathered, his hair longer and messier, his frame somewhat leaner. He looked the same but was entirely different.

Still, his anger was real. It was a good thing Kyle hadn't mentioned the flight to the Hunter Capitol and how he'd nearly been arrested there. He nodded meekly and mumbled "yessir" as the tirade came to an end.

". . . And just know this," Mr. Orm finished. "I'd say the exact same thing to Logan if he were here. You're both as stubborn as grazing hustles."

Kyle gaped. *Stubborn? Us?* He felt a surge of anger as he remembered the way his own dad had given him up for repurposing rather than let him take his chances in the Ruins. His dad was as stubborn as they came, and so was Logan's.

Suddenly, Kyle was done with both dads for the moment. He stiffly apologized, excused himself, and fled the kitchen.

* * *

Kyle spent an hour or so out back with Logan's younger brother, and again he found himself marveling at something as ordinary as the boy's face, certain Byron would have looked like Kiff if he hadn't lost his body in that accident.

Kiff went off to his class around mid-morning, leaving Kyle alone to kick about the house and mull over his dream. Prima had said to rest, and he intended to do so, especially now that Mr. Orm had gone off to work.

The dream had come back to him like a lightning bolt when his mind had turned to the guards posted at the cavern in the rock quarry. The tunnels! The underground stream, the creeping mist, the eerie vapors of light—and Abe, beckoning to him.

It had to be a deliberate vision rather than a random dream. Abe had sent it. But what did he want? The old man had said Kyle and Logan were now phased in with their origins, returned home a dozen years after being swapped as toddlers. In his rightful place, Kyle now had the full powers he'd been born with, and he was supposed to stay in the enclaves where he belonged.

So why did it feel so wrong?

The old man was remarkably short-sighted when it came to the strong bonds of family. Kyle could probably get used to Apparata's way of life—the clean air, the simpler lifestyle, the weird tethering to phantoms from another plane of existence—but was he really expected to live out his life with a new set of parents? Without Byron?

Kyle sighed. Despite his impressive powers, he didn't belong here. He'd rather be a perfectly ordinary boy in the city if there was a way to achieve that without being repurposed. But could he go back? Abe had said no, that it wasn't possible to keep phasing back and forth.

Then again, the old man couldn't know everything.

When Prima returned home later that afternoon, more than a little tired, she grabbed a bite to eat and immediately led Kyle out of the house. She had flecks of blood on her pale-green frock, and when Kyle asked what had happened, she said everything was under control. It had taken three Fixers working together to control the fast-spreading, unseen fire-plague, but the nosebleeds and fevers had finally stopped and now the patients were on the mend.

"Or should I say three Fixers *fighting* together," she muttered as she led the way down several dusty streets and alleys. "I do wish mine would settle down."

She'd complained about this before. Her Fixer got along all right with Nomi's but tended to bicker with all the others.

Kyle changed the subject. "What's the Guardian look like?"

She frowned. "Why the sudden interest?" Sighing, she added, "Leet was quite upset about your antics yesterday, attacking the Guardian's servant and everything. Why are you so interested in him all of a sudden?"

"I just want to learn some history about Apparata."

She didn't look convinced. "Nobody knows for sure what he looks like," she said with a shrug.

"Why?"

"Because nobody in our lifetime has seen him."

Kyle slowed to a stop in the street. "Nobody? Even the servants?"

She paused and turned to face him, smiling faintly. "Well, obviously *they* have. But nobody else. The story goes that the Guardian sacrificed mortality for the good of the enclaves, leaving him with a long-living but crooked, ugly body that none should ever look upon. We respect his privacy. His home is called the Hallowed Spires for a reason. The place is revered by all. They say the Guardian has been there for hundreds of years, watching over us all, protecting us from evil."

"Evil?" Kyle repeated. "Do you mean tech?"

She gestured for him to keep walking. "I mean evil. Long ago, the Guardian shut himself away and vowed to watch over us all with his magic and great wisdom. The servants fetch everything he needs, and they're sworn to absolute secrecy. Becoming one of the fabled servants of the Guardian is no simple matter. On rare occasions, those who fail on Tethering Day are allowed to apply for a position in the Hallowed Spires as an alternative to being exiled to the Broken Lands or put to death. It's a slim chance, for there are never more than seven servants at a time, one representing each enclave."

"So they sidestep the system," Kyle mused, wondering if there was a similar alternative back in the city. According to Abe, there was a Guardian there, too.

"Being a servant is a form of exile in itself," Prima said. "Those poor souls live like hermits, outside normal society, committed to serving the Guardian."

"Doing what, exactly?"

"Monitoring. Reporting back to the Guardian should anything put the Hallowed Spires and the enclaves in potential danger."

"Like exploring the tunnel in the rock quarry," Kyle muttered. When she shot him a glance, he said quickly, "But what's this evil you're talking about?"

"A return to the ugly days of old when flying machines came to shoot agonizing fire from vast distances, hunting for fun and endangering wildlife. Morribies used to be far more plentiful across the land. Now the damage is done; herds are greatly diminished. Those dark days are all but forgotten now." She cast him a glance. "Were, anyway. Now that you're here, people are remembering, digging up old stories, questioning just how much is true and how much has changed in the last few hundred years. Are things better now? Are your people more . . . respectful with their flying machines?"

Kyle snorted before he could stop himself.

"Well," Prima said, "then perhaps you can understand why the Guardian is so important to our enclaves. To protect us from your people."

Troubled, Kyle realized he'd left her with a skewed impression of his world. Yes, there were irresponsible, dangerous individuals as well as general corruption and evil, but it wasn't all bad. Far from it. The enclaves and the city would do well to merge together and share the best of both worlds . . .

This gave him pause for thought. The two worlds had once been whole. Their slow but dramatic separation had come about through a stark difference of opinion regarding their way of life. Now, hundreds of years later, legends suggested that tech bred evil. On the other hand, the people here seemed somewhat primitive. Perhaps there was a happy medium where tech could go hand in hand with the simpler, more spiritual lifestyle—if the two worlds could ever be attuned to one another.

They left the streets and headed into the woods to the south. In the trees stood a cottage, obviously the home of their patient, Grelda Rimpor. Apprehension filled Kyle once more as Prima gently knocked and pushed the door open. He followed her into a dark living room, squinting as his eyes adjusted to the gloom.

Walking silently across the cluttered room to a bedroom at the back, Prima called out, "It's just me."

She entered the bedroom and moved aside so Kyle could see past her. On the bed, wrapped up in thick nightclothes and bundled under several layers of sheets, a middle-aged woman turned her head and gazed at them. She smiled. "Hello, Prima. And you must be Kyle. I've heard so much about you."

Kyle mumbled his reply. It wasn't the sight of the dying woman that distracted him, nor her Weaver spirit floating over the bed tethered only by a wispy strand of green light. What distracted him was the pretty girl sitting by her bedside.

"I take it you had a restful day?" Nomi asked. Her meaning was clear. She, like Prima, wanted him to be at full strength for Grelda's healing.

He nodded. "I'm ready," he said, not ready in the slightest.

Chapter 11
Logan

Logan crouched in the tall grasses, eyeing the grate that led to the underground passage. It was still daylight, but the park was largely abandoned. Situated low in the ditch, he was practically invisible to anyone walking or jogging on the nearby path. He did another quick scan for implants in the vicinity and found one moving swiftly out of the park at its entrance. Maybe a jogger spooked by Logan's rustling in the grasses.

He had suffered through school, including a weird confrontation with Rissa at lunch. She had tried to talk him out of presenting, citing how, as the daughter of a general, she had much more experience with public speaking. He had dismissed her and wandered back to class, going through the rest of his day without incident.

He hadn't even run into Byron. His brother was giving him a wide berth. Was he upset? Hopefully he could make it up to him after he returned home.

I'll just go in and nose around. Two hours underground was his goal. More than that, and he risked upsetting his parents. He paused. Weird how much it mattered what Josef and Loreena thought of him. They were practically strangers and yet were his flesh and blood.

His thoughts turned to Kiff, his brother back at the enclaves. Kyle had to have fixed things with him. One of the reasons to send Kyle to the enclaves was to have him use his powerful talents with spirits to exorcise the Breaker that had overwhelmed Kiff's young mind and body, a feat Logan was unable to accomplish. *But I did save Byron and give him a new body. That's something Kyle will appreciate when he returns to the city.*

Logan brushed aside thoughts of his two brothers and assessed his supplies. He'd brought along very little. This was a simple scouting excursion after all. If he found something that required a longer trip below ground, he'd stock up better for next time. Bought at a nearby market, the clip-on lantern, the extra-sized water bottle, and the hunting knife would do.

The shop owner had questioned him about the knife until he had recognized him as Logan Orm from the Wild, the clunky name the media had given him. Then, the man had been all questions, gleefully wanting to hear all the particulars of surviving out in the Ruins. Logan had shared dribs and drabs of his experience, mostly his encounters with the wildlife and not his run-in with Abe and the Tower. The man had been riveted to his account of fending off kalibacks and orb scavengers, so much so that he had given him the knife at half price.

It was a good blade, lighter and more durable than any made by the Weavers in his enclave. He patted it, thankful for the thick sheath tied to his leg and looped through his belt.

He hefted the last item he had bought: a crowbar. Satisfied no one was coming out of the passage, Logan approached.

The lock and chain on the metal grate required his physical efforts and not his tech prowess. He wedged the forked end of the bar between the looped chain and the metal frame of the grate. Pausing, he looked into the tunnel. What if it was simply an access point to the sewer system? Maybe Apparati had a small population of castoffs who had set up dominion in the sewers. For some reason, that notion didn't make sense to him. It didn't explain how the stranger, an adult, was moving about minus an implant.

The bundle the man had delivered to the Guardian also bothered him. What did it hold within? Another mystery to expose. He felt a little foolish pursuing this entry point to the underground when he knew what he had unearthed earlier was riddled with tech and more likely to be of importance. After all, it had gotten Trilmott riled up.

Logan shook his head. Was he getting off track? He had to move on something, and what stared back at him was the most obvious place to try next: underground. His vision this morning confirmed such a quest was logical if not wholly sensible. The grim end of the dream no longer bothered him. He was certain that had not been part of Abe's transmission but his own mind warping the imposed vision.

Bringing his concentration back to the chain and lock, Logan jerked the crowbar down. The rusted links broke with ease. If the man regularly traversed this passage, he'd find Logan's handiwork. What if he came by while Logan was deep underground? Then bringing the crowbar made sense. It would serve as a weapon and as liberator if the stranger secured the entrance with new chains. He kicked the lengths of the chain free and swung the grate open.

Clicking on the lantern, he took a deep breath and stepped into the tunnel. He hunched slightly to fit but found it wasn't as cramped and closed in as it had looked from the outside. The air was cool and pouring steadily up and out of the passage.

About thirty seconds later, the tunnel curved and sloped slightly downward. He looked back at the exit, the grate still hanging open. That wasn't good. He raced back and slipped the grate shut, ignoring the squawking protests of the two large hinges on its right side. He looped a salvageable length of chain around the grate and tucked the useless lock in place. If not closely inspected, it looked fastened and adequately performing its duty.

He turned about and stepped lightly, heading deeper into a new world.

* * *

The path ahead branched left and right. This was the third time he had reached a juncture. He had gone left each time, thinking that would make it easier when he retraced his footsteps.

The tunnels so far had all been constructed of stacked stone, except for the one to his left. At first glance, the walls appeared to be packed dirt. How had the tunnel not collapsed? Looking closer, he saw why the tunnel was still in use. Crisscrossing spans of dirt raced all over the walls, revealing it had been hardened by Weaver magic. He could be assured it would hold if the Weaver had reinforced the entire length of the passage. Another encouraging aspect: it was taller than the others, and he wouldn't have to crouch while exploring it.

He took his knife and scratched an X on a cornerstone at eye level. He had marked each new path such and wondered how he would do so if the walls were simply earthen from here on out.

So far, his lantern had been the sole source of illumination. His breath had not produced any light whatsoever like it had in his vision. Had he taken a wrong turn? If he had made all rights, would he be exhaling light at this point?

He grabbed his knees and caught his breath. He felt cut off and alone, even more than he had when out in the Broken Lands. He reached out and could sense no tech above. He didn't have his wrist tablet, having left it at school deliberately. They could track him with it, and no amount of manipulation led him to thinking he could disable its tracking system. It was far more hardened against intrusion than most devices. *Probably specially made for me*, he thought.

At the enclaves, he had always craved solitude. A week in a bustling city had not changed that, but the isolation he experienced now was intimidating. Logan tried to settle his thoughts, tamping down the frazzled worry that threatened to overwhelm him.

I'm just underground on another trek that will lead to something important. I'm needed here.

His heartbeat lessened, and he again stood, his confidence reinstated. Had Kyle received a similar vision the previous night? If so, was he also braving the world below? Would his mental state be more fragile, having lived all his life among the comforts of the city?

Logan forced himself to enter the rough-hewn tunnel. Forty feet in, it happened: he exhaled, and the air in front of his face filled with light. The bright green reminded him of the petals of the ladyfire flowers, a key ingredient in several of his mother's healing salves. The veins of the petals glowed that same green.

He exhaled again and more closely examined the phenomenon. It looked like his breath was causing small airborne spores to glow, their light ebbing away in a matter of seconds. Would it be bad to keep inhaling the spores? What if they got caught in his lungs? So far, his breathing was normal, no obvious discomfort. The stranger who had retreated underground hadn't worn any special filtering mouthpiece, so exposure must be tolerable. If he encountered any labored breathing, he would turn around.

He spouted forth a few more bright breaths, fascinated by the act. He tried short gusts and one longwinded exhalation. Either way, the light shone for no more than ten seconds. He tried holding a breath for thirty seconds and releasing it, thinking the longer it spent in his body, the longer the glow's duration. It didn't matter. The limit seemed to be ten seconds, and a few winked out in as little as five.

Satisfied he was reasonably safe, Logan moved through the tunnel with a lighter step and a much lighter breath. While he was still alone, the intermittent production of brilliant clouds gave him a sense of companionship, one that he could cause to reappear as long as he lived and breathed.

Hopefully nothing he encountered down here would put a halt to either.

Chapter 12
Kyle

Grelda Rimpor smiled and patted Kyle's hand as he perched on a chair by her bed. "Thank you for coming to see me," she said weakly, dry and rasping. "I'll understand if you can't heal me. I prepared myself for death months ago. I'm ready to go. So don't feel bad if . . . well, you know, if things go wrong."

Kyle's stomach knotted up. He glanced across the bed to where the red-haired Nomi sat. Prima now stood behind her. Both their Fixer spirits squirmed on their shoulders, impatient to get to work, growling and hissing at one another. No matter how far they strayed or bounced around, a wispy contact with their hosts remained at all times.

Hovering over the bed, Grelda's spirit, a Weaver, waited motionless as though sensing it would soon be time to move on. If Grelda died, it would no doubt go off and roam the enclaves looking for another host, and then perhaps the Banisher would be called to repel the errant spirit back to the Broken Lands.

"I might need help with this," Kyle said after taking a deep breath. He looked at Prima and Nomi. "Help from your Fixers, I mean."

Prima shuffled forward an inch or two. "You can borrow them anytime."

Nomi nodded her agreement. "Yes, please do. They're getting on my nerves."

Kyle took Grelda's hand. The problem with this kind of healing was that he had nothing to focus on. Her illness was unseen, perhaps spread throughout her body. Prima had told him it was cancer. She'd suspected this months ago based on various basic symptoms, but it was largely guesswork on her part. Her Fixer had been sure, though. Although agitated, it had whispered in her head that the patient was terminally ill, that the disease was inoperable.

Kyle was her last hope. He allowed his Fixer to hop out onto his shoulder and scurry down his arm. He noticed it kept its stalklike legs firmly planted in his flesh as it sniffed at Grelda. Recoiling, it let out a high-pitched clicking that Kyle somehow understood: *The patient is too far gone.*

"No," he said firmly. "Look again."

He was aware that all eyes were on him. Grelda looked a little puzzled at his apparent one-sided conversation. However, Prima and Nomi looked on impassively. Either they understood the clicking noises or their own Fixers were offering translations.

Kyle's semi-transparent creature grumbled and moved closer to the bed. It ducked its head through the sheets and into the flesh of Grelda's abdomen. Her own spirit, the Weaver, snarled at this intrusion and rose higher on its intangible but very real thread.

Without waiting for a response from his agitated Fixer, Kyle looked toward Prima and Nomi and said softly, "To me."

They both jerked as their spirits leapt off their shoulders and bounded across the bed toward him, their tethers completely severed. A second later, they were part of him, side by side with his own Fixer, and his head suddenly filled with angry clicks and screeches as the three furry creatures bickered.

"Quiet!" Kyle yelled, and Grelda's eyes widened.

He cast a glance at Prima and Nomi. White-faced, they were probably feeling empty right now.

The three Fixers finally agreed to work together, though for a minute Kyle seriously considered tossing Prima's back to her. The little creature really had a selfish streak and a sore temper. But eventually all went quiet as they dipped their faces into Grelda's body as though taking a peek underwater. Images started popping into Kyle's head, and what he saw horrified him.

He pulled back, bringing the Fixers with him. "I . . . I can't," he said.

In the silence that followed, Kyle released the visiting Fixers, and they darted back to their hosts as though afraid of something in the air. He hung his head in shame as they snuggled meekly back into Prima's and Nomi's shoulders.

Nomi got up. "A word?" she said.

Kyle followed her out of the room. When he glanced back, Prima was sitting on the side of the bed leaning over Grelda. Surprisingly, the older woman was smiling and shaking her head. Kyle caught her hushed words: "It's all right, my dear. I'm ready to go."

Nomi turned to face him. A few inches shorter, she peered up at him. "I know it's scary. I know you think you're going to make everything worse somehow. Trust me, I was terrified when I did my first healing, and that was just a broken finger!" She poked him gently in the chest. "You have a gift. You're far stronger than all of us, especially since you can borrow other Fixers as well. That's . . . that's *amazing*."

Kyle sighed. "She's riddled with sickness. Even three Fixers together seemed out of their depth. I'm not saying I can't do it, just that—"

A gasp came from the bedroom.

Kyle and Nomi swung around to see Prima staggering back from the bed with her hands to her face.

The bed was empty.

* * *

"Kyle!" Prima shouted as he dashed out of the cottage. "That wasn't your fault!"

"I know," he said breathlessly. "Grelda winked out. I get it. It means her counterpart died back in the city. Maybe she died of the same cancer."

Both Prima and Nomi were speechless at this. Wink-outs happened at random, and nothing could be done about them. It was an accepted fact of life. But the idea that wink-outs were caused by the death of a twin in a faraway place . . . well, it was hard to digest.

"I have to go," Kyle told them. He looked up at the trees all around. He was sure his Glider could navigate a way out. "There's something I need to do."

"But *what*?" Nomi asked, hurrying toward him.

"It's hard to explain."

"Try."

Kyle had no idea how to sum up what he felt. He wasn't exactly sure himself. "The city could have saved Grelda. We have tech that can eradicate cancer in just a few minutes. Cellular regeneration is getting more and more advanced." He thought briefly of his brother Byron. "It doesn't grow back limbs, though. That's what repurposing is for. But these machines can identify malignant masses and sort of *dissolve* them, leaving healthy tissue to—"

"If that's true," Prima said, her face still white, "then why did Grelda's twin die of cancer?"

Good catch, Kyle thought. "She might have died of something totally different. An accident crossing the road, a heart attack, anything."

"At this exact moment?" Nomi said with a raised eyebrow.

Kyle had to admit it did seem coincidental. But then again, even dying from cancer at this exact moment boggled his mind. These people had led entirely different lives. Surely something in their diets, local medicines, or just the way they'd lived would have impacted the timing of their deaths? It would be fascinating to see a study of wink-out victims throughout history. Most seemed to happen randomly, but occasionally a person winked out right at a critical moment of danger as though a similar hazardous event had occurred far away and killed the counterpart. This was certainly true of Mayor Baynor and

General Mortimer along with their equally corrupt doppelgangers in the enclaves. Some people were simply closer to their twins, their situations somehow tied together.

Purebloods, he thought, remembering what Abe had once said about that. *Like Logan and me. Inextricably linked in every way.*

"It was cancer," he concluded aloud, realizing he'd been staring into space. "And medical equipment like that is only available if you can afford it," he added grimly, finding himself ashamed. "Not everyone can."

He grimaced, thinking of his dad's endless dinnertime rants whenever the subject of medical costs came up—the great divide between the rich and the poor, how even those in between had little hope of affording much-needed high-tech surgery. For years, the late Mayor Baynor had promised ImpartialCare for all, but he'd never delivered on that promise. Mayors and generals and the like lived in the tallest building in the heart of the city center, which boasted its own hospital wing and operating theater.

"I don't understand," Nomi said, reaching for his hand. "Logan—I mean, *Kyle*—let's sit and talk about this."

Her slip was perfectly understandable, but somehow it strengthened his resolve. He gently extracted himself from her grasp and said, "I'm not Logan. But I'll bring him back to you."

"What? What do you mean? You're not . . . you're not *leaving*, are you?"

It had occurred to him, not for the first time, that many folks in the city would be far better off if the inhibitor didn't keep spirits away. If Fixers were allowed to roam free wherever they liked, mingling and tethering with the poorer people out near the Wall, many hundreds of minor ailments could be healed every day at *absolutely no charge*. That is, if the mayor didn't cash in on the situation. An influx of free medical help? Baynor would certainly have turned that to his advantage! But maybe the new mayor wouldn't be as greedy as the old one. Maybe he would appreciate the Fixers, accept their help, and in return open up some of his high-tech cancer equipment to those who couldn't afford it—including the people here in the enclaves.

Both Prima and Nomi looked aghast. "You're going back to the city?" Prima said. "Is that it? You're leaving us?"

"I don't belong here, and Logan probably doesn't belong in the city."

I hope, Kyle added in his head. It would be awkward if he arrived home and found Logan quite happily sitting at the dining table, the entire family getting along just fine with their new, tech-powerful son.

"You're going home," Prima said again, looking deflated now.

Kyle shook his head. "Not just yet. First I'm going to destroy the inhibitor."

It took a moment for Prima to react. "You can't! Kyle, the Guardian—the Hallowed Spires—you can't get in there—you mustn't!"

"Abe Torren told me there's an inhibitor at the Hallowed Spires that prevents tech from working anywhere near the enclaves. If the inhibitor was destroyed, then I could go to the city and bring back equipment that you can use here to heal other cancer patients. Fixers can only do so much. You need technology."

"And how are you going to fetch all this equipment?" Nomi demanded. "You said yourself that you have no powers back in the city, and no implant in your neck. You'll be arrested! How will you—?"

"Logan will help me," Kyle said, hoping that were true.

As both Prima and Nomi opened their mouths to argue, Kyle stepped back and held up his hands as if to say *enough*. He called on his Glider and waited while the tall, birdlike creature eased its way into place. When translucent wings sprouted from his back, he began to float easily on the air.

"This isn't the end," he told Prima and Nomi, distressed at how unhappy they both looked. "Coming here was just the start for me. I'll see you again—and I'll bring flying machines filled with expensive medical tech. You'll see."

As he flew away, one doubt after another nagged at the back of his mind. If what Abe had told him and Logan about "being phased in" was true, there *was* no going home. Kyle was no longer tuned to the city. He would be a ghost there—or rather the entire city would be a ghost to him, a mass of insubstantial buildings at best and absolute nothingness at worst. And Logan could never return to the enclaves with tech, so Kyle's promise to Prima and Nomi was empty.

But he had to try. Something told him there was a solution to all this. Maybe Abe knew what that solution was, and maybe he didn't, but he'd sent a powerful vision of the tunnels for a reason. He wanted Kyle to meet him there, presumably to talk to him about a new mission. Perhaps his mission was the same as Kyle's.

His mind made up, he angled to the south, heading for the rock quarry. Before he went on a rampage and broke into the Hallowed Spires in an effort to destroy the inhibitor, he'd listen to what Abe Torren had to say. *Abe first, then the inhibitor, and then home.*

Of course, it still meant forcing his way past guards to get into the small cavern where the manmade wall had been exposed.

He sighed and put on a burst of speed. As he flew low over the Fixer Enclave, he felt like he was planning to disturb a deadly nest of orb scavengers.

Chapter 13

Logan

The tunnel went on and on. So far, Logan had not encountered any splits, just one long trek steadily downward. The slope of the passage had increased to the point that he had to watch his footing. Slipping now would send him sliding into darkness.

His bright breath persisted. Apparently the spores were everywhere.

Logan stopped and leaned against the curved wall to his left, his breath blasting over a colony of the spores clinging to the wall. This resulted in a large expanse of light flaring up across the earthen wall. He wondered if carbon dioxide triggered the glow. It made a certain sense because they didn't glow on the way into his lungs, only on the way out.

He imagined he had been walking for a good hour. He'd need to turn around soon if he wanted to get back on time. He had come across no signs of the pale stranger from the other day. Logan didn't know what he had expected to find—a bustling population of subterranean people who served the whims of the Guardian and refused to be implanted? An underground society of exiles bent on mounting a rebellion? Either were a bit of a stretch given he knew so little about the stranger. What if the man didn't even live down here? Maybe he had sensed Logan on his tail and deliberately led him below. But his skin had been so pale. He had to live here.

He resumed walking, holding his lantern out. While the bright breath gave him some light, the lantern was better, persistent. His boot kicked something, sending it skittering ahead. Logan crouched and thrust the lantern straight ahead, inspecting the ground for the unknown object. *Probably a rock.*

He shuffled awkwardly forward, expanding the radius of his light. He also puffed out several deep breaths, temporarily filling the passage with added light.

Logan spied it instantly. Tech. He scrambled on all fours, hoping to avoid sliding past it. He wedged the lantern into a soft section of earth and peered closer at the object.

Some sort of glove. It looked clunky and dated, not as sleek as modern tech. He reached out with his mind, attempting to sync up with it and read its design and purpose. He registered a glimmer of data, but nothing that he could decipher. Its programming code didn't conform with what he was accustomed to from his city experiences. That made the tech very old.

He touched the twin crescent-shaped plates mounted on the upper part of the forearm extension. Armor? He rolled it over, watching the reinforced fingers of the glove sweep slightly open as if it was alive. Logan jerked back, briefly thinking the glove was somehow powered up. The image of it leaping at his throat and strangling him entered and exited his mind lightning fast.

It's a tool. It doesn't have a mind of its own.

A voice from behind made Logan stiffen. "Are you going to keep poking at it or simply pick it up?"

Logan exhaled sharply, casting the person behind him in light. "Byron!"

His little brother stood tall in the tunnel, looking down at Logan with restrained judgment. It was weird how much of Byron's intent Logan could read from his body language. While his new body featured some facile articulation, it was far easier to decipher the boy's mood from how he carried himself. Right now, Byron was ticked.

"We shouldn't be here," Byron said, his words echoing.

Logan retrieved his lantern and stood. "*You* shouldn't be here. You followed me."

"I did."

"But how? I should've sensed you." He knew why as soon as he asked the question. He had disabled Byron's tracking devices when he had put him in his new body. Better to not let the Hub and mayor know Byron's comings and goings. But it meant Logan was blind to Byron as well unless he was close.

"You made me invisible, even to you," Byron answered.

"Yeah, yeah. Brilliant move on my part. At least when you're this close, I can read some of your basic support systems."

"But only if you're looking for me, which you weren't."

Logan nodded. "I have to get you back. It's late. Loreena has to be freaking out about you being gone."

"Not at all. I did what you did, I lied. She thinks I'm with you, which I am."

Byron didn't move as Logan brushed past him. "Let's go. Turns out nothing's down here anyway. Just old, useless tech."

Byron chirped, "That's not all. Look." He pointed beyond the abandoned glove.

Logan whirled around, catching a glimpse of a patch of glowing light. It flickered and reappeared. Someone else was in the tunnel, breathing in and out.

The patch of light appeared again, this time moving closer. Actually, as Logan studied it further, he realized it was two patches of light and far too high to be someone breathing. "What is that?"

The glowing mystery came closer, flickering in and out.

Byron figured it out first. "They're wings. The underside is lit up!"

Once he said it, Logan saw what Byron meant. He also saw a small puff of bright breath expel from the dark area in the middle where the head must be. "It's coming this way."

Logan brought up his crowbar and dropped the lantern to the ground.

The sound of the wings flapping suddenly became noticeable, even though they had to have been there before. In all the craziness, he hadn't registered the distinctive noise. *Funny how so many details you notice when you know what you're looking at,* Logan thought.

It was close enough for him to make out the unlit parts of its body. A squat head swiveled about on a fat furry torso. Maybe three feet from wingtip to wingtip. A pair of legs, each ending with four clawed toes, hung down. The wings were webbed, and the glowing pattern peppered across the taut sail-like flesh was more of a blue than the green of its breath.

The creature flew at Logan. He ducked and swatted blindly at it with the crowbar. His attacker squawked and spun about with practiced ease in the tight tunnel.

"Don't mess with it," Byron said. "Stay down."

Logan dropped to the ground, feeling the claws of the creature graze his hood.

He crawled around to watch it, positive it was going to dive-bomb them again.

Instead, it chattered frantically, then fled deeper.

Logan got back up and grabbed his lantern. Surprisingly, Byron moved to pursue the creature. "What are you doing? Leave it."

Byron ignored him and trundled down the tunnel, projecting a cone of light from his chest. "I want a picture of it. I didn't take one."

"What? No. We're going." He didn't want to chase down the thing. Too much like an orb scavenger for his liking. He thought back to his encounter with the Broken Lands' ruthless airborne scavengers. They hunted in packs. What if this thing did the same? Maybe it had torn off to summon reinforcements. "Byron, don't."

Too late. His brother rounded the corner, disappearing from view.

* * *

He had to give Byron credit, the boy was sure-footed. The decline Logan now navigated was the steepest yet. He dug his fingers into the cave wall as he took careful steps forward.

Byron was still ahead of him, his chest lamp bobbing up and down comically. So far, the winged animal hadn't returned with friends, but Logan was certain their luck wouldn't hold much longer.

"Byron, this is silly. Get back here."

The robot boy didn't look back. "I think I've almost caught up to it. It's just ahead, hanging upside down from the ceiling."

"By itself?"

His brother froze, and Logan could make out a small tube extending from his forehead, his sound refraction array. With it, he could map out areas, determine room dimensions and such. "It's hanging in a chamber. Its wings are closed, but I can tell from its breath that it's still facing me."

"Watching you, waiting for you to get close enough and sink its teeth in you." *Of course, not that you have anything to worry about, Byron.* "C'mon, not all of us are armored up."

Byron said, "Next time, be better prepared."

The sound refraction array retreated back into his forehead as Logan finally caught up to him. They were less than ten feet from the creature, its breath spilling forth in short bursts, its beady black eyes trained on them.

Byron straightened up and took a step back.

Alarmed by his brother's sudden stiffening, Logan said, "What's in there?" He squinted and risked pointing the lantern at the hanging animal.

This provoked it. The creature swept open its wings and hissed. Behind it, all along the ceiling of the chamber, other wings opened up, revealing a glowing army of the beasts.

Byron chirped, "Trouble."

Logan spun around and began climbing up the harsh slope. He didn't need to look back to know that all of the roosting things were in the air heading straight for them. He could tell as much from their keening screams and the frenzied flapping of their leathery wings.

Byron scrambled up the slope, taking the lead. Logan moved as fast as he could but refused to let go of his lantern or his crowbar.

He expected hundreds of claws to grab at him, sink into the yielding flesh of his back. But none did. Instead, the creatures flew above them and dealt with the invasion of their dark home in a thoroughly unique way.

Logan glanced upward to see a volley of excrement dropping toward them. It splattered all over him and the ground, the odor sharp and reeking of ammonia and something else. Their beating wings created a strobe effect that confused Logan even more. It was hard to see which way to go with all the flashing light.

Byron said, "Elevated traces of nitrogen paired with oxygen."

"Yeah, I get it. Really stinky."

"No, it's not just that. When combined, they make the perfect knock-out gas."

Logan's vision swam. He reached toward Byron as a dull whine grew in intensity in his skull. He blinked several times, gulped in a few tainted breaths, and then lost consciousness.

Chapter 14
Kyle

As Kyle descended upon the rock quarry and noted several guards tracking his approach, he wondered how he was going to deal with the manmade barrier in the cavern. He'd only had time to knock a four-inch hole in it before being interrupted. After that the cavern had been off-limits. The wall was supremely tough. He wasn't strong enough to widen the hole without the combined strength of at least a few other Breakers.

He circled around, counting two archers high on the quarry walls and another three guards standing by the cavern entrance. Were there more inside?

I need more Breakers, he thought, knowing the bulk of them were spending the day at a demolition site to the east of the enclave. They had been enlisted to tear down decrepit cottages to make way for new ones. Weavers would be loitering there, too, eager to get to work.

He flew away, leaving the archers to relax and lower their bows.

Over to the east, nestled in a clearing in the woods, a twenty-strong workforce broke the peace with their hammering and shouting. Kyle counted five or six Breakers and plenty of Weavers. At least a Hunter or two as well, if the campfires and gently roasting carcasses were anything to go by.

The Breakers were busy pummeling the walls of the old cottages, knocking out great chunks of stone and easily snapping thick, partially rotted timber beams. A few of these derelict cottages had already been obliterated and cleared away, and Weavers had started work on new buildings, reusing materials from piles of rubble, somehow making all those irregular chunks fit perfectly and fuse together to form brand new walls.

Kyle flew in closer, trembling with apprehension.

He knew what he was doing was wrong and would infuriate a lot of people, including Mr. Orm, but he doubted anyone would go along with his plan if he asked. And even if workers agreed to help, the guards at the rock quarry would get in the way. So he swooped toward a crumbling cottage that three Breakers were in the process of demolishing and landed on the warped, moss-covered roof. They didn't notice him, though a few other workers did.

"To me," Kyle whispered over the heads of the Breakers.

The fiery red spirits jerked and looked up at him, each rising out of the bodies of the workers. As one, they shot toward Kyle as though he were their undisputed master calling them home. The workers—two men and a woman—gasped and staggered as their Breaker spirits abandoned them, and they looked around in shock. It was several seconds before they spotted Kyle standing just out of reach on the roof above them.

"What are you doing?" the woman exclaimed angrily.

By now, most of the workforce had paused to watch.

"I need to borrow your Breakers," Kyle said. "I'm sorry, but it's for a good reason, I promise. You'll get them back." As an afterthought, he added, "But you'd better hurry to the rock quarry. You need to be somewhere close when I release them."

"You can't do this!" one of the men shouted. "That's *stealing*!"

Kyle muttered an apology and, confident the three new Breakers were settled within, set off high above the woods.

He could feel hostility brewing as all seven of his resident spirits, apparently now a strong family unit, muscled in on the newcomers, putting on a united front and making it clear there was no room for others. "Settle down," Kyle told them all. "It's just for a little while."

He returned to the quarry. There was no changing his mind now. He doubted there was an actual written law against stealing tethered spirits, mainly because it had never been possible to do so before, but Acting Sovereign Durant would surely introduce such a law very soon. In the meantime, he'd concoct a number of suitable charges and throw Kyle in the Pens to await punishment.

He didn't want to be around when that happened.

To his surprise, he spotted Kiff just before he began his descent into the rock quarry. The boy was ambling along, hands in pockets, inadvertently heading into danger—because in just a few moments there would be arrows flying and swords flashing as Kyle fought his way past the guards. A little annoyed and worried, he knew he'd have to get this done quickly.

The archers again readied their bows as Kyle flew in. "Stay away!" one shouted, his voice echoing around the low cliffs.

Kyle ignored him and hurtled down to land at the feet of the other three guards by the cavern entrance. They drew their swords immediately, their eyes wide as they recognized Kyle Jaxx of the City, the most powerful individual in all of Apparata.

Two arrows thudded into the ground in front of him, close enough that it momentarily blocked him from taking another step. Then another couple thudded down so that all four, their feathered ends still quivering, formed a neat barrier with a very clear message for him to stop where he was. Those archers were *good.*

"Walk away," one of the three guards said with his short sword raised. "The archers won't miss if you take another step. We have orders to kill if anyone comes close—especially you. Please don't make us."

Kyle allowed his Creeper spirit to slip into place. Then he was on the move, darting sideways and forward, leaping as one guard went to tackle him, ducking as another swung his sword, then twisting as the third thrust and jabbed. Two arrows *thwipped* past, mere inches away, but in the brief two seconds the archers needed to reload, Kyle danced and slid past the three guards until he was behind them. He ducked into the narrow passage before the guards got themselves turned around.

Seconds later, he realized the passage into the cavern was blocked about halfway along. Weavers had been here, no doubt on Durant's command. Kyle knew he could break through, but first he needed to delay the guards.

He turned and faced the first of them as they squeezed single-file into the passage after him. The guard's Hunter glowed, illuminating the darkness. It looked angry, its horn lowered as if ready to charge. Kyle didn't dare underestimate the guard or his spirit. Hunters were experienced killers, after all.

He switched to his resident Breaker and took a number of swings at the passage wall to his side, bringing great chunks of rock down between him and the Hunter, backing up as he did so. The guard faltered but immediately tried to climb over. Kyle brought more rock down, practically flinging it onto the growing mound so that the guard had to pause and shield his eyes from all the dust.

Then Kyle switched to his Weaver spirit. Using the dislodged rubble as a base, he started building a more permanent wall, his hands a blur as he moved one loose piece after another, somehow finding the exact right place for each chunk and magically fusing them in place higher up. Through the choking dust, he could see the guard squinting and trying to clamber through the remaining space at the top of the pile, a space that narrowed with every passing second.

Then it was done, the space far too small to squeeze through. Kyle slowed a little, taking his time and making sure the mound of debris and the construction on top were thoroughly locked together. Every piece he laid hands on toughened the barrier between him and the outside world.

"Don't be an idiot!" the guard shouted through the small gap at the top. "We'll be in there in no time!"

Kyle said nothing. He could close the gap completely and shut out the voices, but there was no need. Besides, even though spirits could phase through solid structures, he felt his three guest Breakers would be happier with an actual hole to squeeze through when they returned to their hosts after he was done.

Now that he'd blocked off the guards, he called on his resident Breaker again and turned to face the wall that lay between him and the cavern. He quickly realized it was a far superior wall to the one he'd just thrown together, probably built by several Weavers working as a team. It had been crafted to last a lifetime.

He called all four Breakers together and concentrated their energy into his hands, which then glowed red and lit up the confined space. He plowed into the Weavers' wall with abandon, tearing at it, digging in and yanking hunks out, faster and faster until he found himself three feet in and still tunneling. Durant, or more likely the Guardian's servant, had *really* wanted this place shut down.

He made it through half a minute later. Sweating profusely, choking from the dust, he struggled through the wall and glanced back. At least six feet thick!

His hands still glowing with vibrant energy, he stumbled down the sloping passage and into the cavern. The rock had been stripped away on the far side, and there the smooth, manmade wall glinted, some kind of metal, extremely tough. He stood before the four-inch hole he'd made the day before.

"Ready?" he asked the Breakers.

They clamored and barked.

He attacked the wall by inserting his hands into the bowl-shaped hole, gripping the edges, and yanking hard. Even with the strength of four Breakers, he found it almost impossible to widen the gap. He guessed these spirits just hadn't evolved to tackle such an unnatural, manmade material. They could shape metal, but only in small amounts. This wall was *tough*.

Slowly, very slowly, the metal began to warp. It became soft in places as though melting, brittle in others, and he ended up pulling and punching with all his might until he was panting, sweat dripping off his forehead and down his nose.

But he got there in the end. He fell back and stared in glee at the hole, now just about wide enough to climb through.

"Thanks, boys," he gasped. "You can go now."

The three borrowed Breakers shot free. They turned to glance at him, then floated away along the passage, following the path of least resistance rather than phase straight out through solid rock. A few seconds from now, they'd emerge into the rock quarry where the guards were probably sending out alerts and calling for help. Hopefully the Breakers' masters would be here shortly, perhaps within sniffing distance already.

Kyle turned back to the metal wall and began climbing through the hole into darkness.

Chapter 15
Logan

Logan woke up and scrambled to his knees, his breath the only form of illumination. He swayed, still groggy from the gassing. He exhaled and looked at the ground. No signs of foul waste, although he could still smell it on his clothes.

He patted his torso. Most of the excrement plastered all over him was dry. Several thick patches flaked off, releasing some residual stench. He stood, being careful not to move suddenly as he still felt lightheaded.

He filled the air with bright light, almost hyperventilating in the process. But the abundant glow helped him assess his predicament if only for a few seconds. He was back in the main tunnel with no signs of the creatures or their waste anywhere nearby. He paced around, looking for his supplies. He still had his water bottle clipped to his belt and his knife in its sheath, but his crowbar was gone. He found his lantern, broken, wedged up against the tunnel wall.

He did make a surprising discovery along the wall to his right. Spaced evenly apart along the wall were four metal brackets hammered into the wall, their ends a curved loop. The closest one held the charred remains of a torch, no more than a blackened splinter, cold to the touch. He had not passed this on his way down. Was he deeper underground? How?

"Byron?" he said, his voice raspy and dry.

No response.

He took a drink and tried again, louder. "Byron?"

Checking himself all over, it surprised him to see no teeth or claw marks from his attackers. They just dropped their spurge on him and left? Not the predators he thought they were. Orb scavengers would've gnawed him to the bone by now.

Although, he had no idea how long he'd been out. *Long enough for someone to move me and nab Byron.* Or maybe his brother had dragged him out of the polluted passage and gone back for his supplies. His new body could certainly do that.

The tunnel continued downward to his left, not nearly as steep as before. Logan moved uphill, thinking the chamber with the nesting creatures would be close by. Whoever had moved him—the pale stranger?—probably hadn't dragged him far. They just needed him out of the fouled air. That indicated that whoever they were, they didn't want to bring him harm. At least not yet.

He trekked upward, breathing regularly to produce suitable light. He soon came across the chamber where the winged creatures had nested. He moved quietly, fearful they were again hanging from the ceiling.

He got within three feet of the chamber entrance and froze. While he couldn't see them, he could hear the creatures rustling about above, chirping and cooing periodically. The strong odor of their spurge assaulted his nose, and he backed away, fearing he would be knocked unconscious again.

No way can I go through there without being detected. He'd endure another spurge storm and maybe not wind up as lucky as before. Maybe they'd feed on him the second time.

He shivered and returned to the part of the tunnel with the four metal brackets.

Where was his brother? Had he gone back to the surface to get help? Logan crossed his arms, frustrated. While his lantern was now useless, his bright breath was providing adequate lighting. He could explore a little farther, maybe come across some clues as to Byron's whereabouts. If he didn't see anything in the next ten minutes, he'd race back to the surface. By then, maybe the coating of spurge in the passage behind him would be dry and nontoxic. The dried excrement remaining on his clothing didn't seem to affect him.

Armed with a plan, he strutted confidently onward, creating a guiding light with each passing breath.

* * *

Without his wrist tablet or the sun overhead, it was hard to determine how long he had been walking. Plus, his head was still out of sorts from the winged gassing. It felt like he had been walking for at least ten minutes, but he wasn't so sure. The consuming darkness played with his senses.

He had quickly adjusted to seeing with the aid of his breath. The tunnel was now wider and parts of the walls were covered in a fungus that glowed a bright blue. Actually, the toadstools jutting out of the walls had yellow caps; their gills underneath produced the blue glow. Thankfully, they did not seem to emit any dangerous odors.

Up ahead, the walls were covered with the mushrooms. As he approached the wall-carpet of fungus, he spied small insects flying from toadstool to toadstool, their large translucent wings reflecting the blue glow to great effect. No longer than his pinkie, he was pleased to see they were harmless. None came at him with pincers at the ready. They whizzed by, their tiny brains focused on visiting the many toadstools. He wondered if their relationship to the fungus was similar to bees and other topside insects to flowering plants.

He would've investigated further, but his attention was drawn to the large cavern that opened up before him. The tunnel spilled into a grotto that had to be thousands of feet across. It was surprisingly well lit thanks to its ceiling being coated in the glowing mushrooms. Not only that, but the sprawling jungle emitted even more brilliance. It was like nothing he had seen before. Massive spires over thirty feet tall made of a rust-colored fungal growth reminded him of the impressive verspit mounds that riddled the outskirts of the Glider Enclave.

Mushrooms with caps wide enough to sit on and as tall as Logan himself stood next to many of the mounds.

And the cave was not without fauna. Birds and other winged creatures, thankfully none of the spurge-dropping variety, glided through the air, their breath adding explosive light like a commuting fireworks display.

A small creek ran through the fungus to his right. He spied a herd of knee-high creatures drinking from it as some also gnawed at a rather gummy-looking pink fungus along the water's edge. The grazers had brown fur, and their long necks bristled with quills. Defense against a predator Logan couldn't spot, maybe? Standing on four slender legs, they were built for speed. As they ate, they maintained an air of vigilance that confirmed this ecosystem had to have predators. When they would show themselves, Logan had no idea. *Hopefully after I find Byron and am well away from here.*

He was disappointed that this was not the exact cavern from his vision. It was half the size and the environment far more colorful. He saw no tunnels that might lead to the troublesome shaft that had ended his dream. *Fine with me. Not looking to take a fall anyway.*

In the distance, almost at the opposite end of the cavern, a spiral of smoke lazily rose toward the glowing ceiling. He darted to the nearest fungal tower and risked climbing it, never taking his eyes off the telltale curl of smoke. Halfway up, he got a good look at the smoke's origin—a small chimney sticking out of a crude roof. He worked his way even higher and soon saw, amid even more exotic fungal growth, more rooftops of varying colors.

Had he found the pale stranger's home?

Chapter 16
Kyle

"I wish I had a flashlight," Kyle muttered as he stood in the darkness and tried to make out his surroundings. The air was cool on his skin, the slightest of breezes tugging at his clothes as it whistled through the newly created opening in the metal wall. He smelled grease or something similar.

He remembered that lanterns hung in the cavern, but they'd been extinguished before the Weavers had closed the place up. The four Breakers channeling their power into his arms had caused a bright aura while he'd worked, plenty of light to see by. Now that he was through the hole and standing quietly in darkness, he realized he hadn't prepared very well for tunnel exploration.

All seven of his spirits nudged up inside him, coming together, and the blackness began to lighten. His aura, mostly green with some hints of red and blue, turned out to be far better than any flashlight or lantern, and he had his hands free.

"Cool," he said, feeling much more cheerful now.

Oddly, when he spoke, an extra plume of light appeared before his face. He watched it for a moment, and it gradually faded. Then, as he said "Huh," another plume appeared.

I'm radioactive, he thought with a degree of horror.

It was hard to ignore the glow every time he breathed out, but he tried to set it aside while he focused on his surroundings. To his surprise, he found that the metal tunnel was octagon-shaped, about twelve feet in diameter, the walls a little greasy to the touch. A single rail ran the length of the tunnel, firmly seated to the floor.

He scratched his head. This wasn't what he'd expected. And it wasn't what he'd seen in his dream-vision.

A tunnel like this couldn't have been dug with picks and shovels. It had been machined. The pod tunnels back in the city were almost exactly the same. One of those giant, automated drillers that construction crews used could bore through miles of rock at a steady walking pace without a stutter. They shot debris out the back in a fine spray of gravel that was collected by other machines known as scoopers.

If such an automated driller had been used, followed by the long, cumbersome contraption that installed the prefabricated metal panels and welded them in place . . . well, obviously tech had worked in this region a long, long time ago. This tunnel might have been here for centuries, perhaps cutting across the entire length of the land from east to west—from the enclaves to the city!

His Hunter whispered that the tunnel actually led northwest to southeast.

"Really?" he said, a little disappointed. Maybe the tunnel had a bend in it somewhere . . . But he was getting ahead of himself. "Okay, which way do we go?"

Either the Hunter, intuition, or plain common sense told him that northwest would be the better option. Any westerly direction was good if it meant a step closer to his city. After meeting with Abe, he could emerge well into the wastelands and continue home from there.

His Hunter nodded its approval, warning him that the Hunter Capitol lay in the other direction to the southeast.

Kyle froze, remembering his brief vision of a tunnel below the Hallowed Spires. Was this it? Did it lead straight to the Guardian?

He steeled himself. "We'll go southeast, then, toward the Capitol." His voice sounded oddly flat in the confines of the metal-walled tunnel. Also, he realized how weird it was to be talking aloud to spirit creatures that were deep inside him. But he liked the sound of his voice. It was oddly comforting. "There might be a way to get into the Hallowed Spires and destroy that inhibitor."

His Hunter spirit wasn't particularly happy, but it settled in with the others, lending their auras but otherwise remaining dormant.

Kyle's footfalls were noisy. He was surprised at how clean the tunnel was—no truggle rat droppings, no bugs, nothing. The combined auras of seven spirits took his mind off his strange fiery breath and illuminated at least ten feet ahead, and all he saw were the slightly greased walls and the single rail in the center of the floor. And a band of running lights low on each side that probably hadn't shed light in a long, long time.

The pod tunnels back in the city were wider than this one. They had similar lighting as well as a central rail for power, only those tunnels were circular rather than octagonal. Why did the air feel so still? Why was his voice muffled rather than echoing? And why was the tunnel so clean? It was almost as though it had been tightly sealed until he'd knocked a hole in its side.

He sucked in a breath. Could this be a vac-train tunnel? Engineers had long ago proposed that vac-trains could replace the antiquated pods, but the cost was prohibitive and the project never approved. Besides, pods were fast enough for short distances across the city. Vac-trains were theoretically more suited for much greater distances, the idea being that air was sucked out of the sealed tunnels by enormous pumps, and the complete lack of resistance in front of and behind the moving train allowed it to travel much, much faster. Couple that with the usual magnetic levitation to further reduce friction and wear-and-tear . . .

Perhaps that was why the tunnel was so devoid of truggle rat droppings—because those nasty critters would never venture into a sealed, airless tunnel. Of course, the tunnel had air in it now. *I've gone and punctured it*, Kyle thought with a stab of concern. *Air's been leaking in.*

He frowned. There was no way it had been airless all this time. Sealed enough to prevent critters getting in, maybe. Airless? Not likely.

He didn't expect this vac-train had ever been used by the general public. It had to be a private one, rarely used. Even so, the thought of being run down by a fast-moving vehicle sent a chill through him.

About twenty minutes later, he slowed to a stop. A full-height door blocked his way. If his theoretical vac-train had ever traveled through this tunnel, it would have gotten no farther than this unless some unseen operator granted access beyond. This was a security checkpoint.

The solid walls all around had become grilles, extremely sturdy in construction, the hint of huge fan blades beyond. Kyle guessed this was where the air was sucked out of the tunnel. There were probably grilles at the end of every tunnel section. Clearly the pumps were inoperative at the moment, the air still.

The door was absolutely immovable. At first glance it might be mistaken for an end wall, but it was designed to slide upward, admitting passengers with the proper security clearance. He rapped his knuckles on the metal, knowing there was no way he would ever shift it. It had taken four Breakers just to widen a four-inch hole in the wall. The door was equally as strong. It could only be opened by someone with the correct access code, or someone with an implant who could—

Logan.

Kyle sighed, and a glowing breath puffed out, startling him again. He shook his head and batted the glow away.

Logan could open the door without a problem. If he were here, the two of them could go on to the Hallowed Spires and up into the building to destroy the inhibitor.

But Kyle couldn't be anywhere near the Hallowed Spires yet because the Hunter Capitol was at least an hour's walk across land from the Fixer Enclave, perhaps more. This checkpoint was well away from the Capitol, probably a security measure to prevent a train being used to carry explosives by a saboteur or terrorist. A detonation deep under the ground might cause the fortress to collapse.

He turned away, disappointed. He couldn't get through the door, and he couldn't easily return to the surface and find a way back down into the tunnel closer to the Capitol. Even if he could find it, he'd need a dozen Breakers to bash his way through the metal ceiling.

"Well, let's try the other way, then," he said.

He trudged back to his starting point, twenty minutes of dull footfalls and nothing to see. It had to be about a mile, maybe more. Finally he passed the hole in the wall on his right and continued onward into new territory, heading northwest.

The tunnel stretched ahead.

Chapter 17
Logan

Logan weaved between the large toadstools, being careful not to touch the brown layer of dust coating their bright white caps. He had resigned himself to sucking in the glowing spores but didn't want to stir up the brown dust and risk taking in any further alien particles. *No telling what they might do.*

He looked back at the tunnel he had just abandoned. Despite its mouth being filled with the glowing blue mushrooms, it was still in shadows compared to his current surroundings. The grazers hung around the water's edge to his right. While he was closer to them, he was far enough away that they had not reacted to his presence.

The cavern was impressive. He had a working knowledge of the ecology on the surface from living in Apparata and his up-close encounters with numerous native surface animals on his trek across the Broken Lands.

Thanks to his constant curiosity and the ease of retrieving information from the data stream, he now understood even more about the ecosystems above. If he had known when he'd entered the Broken Lands that kalibacks communicated crudely with each other by projecting their thoughts, he would've worked harder to avoid them. Knowing they shared thoughts so easily made them even more ruthless.

In his scans of the data gathered by the city historians, he had never heard about any life underground other than the canyon clackers. He discounted the simple organisms found in the rudimentary caves that had been explored above. No one had ever reported on the sheer variety of life like he was surrounded by now. Maybe this discovery alone would embolden the city to send down scientists and researchers to catalog all of it.

But then there was the sticking point of this cavern already having humans who dwelled here. How would they view a sudden influx of nosy people from above? They were down here for a reason. Had they cut ties with the city completely? Was this a colony of ruthless exiles carving out a diminished life in the near dark?

If Byron was anywhere down here, he was with those people. Either he had gone to them for help, or they had taken him. Logan was determined to find out. He had a long walk ahead of him if he was going to reach what he suspected might be an inhabited village. While he could no longer see the smoke due to all the fungus rising up next to him, he knew the general location of it.

While he had only a hunting knife, he would not enter their settlement showing any sign of weakness. He would step up and get his brother back before anything happened to him. They would then head back. He had no idea how long they had been underground. With him losing consciousness, they could've been gone a few hours or most of the night. If that was the case, then Josef and Loreena would be furious.

He entered a part of the fungal jungle that wasn't as well lit. There were still huge varieties of mushrooms and fungi of different shapes and sizes around him, but very few were bioluminescent. He was back to relying on his bright breath. Thankfully, the airborne spores hadn't abandoned him.

There was life all around. He spied small furry rodents with enlarged eyes, their backs topped with hardened shells, feeding on several different varieties of mushrooms. The toadstool with the inverted cap and long thorns jutting from its stem looked the most dangerous, but the shelled creatures simply stood on their hind legs and gorged on its yellow gills with no concern for its fungal defense.

Numerous insects buzzed by him, and a chorus of bird calls issued from the fungal growths that closely resembled large frottle trees, their drooping branches of fungus creating domed, tent-like shelters.

Logan moved in the direction of the homes he had spied earlier.

A large bug, whose antennae glowed bright blue, landed on his shoulder and stuck its proboscis into a hardened patch of spurge. Its antennae glowed brighter as it sucked up whatever nourishment it could from the dried excrement. He shooed it away.

The sound of gurgling water ahead reminded him to again check on the grazers. He could still see the clearing around that particular part of the stream where the fungal feeders had been.

He froze.

They were gone.

Maybe he was looking at a different part of the waterway. He examined the gummy pink fungus along the water's edge. Even though he was almost a hundred feet away, he could see where the creatures had taken fresh chunks from the fungus. There was still plenty to eat. *That's the right spot. They're just gone.*

He latched onto the most obvious reason they had fled: a predator had entered the region.

A predator or predators.

* * *

Logan held his knife out and backed away from the stream. While it was far from him, whatever had spooked the grazers could be nearby.

He exhaled several times, lighting his surroundings. Why had he gone so deep into the jungle where there wasn't as much glowing fungus as along the perimeter? He slid under a drooping limb and found himself feet away from a thick trunk of black fungus, the main bulk of the growth that reminded him of a tree. Looking up, he saw how the drooping appendages created a dome that extended to within a few feet of the ground. The semi-enclosed area was almost fifty feet in diameter and had to be nearly as tall. It was dark within the shadow of the immense tree. Past the hanging sections, he could see jagged patches of other glowing fungus.

He didn't like where he had wound up. *I've cornered myself. This is no better than running back into the tunnel.*

Even with the little bit of light from the outside, the circular patch of terrain swallowed up by the black fungal tree was pretty dark. Would he even be able to see anything that approached him?

He expelled a quick breath, lighting up the area around his face. He put his hand over his mouth. That wasn't good. In this dark space, every exhale relayed his location. All a smart hunter would need to do is look for the periodic plumes of lit spores. Logan was seized by panic. He couldn't hold his breath forever.

But I sure can try. He sucked in a deep breath and held it.

Immediately, he noticed how quiet it was. No bird calls, no twittering and buzzing of insects.

He situated his back against the trunk of the tall growth. It was moist and slick. No easy climb.

A series of clicks erupted far to his left. He listened. It reminded him of the tongue-clicking language he and Kiff had invented. Ahead, something answered, its clicks slower and deeper. Okay, so at least it wasn't kalibacks. They'd come up on him in silence, trading attack plans with their minds. Something else hunted him.

He risked a quick breath, waving off the lit cloud with his free hand.

He froze and peered closer at a patch of glowing fungus outside his dark shelter. Had it just moved?

Seconds ticked by as he kept his gaze on the glowing streaks resembling red stripes. The stripes moved to the right. What? Was he being stalked by a fungus creature, or did the predator have a hide that glowed like the winged things from the tunnel?

A section of red glowing stripes moved off to his far left. He spun around and watched. The unseen creature still moved, creeping closer. Behind him, Logan heard more muted clicking.

Whatever he had his eyes trained on responded, its clicking loud and blatant. *Not even trying to hide that they're hunting me.*

His lungs burned, and he had no choice. He exhaled sharply and drew in two short breaths.

This triggered an immediate response from the predators. The noisiest one pressed through the sheltering black fungal branches and entered the circle of darkness.

Thanks to its glowing coat, Logan could make out most of its features. It was small, coming up to Logan's waist. Its neck was long, extending its overall height by another two feet. All four legs were black and blended in with the darkness. Its torso was riddled with glowing red stripes that turned out to be areas of fungal growth. He wondered what benefit having the fungus all over its short black fur could hold for the predator. It stared at him with tiny eyes, a mask of white fur around each. Its ears drooped down, terminating in a curled length of hardened cartilage or bone that was also speckled with the red fungus.

The creature shook its head and stretched leisurely, keeping its gaze on Logan the entire time. Clicking from behind him caused Logan to turn. Two others had now entered his hiding place and stood still at the edge, eyeing him with curiosity. The left side of the nearer one's face twitched periodically.

He went back to staring down the most aggressive-looking one. It hadn't moved closer, but Logan sensed its hesitation wasn't out of fear. The apparent leader emitted several short clicks and flicked its stubby tail at the others. They responded in unison.

He could take down one or two of them with his knife, but who knew if there were others waiting beyond his ill-chosen fungal shelter.

The leader took another step closer and sniffed in Logan's direction. It wrinkled its face in obvious puzzlement.

Does it not like how I smell?

The creature continued testing the air. Logan didn't like how worked up it was getting. A thin tendril of drool dripped from the edge of its mouth. *It definitely likes what it caught a whiff of. Why isn't it pouncing on me?*

The pair behind him clicked their tongues impatiently.

Logan frowned. They'd cut him down swiftly if he ran. *Stand and fight. Take a few of them down before they sink their teeth in me.*

The solitary predator exhaled, framing his flat face and his rows of sharp teeth in a temporary cloud of glowing spores.

Logan spoke, "Just *do* it! Attack me and see what you get!" He waved the knife slowly in front of him.

The creature snapped its jaws closed and sprang at Logan.

He jabbed his knife at the creature's underbelly, hitting it against a solid patch of the red fungus. The blade didn't sink in. Instead, it glanced off. The fungus was rock-hard.

Logan fell to the left, following the momentum of his lunge. The creature flew past him, its raking claws missing his back by inches.

It stared at him, confused by Logan's attack.

So that's why it doesn't knock off the fungus. Armor. He sighed, knowing he was about to be done in by a scientific relationship he had just read about the other day—*symbiosis.* The hunter benefited from added protection. And the fungus? A means to deliver its spores across the cavern and onto other hides? He briefly imagined the creatures rubbing up against each other, spreading their fungal armor to all in their pack. It would've been an amazing discovery except for the fact that it practically ensured Logan's death.

The other two watched their leader, waiting for its next move.

Logan prepared himself for another attack. *Go for the eyes. No fungal growth around them.*

The lead predator warbled, its call reminding Logan of a kaliback's, more shrill but still similar. He heard a response from beyond the wall of drooping fungus. *Definitely more out there.* If he judged the acoustics right, they were all behind the pair now to his right.

His attacker squared off with him and tensed, lowering its shoulders and tightening its front paws.

A shrill scream sounded behind the pack, off in the distance. This drew the attention of the three he could see. They spun about and stared in the approximate direction of the wailing. It was still going, sounding like an animal in pain, maybe even several.

The animals seemed to grow excited at the howling. All three abandoned Logan's hideout. He watched their glowing stripes disappear into the jungle along with hints of others following them, the rest of the pack that had stayed outside.

Logan breathed out several times, attempting to catch his breath. Realizing he wasn't going to do any damage with his knife, he stashed it back in its sheath.

He moved out from under his poorly chosen hiding place in the opposite direction of the pack. He needed to find Byron and leave before more of those creatures decided he was worth hunting down.

He pushed through another wall of drooping fungal branches, these from a smaller tree than the one he had used.

Logan glanced back at the stream. The grazers hadn't returned. So the threat was still there.

He looked forward and plowed into the chest of someone standing in his way. He staggered back and held out his fists.

The pale stranger who had left behind the mysterious bundle at the entrance to the Guardian's lair stared down at him, his expression barely able to hold back his amusement.

Logan didn't know what to do. Was he a threat?

The stranger threw back his head and laughed deep and hard. He took a few seconds to restrain himself. When he looked at Logan again, it was with the utmost concern.

"Your robot friend is distracting them, but they won't be fooled for long." He grabbed Logan by the hand and pulled him to his feet. "Come, let's wash the stink of minquin off you. That way the vulpers won't find you as appetizing."

Logan reluctantly followed, his anxiety over the man's intentions held in check for the moment. "That was Byron making that awful noise?"

"Yes, your brother is a wonderful mimic. Perfect rendition of a horde of minquins crying out as they execute their mating dance. Vulpers can't resist easy pickings like that," the man said. "Hurry, to the creek. With all that minquin manure heaped all over, you're far too much of a lure for them."

Logan grinned and stuck close to the fast-moving man as he crashed through the surrounding fungus.

Chapter 18
Kyle

Walking along the twelve-foot-wide octagonal metal tunnel became such a chore that Kyle started to wonder if he could fly instead.

His Glider slipped into place. Its translucent wings spread wide, touching the sides of the tunnel, but Kyle wasn't worried; the wings seemed to be for show anyway. He tucked them back slightly, finding that his control over them came naturally as though he'd had wings attached to his back all his life.

Flying inside a confined space struck him as odd, but he picked up speed, occasionally pushing off one wall to correct his trajectory, then the other, sometimes bumping his head on the ceiling. It was the strangest journey he'd ever had, stranger even than flying high above the ground. He guessed he was traveling at fifteen or twenty miles per hour now, his aura lighting the way.

The tunnel remained dead straight, heading in a northwesterly direction according to his Hunter. He lost track of time. It might have been five minutes or ten, but at this speed he must have covered a pretty good distance. At this rate, he'd cut diagonally all the way across the land and out to the northern coast somewhere deep in the wastelands.

But the tunnel ended abruptly.

He slowed himself by dragging his toes on the metal floor. At the end of the tunnel, completely blocking his way, stood his theoretical vac-train. It was glass-fronted rather like a bus only octagon-shaped with barely a few inches of space all around. It was fitted with the usual maglev tech for propulsion, though the train was inoperative at the moment, resting on the single rail.

In front of the train, Kyle found a service door set into the left-hand tunnel wall, a palm pad to the side. He knew that exits out of potentially dangerous environments such as airless vac-train tunnels should have minimal security protocols. The door should hiss open without a fuss. The problem was that tech didn't work this close to the enclaves. Obviously it had long ago, but certainly not anymore.

He swallowed and reached for it anyway. When the power went out back in the city, most exit doors had an override switch. If he pressed down on the pad, it should yield with a click, releasing the manually operated—

The palm pad lit up green, and the door hissed open. Jerking backward, he gasped and blinked in shock. At the same time, small running lights flickered on throughout the length of the tunnel behind him, a soft red glow that his eyes had no trouble adjusting to.

Tech *worked* down here? He'd had the use of electrical lighting the whole time and hadn't realized it?

He stood gaping for a moment, trying to figure it out. The green light flashed in warning, and the door slowly closed again. The pad dimmed.

Tech *worked*?

It didn't make sense. The inhibitor covered an *enormous* area, stretching from the Hallowed Spires all the way out across the wastelands to the west, reaching almost as far as the city. Kyle clearly remembered walking barefoot over the ridge of dead machinery and weapons that marked the perimeter of the inhibitor's tech-free zone. Where he was right now couldn't be more than a few miles outside the enclaves. He was well within the inhibitor's range. Tech shouldn't work.

So how . . . ?

"Lights out," he called.

The tunnel's running lights winked out, and he was plunged into darkness again.

"Lights," he said, shaking his head.

They came back on. This time, something went wrong. He heard a buzzing sound, and the red glow brightened to white, flickered, then went out. He frowned, noting that the running lights were still illuminated farther along the tunnel. It was just the first fifty feet or so that had gone out.

Still, electrical problems or not, it seemed the majority of the tunnel worked fine. "I'm such an idiot," he muttered. The simple commands, "Lights" and "Lights out," were perhaps the most rudimentary in all walks of life across the city. A week in the backward enclave community had caused him to forget simple conveniences. Then again, it hadn't occurred to him that tech worked underground.

He placed his palm on the pad again. As before, it lit up green, and the door hissed open. If the tunnel's running lights had been out right now, they'd have flickered on again to aid the service engineer.

"Lights out," Kyle muttered as he stepped through and found himself in a narrow room. To his right, farther along the wall, was a set of glass doors designed to facilitate train boarding.

Welcome to the vac-train station, he thought in amazement.

He was still battling with the fact that tech worked. Then again, with the control panels and surfaces covered in dust, Kyle knew the system hadn't been used in a very long time. He jabbed at a few buttons, and they lit up in a variety of colors. One flashed a message: VACUUM BREACH.

Yeah, there's a hole in the tunnel wall. Sorry about that.

Since he had no security control codes or even an implant to try to override things, the control panel soon timed out, and the lights went dark again.

He turned to the station exit. As he approached, the door slid open with ease. There had to be solar panels on the surface above keeping the station fully charged. He marveled at the idea of tech working alongside his spirits. Surely this was a first! The seven creatures within him were strangely quiet and apprehensive, sniffing at the air as though they could taste the charged, manufactured energy.

On a whim, he said loudly, "Lights."

As the ceiling flared into brilliant white light, he chuckled and shook his head.

Leaving the lights on, he stepped outside into the darkness of a vast cavern. Peering around, Kyle couldn't quite see the roof, nor its far walls. He knew only that it was hundreds of feet across. A breeze tugged at his clothes, and he heard . . . *something*. Noises. A scuffling here, a *tap-tap-tap* there, a mixture of different sounds from different places as though the place were alive with insects and rodents.

He summoned his spirits and brightened his aura, but it didn't help much. "I'm probably just attracting the bugs," he muttered.

Staying in the light that streamed from the station door, he took twenty paces into the cavern, careful to watch his footing on the uneven rock floor. He paused and glanced back, squinting to see. The station, basically a square, metal-walled building with a door in the side, looked completely out of place in the subterranean environment, especially with the blinding white light from the doorway.

He moved farther into the cavern, the light on the ground and the shadows it cast fading with every step. Soon he had to rely on his glowing spirits again—or his breath, which he suddenly realized must come in useful for those without a built-in aura.

"Lights?" he said hopefully.

To his surprise, old bulbs buzzed and flickered into life. A set of workers' lamps had been strewn across this section of the cavern, six or seven of them, their cords strung up high so that the bulbs dangled well above head height. There were even the remains of old campfires, one complete with a large, iron pot hanging from a tripod spit. One or two looked recent. Kyle immediately thought of Archie, that crazy guy he'd met in the wastelands. Perhaps people like him, exiled from the city or the enclaves, came down here from time to time.

"How cozy," Kyle muttered. "Cooking out under the—" He glanced up. Instead of a starry sky, he saw flecks of faint blue light. "What *is* that?"

He stared and stared, but he couldn't figure it out. It looked like the rock itself, the ceiling of the cavern, was alive.

He shook his head. "Okay, so where are we headed now? Any ideas?"

None of his spirits ventured a guess.

"What about you, Hunter? If you were hunting for Abe Torren, where would you look?"

The spirit shifted into position and sniffed around. Kyle couldn't see it, but he imagined it narrowing its eyes and lifting its snout. He got the sense it was picking up a plethora of interesting smells and sounds, and it seemed out of sorts for some reason.

"Okay, listen," Kyle said quietly. "If anything jumps out at us, I want Creeper to take over so I can hide really fast. I'd rather hide than fight. Got that, Hunter?" he added, remembering how the spirit had once made him kill an armor-plated shuffler in the woods. "So no stabbing things in the neck, all right?"

Stabbing with what? an inner voice questioned.

"Good point."

Kyle again conceded that he'd come along on this journey woefully unprepared. No lantern, no knife, no food or water, no blanket in case he needed to sleep . . .

"Not much of an explorer, am I?" he said. "Logan would be in his element here. Not me. I'm a city boy."

Still, despite everything, he knew he was a step closer to the dream-vision from which Abe had beckoned.

Shuffling sounds caused his Hunter to grow excited, but Kyle refrained from running over and leaping on whatever rodent it wanted to strangle. He continued his slow pace, following the contours of the rock, stumbling here and there as he left the light of the campsite behind. "Lights?" he said again, but this time nothing happened.

He began to make out huge shapes ahead of him, but he couldn't figure out what they were until the light from his spirits picked out the details. With a sigh of understanding, he approached the hulking machine.

"The driller," he said with awe.

The machine was only a little taller than he was but very long, at least twenty feet. Mostly rounded like a tube, it had dozens of small wheels and tracks. A vicious-looking twelve-foot drill bit protruded from the front end, larger than the main body. It reminded Kyle of a canyon clacker. Indeed, these driller machines emitted a similar sound frequency that caused the rock to vibrate and crack seconds before the drill plowed through.

He wished he could see it better. "Lights!" he yelled.

Again, nothing happened. In the distance, the workers' campsite remained lit in a pool of orange. Beyond, a rectangle of bright white light still streamed from the vac-train station's entrance—but only for a few more seconds, at which point the motion sensors apparently determined nobody was around and dimmed the lights.

He returned his attention to the machine. It had been dead a long, long time, absolutely smothered with what looked like fungal growths, hiding the yellow paintwork under a mass of ugly white and grey. Other machines and equipment lay behind the driller. Everything needed for creating a tunnel was right here, abandoned. Which meant . . .

Kyle spun about and scoured the darkness. If these machines were here, there had to be an entry point, a way for them to drive in and out. Or in at least.

He spotted a faint glow at one dark side of the cavern. He squinted, then headed toward it, his excitement growing. There he found a yawning hole about six feet up the cavern wall, rounded and sloping skyward. The driller had come in this way a long time ago. That was *daylight* up there!

Kyle hurried up the smooth, rounded tunnel, panting as he went. At about twelve feet in diameter, it was more than tall enough for a standard train tunnel—not that anyone would install one on an angle like this. The tunnel was merely the entry point for the massive driller machine. Kyle slipped on loose gravel but picked himself up and continued on, noting that the glow at the top of the tunnel was getting brighter.

His spirits began to squirm. Agitated, they seemed to swirl around inside him like fish in a tank during a water change, darting this way and that. It was all in his imagination, of course; there couldn't be room for such movement. He'd marveled at this phenomenon many times. Most of these spirits were larger than him. They crowded the same small, physical space, their individual essences superimposed on one another, jutting faintly out of his body here and there. He'd decided that six of the spirits shrank down small while the seventh, whichever it was at any given time, filled his frame and asserted its presence.

Right now, though, all appeared to have hidden deep down inside.

Afraid.

He soon found out why. As the daylight flooded over him, warm and glorious, he picked up his pace and climbed the last few yards to the top of the tunnel. He could see long grass and bushes overhanging the rim and knew he was about to emerge into the wastelands. He still wanted to find Abe, but right now he had to do this, to see where he ended up.

As he clambered out, his spirits began screeching. He faltered, suddenly aware that something was very wrong. He caught a glimpse of derelict buildings on the hills behind him, and a raging river at the bottom of the slopes to the east. But he had no more time to look because one of his spirits fled from his body.

It felt like it had been yanked from him. The serpentine Skimmer howled as it spun through the air, whisked away by a powerful, unseen force, hurtling toward the river. A second later, another spirit was wrenched from his body—his Fixer, small and furry yet insubstantial, spinning uncontrollable as it followed the Skimmer on its tumbling, twisting journey through the air, leaving pale green contrails.

Kyle fell backward into the tunnel, gasping as he slipped and skidded down the loose dirt and gravel into darkness. The five remaining spirits, still agitated, began to calm themselves as he hurried down the slope away from the daylight.

He mentally kicked himself. He'd recognized that river. Its eastern bank marked the spirit barrier—the spell that kept the spirits from crossing the wastelands and entering the city. His underground journey had taken him past that barrier, only it hadn't affected him while he was safely underground. His spirits might have sensed it, but they hadn't fretted about it.

Until he'd popped up aboveground. Then the spell had kicked in.

And now he'd lost two of his friends.

Chapter 19
Logan

After the third dunking, Logan kicked free and drew away from the stranger. They stood facing each other, knee-deep in the river that had previously played host to the grazers.

Logan wiped his long, waterlogged hair away from his face and sputtered, "I think you got it all."

Shirtless, Logan waded toward shore, his pants soaked through and weighing him down.

The man held Logan's shirt high. "It'll do, but this still smells like minquin. Say goodbye to it." The pale man's eyes darted to the article of clothing in his hand. "I have one back home for you."

Logan stepped over the gnawed-at fungus lining the water's edge and attempted to wring out his pants. "Just get me to Byron, and we'll get going. I don't need anything from you." He didn't want to come across as difficult, but he was tired and wanted to get Byron back home. Nothing from Abe's vision was down here. *Just crazy hermits and glowing mushrooms. And minquins and vulpers, too.*

"You're safe now. The vulpers thought you were a minquin. You had their stink all over you."

"Pretty dumb of them. I don't look like those crazy flying rats." That explained the predator's confusion. "Vulpers don't bother you at all?"

"No, they feed on minquin. They rely on their sense of smell because their sight is so poor. Some get lucky and bring down a rackle once in a while."

Logan wondered if the grazers he'd seen down by the river had been rackles, but he didn't want to prolong their conversation. As much as he had been fascinated by this world minutes ago, he also wrestled with wanting to get his brother home safe and sound. If this man would even let them go.

The man's expression softened. "So sorry you and Byron ran afoul of a minquin colony. I honestly didn't think you'd agitate them to the point that they'd foul the two of you up so badly. Your brother pulled you out of there. That's when I came across him. He's quite the amazing technological wonder. He was quite shaken, babbling on about the excrement being corrosive and wanting to get it off as quickly as possible."

And yet he was okay with it staying on me? Thanks, Byron. Although, Logan couldn't blame his brother. If any of the manure had worked into Bryon's joints through his numerous seams, it could cause extensive damage, something Logan didn't have to worry about himself.

"We left you because vulpers don't enter the tunnels. They prefer to feed on minquins when they fly into the main cavern to feed or mate. Anyway, it took longer than expected to wash him off. He insisted he couldn't be dunked, so I had to work him over with a wet rag." He pointed to a discarded piece of cloth draped over a large green mushroom. "We were on our way back to get you when I heard the vulpers getting worked up. Good thing vulpers aren't the quietest hunters. Their noisy clicking brought me to where you were hiding. They had you thoroughly boxed in. Knowing you were far too enticing in your coated condition, I got Byron to lure them off."

The fake minquin screams supplied by Byron some distance away abruptly stopped. Fearing the vulpers had gotten to him, he said, "Where's my brother? Did they attack him?"

"Safe, and I doubt they would undertake chomping down on any part of him." The man stepped onto the shore, skirting by a patch of the thorny mushrooms. He flung Logan's shirt downstream. It sank as the current dragged it away.

"Who are you?" Logan asked.

"Yando Vril." Still dressed in the same clothes as he had been wearing the other night, the man appeared stronger amid the glow of the fungus, much more so than when he had been sneaking around the city. Even his pale skin didn't look as sickly here. His eyes were a bright green, and his hair would've been longer than Logan's if it wasn't in a knot top. The man extended his hand.

Logan shook it. "Logan Orm." Almost an afterthought, he added, "Of the Fixer Enclave."

The man feigned surprise. "You're not from Apparati? Then why were you nosing around in the city?"

Logan couldn't tell if Yando had made a lucky guess, or seen him by the Guardian's home. "I'm from Apparata."

He turned his back on him and threw up his hands. "Apparata. Apparati. Doesn't matter to me."

"And where do you call home? What is this place?" Logan failed at hiding his frustration.

"Apparatum, either what's left of it or what's to come."

Yando was as perplexing as Abe. "Another crazy," he mumbled.

He drew up next to Logan. "Do well to respect your elders. Some of us see more than what's in front of us."

Logan resisted the urge to pull away. He held fast, never once blinking.

The man's mood lightened. He clapped Logan affectionately on the back and steered him down the crude path they had just walked. "Let's go reunite you with your brother." He whispered, "And show you off to the family."

* * *

He didn't get much from Yando on the trek to his settlement, mostly details about the wildlife they encountered. The man pointed out several fungi that were edible. Logan tried a stem of ligglescratch. It was oily and left a faint aftertaste. Yando assured him it was better grilled. When Logan asked him what they used to fuel their fires, Yando didn't answer.

When they arrived at the settlement, Byron stood in the small town's center. Two young children climbed all over him, tapping at his arms and legs.

The youngest, a boy with brown hair, raced up to Yando and hugged the man's leg. "Father. Another stranger."

The boy stepped over to Logan and sized him up. His face drooped in disappointment. "Where's your armor? You look like me."

Byron walked over with the girl. From their similar features, Logan guessed they were siblings.

The girl said, "Mind yourself, Pront. Byron is a robot, not a knight." Wide-eyed, she looked at Logan. "Byron's wild. Is his brain really tucked away in there?" She pointed a thumb at Byron's head.

Byron supplied the answer, "Anchored in a stasis fluid to lessen impacts."

Pront jumped on Byron's back and thumped his fists on the boy's cranial plating. "Like this?"

Logan's brother went along with the boy's hijinxs. "Very much so."

Yando grabbed his son to prevent further testing of Byron's patience and slipped him onto his own shoulders.

"Who are you people?" Logan said.

A feminine voice answered from behind him. "Seekers."

The woman, her hair jet-black, stepped out of a doorway and into the glowing light of the many mushrooms growing all over the open area. She wore a simple blue dress and had her hair up in a tight bun. Her long narrow nose was in contrast to her large eyes. She smiled, and Logan sensed she was important. She walked up and took the little girl's hand. "Milene, take your brother back to class. He's not done his lessons."

Milene straightened up and sent her mother a playful salute. "Right away."

The two children ran into a squat red building, a good part of its roof covered in the blue-gilled mushrooms.

Logan took in the settlement. Twelve buildings in all. Several were two stories. Most appeared to be a mix of fungi, stacked stone, and in places, stout timbers.

"Is it just your family down here?" Logan knew that couldn't be right, not with the many structures he saw.

"No." Milene clapped her hands in rapid succession and glanced around. "Come out, everyone. We must not shrink from one who can bring us a new future."

From four other buildings, a total of nineteen adults stepped out. They walked over to stand behind Yando and his wife. A few held axes and spears in hand. All were pale but well-nourished.

Yando whispered in his wife's ear for an uncomfortably long time.

At a certain point, she held up her hand, and he stopped. Either he had said enough or far too much. It was hard to tell from her expression. It wasn't that she was cold or radiated aloofness. Of all the people gathered around him and Byron, she was the only one who was all business.

Yando's wife looked directly at Logan. "My husband accomplished his mission. He led you to us unscathed." She gave her spouse a sideways glance. "Although, he could've avoided the whole vulpers situation by meeting up with you in the tunnels."

Yando didn't say anything.

"I don't understand. Led me here?"

"Well, your ultimate destination isn't here. Our meager home is a way station on your journey. It's the Well. Abe Torren wants you at the Well. You and your counterpart are far from finished. More tasks await the two of you, one of which you must undertake together. I only hope that Makow will deliver Kyle. He's not terribly reliable, but he's fast and knows the route like no other."

"I don't understand. I need to get Byron home. Who are you to tell me what to do?"

She leaned in, close enough for Logan to catch a pleasant whiff of her scent. It reminded him of his mother's after she had spent the day pressing muva weeds for their rash-relieving juices. He found the smell comforting. "I am Gracil. You can't return home yet. There's still more to do."

At that moment, a Breaker stepped out of the largest building in the entire settlement. It didn't float over to them. It marched over, its broad three-toed feet delivering a satisfying crunch to the gravel underfoot. The Breaker's tusks were longer than any Logan had seen before, jutting out from its cheeks more than three feet. Its eyes were sunken deep, and a pronounced brow kept them in shadows. It was easily twice Logan's size, its thick arms swinging slightly as it lumbered toward him. The spirit wasn't tethered. It also wasn't transparent. It was solid.

It shouldered past several villagers, its physical form clearly not at all ethereal. It came within inches of Logan and expelled a breath, triggering an impressive cloud of illuminated spores. The creature had scales all over, something Logan had never noticed with the more intangible form he was used to.

What it did next defied everything Logan knew of the spirits.

It spoke.

"He's *weak*. No *resolve*. Not the answer the old man should've delivered to us." Its voice was almost human but contained a mild echo, a reverberation that followed every other word or so, especially the ones it emphasized like *weak* and *resolve*.

Having said its piece, it turned around and walked back to the building. Logan saw a Skimmer and Weaver hanging their heads out the entrance of the building, both equally as solid as the Breaker had been.

"What's going on?" Logan said.

Chapter 20
Kyle

Kyle walked with his eyes on the rocky floor, his remaining five spirits subdued. How quickly he'd become attached to his tethered guests. Losing two of them hurt more than he ever would have expected. Now he understood how it had felt for those workers back at the rock quarry when he'd borrowed their Breakers—and how Prima and Nomi had felt when he'd made use of their Fixers.

No more, he vowed. *Never borrow anyone's spirit again.*

At least they'd got them back. He doubted he'd ever see his Skimmer and Fixer again. They were out in the wastelands among the rest. Kyle couldn't imagine seeing them again. To do so safely without losing his other spirits in the process meant going back the way he'd come, staying underground until he could emerge somewhere on the safe side of the spirit barrier by the river. Even then, what were the chances of finding those two particular spirits among the hundreds of others that clamored there?

Maybe they'd find me, he mused.

He sighed for the umpteenth time. Even without the spirit inhibitor, he couldn't exactly take his friends into the city anyway. He'd have to let them go at some point.

For the past twenty minutes, he'd walked with his head down and hands stuffed in his pockets, barely paying attention to his surroundings. His five spirits were quiet, their glows so diminished that darkness crowded in on him.

Only he still had the light of his weird breath vapor.

He held up his hands. Previously, his spirits had shed an aura bright enough to light his way for ten feet ahead. Now they didn't, yet he saw his hands and arms clearly thanks to his own breath. It was the strangest thing to see the expelled air from his lungs react with the atmosphere and light up, then fade after five seconds or so.

He faltered. It wasn't the air itself that was lighting up. It was something *in* the air, tiny particles everywhere he looked, floating on the slightest breeze. Some sort of dust?

The miniscule specks flared again when he breathed out, reminding him of the white puffs everyone experienced on the coldest days of winter. This underground phenomenon defied explanation. It was both fascinating and a little worrying.

Still, he hadn't died yet. If this were some form of radiation, he felt absolutely fine.

He slowed his pace, putting his woes aside and focusing on his surroundings a little more. He'd left the vast vac-station cavern behind. It had funneled him into an ever-decreasing tunnel that meandered upward and down again, left and right, sometimes spacious enough to fit a maglev train through but mostly no wider than four feet. When the walls closed in on him, his breath lit the way quite easily.

But there were other light sources. When he stopped again and peered ahead, holding his breath and urging his spirits to dim themselves, he thought he could see vague dabs of light all around, though he couldn't quite focus on them. He'd seen faint blue light on the ceiling high above the train station, too. Much of the rock here was covered with a mosslike growth, green and spongy-looking. He couldn't be sure, but he suspected the moss was reacting to his presence somehow.

The tunnel had been pretty straightforward for a while, and he'd trudged along without a care, his mind on other things. As soft crunching sounds accompanied his footfalls, he noticed that the ground was becoming slippery—not so much from moisture but something else, a bit like a carpet of nannel tree needles. He paused and squinted, seeing only smudges of darkness at his feet. He leaned over and blew softly, and the vapor gave him a brief, faint sighting of something underfoot.

Suddenly worried, he called on his spirits. "Wake up, guys. Come on, give me some light here."

The spirits seemed reluctant to stir, but they mustered themselves and came together to give him back his aura. It was like turning up the flame on a lamp; the tunnel steadily brightened, and he gasped.

He was walking on a teeming mass of insects, each the size of his thumb, shiny and black. He remained still, horrified that they were crawling all over his shoes in absolute silence. Peering over his shoulder, he wondered how many he'd squished dead over the last few minutes. He half expected to see footprint-shaped indentations where flattened corpses lay, but the army of bugs simply walked all over their dead as if they weren't there.

"They're harmless," he whispered to himself. He still liked the sound of his own voice in this lonely, depressing place.

He hadn't detected any bites on his ankles, though he felt a few bugs crawling up his legs. He shivered and batted at his pants, then shook his feet one at a time and carried on marching. He demanded his spirits keep their aura as bright as possible so he could see what he was walking on. The bugs—thousands upon thousands of them—blanketed the tunnel floor.

He passed a fissure in the right-hand wall, and it was from there the bugs spilled, almost like a torrent of oil from a cracked storage container. He hurried past and up a slope, leaving the creepy-crawlies behind.

The tunnel rose steeply and emerged in a circular chamber about twenty feet across. Sound was oddly muffled here. His click-clacking, echoing footsteps became dull thuds as he walked across the smooth rock. He stopped in the center of the chamber, the middle of the dome, and craned his neck to look up. Something clung to the ceiling there.

"Mushrooms," he muttered.

They had yellow caps, but what fascinated him was the blue glow emitting from underneath around the stems. The overall effect was a wash of bright-blue light pockmarked with dabs of yellow. The mushrooms clustered together and smothered the entire ceiling, thickest in the center, more sparse nearer the floor. They lit up the chamber in such a way that Kyle felt nothing but awe and delight. Breath that glowed and now *this*, nature at its most beautiful.

The journey had become bearable. The despair he'd begun to feel dissipated. Perhaps he was only just now reaching the interesting part of this subterranean world. There might be plenty more wonders ahead. And it had to be pretty safe if Abe was down here somewhere.

He moved on, passing through the chamber into another tunnel. Again the rounded walls were surprisingly regular, the floor easy to walk on. The place couldn't be entirely natural. Breakers had worked here in the past. The wall surfaces had telltale ridges caused by the claws on the Breakers' stubby digits when they scooped out handfuls of rock. They'd dug their way through the ground over many, many years, perhaps widening existing fissures and ravines, making it accessible for—

For what?

He puzzled over that as he entered a far more irregular cavern filled with long stalactites, lumpy columns, and a pale white mist that rolled toward him. The ceiling looked like the maw of a fanged giant, which meant he was walking across its tongue. Oddly, his feet sank into the ground a little, and for a second he feared he might actually be right, that he was about to slide down the throat of an underground monster. The thick moisture in the air and the creeping mist all around didn't help alleviate this cheerful thought.

He sucked in a breath and skidded to a halt as a figure rose in the gloom ahead. "Don't move," a man's voice said.

Kyle froze. "W-what?"

"Don't move. You're about two steps away from a horrible, painful death."

Chapter 21
Logan

Gracil stood while Yando sat with Logan at the small table, a square rectangle of stacked stone, its top surprisingly smooth. They had taken him into a nearby house, their home if he had to guess. The shirt Yando had given him was large and well worn. At least it wasn't scratchy.

Lit by lanterns and a variety of bioluminescent mushrooms on the wall and ceiling, the atmosphere was kaleidoscopic.

"Those were spirits. They were solid," Logan said, barely above a whisper.

Yando responded, "They are the first, the Forerunners."

His wife shot him a look.

Byron said, "These are the things Kyle can tether with?"

Logan nodded to him. "I don't understand, though. Forerunners? What is that?" He knew what the term meant but didn't see how it applied to the spirits. They had always existed side by side with his people, hadn't they?

Someone behind him hissed, "Let me show him."

A Skimmer slithered in from outside. Logan was not used to seeing one travel along the ground. The Skimmers he knew darted around in the air, wiggling their long, serpentine spirit forms with slow, hypnotic undulations. This one did the same, but its movements didn't captivate Logan. He sensed they could if the creature wanted them to. Its skin pigment was a more vibrant purple, not muted like its spiritual brethren.

It looked exactly like a topside Skimmer, just solid. The spiny gray ridges along its back ran from head to tail and were much longer than any he had seen before. Its drooping whiskers on either side of its mouth were tinged yellow on the ends. He saw red clusters of the same fungus armor the vulpers had crisscrossing their hide, although not nearly as much.

He knew the creature planned to tether with him and broadcast some past history, share important memories to get him up to speed. He cringed. "Wait. I can't tether."

The Skimmer reared back and slowly bobbed left and right, sizing him up. It squinted and said, "Yes, you lack the affinity to tether with those above, but down here, I can draw you into me."

"What?"

"I can tether you to me."

Yando said, "It's okay, Logan. We do it all the time. Our races work alongside each other down here. Sometimes that requires joining to accomplish a task we could not do alone."

Byron stepped next to Logan. "I'll record what happens. If it hurts you, I can try and displace it with a stun blast."

Logan eyed the robot boy's chest cavity. The small compartment containing his neural stunner was open and the device extended, hovering inches above his shoulder. Classified as medical tech, it was not considered a weapon. Thanks to Logan, the stunner Byron housed was amped up to do more than numb an injured area. He kept his panic in check, knowing his brother didn't need to poke him with the weapon's sharp point, that he could deliver an electrical current without touching the tip to his skin. *No sense recoiling from his brother and hurting his feelings.*

"I will not hurt you," the Skimmer said. "This is the fastest way to help you understand." It added, "Abe would insist."

Did everyone down here know the old man? Abe certainly got around. For someone so ancient, he was well traveled. It wasn't like he could teleport to where he needed to be. Abe's metal collar allowed him to phase in and out between different worlds. He still had to get to his destination on his own.

Logan looked around, half expecting Abe to phase into being next to the Skimmer. "Could we ask him?"

"When you are at the Well," Gracil said. "He will be there for you and Kyle."

"Can't he fill us in there?"

"Not in the way I can." The creature narrowed its eyes and drew in a long breath. It was weird watching it inhale and exhale. Its kin aboveground didn't do that. They didn't need to. Logan couldn't recall any spirits ever doing normal functions like breathing, eating, expelling, or even dying.

The Skimmer loomed over Logan and darted its head back, preparing to . . . what? Dive into his body? That was how tethering worked; his people drew the spirits into their bodies. But the Skimmer had said he would pull Logan in. How?

Logan suddenly felt lightheaded. He looked up at the Skimmer to see it now had its eyes closed and was deep in concentration.

He lifted off the seat. "Hey, what?" A sweeping numbness traveled down his body. He couldn't move a muscle. *I'm helpless. Is this how a spirit feels when it's being tethered?*

His skin and clothing faded, every part of him growing paler. He was becoming a spirit.

Abruptly, his consciousness whisked toward the Skimmer. Logan entered the creature through its skull.

In seconds, he was trapped within. It was then that the impressive show-and-tell began.

* * *

Logan had no body. He was a hitchhiker within the Skimmer. All around him the darkness faded away, and he saw the land from far above as if looking down from a Glider's perspective. Apparatum was the solitary continent in the Great Sea.

Wonderful view, isn't it? Gliders are fortunate.

He didn't know how to send his thoughts outward, so he spoke aloud. "You can tether with each other?" His words were muted and faint.

Of course. I'm showing you memories of past tetherings from the past three hundred years of my limited existence. I tend to favor the Glider perspective. The view disappeared as the Glider dove through a thick layer of clouds. *One world, two races. Never were there to be three. Never were any to be divided.* It was the Skimmer's voice, its words pushing in all around Logan. While he had no physical form here, he did have a presence, one that filled a very small space.

"Who are you talking about?"

He felt the Skimmer rooting around in his mind, sifting through his memories. He didn't like being inspected so.

Its thoughts slid into place. *Abe gave you only part of the task. He wanted you to bring down the corrupt, those who would resist change.*

"The mayor and the sovereign."

Yes. The scene around him swirled, the Glider view of the world replaced by a glimpse of a sprawling society, neither the city nor the enclaves.

There were odd mounds of purple fungus sprinkled throughout the city, often in large stretches of parkland. Despite the buildings looking untouched, he recognized the overall architectural look. "The Broken Lands."

Broken or ruined, it matters not the name now. What it was called then was Apparatum.

Logan sensed someone else beside him. A hazy image of Byron appeared and winked out. What did that mean?

My people came first. Solid versions of all seven spirits moved through the streets. The scene abruptly changed to show the city, now even larger. In this shot, people moved alongside the Forerunners. *Your kind manifested next.*

Manifested? Such an odd word choice. Logan wanted to ask, but sensed whatever history lay behind the word was not of immediate importance and might not even be a part of this creature's impressive memories.

The city grew larger and more developed, the fungal mounds now scattered everywhere there was greenery. Now humans and solid spirits interacted and conducted business with each other.

"Did my people tether with you Forerunners?" He watched a boy, younger than Kiff, approaching a large Breaker. That wasn't good. The spirit would overwhelm him. Instead, the Breaker smiled and patted the boy on his head.

They worked together, each sharing their gifts. The scene sped up and shifted to the site of a new building being erected. Weavers and Breakers shared the bodies of humans, working in tandem as they did in the enclaves.

Before he could digest much more, the scene changed to a young woman standing alongside a Skimmer. The serpent pulled the woman into its body, and he watched as the woman's arms, ghostly and slender at first, became solid and picked up a brush from the tray of an easel. The Skimmer, now outfitted with limbs, approached an untouched canvas perched atop the easel. It manipulated her arms first to load the brush tip with blue paint and then swept it across the canvas.

We each assisted the other in areas of need.

"Symbiosis, mutualism," Logan said.

For a very long time it was just that.

The next scene was many years later. *Your people dabbled more and more in tech, seemingly working hard to find a replacement for us.*

Logan saw the expansion of the city being done by large excavators and other tools. Very few Breakers and Weavers were in attendance.

They turned on us. Devious minds drove us to the sporecore, the primary source of our magic.

The vision showed the center of the city and a massive hole at the apex of the hill Logan recognized as the site of the Tower. The edges of the hole were riddled with roots that crept up out of the hole and almost seemed to grip the ground, anchoring whatever was in the shaft. He couldn't get a good look at what was down the hole, but the color of the roots was the same purple as the mounds he had spotted earlier. Logan looked around. A strange blue cloud was being sprayed by flying machines.

The chemical they spread didn't cause us immediate harm.

The scene zoomed to a mound of fungus, somehow related to the Well at the center of the city.

While the chemical was a nuisance to us, we soon bore witness to its true target.

The blue cloud spread throughout the land. As it rolled through an area populated by the distinctive purple fungus, the mounds died off astonishingly fast. *The chemical attacked the progenies of the sporecore that were a fixture of our land.*

He watched fungus after fungus wither and die. Even though there was no sound, it was clear the Forerunners were screaming and howling in outrage and fear, especially the more sensitive Fixers and Weavers.

The Skimmer sped up the scene. Hundreds of Forerunners fled down a shaft into darkness, many using numerous protruding roots and fungal veins, some taking great, haphazard bounds from side to side as they descended, others helped by Gliders. The walls of the shaft teemed with frantic movement. Logan had a hunch this was the Well. The Tower stood there now.

Logan reached the inevitable conclusion. "Without the spores, you became spirits, lost your minds."

The Skimmer let the scene go dark.

Logan saw movement out of the corner of his eye and looked left. He again caught a fleeting image of Byron before it dissipated. Was his brother trying to wake him?

"There aren't any of those mounds anymore?" Logan felt drained.

Only the sporecore, the Well. We have Abe and the Tower to thank for its survival. But you and Kyle can change that. You can bring the mounds back, and my people can return to the surface, whole and complete.

"So if you go topside you become spirits?"

Yes. It is when the fungus once again covers the land that my people will be solid again. Only down here do we have any substance.

He felt his mind being pulled in every direction. Abruptly, he was yanked from the Skimmer. He opened his eyes to find himself on his knees by the serpentine Forerunner. It looked at him with distress.

"Rest a moment. The first tethering is the hardest."

Logan sucked in lung after lung of fresh air.

Yando eventually helped him to his feet, while Byron handed him a cup of water.

"I don't know what you want me to do," Logan said.

The Skimmer grinned generously. "The task to show you the past fell to me. Once at the Well, Abe will share with you our future."

He slowly nodded at the Skimmer.

Logan knew he couldn't turn back. He had to keep going. He was needed. He looked at Byron. Could he leave his brother with these people? Maybe ask Yando to ferry him back to his parents?

The Well was the sporecore, the primary source of magic buried for hundreds of years, the surface denied its magic. But how was he to bring the magic back? The image of him trekking far and wide over the land planting seeds or spores didn't seem to make sense. He knew something grander was expected.

Byron tugged at his sleeve. "Logan, that was amazing. I saw it, too. He pulled me in with you. I know everything like you." Byron's photoreceptors dimmed slightly, and he dropped his chin. "We have to go to the Well."

Logan responded, "We do."

Chapter 22
Kyle

The mist crept around Kyle's feet and up to his waist. He stood perfectly still while the stranger edged forward. *Definitely a man*, Kyle thought, straining to see. *Probably in his twenties. Incredibly skinny. Taller than me.*

"My name is Makow," the newcomer said. "I'm here to guide you. But at the moment you're standing at the edge of a chasm."

Kyle glanced down, seeing nothing but thick white mist around his legs. He inched forward, shuffling his feet, feeling with his toes. Sure enough, the spongy ground dropped away. He inched back again.

"It's a pit of scalding-hot water," Makow explained, his voice thin and reedy. "Very deep. Rivers and streams run everywhere down here, but this one bubbles up from the depths of the world. There's a magma chamber down there somewhere."

"Who *are* you?" Kyle asked, wondering how wide the chasm was. The man stood twenty feet away. Was he right on the edge? If so, it was too far to jump—not that he relished the idea even if it were just a short hop. "Your name's *May-cow*?"

"Makow, yes. Gracil sent me. I'm here to guide you the rest of the way."

"The rest of the way to where?"

"To see Abe Torren."

Kyle felt a flutter of excitement tinged with relief. So he hadn't imagined his dream-vision after all. Abe had really sent him a message. "Okay," he said slowly, "so how come you've been waiting here? Why didn't you meet me back at the vac-train station?"

Even with the mist creeping up as far as his chest and partially obscuring his face, Makow looked sheepish. "I, uh . . . well, this chasm is fairly new. It opened up a few months ago. There's no bridge or anything, and nobody has cared until now. I dragged a mushroom stem all the way from the grubberming caves, and it would have been perfect as a bridge—about as thick as my waist, springy but tough, pretty lightweight considering its size. But . . ." He trailed off and sighed.

"But what?"

"It fell in."

Kyle tilted his head. "It fell in? The bridge fell into the chasm?"

"Well, I stood it on end, right on the edge here, and carefully tipped it over. It landed just fine, reaching the other side with a foot to spare, only it bounced and rolled sideways. I tried to grab it but, well, there's not much to get a hold of . . ."

Shaking his head, Kyle tuned the man out. He had his own means of getting across. He called on his Glider and waited for it to ease into position. It seemed oddly reluctant. As it took up control of his body, he realized it felt different, somehow heavier.

He glanced over his shoulder, seeing the reassuring blue glow and the ethereal wings with their hazy webbing. Frowning, he beat the wings a few times. Was it his imagination or did they somehow feel more substantial? For the first time, he could sense resistance as he moved them. In any case, his feet left the spongy floor, and he drifted across the chasm without effort.

Makow's eyes widened. "Abe said you had mastery over all the spirits at once. Is it true? Are they all within you at this moment?"

"Most of them," Kyle muttered as he landed on the other side.

The ground here was just as springy, and when he leaned down to touch it, Makow said, "It's just moss. It loves the moisture."

The Glider eased back into its dormant state, leaving Kyle feeling strangely relieved. Something was off with his spirits, but he couldn't quite place what it was.

"Let's walk," Makow said, bypassing any formalities such as shaking hands. He had an untidy mop of light-brown hair, a youthful face, close-set eyes, and ears that stuck out. He exhaled the same illuminated vapor that Kyle did. "Abe Torren has sung your praises, Kyle Jaxx. And Logan Orm's, too."

Kyle grabbed his arm. "Logan's here?"

"Somewhere, yes. He's obviously coming from the west. I haven't seen him, though. Yando is bringing him. I wanted to make sure I got here before you took a wrong turn." He pointed back the way Kyle had come. "So far you've only had one possible route to take, and a safe one at that. But from this point forward it gets complicated and dangerous if you don't know your way around."

"Dangerous," Kyle repeated, grateful they'd left the mist behind. Now they were in a low, steadily widening passage. It seemed to be opening out into another of those vast caverns.

"Yes, lots of choices to make, wrong turns and dead-ends, unseen dangers . . . So I'm here to guide you. Abe wants you in one piece."

"That's nice of him. What does he want me for this time?"

Makow walked fast, hopping over mounds of red-and-blue mushrooms and clusters of ugly, tumorlike growths. Some of the ones he stepped on popped without resistance and sent up puffs of spores. He didn't seem to care, though. "Abe will explain everything."

"But who *are* you?" Kyle demanded. "Are you from the enclaves? You don't look like you're from the city."

The man gave a wide berth to a monstrous, brightly glowing fungus, not quite a mushroom or toadstool but something egg-shaped standing about thirty feet tall. Kyle gasped as he craned his neck to peer up at it. The giant fungus seemed to be in the process of shedding a thick, grey, lumpy skin to reveal a smooth, vibrant-orange inner shell with splashes of yellow. It quivered when Makow passed it.

Kyle followed in his footsteps.

"That's a fruiting mindsapper," Makow said. "It's already tall, and it's going to spread wide when it shrugs off its veil and expands. Probably later today or tomorrow, I should think. I wouldn't like to be around then. You got here just in time, my friend."

Kyle wanted to ask about it, but more important things were on his mind than biology lessons. "Who *are* you?" he asked again. "Where did you come from? Where do you live?" Other questions bubbled up. "Why is there a metal tunnel back there? And an old drilling machine from the city? How come tech works down here?"

Raising his hands, Makow grinned. "Slow down. The metal tunnel is there because Diggers never dug that far east, and the drilling machine was the only way to connect to the enclaves. Tech works down here because . . . well, we're underground. As for where I live—"

Just then a distant shriek brought both of them to a standstill.

Kyle spun around, looking back the way they'd come. He listened hard, and his spirits roused and grew agitated on his behalf. A chill had seeped into him. It had *almost* sounded like someone was yelling his name . . .

"Kyle!" the voice shrieked again.

He gasped. Kiff? What was *he* doing here? And how had he gotten past—?

Ask questions later, he thought as he took off running. He raced past the massive fruiting mindsapper, causing it to shake and wobble as though stirring in its sleep.

He didn't bother checking to see if Makow was behind him. All he could think about was Kiff's panic-stricken voice.

"Kyle!"

"I'm coming!" he yelled.

Back in the cave of fangs, he launched himself into the white mist and skidded on moss. He saw no sign of Kiff, but the mist was thick and completely hid the chasm. He feared Kiff had fallen in.

"Glider!" he ordered, and leapt.

Plunging into a mist-filled chasm with boiling water far below didn't fill him with joy, but his Glider stopped his fall. Still, the heat was unbearable. Steam threatened to blister his skin as he fought to rise back up out of the pit. As he did so, he flailed with his arms, seeking the source of Kiff's awful shrieking.

"Kyle!"

"I'm right here," Kyle shouted. His fingers brushed against fabric, and he threw himself in that direction until he was pinning his half-brother to the slippery chasm wall. "I've got you. Let go. I've got you."

Kiff refused to release his grip for a moment, but after a bit more gentle persuasion, he did so and allowed Kyle to lift him up and out. Once safely on firm footing, the boy threw himself at Kyle and hugged him tight around the waist.

"You all right?" Kyle said after they'd both calmed down.

"Yeah," came the muffled reply. Kiff untangled himself and stepped back, furiously rubbing his eyes. "Sorry. I . . . I was fine. I had a good grip on that rock. I would have pulled myself out once I got my foot on something."

"Right," Kyle said. "Well, I happened to be nearby, so . . ."

Makow appeared in the mist behind them. "What's going on? Who *is* that?"

Kyle reached out and ruffled Kiff's hair. "This is my half-brother. He has this annoying habit of following people into dangerous territory. Last time, he followed Logan into the Broken Lands and wound up prematurely tethered to a Breaker. This time he followed *me*." He glared at the boy, who in turn shuffled and stared into the mist. "What are you doing here,

Kiff? And *how* are you here? There's no way you could have followed me through that rock quarry entrance."

"Did too," Kiff muttered.

"I don't understand."

With an impatient sigh, Makow wrung his hands and gestured to the tunnel he'd emerged from. "We really need to get moving. Abe will be waiting on us. I really hoped to have been back at the Well by now. We're going to be late."

"Fine, let's go." Kyle gripped his half-brother's shoulder. "But Kiff, you'd *better* explain yourself."

Chapter 23
Logan

The Seekers, as they called themselves, fed Logan a large slab of rackle rump and a helping of mushrooms that had much more flavor than the ones Yando had let him sample. The meat was fatty but tasty. He chose not to ladle the green sauce they offered as its smell was off-putting.

Yando's children hovered over Logan the entire meal, mostly asking questions about the city and Byron. His brother fielded the questions about his robotic housing, not the least bit ashamed.

Gracil explained their underground refuge as Logan ate. No solid spirits interrupted their meal.

"We seek to bring the Forerunners back to the surface," she said.

"But won't they just be spirits?" He thought back to the image of the solid Breaker being compassionate to the child in the Skimmer's vision. "My people only tether when we can safely control one. Anyone under fourteen can lose themselves in their spirit. More of them running around might mean more danger for my people." Could the meager magic the Banishers employed keep solid spirits away from the enclaves? Logan somehow doubted that.

"The Forerunners you tether with are broken, lost. When they are away from the Well, they lose their minds, resorting to animal instinct. Those your people bond with are not healthy. It's a miracle they haven't caused more harm than good to your world."

Well, they have. He thought back to Kiff's encounter with the Breaker, one of the main reasons Kyle had returned to Logan's true home. Had the city dweller fixed his brother?

"But what's this Well? How is it going to bring the Forerunners back to their right minds?'

"That is for Abe to relate to you and Kyle. He was very clear on what we could divulge." She sighed, upset that she couldn't reveal more.

Logan pushed his plate aside and stood. "Then there's no reason to delay. Let's get this done with. I have to get Byron back as soon as this is all over."

She nodded and took his now empty plate.

Logan looked at his brother. "You're coming with me. I can't risk anything happening to you." Was Kyle making his way underground as well? If so, he hoped Kiff was not by his side. It would be too much for him. At least Byron was protected by his hardened robot body. What would Kiff do against the vulpers or minquins in his tiny body? "Show me the way," he said to Yando.

* * *

Logan felt silly sitting in the back section of the boat. It was not made of wood like those used by the coastal enclaves to fish in the Great Sea. Bobbing in the water on an upside down mushroom cap had to be an absurd sight. The gills of the nearly ten-foot-wide grubberming, the name the Seekers gave the fungus, had been scooped out and the cavity outfitted with a bench hewn from precious wood.

Yando handed him two long oars made from another type of fungus, surprisingly thick and sturdy, and pointed downriver. "The Wiscuppa will pour into a tunnel." He tossed several of the mushrooms that gave off a bluish glow into the boat. "It's the fastest way to the Well. Otherwise, your trek would take more than a day. Using this, you can be there in a few hours."

"How will I know when to go ashore?" Logan fiddled with one of the oars, dipping it into the slow-moving current.

"A string of bright orange fludda mushrooms have been hung along the ceiling to mark your destination." Yando untied the boat from the rock-sculpted dock. "From there, take the leftmost passage. It will get you close. I suspect Abe will escort you the rest of the way."

Peering over the rim of the cap, Byron's body language indicated apprehension. "And there's not another way we could travel with less water?"

His brother's body could withstand a soaking but perhaps not a prolonged submerging.

Yando grinned. "Not unless you want to risk a run-in with a clacker?"

"Clackers come this deep?" Logan said.

"Some do, but the other tunnel is much closer to the surface. It's where my father fled when he was exiled. He was lucky to find the Seeker settlement."

"Was he from the city?" Logan asked.

"No, my father came from your land. He couldn't tether, and they cast him out. What kind of people do that?" Yando scowled at Logan, directing blame by association. There was a lot of frustration stored up in this man. "He found his way down here and chose to live among the Seekers."

"It happened to me, too."

"So Abe said."

The old man was not done with him. Logan was unsure the next task he required was within his means. For some reason, despite having greater power, he felt small and weak in this strange world. Unable to tether with spirits and with no tech around, he felt exposed.

Yando waved at them. "Be safe. Abe is wise. He will reveal a clear path for you, both of you."

Logan plunged the oar deeper and began rowing.

* * *

Thanks to his bright breath and Byron's chest lamp, the narrow passage they glided through wasn't as foreboding. With the current much stronger, Logan had little need to row. Instead he used the oars to keep them from knocking into the walls. This gave him time to take in the sights. Despite occasional fungi on the walls, the real light show was underwater.

Fish with glowing antennas and fins skirted clear of their progress. Lumpy, shelled creatures darted around on the river bottom, snapping their four sets of large claws silently in the current. Above water, he was certain their actions would make a horrible racket. Several insects skated along the water's surface, their six legs providing their luminescence.

Byron seemed to have conquered his fear of the water and was leaning over the edge, scanning the aquatic world. "I'm recording a lot of what I see. Maybe someone will have a use for it back in Apparati. This is amazing."

"Not like you can share it with anyone."

"Why?"

"Think of the trouble you'd get into if you strut around telling people about all the life below ground. The mayor came right out and forbade me from sneaking down here."

"Oh," Byron said, softly.

Knowing a change of subject was needed, Logan said, "The man we're about to meet up with is a little intense."

"Abe? He's the one who helped you and Kyle get synced up to your right birthplaces, isn't he?"

Logan had told Byron all about his trip through the Ruins. The boy knew his story in and out. "Yes."

"And he sent Kyle away. He can't come back to me in any way that I can see him again." Byron didn't phrase either as a question. There was lethargic resignation in the way he dropped his shoulders.

"I don't believe that. There has to be a way. Maybe that's why he's calling us to the Well. Maybe it's the opposite of the Tower and puts us back in our proper places." Logan regretted his wording. Byron would take his comment to mean that Logan didn't see the city as home. But it wasn't. He had been born there, true, but the enclaves were where he had been raised. It was where Kiff and Nomi were. And his parents.

"They said Kyle was meeting us at the Well. Maybe I'll be able to see him."

Maybe, thought Logan, but what would be the price?

With Abe, there was always a price.

* * *

Logan spotted the string of glowing mushrooms draped over the river ahead. He pointed at them and steered their boat toward the glowing embankment. One of the clawed creatures from the riverbed scuttled across the rocky shore and dove into the water, clacking its claws at them for driving it away.

Despite the swift current, Logan navigated the boat safely to shore. Its bottom ground against the shallows, wedging itself between two submerged rocks. Logan hopped out, splashing a little in the water as he tied the boat to a rock outcropping similar to the one Yando had freed it from earlier.

The lighting wasn't as prevalent. Logan exhaled enough to see there were three distinct tunnels leading away from their landing spot.

Byron jumped out and landed on dry land.

A voice from the darkness ahead said, "You brought a friend. Not what I expected."

Logan stepped between his brother and the old man emerging from the shadows, Abe Torren. His eyes looked more manic, and the play of colors across his face from the various glowing fungi made his wrinkles appear deeper and more pronounced. He wore the harness that swooped upward behind his head to almost look like a cowl.

Byron held out his hand. "I'm his brother, Byron. Pleased to meet you."

Abe didn't shake his hand but clasped it from above and squeezed it with a surprising air of warmth. "A pleasure. I trust you are helping Logan adjust to his new home."

"I think so," Byron said.

"I'm sure you are." Abe looked at Logan, his eyes narrowing. "But we're not here for social reasons. I have need of you and Kyle one last time."

"It's got something to do with a well. What is it? Gracil and her people weren't very forthcoming." Logan crossed his arms.

"Then they abided by my wishes." He turned and strolled down the leftmost passage. "In truth, if they had told you everything, I doubt you'd have agreed to come."

"I don't understand. Am I in danger? Is Kyle?"

"We all are, Logan." He expelled a breath and briefly eyed the glowing spores erupting from his mouth. "But you and Kyle can makes things right. You can reinstate the world of Apparatum."

He pointed his staff forward and took off at a faster pace than Logan expected. He moved at a brisk jog to keep up. Byron's servos effortlessly propelled him forward. At this pace, Logan would quickly get winded, but his brother wouldn't. For some reason, he doubted Abe would suffer any shortness of breath. He was of sterner stock than he looked, hardened in ways Logan could never understand.

Chapter 24
Kyle

Kyle shook his head as he traversed the ever-widening tunnel for the second time, following in Makow's footsteps.

"I don't get it, Kiff. How did you get past the guards at the quarry? There were three of them, plus the archers on the cliff. Even I had trouble. And then there's the Weaver wall blocking the passage. I tore through it, but I built a new one of my own as well. You *couldn't* have come after me that way."

Kiff had discovered that he'd cut his hand while clinging for dear life in the chasm. He waved it in Kyle's face. "Can you fix this for me?"

"Sorry, no, I lost my Fixer. Keep moving and *talk*."

By now, they were in the giant cavern, stepping over the red-and-blue mushrooms and nasty grey-and-white growths that looked like tumors. Again, Makow stomped on some as he went. And again he was careful to navigate around the thirty-foot, egg-shaped mindsapper with its vivid orange hue and splashes of yellow. Now it seemed to have woken, and the veil, as Makow had called it, was beginning to come adrift, sliding off inch by inch as the monstrous fungus began to swell outwards. Kyle eyed it warily as he passed, making sure to guide Kiff well away from it.

"I saw what you did," Kiff said at last. "I saw you land in the quarry. I got there just as you were giving the guards the runaround. It was funny." He grinned. "Then you were gone. One of the archers ran off to get help, and news spread around the enclave, and everyone started showing up. The first to arrive were Breakers from the construction site—just in time, because the spirits you stole from them were flying around the quarry."

"Did they make it back to their hosts?" Kyle asked.

Kiff nodded. “They tethered fine. Or re-tethered, I suppose. Anyway, I heard the guards say you’d blocked the passage behind you, and they ordered the Breakers to clear a way through.”

Kyle pursed his lips. When he’d urged the construction workers to hurry along to the quarry to retrieve their stolen Breakers, he hadn’t meant for them to be so helpful undoing the wall he’d built!

“The Breakers had trouble getting through your wall,” Kiff explained. “They said it was ugly but strong.”

“Not bad considering it only took a minute.”

“The guards noticed me watching. There were at least twenty of them by now. Acting Sovereign Durant showed up, too. And a man in a black robe and hood.”

“Nailor,” Kyle growled.

“Yes, Nailor,” Kiff said. “Him and Durant talked for a bit, then came over and asked me if I was your brother. I said kind of. Nailor asked if I’d like to go after you, and I said yes.”

A horrible feeling crept over Kyle.

Kiff went on. “He was quite nice. He said he works for the Guardian at the Hallowed Spires! Can you imagine? So anyway, he got four guards together. Grib Lottle was one of them. I didn’t know the other three; they were from the Hunter Capitol. As soon as your wall was halfway down, me and Grib and those other three Hunters came after you.”

Kyle stopped dead, his fears realized. “You came after me? All of you?”

Ahead of them, Makow turned and huffed his impatience again. “Please keep moving.”

Kiff snorted with laughter and lowered his voice. “Did you see Makow’s breath when he breathed out of his nose? It lit up really bright! Why does the air do that, Kyle? It’s amazing!”

“Spores,” Kyle told him shortly, repeating something Makow had mentioned earlier. “Stay on topic. Are you saying you and the four guards followed me?”

"All the way," Kiff said proudly. "Grib carried me on his back the whole time, and all four Hunters ran without stopping. I could never have done that. Grib said Hunters train for this sort of thing because it's the only way to catch gallumpers—by wearing them down."

Kyle didn't know anyone called Grib, but he did know that anyone tethered to a Hunter spirit tended to be pretty fit. So they'd caught up with him simply by breaking into a run? He'd underestimated their persistence.

"We ran all the way along the metal tunnel to the end," Kiff went on. "There's a big machine there, Kyle. They called it a *train*. It carries people from one place to—"

"I know." Kyle rubbed the bridge of his nose. "Do your parents know you're here?"

"No, but Nailor promised to tell them."

"Sure he did."

The terrain had gotten difficult. No more easy walking through flat-floored caverns. Now they were in what Makow explained was Apparatum's equivalent of a jungle—endless fungal monstrosities that squished under their feet or towered over their heads, many of them harmless but some deadly. "Steer clear of that red-and-white one," he warned, pointing. "It reacts to movement. It detects vibrations in the air and turns upward, revealing its gills. Then it gases you. When you die, your rotting corpse attracts—"

"All right, all right," Kyle snapped. "Kiff, go on. What happened next?"

Kiff shrugged. "The Hunters stopped outside the station and argued about something. One said, 'Do it,' and Grib said, '*You* do it.' I didn't know what was going on, but in the end, one shouted 'Lights!' really loud." At this, Kiff's eyes widened. "You'll never guess what happened next."

Kyle rolled his eyes. "The lights came on?"

"Yes! It was amazing. There were lots of lamps hanging around the place on strings, and they all came on the moment someone shouted 'Lights!' It was like magic! Grib and the others all ducked down at first, really frightened. It was funny. I wasn't scared at all."

"And then . . . ?" Kyle prompted.

"Well, then they found a log pile and got a fire going. Grib told me they weren't allowed to go any farther, and the rest was up to me. He said I just needed to follow the tunnel and catch up with you."

"Why?" Kyle asked, suspicion bubbling up. "Why would they just let you go off after me?"

"Because they were scared you'd get eaten by minquins, whatever they are. They said the tunnel only led one way, so there was no chance of getting lost, and I'd be safe if I hurried and caught up with you." Kiff grimaced. "I guess I should have taken my time in that mist."

Kyle sighed. "And you just went along with them?"

"I . . . I was afraid I'd never see you again," Kiff mumbled. "I thought maybe you could take me to the city and let me see where Logan's living now."

"If we can see anything at all," Kyle said. "Abe said the city is out of phase to people from the enclave, even me now." He shook his head. "Never mind. What's Grib up to? Why didn't he come after me himself? Why send you?"

He stopped suddenly, struck by a thought. He grabbed Kiff and turned him around to face him. The boy's eyes opened wide.

"Did he give you anything?" Kyle demanded. "Like a piece of tech?"

Kiff's eyebrows shot up. Without a word, he nodded and hitched up his left pant leg. Around his ankle was what looked like a metal bracelet. A small light indicated that it was activated. "Hey," he said, awed. "What's that bright red dot? That wasn't there before."

"I knew it," Kyle muttered, feeling sick. "It's probably a tracker. Now he knows exactly where we're headed."

Kiff screwed up his face in confusion. "You mean it's tech that *works*? But I thought—"

"It doesn't work aboveground, but it works down here. Which means the guards can track your whereabouts. That's why they're underground. Nailor must have given Grib a tracking device, and it will only work down here."

"Where did Nailor get tech like that?" Kiff asked, looking astonished.

From the Guardian, Kyle thought, recalling his vision of a tech-filled chamber at the Hallowed Spires. *His servants probably have all kinds of dormant gadgets lying around.*

"We need to get that bracelet off," he said.

He knelt down to tackle the problem while Makow snorted and huffed some more, sending bright flurries of spores whirling around the place.

"Grib said it would ward off minquins," Kiff said, sounding a little sullen now. "He said it was magical, that it would put out a high-pitched screech that we couldn't hear."

Kyle ground his teeth. "And you believed him? You know, Byron's the same age as you but would never—" He broke off, realizing he was about to say something that would cut the eight-year-old boy to the bone. He continued in a more gentle tone. "Well, he wouldn't care about minquins, whatever they are. He's made of metal, so they wouldn't bother him."

The bracelet was tough. Kyle called on his Breaker and put his strength into it—but then an odd thing happened. His hands, which gripped the metal, suddenly bulged and expanded in size. He jerked and threw himself backward in shock. His Breaker howled and tore free, and Kyle couldn't help gasping at the terrible wrenching feeling as he lost his tether.

He stared in amazement at the spirit creature that stood nearby, untethered and surprisingly solid-looking in the dim, subterranean light. More than that, it appeared to be standing on the ground rather than bobbing about in the air. At twice Kyle's height, it cut a brutish figure. How something like that fit inside anyone's frame was a mystery. Still, substantial though it was at the moment, its features remained a one-tone reddish hue, difficult to make out.

Makow strode over to Kyle and gripped his arm. "We need to *move*. Please. No more delays. We'll talk as we walk."

"But—what *is* this?" Kyle said, gesturing to the Breaker. It stared back at him with a tilted head, strangely calm. "What's happening?"

Perhaps a little childishly, Makow refused to answer and instead gestured sharply for his guests to keep moving. When Kyle and Kiff reluctantly followed, Makow picked up the pace, navigating his way carefully around dozens of luminescent tendrils that hung from an unseen cavern ceiling far above. "Don't touch those," he said. "They sting."

Kyle had so many questions that he didn't know where to begin. And Kiff's tracker was a serious problem. He didn't want to lead Nailor's henchmen to wherever he was supposed to meet Abe.

The guards could kill us all in one go. Logan as well!

That was a horrible thought. He had to remove the tracker before arriving at the Well, if indeed he could. His Breaker had been unable to loosen it.

He glanced back. The creature was shuffling along, actually walking on solid ground, looking about in silence and glowing fiercely. A spirit that wasn't quite a spirit.

Makow spoke. "The air you breathe, this illuminated breath-vapor? It's because of the sporecore. It pumps magic into the air. It surrounds us and keeps us grounded. And we're getting close to the Well where the magic is strongest. The fact that your Breaker wants out means it's feeling the effects. It's starting to feel real again."

As he said these words, Kyle felt a stirring within as another spirit, his Creeper, grew claustrophobic. Oddly, he felt the same way, a need to exorcise what seemed to be a more-than-ethereal being. Sweating, he had to pause and politely suggest the Creeper step out.

It did so, erupting in a flash of light. It was a hideous-looking thing, about his height but utterly inhuman. Kyle realized he'd never gotten a good look at one before because of the way they ducked and dived in their phantom state, usually a blur of green light, their only obvious feature being tentacles around the middle. Now, through the hazy aura, he identified the creature as some sort of giant insect with segmented armor plating and bulbous compound eyes—but what kind of bug had three pairs of fleshy, slippery tentacles? They wriggled and undulated as the Creeper stood there jerking its head from side to side, mandibles snapping.

It stood upright for a few seconds longer, frozen in place, somehow balanced on what looked like three tails. Then it bent forward and crouched low, using its tentacles as legs and raising those tails high. Two splayed out to the sides while the middle one arced over its shiny, black armor. Kyle thought he saw a needle poke out from the end . . . but then the Creeper relaxed and eased back upright, standing tall as before, its tentacles moving eerily.

Kyle winced as a stabbing pain shot into his forehead. He reached up and was startled to find a horn sticking out. He felt his face beginning to contort and stretch . . .

"No!" he shouted, fighting it. "This is *my* body!"

He ejected the Hunter, and it staggered and reeled. Kyle squinted at it, and through the ghostly green light saw something a whole lot more familiar: a long snout and single deadly horn, vicious razor-sharp teeth, and hideous flaps of skin behind its ears that puffed out as it twisted around to face him.

"This is amazing," Kiff whispered. "I've never seen a spirit look so . . . so . . ."

"Solid?" Kyle finished, his heart pounding.

Unperturbed, Makow led the way up and over mounds of dull-grey mushrooms, some of them ten feet wide. "These are grubbermings, about ready to burst. Don't puncture them. They're harmless, but you'll probably choke on the dust."

Small flying creatures screeched from above, and Kiff gave a yelp and put his foot through one of the mushroom caps. It broke easily, his foot disappearing inside and a cloud of fine spores puffing out. As Makow had promised, the cloud choked them as they stumbled onward.

"That way leads to a minquin den," Makow said, pointing to a gaping hole of blackness to their left. "There's a lot of them around. We're okay if we stick together as a group and avoid their habitat. That's why you need a guide. There are a dozen different tunnels you could blunder into, and only one is really safe. That tunnel over there, for instance, leads down into the firepits where orb scavengers live. They're not like the cuddly ones on the surface," he added. "These ones are dangerous."

Kiff hung close to Kyle the whole time, a mixture of fascination and fear on his face.

"Who *are* you people?" Kyle asked his guide, not for the first time.

As the Glider and the Weaver began to squirm with increasing unrest deep down inside him, the others trailed behind, sniffing and touching things. Makow forged ahead into the narrowest tunnel yet. At last he began to talk about himself.

"My people live on the other side of the Well. Gracil is our leader. We stay close to the Well because that's the only place the Forerunners can exist."

"The Forerunners?"

"Them," Makow said, jerking his thumb back toward the three semi-solid creatures that trailed behind. "You know them as spirits, but in their proper non-phantom state they're called Forerunners. There are nine distinct species, and they—"

"Nine?" Kyle interjected. "I know only seven."

Makow sighed, his breath lighting up the tunnel ahead. "Do you want me to talk or not? If so, please stop interrupting."

Chapter 25
Reunion

Logan worked to keep up as Abe continued to move with a sense of urgency. He noticed the spores in the air were much more plentiful and seemed to hold their glow longer. Because of this, the tunnel was easier to navigate. That was a good thing as the ground, walls, and ceiling of the passage had hundreds of tiny purple nubs and roots sticking out, in some places nearly a yard.

"What's with the roots?"

"Part of the Well. We are close."

"The Skimmer showed me the Well from above. Is it made of fungus?" Logan ducked under a root that reminded him of a purple noose. *The same color as the mounds from the vision.*

"Yes," Abe said but didn't elaborate.

"It's called the sporecore, too. Is that why there are more spores flying all over the place?" Byron asked.

Abe grunted. "Smart little man. Your observation skills are sharp. I'm happy to see Logan was able to give you a new body, a big improvement."

Byron didn't reply.

Logan eyed his brother, who was probably thrown by Abe's extensive knowledge. The old man's observations came across as invasive at times. Who was he to be keeping tabs on them?

The roots continued to intrude more and more into the tunnel. Soon, the trio were climbing over much thicker ones.

"You built the Tower over the Well, didn't you?"

Abe pressed forward. "Really, I'm happy to answer your questions, but I'd prefer to do it only once. If I blather on to you now, I'll just have to repeat myself when Kyle joins us." Abe pressed a particularly long and resilient root out of the way, being careful not to bend it so much it would snap off. If Logan didn't know better, he'd say the man handled the growths with a degree of reverence. "Entrance to the Well is limited to three points. Mind the drop when we step out into it."

Abe squeezed by a throng of roots, almost a web, and through a narrow opening no more than four feet in diameter. Logan realized the tunnel itself had slowly diminished in size, tapering down to the narrow access point. He hadn't noticed because of being preoccupied by all the roots. The surface of the tunnel was no longer earthen. Now covered in a layer of purple fungus that clustered in small mounds like the ones from the Skimmer vision, it was decidedly claustrophobic. The air was thicker and the floating spores even more pronounced. He wiggled through and stepped out onto a ledge no more than three feet wide. Byron emerged next to him.

The bright breath clouds Logan and Abe produced were immense plumes. The Well was filled with the light-bringing spores. The walls extended upward and downward, disappearing into darkness. The Well had to be filled with a healthy amount of carbon dioxide to keep the spores lit for so long, though Logan had no trouble breathing.

Purple fungus covered every surface. He realized what he had mistaken for a ledge was merely a thick bulging vein. The veins stretched out all over, some wider than the one they stood on while others were no thicker than his arm. They glowed slightly but not nearly as much as the spores. The green light against the massive expanse of purple was a ghastly color affair.

Abe didn't linger on their ledge. He hopped to a narrow one higher up and used his staff to assist him in climbing to another ample vein, the underside of which had thousands of small roots swaying in the updraft. He made his way up several more veins, exploiting the horizontal ones the most.

The old man looked down at them and shot an arm out to wave Byron back. "Stay there. I need to fetch Kyle. He should be here by now. His guide's a little off, but he knows these tunnels well, and I impressed upon him the importance of getting you two to the Well without delay. Probably some minor setback. I will be back momentarily." He ducked into a dark opening in the wall, one of the other access points. Was the third above or below them? For some reason Logan thought above. Maybe it even led to the Tower.

He took in the Well again. On his second inspection, he noticed a thick metal rod coming down through the center of the shaft about fifty feet above. It looked to be as thick as an upper branch of the slender wugga tree and ended with a silver ball at its tip.

Byron noticed it as well. He pointed and said, "Do you think that's tech?"

"I don't know. Maybe. Let me check." Logan closed his eyes and cast his mind toward the structure. Contact. He probed around, surprised at what he found. While he couldn't extend his investigation much more than a hundred feet or so, he was confident the rod met up with the Tower in some way, that the two were connected.

"What's it do?" Byron asked.

Logan rubbed his eyes. "I don't know. It's not easy to figure out. But I know one thing, it's tech of some sort and so much more."

* * *

". . . And now you know all about us," Makow said, panting as he climbed an earthen slope.

Clods of soil tumbled loose, skittering around Kyle as he climbed after him up one side of the cavern, following by Kiff and the three partially solid spirits. He likened this place to a vast bowl filled with dirt and hideous fungi, with another bowl turned upside down and placed on top to form the cavern ceiling. Dozens of mysterious openings at many different levels all around made him thankful Makow was here to guide him.

"I don't know *everything* about you," Kyle argued, his fiery breath beginning to get on his nerves. It was like a constant flashing before his eyes. "Okay, so I kind of know about the Forerunners and how they were driven below, and the spores in the air, and why my spirits are changing form. I don't really get the phasing stuff."

"Yes, well, it's complicated. Abe is the one to ask about that."

"Tell me more about the Well, then," Kyle pressed. "Tell me what Abe wants with Logan and me."

"All in good time, my friend," Makow said. "That's something Abe wants to explain himself. He wants to show you. You'll see the Well soon enough."

Kyle winced as his Weaver again threatened to slip free of his physical form. "No," he growled. "Stay put. I can't lose you as well. Nor you, Glider."

The other spirits still trailed behind as though they hadn't yet committed to a course of action. Would they leave Kyle soon? Until then, they followed like obedient pets.

The group finally crested the hill and arrived at the far-end wall of the enormous cavern they had crossed. Makow led them into the darkness of a passage that looked exactly like all the others, his breath lighting the way.

"Tell me about the vac-train tunnel," Kyle said. "Why would anyone want to connect to the enclaves underground? What's wrong with just walking through the wastelands?"

"When our ancestors first arrived in Apparatum and began exploring, it wasn't enough to roam about on the surface. They found all these tunnels below ground and felt a need to extend them to the east. The first enclave, the Hunter Capitol, was built where that old vac-train tunnel emerged."

"I knew it!" Kyle exclaimed. "Does the tunnel end at the Hallowed Spires?"

Makow shrugged. "I don't know. Maybe. Save that for another time. We're here now."

Kyle felt a jolt of surprise. "We are?"

The passage was short. To Kyle's surprise, a figure stood at the end of it, silhouetted by a light shining from the top of his staff. Abe Torren! Here he was at last.

"Good to see you again, Kyle," the old man said in a gravelly, echoing voice. "Step this way. Logan is waiting."

"But hold on," Kyle called to him as he faltered. "Kiff has a tracker on his leg. I can't get the thing off, and nor can my Breaker."

After a pause, Abe sighed. "Then it's too late, they already know where we are. All the more reason to hurry. Come along."

Makow walked with them to the end of the passage where Abe waited. It seemed to be a juncture of four different routes, the passage ahead strangely purple. The others looked more like a main thoroughfare, much wider. The one to the left led down into soft yellow light. Kyle could hear the rush of distant water.

A metal platform hovered in the middle of the intersection, completely out of place and illuminated quite clearly with the light from Abe's staff. These platforms were common in the city, about the size of a table with fencelike sides and an upright push-handle. The floatpad was filled with distinctly shiny metal objects and other things that made Kyle frown. Obviously tech, but . . . He peered closer. Grenades and raze bombs, some thermal detonators, an arc lance, a wide-muzzled stump pistol, and various other weapons buried underneath. He thought he recognized a molecular disruptor, but those things had been outlawed decades ago. And was that a skip pack?

Makow cleared his throat and turned into the left-hand tunnel toward the distant light, walking backward while he bade them farewell.

"Oh, you're going?" Kyle said, tearing his gaze from the pile of weapons. "Thanks for . . . you know, coming to find us."

Makow shrugged. "Simple enough task. I'll try not to drop the bridge into the boiling pit next time. Look, I won't be far away. See you soon—and good luck."

Abe frowned after him. "Bridge?" he muttered. He shook his head. "I wonder about him sometimes."

After Makow had trudged away, a silence fell as Kyle took a good long look at the old man. He seemed to have aged a few years, unless it was just the way the shadows fell across his wrinkles. His head was bald, but he had flowing white hair at the sides, and a grey beard that desperately needed trimming. He still wore the strange metal collar that swept high around the back of his head. That contraption somehow helped him phase in and out between worlds, something he claimed took a lot of practice. He held in his gloved right hand the familiar staff, resting it on the floor as though it were a walking stick. Right now, the ball on the top was putting out a dazzling light that flickered and buzzed occasionally.

"What *is* that thing?" he asked, suddenly curious. "It's not just a glorified flashlight. What's it do?"

Abe raised an eyebrow. After a pause, he switched the staff to his left hand, which wasn't gloved. The moment the staff touched his skin, Kyle received a powerful image in his mind—an old, cluttered desk in the shadows of a cobwebbed room filled with tools and dusty electronic equipment, the shelves on the wall jammed with tomes. On the desk lay a small, rectangular piece of tech, its casing removed to expose circuit boards and wiring. A pair of wrinkled hands tinkered with the device in flickering candlelight . . .

The vision ended as Abe switched the staff back to his gloved right hand. "That was my little den," he said with a smile.

"How—?" Kyle shook his head. "That's some powerful tech. I heard something about thought projection on a documentary once. It's totally theoretical."

"Of course it is," Abe said. "Something like this in the wrong hands would be dangerous." He thumbed a small switch on the shaft, and the light dimmed. "Better save the battery. Now then, I see you brought Kiff along. While it's a pleasure to see you, young man, I wish you hadn't come. Still, perhaps you'll keep Byron company while these older boys do their job."

Kyle sucked in a breath. "B-Byron's here?"

"Just along this purple-colored passage behind me. I suggest we—"

But Kyle had already stopped listening. He shouldered past the old man and headed into the passage. It was narrow and festooned with what looked like purple roots poking out of the walls and ceiling. As he ducked and weaved around them, he realized his breath was brighter than ever before. A gentle breeze tugged at him as if to help him along.

He didn't stop to see if Kiff and his spirits were following. He was sure they were, with the old man bringing up the rear. All he could think about right now was Byron.

He burst out of the end of the passage and gasped when he found himself on the brink of a massive shaft filled with hideous purple growths and what looked like green-glowing veins. His breath plumed spectacularly, floating upward on a draft.

Through that plume, he spotted two figures perched on a fat veinlike ledge low down on the far side. Logan! Not just a ghostly phantom but a fully fleshed-out mirror image of Kyle himself. If anyone could remove the tracker bracelet from Kiff's leg, it was him.

As for his companion . . .

Was that *Byron*?

He blinked in amazement at the tall, sleek robot figure. A vast improvement over the last model. Logan had done it. He'd upgraded Byron's worn-out frame and given him a new lease on life.

Kyle could barely speak. He grinned broadly and waved, and Byron rather comically gave him a metal thumbs-up.

At that moment, Kiff arrived in his own plume of breath. Unlike Kyle, he leaned out over the endless pit and shouted at the top of his lungs. "Logan! You're here! It's me! Kiff!"

"Careful, boy," Abe warned from behind them. "The shaft is a thousand feet deep. We're just above halfway, but that still leaves quite a drop, enough to break a bone or two I should think."

Logan laughed. "Kiff, stop jumping about or you'll fall in." Then his eyes nearly bugged out. "Wait—you're *jumping about.*"

Kiff nodded vigorously. "Kyle fixed my leg."

And in that moment, Kyle and Logan shared a look of gratitude and joy that no amount of words could convey.

* * *

Logan watched with envy as Kyle used his Glider spirit to fly Abe and Kiff across the shaft to where he waited with Byron.

No sooner had Kyle deposited Kiff than he blurted out, "Logan, you have to disable Kiff's bracelet!" He grabbed the boy's pant leg and exposed the tech secured to his left ankle. "The Guardian's servant gave it to him and said it would ward off minquins. I don't think it does that."

Logan read the panic in Kyle's face. He responded quickly, sinking his mind into the small tech. Immediately, he identified it as an explosive keyed to go off when its one external sensor registered a certain level of spores in the air. Luckily, the concentration required to trigger it hadn't been reached. It was only at fifty-four percent. The Guardian expected Kiff to work his way to somewhere that had a high spore content—but where else was the air thicker with spores than here?

Logan helped Kiff to lie down on the ledge, situating him as far from the edge as possible. “It’s not a minquin warder. It’s set to blow if it registers a high level of spores in the air.”

Abe replied, “An eruption from below would surely trigger it.”

The boys looked at him, perplexed, and Kiff said, his voice strained, “Why? How?”

“I’ll explain, but right now we have to safeguard all of us.” Abe nodded at Logan. “Can you disable it?“

Knowing Kiff was near panic, Logan responded calmly. “Not a problem.” He concentrated and easily disabled the lock. The bracelet fell off into his hands. He subverted the detonator impeller and held the inert bomb in his hand. “All done.”

Abe took it from him and said, “I will dispose of it.” He tucked it into his robes.

Kiff jumped up, looking relieved. A second later, he seemed to have completely forgotten about the bracelet and had turned his attention to Byron, clearly taken aback by the tech.

Kyle, with Byron clinging to his side, wore more traditional clothing than the last time he had seen him. At the Tower, Kyle had been outfitted in city garb.

Logan slid his fingers over the fine weave of the city shirt he now wore. It was soft to the touch unlike his enclave clothes, which Loreena had tossed. He said to Kyle, “Thank you for healing his leg.”

Kyle smiled. “My pleasure.” He nodded at Byron. “And thanks for saving him and giving him an upgrade.”

He smiled back and tipped his head.

With Kiff’s bracelet no longer a threat and the thank-yous out of the way, Abe stepped in again, his voice echoing as he projected it with more fervor. “You’ve both been told of our past and how the Forerunners were driven from the surface.”

Kyle said, “Yeah, Makow said they ended up down here and the Well was blocked, and everything aboveground has been out of phase ever since. Is this why we can see each other now? Because we're in the Well? We're aligned in the same reality like we were in the Tower?"

Abe nodded. "The Well brings you back to the one true reality. If you'll let me speak my piece, I will answer all your questions."

Logan and Kyle nodded in agreement.

Abe pointed his staff up to the rod Logan had earlier interacted with. *Good, start there because that thing is just weird.*

"This Well holds magic. Without its influence above, the people fell out of step. You know how our people drove the Forerunners below and killed the fungal mounds. Those mounds and the sporecore generate millions of spores. The fungus you saw in the vision spreads them into the air in small amounts, but the true spectacle is when the sporecore fires out its spores. If the Guardians suspected plans were afoot to revert the world to its former state, they would certainly try to finish what they started and destroy the Well for good. I'm sure the bracelet was a case of seizing an opportunity when it arose, but the Guardians will be alert now. I don't expect this to be the end of it."

Logan exhaled, producing a blindingly bright cloud. "What do you mean fires out?"

"The Well is the main organism. It's a fungal cannon. The bulk of its mass lies below in what we call the sporecore. Through a series of chambers and synchronized valves, it builds pressure and then expels the spores upward." Abe waved his free hand with a dramatic flourish. "Casting them far and wide over Apparatum. They land and create the mounds, which also produce more spores but at a smaller scale."

"And what do the spores do?" Kiff asked.

"They keep the world bound together and allow the Forerunners to be intact, physically and mentally."

Kyle appeared flustered at the last comment. Logan noticed the various shapes of the spirits rising in and out of Kyle. How many did he have tethered to him anyway?

Seeing him staring, Kyle said, "I've had a few escapees." He nodded at the solid Breaker, Hunter and Creeper hanging back by the access tunnel, each giving Kyle confused looks as if they still wanted to be connected to him. The Breaker had a rebellious air to him, like he would be the last one to want to tether again with Kyle, but even this brute didn't look like he would abandon him just yet.

The slender, yellow arms of a Weaver slipped out at Kyle's waist. The boy concentrated, and they popped back in. Next, the Weaver's narrow head wiggled out from Kyle's left shoulder, its large round eyes staring at Logan, unblinking. Kyle forced it back in. A Glider's lower leg stuck out from his right knee, almost kicking Byron off the ledge. Kyle sighed and managed to again store it within himself.

Abe eyed the spirits jumping in and out of the boy's body. "If you released them completely, their exposure to the spores down here would make them whole. Tucking them away dulls the spores' effect, but I can see they've been giving you some trouble."

A single wing shot forth from Kyle's back, not the least bit transparent. A look of panic fell across his face. He eventually furrowed his brow and drove the spirit back inside himself.

"And the spores bring all of us together? That's why we can see each other now." Logan pointed at Kyle.

"Yes," Abe said and glanced down the shaft.

Logan's sleeves fluttered, the air currents batting them downward. The air no longer rose from below. It had switched directions. What did that mean? This change was noticed by Abe.

"So if we spread the spores all over, the city and enclaves will exist in the same reality?" Kyle asked.

Abe hooked his staff to a sturdy root and kept his attention on the air sweeping downward. The air was forceful. Logan moved Kiff toward a thick handhold and made him clamp on.

Logan did the same, anticipating something dire was about to happen.

Abe now shouted to be heard over the torrent of air racing past them, "I'm afraid we'll have to table our discussion for a bit! Looks like you're going to see the sporecore work its magic. Hold on tight!"

Byron secured himself to a root and used his other arm to hold Kyle tight. Logan knew the robot had the best grip of them all.

The air rushed past them. Then, suddenly, it died away. *The calm before the storm.*

Logan girded himself, knowing whatever terrible thing was about to happen was imminent.

* * *

The silence was palpable, almost suffocating. When Kyle breathed out, barely a flicker of light puffed from his mouth. Some sort of vacuum had formed far below in the sporecore, and the Well was busy sucking the air down into it.

Kyle felt his Weaver and Glider spirits stirring deep within. They seemed to have gotten restless, probably because of the density of spores in the air. They wanted to escape like the other three. "Stay put," Kyle told them in a low voice.

"Me?" Byron said, his head swiveling around.

"Not you. My spirits."

He thought he heard whispering in his head as though the ghostly Forerunners were conspiring. He tensed, sure he was about to lose them . . . but then a voice floated into his mind: *We will stay for now. You have given us the promise of life, and we owe you for that. However, understand that our union with you is by choice. We are not slaves.*

"Fair enough," Kyle muttered, taken aback. The spores had not only made these creatures more solid but also returned their sense of pride. A second or two later, the spirits relaxed, apparently satisfied now that they'd asserted their rights.

He winced in the grip of Byron's metal digits, noticing that his robotized brother had clamped onto a thick root as well, securing them both. As for the Orms, Kiff had a tight hold of a similar root while Logan gripped the boy's shirt collar just in case. All four of them flattened themselves against the wall while Abe simply hunkered over his staff.

"Here it comes," Abe whispered. He grinned at Kiff and Byron and winked.

"What exactly is—?" Kyle started to ask.

A dull boom sounded deep below. It shook the walls hard enough for thick veins and nodules to quiver. Dirt sprinkled down, but the fungal roots above provided shelter against the worst of it.

A massive cloud appeared below, rising fast. Mostly green, it billowed and rolled, a dense mass of spores. The cloud shot past them all, and they squeezed their eyes shut.

Kyle risked a peek. The spores were larger than expected. As he shielded his eyes, spores collected in his hand, light and fluffy, some of them the size of his fingernail. A sudden blast of rising wind whisked the spores away and upward, and he gasped as the gale whistled past.

It lasted about a minute, and then all fell quiet. In the blissful silence that followed, all five of them craned their necks upward, trying to see in the darkness. Kyle noticed his illuminated breath vapor was returning, growing stronger and brighter by the second as the wind died to a breeze and spores began to float back down the shaft.

"The sporecore does this every half hour or so," Abe said, his voice oddly loud now. "This eruption, like all others for the past few hundred years, has been utterly wasted. All these spores will spread throughout the caverns and tunnels and enrich our lives down here, but they'll never reach their intended target, the vast outdoors up above."

"Because the Well is blocked," Kyle said, looking skyward to where the strange silver ball hung about fifty feet up.

"Yes—a massive, immoveable plug. After the city drove the Forerunners down this shaft with their toxic gas clouds, they demolished some of the nearby buildings and shoved the structures into the Well, expecting to fill it and destroy the sporecore at its base. Only the debris never fell that far. Some of the structural supports jammed partway down, a tangled mass of metal girders. It didn't take long for the blockage to build up, and the shaft quickly filled to the top, about a hundred feet of debris in all. The city realized they hadn't been fully successful in their task, but it was too late. They resigned themselves to partial success. The Forerunners were gone no matter what, and the Well blocked."

They all stared in silence as more and more spores whorled like a green snowstorm. The gentle, upward breeze couldn't quite hold the larger spores aloft, but the tiny, dustlike specks moved slowly around, a hazy cloud following the ever-changing air currents.

"Why are the spores lit up here?" Kyle asked. "Not just in front of our faces but all the way up and down the shaft. It's not like we're breathing on them."

"You're not, but the sporecore is," Abe said. "Fungi take in oxygen and give out carbon dioxide the same way people and animals do, only through gills. Think of the sporecore as pushing out a constant, slow breath. Every half hour or so, it inhales, then sneezes."

"Sneezes!" Kiff said with a laugh.

Abe smiled at him.

Logan didn't look convinced. "You're saying a giant mushroom *breathes*?"

"The sporecore does. It's unique, an enormous fungal growth stretching across and growing inside of a natural geological anomaly, an air blowhole that vents to relieve the pressure of a closed underground system." When nobody responded, he sighed. "Let's just say the sporecore has adapted to use the blowhole's power to its advantage. Now, where was I?"

"The blocked Well," Kyle offered.

"Ah, yes," Abe said, nodding. "As time passed, the majority of the Forerunners gradually made their way back to the surface, only they found themselves to be insubstantial, floating around like phantoms. Without spores in the atmosphere, this ancient race was reduced to intangible forms."

Logan nodded. "Spirits. That's how my people have always known them."

"Yes, your ancestors welcomed them back," Abe continued. "All those people who had migrated to the east were delighted with the development. It meant tetherings could be re-established. However, the city folk in the west were most upset. They came out to destroy the Well properly. Only . . . they couldn't find it."

"They got *lost*?" Kiff exclaimed.

Abe smiled. "Not quite. From their point of view, the Well had simply vanished—not just the mound of rubble they'd left behind, but all the surrounding buildings as well. The city people were by now out of phase, and the old towns in the center of Apparatum had faded away like a distant dream. Yet the ghostly Forerunners persisted in roaming the streets of the fledgling city, trying to tether with people who wanted nothing to do with them. To combat the problem, Mayor Liggerman ordered the construction of a machine. They called it the Sentry."

Everyone stared in silence as he peered around at them one by one. After a while, Logan said, "Which was what, exactly?"

Abe leaned closer to him, his voice lowering. "A fully automated, intelligent mobile weapon. It would take months to build, and it would be programmed to search the land and seek out the Well." He straightened, his voice now reverting to normal. "Of course, while they were building this machine, I was busy here at the Well."

"Busy how?" Kyle asked. He hated that Abe kept stopping. The old man seemed to enjoy his storytelling despite the urgency of their mission.

Abe took a long breath and exhaled, and they all watched the extra-bright glow slowly drift away. He pointed upward. "See the harvester hanging down the shaft fifty feet above?"

"The shiny ball on the end of a metal stick?" Kiff said.

Abe chuckled. "Yes, Kiff. While the people of the city were having trouble locating us, we in turn were finding it quite a shock to realize that the city buildings and the enclaves were fading from view. We had to do something. We had to return the spores to the atmosphere and restore the balance. However, the blockage high above our heads is significant. We could not shift it by physical means. Our finest Breakers were unable to make an impact on so many tons of metal."

Kyle understood that. Metal was tough.

"Breakers tunneled around the blockage, allowing us access to the surface. We cleared the area above the Well and, commandeering a heavy-duty portable laser drill used in construction, we atomized a six-inch hole all the way through the hundred feet of debris jamming the shaft. We constructed the rod and developed the harvester, which attracts and boosts the spores' magic all the way up through the plug to the surface. Our hope in those confusing days was to phase out the debris and re-open the Well."

"Oh!" Kyle said. "Like turning it into a *phantom* plug."

"Precisely. Of course, we understood very little back then, and the plan didn't work. The spores were still trapped down here because, relative to the sporecore, the plug and the surrounding land remained as solid as you and I." Abe sighed. "Meanwhile, in the absence of spores in the atmosphere above, Apparatum on the surface drifted even more out of phase . . ."

* * *

"What about the Sentry?" Logan pressed. "Did it ever get built?"

"Oh yes. It rattled and whirred its way out of the city one day, a monstrous metal bug. It headed east into what people had started calling the Ruins . . . and promptly vanished. After all that fanfare, the city techs lost the Sentry's tracking signal. It just faded away. They feared their machine destroyed."

Kyle shivered. "But it wasn't, was it? It's still around."

Logan nodded in agreement. "I can't sense any tech nearby, but I have a feeling it's what I'm here for."

At this, Abe nodded gravely and placed a hand on Logan's shoulder. "The machine did in fact find its way underground, squeezing through endless tunnels before arriving here at the Well. It reported back and awaited instruction. Should it destroy the Well or guard it? It's still waiting for a response, because the city never heard it."

"It's out of sync!" Kiff exclaimed.

"Indeed. During its underground journey, it phased in with us here below. Until it receives an instruction to self-destruct and destroy the Well for good, the Sentry will continue its guard duty. It's been here three hundred years, just waiting, preventing anyone from getting close."

"So it's *up there*?" Byron said, suddenly coming alive. He made some clicking, whirring noises as he scanned the shaft above. "I don't detect anything. Do you, Logan?"

Logan shook his head. "My range is limited."

Abe pointed upward. "It's somewhere high up, nesting among various gaps in the blockage." He paused. "With the apparent loss of their Sentry, those in charge of the city eventually resorted to an inhibitor, designed to repel spirits to the far eastern end of the land. It worked well. Every spirit in the land was flung to the east. And suddenly our Forerunner friends could no longer safely step outside without being whisked violently away. They've been down here ever since, separated from their spirit-form brethren on the surface."

They all peered up the shaft. Everything was quiet, and it seemed hard to believe some kind of machine lurked in the shadows, still awaiting orders from the city after hundreds of years.

Abe spoke again, softly now, sounding tired. "We found that the harvester was helping to bring the local area back into sync. If we could only amplify that technology . . . So, keeping the hundred-foot plug between us and the Sentry, we built the Tower over the Well in direct contact with the harvester's rod. We hoped it would act as a substitute for the spores themselves, a beacon spreading the magic across the land and bringing everything back into sync, restoring normality."

The old man looked upward for a moment. Following his gaze, Logan studied the silver ball and the cloud of spores around it.

"It partially worked," Abe said. "The Tower brought most of the land back to us. The wastelands, the Ruins, the Broken Lands . . . all of it is now correctly phased with us down here in the underground. It's what we call true Apparatum, the old world. It didn't help the Forerunners, of course. No, they still turned insubstantial after a day of being on the surface. They needed a real spore-filled atmosphere, not just some diluted semblance of it."

Logan could almost picture the Forerunners sneaking up through tunnels to the surface and spending a day running around in glee before slowly turning into ghosts and losing their minds.

"But it seemed the city and the enclaves were unaffected by the Tower's reach and remained stubbornly out of sync," Abe went on. He threw up his hands in disgust. "Why? The rest of the land had phased back into normality, so why not the city and the enclaves? We eventually came to the conclusion that the *people themselves* were affecting the stability of the land: the scornful mindset of the city refusing to acknowledge the techless, spirit-loving people of the enclaves in the east; and the simpler people of the enclaves wanting no part of the filthy machine-driven city of the west. They simply blocked each other out and drifted apart."

"But the inhibitors still work against each other," Kyle argued. "How can they if—?"

"Exactly!" Abe exclaimed, almost indignantly. "There does seem to be a tangible connection in that respect alone. The inhibitors still work to this day even though the people of the city and the enclaves have all but forgotten each other and are out of sync. I guess it's exactly what the people wanted—to push each other away and forget. It's a curious thing, isn't it? The power of suggestion over centuries . . ."

Abe let that hang in the illuminated air for a moment.

When he continued, he sounded tired. "The Tower has its uses. We're effectively alone down here; it's just us and those exiled to the wastelands. But with the Tower, we can tune ourselves to the city or the enclaves and see them from afar. And with careful manipulation, we can permanently alter a person's state and change their zone—as we did with you two boys." He tapped his collar. "And this device does the same thing for me. Over the years, and with much practice, it's allowed me to physically sync with the different zones. Until the battery runs down, anyway."

Logan sighed. "So now what?"

"Now, my boy, we are in a position to set things right. You're going to destroy the Sentry for us, unplug the shaft, and blow up the Tower."

Logan's heart sank.

Abe grinned and turned to Kyle. "And you, my boy, have an equally important task. When the Well is unplugged, you're going to have to do something about the mess Logan sends down to the sporecore. And for that, you're going to need the help of a tethered friend."

Kyle swallowed. "Which one?"

"One of the two you haven't met yet. One nobody has ever tethered to before."

Abe's crazy, Logan thought. Blow up the Tower? Fight some sentry the city had squirreled away here in the Well? Not that Kyle's mission sounded any easier—locating two elusive spirits, new ones with unknown powers, that Kyle would somehow figure out how to clean up Logan's mess, whatever that might be.

Logan asked the question that had been nagging at him since Abe started talking about the spores reuniting everything. "What about the counterparts and the wink-outs?"

Abe gave him a serious look, his beard lifting slightly thanks to the air current moving upward. "What about them?"

"Will the counterparts merge?" Logan pointed at Kyle, his twin for all practical purposes. "Will we suddenly be one person?"

"No. In theory, the wink-outs should stop." Abe added, "The two of you have been immersed in spores since you began your trek underground. I don't see either of you merging together right now, do you?"

Logan shook his head. Kyle did so as well, just slower.

"And will the wink-outs stop?" Kyle said.

"I am confident they will. Wink-outs only started happening with the absence of the spores. I see no reason they should continue once we set things right."

Abe moved toward the access point the old man and Kyle had exited. "Let's get on with this then. Kyle will take your brothers to Makow, who will keep them safe." He nodded upward. "I'll dispatch the Tower. Once the two of you perform your tasks, you can return to your respective homes. You, Kyle, to the enclaves; and you, Logan, the city."

Kyle put his hand out and snagged Abe's staff. "No. That's not what's going to happen. I'm not going back there."

Abe grimaced and waved dismissively at Kyle. "Don't be absurd. The inhibitors are still in play. You are needed back at the Hallowed Spires to defeat the Guardian. And Logan's tech abilities are required in overthrowing the Guardian in the city."

Logan surprised himself and said, "I'm with Kyle. I'm going back to the enclaves with Kiff. That's my home."

Abe's face reddened, and he howled, "Absolutely not!"

* * *

Abe stormed down the tunnel Kyle had come from, leaving the Well behind. There was a moment of confusion as three dimly lit spirits shuffled aside to let him pass. Kyle hurried after him, squeezing between the Hunter, Breaker, and Creeper. With a shock, he noticed they were far more solid now than they had been earlier. Their auras were dimming, their features fleshing out. As he noticed this, he felt a pressure from within and knew his Glider and Weaver were squirming for release.

"Stay," he muttered to all of them as he brushed past and caught up to the old man. He raised his voice. "Abe, I'm telling you, it'll be *much* better if Logan deals with the Guardian at the Hallowed Spires. There's a massive metal door in the tunnel that I can't get through. He's the one with tech powers. He'll get through in no time. And the Guardian lives in a room of metal and tech. Logan's better equipped."

Abe slowed. He reached the intersection where the weapons sat atop the floatpad. There he paused and turned to Kyle with a thoughtful look on his face.

Logan came hurrying up. "Yes, and Kyle's better suited to deal with the Guardian under the city. There's magic at work there. I think it's our . . . our destiny to go home."

"Pah!" the old man retorted. Yet he still had a thoughtful look on his face. He rubbed his nose and said to Kyle, "A room of metal maybe, but nothing useable. Worthless junk."

"But still tech," Kyle said. "From the outside, the Hallowed Spires looks like an ancient monastery or something, but I read a servant's mind and caught a glimpse of where the Guardian lives. It's all tech. I don't know about the main entrance, but there's definitely one underground at the end of that vac-train tunnel I came along. And Logan could get through that in a second."

He realized he was guessing to some extent, but it seemed likely. The perfectly straight tunnel headed southeast toward the Hunter Capitol near the coast. It *had* to lead to the Hallowed Spires.

"Anyway," Kyle went on, quietly now because the two younger brothers and three near-solid spirits had just caught up to them, "no offense to Logan, but I want to take Byron home myself. And I miss my parents."

"Agreed," Logan said in a stern voice as he stared defiantly at Abe. "Besides, I don't think you have a say in the matter, old man. We didn't ask for any of this. We'll help you with the sporecore thing, but then we'll do things our way."

Abe sighed and nodded. "Fine. Let's not waste any more time talking. Logan, take whatever weapons you need."

Logan blinked in amazement as if seeing the weapons stash for the first time.

While he was standing there gawking, Abe pulled Kyle aside. "Listen to me. Those three untethered friends of yours aren't spirits anymore. You can still tether to them if they'll let you, but the more solid they are, the more vulnerable they'll be to physical attack."

"Attack from what?"

"From the Digger."

Kyle frowned. Makow had mentioned Diggers earlier. He'd said Diggers hadn't dug as far as the enclaves, and so a machine had been used instead and a metal vac-train tunnel installed.

Seeing his confusion, Abe said, "A Digger is one of the two Forerunner types you've never come across in spirit form. The other is a Swimmer—harmless, though difficult to catch up with. If they exist on the surface in spirit form, I'm not aware of it. They're water dwellers, but while in spirit form, I see no reason for them to stay underwater when others can float around and ghost through solid objects. So if there are any Swimmers up top, they stay in the rivers out of a simple desire to feel at home."

"And the Digger?"

"Very dangerous. To my knowledge, nobody has tethered with one. I'm confident you can, though."

"So where do I find one?"

Abe pointed. "Go find Makow. He'll show you before he evacuates the area."

Of the four possible tunnels leading from the intersection, Kyle had explored two. Makow had gone off down a third, one of the wider tunnels, toward a faint glow of light.

"And what exactly am I supposed to do with this Digger?" Kyle asked, unable to keep the cynicism from his voice. He was tired of Abe using him and Logan like pawns in a game.

"These creatures don't just dig. Their jaws are impossibly powerful. They're much worse than the canyon clackers, which you can also find nearby. Diggers are slower but bigger, and their bite is truly incredible. While I'm on the surface blowing up the Tower, Logan will be battling the Sentry and setting charges in and around the plug. You, Kyle, will be ready to clear the debris from the bottom of the Well where the sporecore grows. Nothing else will chew through tons of twisted metal and rock like a Digger."

Kyle digested this news with astonishment. Finally, he said, "Won't the core be crushed if tons of debris falls down the shaft onto it?"

"It will be smothered, not crushed. That's why you'll need to work fast."

"And then what?"

Abe's jaw tightened. "No more questions. Let's get this done. Bearing in mind the bracelet they gave to Kiff here, I'm afraid one or both Guardians will soon be sending people to stop us. Let's not let that happen. If . . ." He swallowed. "If any of their servants or helpers are underground somewhere, they might pick up that confirmation request signal from the Sentry. If they respond with an affirmative, the Sentry could simply self-destruct and complete its mission."

"Well, that would save *us* the trouble of blowing it up," Logan said, turning to face them.

Abe raised an eyebrow at him. "I'm only planning to bring down the plug and open up the shaft. The Sentry will turn Central Apparatum into one gigantic crater."

"So," Logan said slowly, "should I be worried about blowing up the Sentry along with the plug? In case its self-destruct thing goes off?"

"Absolutely you should. Lead it away from here and disable the machine quietly."

Logan nodded. "So you'll take out the Tower while I'm dealing with the Sentry. And then I blow the plug and get out of the way."

"And I'll clear up your mess," Kyle said to Logan.

Shaking his head, Logan muttered, "It all sounds so easy."

Kyle pointed to a small group watching them from the darkness. Byron and Kiff stood there quietly, listening intently with three semi-solid creatures lurking behind them. "And what about our brothers while all this is going on?"

Abe reached into the hovering weapons pile and dragged out a skip pack with lots of straps and controls. "Makow will look after them. And he'll deliver them home for you if we don't make it out."

If we don't make it out, Kyle thought, his heart beginning to thud in his chest. How he longed to be a simple city boy with an ordinary implant like everyone else he knew.

Chapter 26
Realignment

Logan watched as Kyle escorted Kiff and Byron into the tunnel that apparently led to Makow, one of Yando's acquaintances. Though nervous about the younger boys, Logan had to trust they would be safer with the guide than anywhere close to the Well.

With everyone gone, he focused on the weapons at his disposal. The tech Abe had socked away for him was impressive. Piled high on a floatpad was a treasure trove of weaponry. He had scanned all of it a few minutes ago and knew each device's strengths and limitations. That shook him a bit. If Abe had stockpiled so much for Logan's eventual use against the Sentry, then the machine had to be dangerous.

He strapped a skip pack on, a far smaller one than Abe's, but still a vast improvement over the obsolete pack Logan had come across in an alley a few days back. How long had they been underground? Surely no more than a day. Surprisingly, none of the tech featured a timepiece. The timers on the dozen or so raze bombs didn't mark time except in a countdown sense.

He'd cart the bombs up to the plug after dealing with the Sentry. Should he bring along any grenades? He suspected the Sentry had to be pretty well armored. He clipped four to his belt and grabbed the arc lance and a stump pistol, named for its wide flat muzzle. The stumper, as the city troops called it, dispersed multiple projectiles over an impressive spread. If the Sentry was large, it would come in handy.

He powered up the skip pack and thumbed on the arc lance, triggering it to expand out to only a four-foot length. While it could extend to over forty feet, he doubted he would need it to. The lance's battery was weak, good for four or five thrusts at the most.

Logan cinched the stump pistol's holster and tucked the weapon into it, flicking the safety off with his finger rather than his mind.

He felt the skip pack's enhancer bands snake around his upper legs and tighten against his muscles. A small array of needles slipped into his legs, causing a slight numbness but not pain. They would augment his ability to jump, supercharging his muscles in a sense. As long as he kept the jumps to a minimum, he could avoid the rubbery legs that follow any extensive skip pack use—one of the reasons the devices were no longer in favor, even the newer versions. Who wanted to ache after every use?

He'd only employ it if he couldn't reach a thick enough fungal vein. Otherwise, he'd scale the walls. It would slow him down, but it would pay off in the end. Marching back to the enclaves on shaky legs with Kiff wasn't something he wanted to do.

He returned to the Well and scanned the veins above him. He spotted a route that would get him a good fifty feet up before having to resort to the skip pack. He began scaling the sides of the Well, noting the presence of the updraft. Abe had said the sporecore fired off every half hour or so. Would he make it to the Sentry before its next outburst? He hoped so.

Expelling a bright breath, he focused on the handholds and footholds awaiting him.

* * *

With Byron and Kiff in tow, Kyle headed down the steep tunnel Makow had disappeared into earlier. It was strange having not one but two siblings to look after. He felt bad that Logan hadn't had much of a chance to say a proper goodbye to Kiff, but none of them intended this to be a final farewell anyway. If all went well, they'd reunite again shortly.

Soft, yellowish light shone ahead. The tunnel widened into a chamber some fifty feet across with a ceiling so low he had to duck in places. He was surprised to find a circle of campfires way over on the other side. The yellowish glow flickered and sent shadows dancing across the walls. The roar of rushing water increased dramatically as he moved deeper into the chamber.

"This way," he said over his shoulder to the younger boys. Behind them, still in the darkness of the tunnel, trailed the faint auras of three mostly-solid spirits, the Breaker bent double almost the whole time.

Ahead, Makow was leaning against a rock, chewing on a piece of blackened, steaming meat. "Kyle Jaxx," he called, waving. "Come on over. You two boys as well. Are you hungry? I have some fine roasted vulper here. A bit burnt, but not too chewy."

"No thanks," Kyle said, although he realized then that he was quite hungry. He grudgingly accepted some of the pale-colored meat and bit into it. After a few chews, he turned to Kiff and said, "Tastes like durgle. Maybe a bit tougher. Try some."

Kiff dug in eagerly while Byron stood aside and stared with the usual detachment he displayed at mealtimes. Kyle felt almost guilty eating, but he didn't let that stop him from getting a decent fill. He glanced back to where the three spirits loitered. "Hungry?" he called.

They just stared at him, their heads tilted. In the light of the campfires, the creatures appeared far more solid now than Kyle had ever seen them, their green and red auras almost gone. Now they had taken on the skin tones of actual living creatures, and their substantial forms were somehow far more otherworldly in the flesh, and much bigger. The scowling Breaker, standing twice Kyle's height, had developed scaly skin. Its eyes were deep-set, its tusks long and curved. The Creeper's tentacles and constantly moving mouth-pincers set Kyle's nerves on edge. It was far more menacing in the flesh. That ugly thing had been inside him all this time? And the Hunter swung its head from side to side as though looking for something to pierce with its horn.

Kyle returned his attention to Makow. "You'll look after Byron and Kiff, right?" he asked over the roar of the unseen river. He guessed the water lay at the foot of the nearby chasm, which stretched across the chamber.

Makow nodded. "They'll be fine all the way down here."

"But if the Sentry self-destructs—"

"The blast won't reach us. Relax."

Kyle sighed. "All right. Where can I find these Diggers?"

Climbing to his feet, Makow stuffed another chunk of meat in his mouth, wiped his hands on his pants, and gestured for Kyle to follow. He called back over his shoulder to Byron and Kiff, "You boys wait here. I'll be right back. Finish the vulper."

Makow set off along the edge of the fifteen-foot-wide chasm. Glancing in, Kyle finally spotted the source of all the noise, a fast-moving river just ten feet down. Kyle avoided the edge in case he stumbled and fell.

His Glider remained silent deep within him, as did his Weaver. Glancing over his shoulder, he again found the other three spirits following at a distance, shuffling along.

"Careful," Makow advised. "It gets narrow through here."

He was right. The walls closed in tight, leaving only a foot or so to walk alongside the chasm. Kyle again peered down into the rushing water, watching it froth and churn past jutting slabs of rock.

"Diggers like to chew," Makow said. "Much of our underground world has been formed by Diggers over many thousands of years. Some fear they're chewing too much, undermining the structure and threatening to bring everything crashing down. That's nonsense, of course, though it's probably true they created every tunnel and cavern we've ever walked through."

“I thought the Breakers did that,” Kyle said.

“Breakers smoothed them out so we could use them without stumbling about everywhere. Diggers do the bulk of the work, though.”

They turned sideways and shuffled over the narrowest part of the ledge overhanging the chasm. Thankfully, the floor widened again after that. Despite the poor light, Kyle glimpsed something black and shiny in the dark river. It swam by, illuminated only by what appeared to be phosphorescent mollusks plastered all over the tunnel ceiling and walls. The creature in the water had to be the size of an adult hustle, large enough for three people to sit upon its broad back.

“That was a Swimmer,” Makow said. “I wish we could tame one. The Wiscuppa River starts in the far west and runs underground past the city and our settlement, ending just around the corner from here. It’s the route your friend Logan used to get to the Well. It would be much faster to hitch a ride upstream on the back of a Swimmer, but they don’t seem to like us much, and they certainly won’t tether with us.” Makow looked over his shoulder at Kyle. “You, though, might have better luck.”

The idea of running into canyon clackers didn’t sit well with Kyle. Perhaps he could try and tame a Swimmer . . . But he’d deal with that problem later.

“Here we are,” Makow said, lowering his voice.

The roar of the river diminished. They had arrived at a large, gurgling pool. The river emptied out here, but it was hard to make out where the water went next. It had to go somewhere, otherwise the place would be flooded. *Probably continues underground*, Kyle thought. Then he kicked himself. The river was already underground! *Okay, so it goes even more underground, then.*

Rather than stand by the pool’s edge as Kyle was doing, Makow climbed the uneven rock at one side of the cavern, not caring about the sea of bright-white mushrooms that grew all over. With the phosphorescent mollusks above, the gleam of white below, and the shimmering reflection from the pool, it made him think of underground moonlight.

"Up here," Makow said softly, pointing.

Unable to avoid stepping all over mushrooms, Kyle climbed after him to an ominous pitch-black hole in the wall.

"A recent Digger tunnel," Makow whispered. "There are three others I could show you, but this one is closest to the Well. Follow the tunnel until you find the Digger. Then you just need to tame it and ride it back."

"Easy," Kyle said, staring into the black hole. He couldn't help noticing the air was thin on spores here, his fiery breath somewhat feeble.

"Good luck," Makow said, slapping Kyle roughly on the back. "Get back to the Well as soon as you can. The sporecore has a tough shell, and Abe doesn't think falling debris from that plug will harm it. But you still need to clear it as quickly as possible."

"What about you?"

"I'm heading back to the campfires. The two youngsters and me have some vulper to finish and stories to tell. And as soon as you're back, I'm heading home to the settlement to spread the word and get things moving."

"What things?"

Makow spread his hands. "Expeditions to the surface, of course. Good luck, Kyle."

With that, Makow turned and slithered back down the slope, squishing more mushrooms as he went. Down by the pool, he slid past the Hunter, Creeper, and Breaker, who stood looking up at Kyle.

"Are you coming?" Kyle called down to them.

They stared back.

He'd lost them. He had the feeling he could force them to tether to him, but they wouldn't be happy about it. It would be like having slaves, and he didn't want that, especially after promising the same to his Weaver and Glider. Besides, they were almost completely solid now, flesh-and-blood creatures that could easily be harmed by the Digger.

Sighing, Kyle gave a nod. "You're free to go."

He waved his hand and dismissed the creatures, then turned and stepped into the hole. He glanced back only once. The three former spirits were already shuffling eagerly away.

"Down to two," Kyle said to himself. As the Weaver and Glider stirred within, he scowled and said, "Oh, pipe down."

The tunnel was easily ten feet wide, which meant the Digger was too. The creature did the same job as one of those huge driller machines. The idea of a monstrous creature chewing its way through rock filled him with awe. Did it swallow the rock? Pass it through somehow?

He would find out soon enough.

* * *

After only three uses of the skip pack, Logan's legs already felt weakened when not being synthetically motivated to take great leaps. On the last hop he had overshot his target by a good ten feet but had managed to scramble onto a thinner bulging vein. It was a thrill to sail upward twenty or thirty feet at a time but also a challenge. Twice he had landed on his desired destination, even though the landings had been more like smacking his entire body against the fungal walls of the shaft.

On the other side of the Well, he spotted the access point leading to the Tower. Abe was probably already at the surface. The old man had donned a much larger skip pack to hurl himself up the Well to this tunnel. Did that mean Abe's legs were the worse for it? Logan hoped not.

The updraft persisted. He estimated his ascension so far had taken almost ten minutes, finding he needed a few minutes between leaps to allow his legs to recover. He scrambled up and over several veins and sat for a minute on a thick one, catching his breath. Abe had said the shaft was over a thousand feet deep.

Logan had started a little higher than halfway up. He probably had no more than a hundred feet to go to the plug. He dreaded the fact that he'd have to make two round trips up and down to complete his mission: first to defeat the Sentry, then to bring the explosives up to the plug.

Looking back at the Tower access tunnel, he decided it was where he needed to end up before triggering the explosives.

As he rose, he detected scraping coming from above. He tensed, knowing that it had to be the Sentry.

Logan held his breath, afraid he would give away his position as he had when cornered by the vulpers. Of course, why bother? The Sentry was probably equipped with thermal imaging and already had a lock on him.

The scraping stopped and all was still, including the air. For a few seconds, Logan couldn't feel it flowing in either direction. Slowly, the air swept downward until it was gusting past him. He clung tight to the nearby veins and waited. Better to let the sporecore fire off a round before he continued. Or was it? Maybe he could use the rapid expulsion to his advantage, aiding in driving him upward to assault the Sentry.

To do that, he'd need to locate the machine's exact location. If it was too far up, he would fall short.

He reached out with his mind once again, wary of the tech he would encounter. If the Sentry was out of range, it'd be practically invisible to Logan.

Luckily, that wasn't the case. He locked onto the Sentry's tech only sixty-five feet above him. He almost slipped away from it, alarmed at how extensive and overwhelming it was. He probed cautiously, fearful the machine would detect him and lash out. At its core was an ancient but well-built system. His chief concern, the self-destruct mechanism, lay within a reinforced core in the creature's thorax. As long as he focused on the legs and abdomen, he should avoid blowing up most of Apparatum. He catalogued over seven weapon arrays, two of which he had no understanding of. Most were beam- or projectile-based. He retrieved the Sentry's physical specs from deep storage and was amused to see they had modeled its appearance after a zenith spider: eight legs and two long, armored stingers.

The vacuum tore at him now, threatening to pull him off the ledge and plunge him downward. It was a good deal more forceful than the previous time. How was Kyle faring so close to the source of the rapid intake?

Distracted, he suddenly realized the Sentry's defense system had shifted to high alert. *It knows I'm here.*

The intake of air by the sporecore stopped, and Logan once again experienced the brief serenity of the calm before the storm. He slipped the stump pistol out of its holster and pointed it upward. He dropped to a slight crouch, ready to launch with the aid of the skip pack the minute he felt the air rushing upward.

The sporecore erupted with a faint boom. He waited a total of three seconds before launching himself amid what he thought was the most powerful blast. The air around him glowed bright, exposing his target for him to see. He wished it hadn't. With the main mass of the Sentry being black, the sheen off its abdomen betrayed just how large it was. It was a wonder it fit in the Well at all. He caught a glimpse of the machine's impressive legs, eight thrashing armatures that extended the creature's reach. The Sentry was impossibly big and poised to strike.

Logan fired off a single round. The spray of bullets bounced ineffectively off the machine's armor before he slammed into the head of the creature and its large mouth-pincers wrapped around his waist, squeezing tight.

At least he wouldn't fall to his death. He was certain the Sentry would slice him in half before dropping him like so much waste.

* * *

As Kyle had suspected, the air was thin within the tunnel—or rather the spores weren't so dense, making them unreliable as a light source. He urged his Glider and Weaver to wake up and share their auras, and they grudgingly stirred.

The Digger appeared to be asleep. Kyle edged closer, approaching its rear end, aware that his two spirits were squirming with apprehension. What would happen if he died right now? They'd simply become untethered, right? Free to leave? So what were they so upset about?

Maybe they were genuinely concerned for his welfare.

He'd imagined the monstrous creature to be like a canyon clacker. This thing was much bigger and had scales, which surprised him. He'd envisioned something slimy and wet, or perhaps something with horribly matted fur. The sleek, dark-brown scales impressed him for some reason. Perhaps this thing wasn't as hideous as he'd thought it would be.

Its fat, oversized, limbless body ended in a flat tail. The creature's enormous bulk perfectly filled the freshly hollowed-out tunnel, though Kyle saw no debris or chewed-up rock from all the digging it had done.

Puzzled, Kyle stepped closer still, telling himself that the backend of the creature had to be far safer than the front. What could it do to him?

The monster had no scent at all, even up close. Kyle reached out and placed his hand on its flat, scaly tail. It felt cool to the touch.

The Digger reacted by jerking and letting out a thunderous, muffled screech. Kyle immediately backed up, fearing it might reverse on top of him. It didn't, though. Instead, it lifted up its tail.

Kyle's Glider had already slipped into place and taken control of him. He sailed up above the rising tail until he lay plastered against the ceiling. A tremendous blast of foul-smelling liquid shot out from below the tail, saturating the rock he'd been standing on. To his horror, the rock sizzled and steamed as the acid ate into it. The fumes made his eyes water, and he squeezed them shut.

Nice rear-end defenses, he thought.

The Glider held him high above the acid, pinning him to the tunnel's rounded ceiling. Gradually, the sizzling stopped—but the Digger was already on the move, lurching forward several yards at a time, apparently chewing its way through the rock ahead.

Still no debris, he thought as he floated along behind it. *No reconstituted rock, nothing. Where's it all going?*

He wondered if perhaps the Digger used acid at the front end as well, drenching the wall in it before pushing through with its armored hide. But he couldn't imagine that much rock corroding away, and besides, it still had to go somewhere, liquefied or not. Kyle saw no sign of it.

Time to tether.

He reached for the monster and got a grip on the larger scales along the top, which overhung like roof tiles. Hooking his fingers under the lower edge, he held on while the Digger vented another blast of acid. It did *not* like being touched.

"To me," he said aloud, reaching out with his mind.

His Glider slipped back down inside him, apparently realizing it needed to make way for the Digger. With his power of flight gone, Kyle found himself clinging to the rear end and standing on top of the flat tail, which lifted several times to squirt more acid.

"To ME!" he shouted.

Though the Digger completely ignored him and continued surging forward, Kyle found that he'd made a connection with it. He felt the tethering begin, could almost see a glowing green tendril reaching from his body and into the Digger's. And when that tendril snaked around and found something to cling onto, it tightened suddenly, dragging Kyle deeper.

Gasping with shock and revulsion, he sank through the armored shell and into the Digger's flesh. One of them was out of phase, slightly insubstantial, and he guessed it was him. He was becoming one with the monster, *not* what he'd had in mind.

He squirmed and thrashed, feeling like he was trying to swim out of a pool of thick mud. Sure he was about to suffocate in folds of monster flesh, panic bubbled up and threatened to overcome him. It was only when he gasped for breath and took in a lungful of plain air that he faltered and took a heart-pounding moment to assess his situation.

Being pulled through the scaly hide into the depths of this monster wasn't quite what he'd imagined. Then again, riding its back as if it were a hustle wasn't practical while the thing was digging a tunnel. This had to be the only feasible option if he wanted to tether. The giant couldn't possibly fit inside his puny frame, and to gain any semblance of control, he needed to be part of the thing. And that meant sinking into its body, merging with it.

To his surprise, the ghastly shock of being smothered gave way to a feeling of great comfort. It reminded him of his Uncle Jeremiah's old road rumbler back in the city, an antique sports vehicle designed for a driver and one passenger only—a real struggle getting in through the awkward door but supremely comfortable once properly seated.

The Digger's eyes showed him a series of black-and-white tones ahead. He could see through the rock itself, into caverns above and below. He knew exactly which direction to take. He could dig downward a mile to the fuzzy suggestion of a gigantic space, or to the right where various untapped chambers lay. From the point of view of the Digger, Apparatum was much greater than the space above land and the caves below. It was unlimited, endless miles of rock in all directions, waiting to be chewed through . . .

Within reason, he thought as he gained a better understanding of the Digger's subterranean world. *Too deep and there's magma to contend with. Too high and it'll drill out onto the surface like a canyon clacker.*

The Digger roared its disapproval that anyone had been bold enough to tether and worm his way into its mind. Kyle felt a wave of pride at his achievement. Either everybody else was too afraid to get close, or they'd been chewed at one end and dissolved in acid at the other, or they'd simply not been powerful enough to force a tethering.

Kyle was in.

Set course for the Well, he commanded.

Words were unnecessary. The Digger needed only a mental image to figure out what Kyle wanted. Why it obeyed was a mystery, but in that respect it was no different than any other tethered creatures.

The Digger chewed through the rock to the left, starting a new course at a slight upward angle. The Well showed quite clearly in all its black-and-white glory, a vertical dark-grey smudge amid utter darkness.

Kyle mentally punched the air. He would be there in just a few minutes.

* * *

The Sentry was huge, easily the size of three adult hustles. The spores buffeted Logan, slapping against him and shooting upward. They smacked against the Sentry and the plug, coalescing into a choking mass. Logan coughed as he waved the gathering spores away from him. Their illumination gave him his first look at the plug but also made it hard to breathe.

It looked like half the city from above had been dumped into the Well, but he knew better. Abe had told him it was only about a hundred feet of debris. Sections of walls bowed outward, interlaced with twisted girders and quite a few dangling wires. There were several niches that he suspected served as perches for the Sentry.

The machine's mechanical eyes shot out of its sockets, still connected by a thick, remarkably flexible armored tube. The orbs hovered near his head, scanning him. What would it make of him not having an implant?

Once the eruption was over, he'd try and break free. He continued to eye the machine. The schematic he had seen didn't do it justice. It had the rough approximations of the zenith spider's body parts, head, thorax, and abdomen, with most of its weapon systems arranged around its large abdomen. The head had pincers, and Logan also knew from his initial scan that its bobbing, seven-foot-long antennae were razor-sharp as well.

Four shock cannons pointed at him from the top of the abdomen, while the machine's two long tails terminating in stingers swayed slightly, reminding him of a Skimmer's mesmerizing movements. The eight legs tapered to lethal points, and it had all of them jammed into the walls of the shaft, its head twisted to one side to avoid the harvester rod running down the center.

Why isn't it slicing me in half? Maybe it doesn't know what to make of me.

No implant. Did that mean it would equate Logan with not being a threat? Doubtful. If any of the Seekers or exiles from the enclaves had come across the Sentry, it would be familiar with humans missing implants. He wished he could access its protocol files, but the archaic firewalls would take too long to disable.

With the air movement in the shaft almost back to normal, Logan decided it was time to act.

He swept the arc lance around and jammed it into the Sentry's right eye socket, sending rakka energy into the machine's main mass. Thankfully the lance delivered rakka and not electrical current. If it had been the latter, Logan would've been fried as well. Rakka had no effect on organic beings. Smart of Abe to outfit him with such weaponry.

The pincers snapped open, and he dropped. He triggered the lance to extend to its full length as he snapped it into a horizontal position. The ends of the weapon drove into the opposite walls of the Well, extending over thirty feet, and he ground to a halt, nearly forty feet below the convulsing machine.

The rakka wouldn't disable it, only briefly scatter its thought processes. Already, the machine's tremors were subsiding. It swiveled its oval-shaped head and trained its one undamaged eye at him.

The Sentry descended toward him, its eight legs touching the opposite walls of the shaft much like his now useless arc lance. It worked around the center rod with practiced ease.

Logan briefly dangled before gathering his wits and swinging hand-over-hand to the large ledge to his left. He tried to get the lance to retract but something had been damaged inside. He grabbed two grenades, pulled their clips, and heaved them at the Sentry. Both exploded a few feet in front of the machine. The blasts blew away the right frontmost leg as well as the pincer on that side.

The severed leg along with the pincer fell past Logan, its blunt end shooting sparks. What would Kyle make of that? Friendly fire. He hoped his counterpart would not get hit by the appendage. If Logan succeeded in destroying the Sentry, would that complicate Kyle's mission? He'd have to dodge falling debris. Logan cleared his head. He needed to worry about himself and trust Kyle could survive whatever was thrown at him.

The Sentry shot its other front leg at Logan. He hopped thirty feet upward, just barely avoiding the piercing tip.

He tossed his remaining grenades at the back of the machine, taking out two of the shock cannons. The other two sent crisscrossing beams at him. He leapt upward again, knowing his legs would hate him later for relying on the skip pack so much.

He was less than twenty feet away from the plug. Carved out of the wall to his left, he spotted a gaping opening, large enough for the Sentry to fit in. Its perch.

Another beam shot past him, slicing into the left side of the skip pack. The tech went dead inside the device.

Logan aimed the stump pistol and fired six rounds, dealing slight damage to the machine's abdomen, disabling one more shock cannon, and sending two more legs to rain down on Kyle.

The Sentry crawled toward him on its five remaining legs. Its stingers glowed. He had no idea what they did; they were part of the two weapons systems he couldn't decipher.

A leg shot forward and knocked the pistol from his hand. Bereft of external weapons, Logan had no other recourse. He needed to come at the machine from within.

He plunged his mind deep into the creature's core, plowing through its systems, violating them in ways that made his head hurt. The creature's motion system shuddered and revolted. The legs suddenly buckled and retracted. No longer anchored to any part of the Well, it plummeted.

Emboldened, he forced himself into the unknown weapons systems and fumbled about. As he did this, the Sentry regained control of its legs and halted its plunge by digging into the shaft walls. It worked its way back to Logan with alarming swiftness. His mind grew scattered as he wove through a strange maze of data. Any second now, the machine would skewer him with one of its stingers and pump him full of whatever energy or poison it held within.

He couldn't get past the security constraints, and even if he could, the tech was beyond him.

Logan retreated, but in doing so, he found a way to turn the Sentry on itself. While he couldn't comprehend the weapons systems of the tails, he could work through the primary motor-servo array that directed them. He dove in, aware that energy was building in both tails. *Another second, please. Don't atomize me before I can finish you off.*

He was in. With surgical precision, he commandeered the skeletal and movement arrays and directed the tails to plunge into the machine's weighty abdomen.

They did as he ordered, sending their strange energies into the bulk of the Sentry.

Logan jumped upward and scrambled into the large alcove by the plug, fearing he would be caught in a lethal blast otherwise.

He rolled away from the edge, deeper into the space.

When no explosion came, he crawled forward and peered over the edge.

The Sentry clung to a girder by one leg, still convulsing from the strange energies delivered into it by its own tails.

It whirled its head around to look at Logan and then, wracked by one massive convulsion, it slipped free and plunged down the shaft.

Watch out, Kyle! Incoming!

* * *

It's phasing the rock out of existence, Kyle thought in amazement.

The Digger plowed onward, chewing a new tunnel straight toward the Well. Kyle was getting a sense of its jaws in his mind's eye, a gaping maw filled with molars. But these molars had to be for show only, because jaws couldn't be strong enough to actually crunch their way through the underworld. Instead, the rock just . . . vanished.

Kyle watched, fascinated, feeling at the moment like he was inside the monster looking out through its throat. As the teeth made contact with the wall ahead, the rock simply faded from view.

It's still there. The Digger's not shifting it at all. It's still there—but no longer in sync.

He imagined a strange dimension with nothing but these displaced tunnels, still connected and unbroken, a network of fragile rocky tubes floating in space. It had to be more than just a little out of sync, a permanent state that no amount of spores could reverse. These Digger tunnels had been here for thousands of years in spite of the spore-filled air.

His black-and-white image of the Well brightened considerably as he neared it. Suddenly he was through the last section of rock, and his vision turned into full color, green hues of light and purple veins protruding from the shaft walls. The Digger stuck its head out and looked around, and now Kyle realized it had four small eyes that could be used in pairs to focus on two different things at once.

The first thing he noticed was a strong downward draft, the air thick with spores. Had he just missed the latest eruption? A dull thud came from high up, and he quickly took stock.

He trained one pair of eyes downward, taking in the sporecore itself: domed and purple, easily the biggest mushroom cap he'd ever seen spanning the thirty-foot shaft just below. Several triangular sections formed the cap, all tightly abutted to form a seamless whole. Kyle guessed those sections must open up when the spores erupted.

His other pair of eyes were already focused on the shaft above, but his brain wasn't used to dealing with two separate images. He ducked back just in time as a huge chunk of metal came crashing down.

Clouds of spores flew everywhere as the object smacked into the sporecore. It was some sort of three-jointed pole, perhaps a severed robot arm of some kind, very sharp at one end, clearly broken off at the other and still shooting out hot sparks. A few other bits of metal joined it, shapeless hunks that rained down all around. Kyle also spotted a bent, fully extended arc lance, which worried him. That had to be Logan's.

The mushroom mound sank under the weight, and Kyle sucked in a breath. The metal contraption lay there a moment, deeply embedded in the mushroom cap, almost as though lovingly wrapped. Then, slowly, the mound pushed upward, returning to its previous shape, apparently unharmed. The thing was tough, flexible and resilient. The metal arm ended up toppling to one side and coming to rest against the shaft wall.

More dull thuds followed, which Kyle now recognized as explosions. *Logan and the Sentry*, he thought. *I hope Logan's winning!*

He smiled. The severed robot arm must have belonged to the Sentry. And at that moment, two more came crashing down right in front of him, once more flattening the mushroom cap and causing the first metal arm to bounce some more. How many arms did this Sentry have?

As before, the mound slowly puffed back up, completely unharmed except for some scrapes on its purple surface and a burn from one of the smoldering metal arms.

Kyle didn't like the tangle of robot arms lying on top of the sporecore even though Abe had seemed unconcerned about damage. The cap cushioned the falling heavy objects, suffering only marginal surface damage, and then expanded again. How would it fare with much heavier objects? What about tons of metal girders from demolished buildings? What about a hundred feet of rock and dirt? There was no way the sporecore would puff back up with all that on top!

Now he fully understood his role. The sporecore might survive the impact and all that weight. It could be squished completely flat and still be able to recover. But it couldn't open unless the debris was removed.

He urged his Digger to slide forward and chew on the metal. To his delight, the robot appendages dissolved into nothingness the same way the rock had, phasing out of this world and into another. Once these random bits of junk were cleared up, he just had to lurk safely in his tunnel and be ready to gobble up whatever else fell down the shaft.

As soon as he was done with the three metal arms, he pulled back into the tunnel and waited.

He didn't have to hang around for long. With a terrible rending of metal and a shower of sparks, the rest of the Sentry came crashing down, bringing with it broken roots and huge clods of dirt and rock. A massive spiderlike creature with only five legs remaining, two nasty-looking tails, eyes on stalks, a pincer . . . The thing couldn't have been any more nightmarish.

But now it was dead. Aware of the self-destruct mechanism inside it, Kyle got to work chewing the thing up. The quicker this ticking bomb was dispatched to another phase, the better.

* * *

Finally, Logan was back at the small armory Abe had left for him. It had been trying, navigating down the Well without the help of the skip pack, but he had done it. What would be even harder would be returning to the plug without it.

As he surveyed the explosives and other weapons, he thought of Abe, who had used a much larger skip pack to get up to the tunnel leading to the Tower and had promised to leave it as a backup. Logan had been so focused on getting back down to the weapons, he had foolishly passed it by. If he could get to that ledge, he could use the pack to cover the rest of the distance to the plug.

Armed with at least a partial plan, he draped the two different bandoliers over his shoulders and across his chest. One had a dozen grenades attached, while the other had six compression bombs and six raze bombs. Both of the latter explosives had liq-stik, allowing him to slap them easily into place. He just needed to break the small pellet of liquid to trigger the quick-dry adhesive, and he could cover the plug with the explosives. He reached his mind into each bomb, making sure their timers worked. He wouldn't set them until he knew roughly how much time was needed to retreat from the plug to the Tower tunnel.

Logan slipped a slender tremble pistol in the stumper's large holster and latched a barrier breach wand to his belt. No telling what might come in handy. Still more weapons were available to him. Abe had really stockpiled his armory. He selected one more, a sonic scrambler. It would work in a pinch if he needed to blast his way free of a caved-in section of tunnel.

Satisfied he couldn't carry any more, he began climbing up the Well. It took all his focus to scale the distances he had previously covered with the aid of his skip pack. The veins in those spans ranged from dangerously narrow to nonexistent. Twice he slipped, the second time falling almost ten feet before hooking his arm on a vein that thankfully jutted out farther than all the others.

Quite a few minutes later, he stood on the vein with the Tower tunnel staring back at him. He exhaled, sending several plumes into it. Behind him, the Well was reversing its air flow yet again, sucking in the air deep below to propel upward its next round of spores. He strode into the tunnel, searching for Abe's skip pack.

He found it about fifty feet in, propped up against the wall. A quick check showed it was fully functioning. While his legs were still a little weak from his previous use of the smaller pack, he needed to use this one if he had any hope of getting to the plug. There was a particular stretch of the shaft higher up that he knew had virtually no handholds.

He donned the pack, wincing slightly as its much larger bands of enhancers secured themselves to his upper legs. His curiosity got the best of him, and he moved farther up the tunnel until the slope became more extreme. Could he just reach the surface and blow up the plug from above? No, there'd be no guarantee the explosion would dislodge the entire section. Not that his chances were any better doing it from below, but that was the plan Abe had laid out for him, and Logan needed to stick to it. He turned around. There'd be time to go to the surface after he completed his mission.

He returned to the shaft. Hanging back about ten feet, he waited, watching and feeling the gusting air driving downward.

The air current petered out, and Logan counted during the short period of relative stillness. Seconds later a thunderous boom sounded and the air pushed its way upward, gaining velocity in a surprisingly short amount of time. He shielded his eyes from the bright lights of the spores. The sporecore must discharge a lot of carbon dioxide when it shot the spores up and out. The light show on the surface would be a magical sight at night. Logan was eager to see just such an event.

A minute passed before he could safely approach the shaft's edge. He stood on the large vein and launched himself upward.

He easily ascended using the pack six times. While larger in size, its effects on his legs were far less than the other pack. That was a good thing. It meant Abe would've been in decent shape after his use of the tech.

Back at the alcove near the plug, the former lair of the Sentry, Logan shed the skip pack and eyed the massive blockage.

Lighting was not an issue. Thousands of spores glowed in the shaft, drifting slowly downward after having been expelled from the fungus deep below.

The rod from the Tower reached down the shaft through the center of the plug. He thought back to his battle and how nimbly the Sentry had used the rod to aid in its attack.

There were plenty of horizontal veins situated near the obstruction that would allow him to make his way all the way around the circumference of the shaft. All he needed to do now was secure the bombs. He mapped out his path. No reason to use any of the twisted metal struts that jutted out of the plug. While they should hold his weight, all it would take is one giving way and he'd fall. Better to avoid climbing on the packed debris of the plug and plant the explosives within arm's reach of the edge. He'd secure the bombs and then reach out with his mind to set their timers simultaneously. Looking down, he thought of how much time he would need to climb down to the

Tower access. He wouldn't be able to use the skip pack, but he'd wear it anyway since he or Abe might still need it.

Logan stepped out onto the first vein and slapped a raze bomb in place, making sure the impact was hard enough to trigger the liq-stik. He had the explosives in place and was back at the alcove after only a few minutes.

He donned the skip pack. It was a better fit now that he only had one bandolier filled with grenades.

He reached into each bomb and set them to count down from ten minutes.

Pleased with himself, he exhaled two quick breaths, adding more lit spores to the dense population still wafting through the air before he scrambled down the shaft.

About thirty feet down, he heard a muffled explosion from above and cringed. His perch trembled, and he gripped the wall tighter. Had the bombs detonated early? He hugged close to the wall, thinking a shower of debris might follow. When none did, he reached his mind upward.

All twelve bombs registered. Then what had happened?

Abe had destroyed the Tower.

Logan glanced at the rod, wondering if it would become a deadly projectile once blown free from its mooring. Not that impaling a giant fungus would necessarily kill it. It wasn't like mushrooms had hearts or other vital organs.

He continued down and reached the Tower access tunnel in very little time.

His legs throbbed. He limped almost a hundred feet to the section of tunnel that sloped harshly upward before removing the skip pack and sitting down to give his legs a rest. While they were sore, they didn't feel like weeba jelly as he had dreaded they would.

Logan couldn't detect the explosive tech to check how much time remained. It was just out of range. He worried that Kyle would be hurt by the falling debris from the plug, but he had to assume he had that under control.

His thoughts turned to their next step. Abe needed them to defeat their respective Guardians. But Logan was in agreement with Kyle. He would take out the enclave Guardian somehow and stay in his rightful home. *Just try and stop us, old man.*

The blast roared down the shaft, followed by tons of debris and metal girders. Logan covered his eyes when he should've covered his ears. The din of the explosion was loud and prolonged. He slipped his hands from his now closed eyes to shield his ears, but the damage had been done. He cursed but couldn't hear a word of his outrage.

He was deaf.

* * *

The Sentry was gone, chewed up and out of sync.

When Kyle heard the first booming explosion high above, he hunkered back into his Digger tunnel and prepared for the deluge of debris. But it never came. Surprised, he urged his Digger to peer up the shaft. It was still almost pitch-black up there despite the swirling haze of glowing spores.

It occurred to him that Abe had planned to bring down the Tower before Logan cleared the plug. That noise might have been the Tower collapsing.

Minutes later, an even louder explosion rocked the shaft, and this one brought with it the deluge he'd been expecting. The noise was incredible, far greater than he could have imagined, and even his Digger reversed deeper into the tunnel as massive chunks of metal and rock hammered the sporecore.

"I hope it's as indestructible as Abe thinks," Kyle said aloud as the deafening racket continued. Whatever hazy green light there had been from the tunnel was gone. Now he was in utter darkness, the noise far more muffled.

He waited as long as he dared. As silence fell, he pushed his Digger forward again, into the shaft—or where the shaft had been. Now the base was filled with masses of tangled debris.

“Eat,” he ordered, and the Digger began chewing.

As everything before him phased out of sync, it created vacuums for more rubble and twisted metal to tumble down in its place, making the work dangerous even for a Digger. They could chew through anything, but they could still be crushed. Feeling as though he were doing the work himself, Kyle altered course and ate in an upward direction until he reached the top of the debris pile a hundred feet up. There he found the long, bent metal rod of the harvester poking out. He chewed through it, then circled around and around, eating his way slowly and methodically back down to the bottom.

He appreciated now why his Digger had been resting when he’d first come upon it. His jaws felt like they were on fire. Chewing was exhausting work! But he urged the creature onward, fearing the sporecore would expire from being smothered too long.

Finally they came within reach of the Well’s base. “Careful,” Kyle warned. “Don’t eat the sporecore.”

The Digger slowed. The debris here was mostly lengths of twisted metal, the reason all the demolished buildings had lodged near the top of the Well in the first place. The Digger kept chewing, making it all disappear, gradually uncovering the giant mushroom cap.

The flattened sporecore began to quiver. As though someone were airing up a tire, the mound slowly began to rise, puffing up bit by bit as dust and small rocks rolled off. Coated with filth, badly gorged and scraped, the mushroom looked like a wounded animal struggling to stand and brushing itself off.

Looking upward with both pairs of the Digger’s eyes, Kyle expected to see daylight a thousand feet above. Instead, it was dark. But perhaps he felt something, a stronger updraft than normal. The blockage was gone, the Well open, the Tower destroyed. And the sporecore seemed unharmed.

But what about Logan?

Chapter 27

Logan

Logan looked up the shaft for the umpteenth time. The cloud of dust had finally cleared, and he could see a small circle of night sky. Abe had really done it. The Tower was gone. And the explosives Logan had placed had been enough, too. The shaft was more or less clear. A few broken girders stuck out of the walls, but none dangerously so. Kyle could easily navigate through with his Glider.

He looked down, half expecting to see his counterpart racing upward. Was he okay? Had he gotten to a Digger and dealt with the tons of debris Logan had sent his way?

So many questions rolled around in his head. And while he couldn't really go down the seven hundred or so feet to confirm Kyle had survived, he could scoot up to see if Abe was okay. *I'm more armed than the old man. I can fend off any kalibacks.*

Checking the skip pack, he saw it had enough of a charge for at least three, maybe four more hops, a much faster alternative to climbing the steep slope in the tunnel.

He climbed up the shaft, using several of the girders to aid in his progress. He was now getting the hang of the skip pack and used it only twice to easily vault him up and out of the Well the last forty feet. He landed on a pile of crumbled curved wall sections. Climbing down from the heap, he surveyed the destruction. Remnants of the Tower were strewn everywhere, flattening much of the tall grasses surrounding the hilltop site. He clambered over a largely intact section of wooden flooring and spotted the massive metal door, the former entrance to the Tower, resting in the tall grasses a few feet away from a wagon. The door had saved his hide from a vicious pack of kalibacks on his first visit here.

Logan walked over and tried to lift it. He managed to raise it a few inches, but without hinges to aid him, it wasn't going to be of any use as a shield or barrier like before. He thought about sliding it up against the wagon and at least creating a better hiding place in case any predators wandered in to see what all the noise had been about, but that was too much work.

He felt a rumbling underfoot and knew what was about to happen even if he couldn't hear the distinctive boom that preceded the event. He spun around as a torrent of green-glowing spores erupted from the recently cleared Well, shooting into the air several hundred feet. The expulsion created a gigantic light cloud that began to spread out. All those spores would be carried off, landing near and far and producing fungal offspring that, while lacking the cannon-firing abilities of their parent, could still spread more spores in their own small way.

Logan almost expected a horde of solid spirits to come thundering out of the Well but knew it wouldn't be so dramatic. The Forerunners would filter out onto the surface, exercising caution at first. After all, they had no idea how those on the surface would view them, not to mention the inhibitors were still in operation. Any surfacing here would be flung east if they didn't die on the way.

With the spectacle of the first eruption of the Well in several hundred years still happening around him, Logan's reason for coming to the surface shook him free from his daze. Where was the old man?

"Abe! Are you here?" His own voice sounded muffled, as if he spoke underwater.

He pulled out his tremble pistol and set it for maximum. If he ran into kalibacks, he'd need to hit them with the strongest setting. They were not small predators like the vulpers below.

He continued to call, "This is Logan! Are you up here?"

Nothing. *Where is he?*

Disappointed that he had not found Abe, he gave a quick glance to the far west at the tech world he had left behind only a day ago. He saw only a vague forest where the city should be. Apparati should've been lit up like a harvest bonfire along the Great Sea.

The reminder of the annual celebration back at the enclaves made him yearn for his home. His father had taken him once, and Logan had marveled at the fleet of fishing boats out on the water, each decorated by hundreds of torches that had been later thrown overboard in unison. It was a ritual he suddenly yearned to see again. Would it change if tech was introduced back into the primitive world of the enclaves? He hoped not.

But the city isn't there. It's still out of phase. Logan knew the spores needed time to work their magic, but how long? A day or two? Weeks?

From out of the corner of his eye, he detected movement from above. He whipped around to see Kyle crashing down in a crumpled heap with all his breath knocked out, his Glider nowhere in sight. Had he ridden the sporecore eruption all by himself? Where were his spirits? Had they run off, or been forced away by the inhibitor field?

Kyle crawled to his feet, surprisingly clearheaded and not as dazed as he should be from such a rough ride. *He's tougher than he looks.*

Logan looked to the east, knowing the spores couldn't have travelled as far as the enclaves just yet. Without their magical presence, he would not be able to see any fires from the numerous villages and homes either. *Not yet but soon.* He and Kyle were aligned with Apparatum now. The city and the enclaves were not a part of their world at the moment, but the spores would change that.

Noticing that Kyle was talking but not hearing much more than muted, incoherent sounds that almost had the cadence of words, he drew closer. At least his hearing seemed to be improving, if only a little.

Chapter 28
Kyle

"See you around, buddy," Kyle said, mentally patting the Digger on its back just before he vacated its body.

The updraft had ceased. Another sporecore eruption was coming, and this time it would be unimpeded.

When Kyle untethered himself, he found himself bouncing down onto the gigantic mushroom. At that moment, the Digger swung its massive head around and glared at him with all four eyes. The monster was half in and half out of its tunnel, resting on the mushroom as the fungal cap tried to open. Some of the purple-colored triangular segments rose easily and peeled back while others remained closed, trapped under the creature's body.

"Okay, back off," Kyle said, aware that he was now within easy chomping distance. "Time for you to go, Digger." He pointed at the half-closed mushroom. "You're blocking the way."

The Digger let out a long, rumbling growl as though trying to decide whether it should chew into Kyle and send him out of phase. Kyle couldn't think of anything worse. Rather than hang around, he allowed his Glider to slip into place and soared upward quickly and silently until he was out of reach.

The Digger rumbled again, then swung around and started a new tunnel adjacent to the first, angled slightly to the north. In moments, the massive brown-scaled monster was gone.

Now the mushroom cap spread wide, clods of earth and loose rocks tumbling to the side or down into the yawning mouth. The inner section of the sporecore began to open. It looked like a hardened shell, and it was this that all the weight of the debris had come down on and squashed the mushroom cap against. The shell opened sideways like some kind of mechanical entrance doors, splitting somewhere in the middle and both sections pulling back. Below, darkness awaited, some kind of gigantic pit—but then, as the sporecore sucked air into that mouth as though drawing a deep breath, green light glowed from within, brighter and brighter . . .

Kyle shot upward, trying to get ahead of the eruption. It boomed behind him, and a second or two later the powerful wind caught up and blasted him even faster upward. He yelled with the thrill of it all, using his Glider only to keep him on track and away from the edges of the shaft.

He experienced seven hundred feet of superfast travel up the newly opened Well before his remaining two spirits began squirming. Remembering the dreaded inhibitor, he gasped with horror at the realization his friends would be whisked violently to the east the moment the cannon blew him free of the Well.

The spirits peeled away from his body. For a second it seemed hopeless—the eruption was unrelenting, the blast of wind too powerful to escape, Kyle's upward momentum too strong. But the Glider displayed surprising forethought. It grabbed the flailing Weaver and yanked it sideways, and suddenly they were gone. Kyle caught a glimpse of them vanishing into the safety of a tunnel at the side of the Well, which he guessed must be Abe's Tower access. Then he was shooting past, up and out of the shaft into the cold night air.

His horror turned to terror as, free of the eruption at last, he flew in an arc and plummeted toward the ground. He barely had time to brace himself before he hit, skidding and tumbling, his breath knocked out of him as he rolled to a stop among some tangleweeds.

He lay on his back fighting for air and wondering if he'd broken any bones. When his lungs finally started working again, he panted hard and check himself all over, watching the sporadic glows before his face as he breathed.

Spores in the air!

Once he'd composed himself, he was able to focus on the spectacle unfolding all around. Spores were being released into the atmosphere for the first time in hundreds of years.

He pushed himself onto his elbows, then sat up straight. The light show was spectacular. With three moons high in the sky, the stars bright, and the spores glowing green everywhere he looked, he couldn't imagine a more perfect evening. If only the city folk were seeing this!

He did a double take. He saw no city lights in the distance. He was pretty sure he should see them even from this distance. He'd seen the city from the top of the Tower last time he was here, and he'd always been able to view the Tower from the city.

I'm out of phase, he thought. Then he corrected himself. *No, it's the city that's out of phase. And so are the enclaves.*

With the spores finally in the air, maybe normality would be restored soon.

The Tower was, of course, gone. Metallic wreckage littered the area, though the bulk of it lay to the north where the Tower had toppled, glinting in the moonlight. Very little remained around the Well opening, and what had been sitting on top would have fallen down the shaft. It was hard to believe such a tall, substantial structure could be reduced to rubble in short order.

What a waste of a good Tower, he thought.

Glancing around, he spotted movement among piles of twisted metal along the top of the small, grassy hill the Tower had once stood upon. Logan! He must have crawled from the Well before the eruption. He had a weapon drawn, but he was looking directly at Kyle with a wide-eyed look of relief on his face.

Why the weapon? Kyle thought. Then he remembered the wastelands were full of predators, in particular kalibacks. He scanned the area to make sure nothing was nearby. It was hard to see much in the darkness though, and the fiery spores were already beginning to fade.

He hurried toward Logan and said cheerfully, "Good to see you. Nice work with the Sentry and everything. It all sounded pretty hairy, but I knew you were all right. Know how I knew that? Because I'm still here. I figured that if you got yourself killed, I'd wink out as well. I know Abe said wink-outs would stop, but right now we're still connected." He looked around. "Where *is* Abe, anyway?"

He realized Logan was frowning and tentatively touching his ears, occasionally shaking his head. He looked a mess, a graze on his forehead and blood dribbling down from his nose, some sort of machine oil on his shirt, one of his shoes ripped open at the toes. He probably didn't even know how beat-up he looked.

"Huh?" Logan said.

He still wore a skip pack, though it must be depleted by now. It would need recharging. Like most tech, it just required a few hours in sunlight . . . which, of course, was something the underground lacked. Instead, Abe probably used a standard thermoelectric generator over a campfire, converting energy from heat instead of light.

"Are you all right?" Kyle asked.

Logan shook his head and blinked as though he had something in his eyes. "What?"

Deafened by the blast, Kyle thought. *Maybe even concussed.* He reached inside for his Fixer before remembering the furry fellow was long gone. Sighing, he wondered if there was another Fixer somewhere down below, maybe in the settlement where Makow lived.

"Where's Abe?" Logan asked in a strangely loud voice.

"That's what I was wondering."

"Huh?"

"I said—oh, never mind."

Logan frowned at him. "What? I can't hear you. I've gone deaf."

"So stop asking me questions," Kyle said, grinning. He turned away before Logan could utter another questioning grunt. "Abe's about somewhere. Let's give him a few minutes."

He peered all around, seeing nothing but darkness over grassy plains with stands of trees here and there. Any civilization that might have been here once was long gone, some of it demolished and shoved down the Well, the rest flattened and lost to nature. He saw a wagon, strangely out of place. That was *his* wagon, the one he'd arrived at the Tower in when he'd first met Abe and a ghostly Logan. How long ago that seemed now.

"Did you say something?" Logan said, raising his voice again.

Kyle sighed.

Chapter 29
Logan

The ringing in Logan's ears persisted. Thankfully, his hearing had almost completely returned. The initial back and forth with Kyle had been aggravating because he hadn't been able to hear him well, and Kyle had grown annoyed at all the yelling.

He listened as Kyle filled him in on his foray below, wishing he had been able to encounter the Digger himself—with Kyle controlling it, of course.

Logan, in turn, recounted his battle with the Sentry and the destruction of the plug. He was happy to hear Kyle had evaded the falling pieces from both.

"So we can't use the Glider to go back down?" he asked.

"No. I had to leave it and my Weaver below. The inhibitor makes this a no-go zone for any Forerunners. We need to find Abe and have him show us where the access tunnel comes out."

Abe's voice cut through the night air. "Boys!"

He slipped out from behind a small copse of trees. Logan was certain he hadn't been there before. The old man must've wandered back from whatever safe hidey-hole he had squirreled away in to weather the explosion, well beyond the blast area.

The old man appeared relieved. "It's done," Abe said. "The Tower's gone, and I witnessed the first spreading of the spores in over three hundred years. Breathtaking."

"Only the inhibitors left, then," said Kyle.

Abe gave them each a concerned look. "So, I can't dissuade you from returning to your true homes?"

Logan spoke up first this time. "No. I'm going with Kiff."

"Try and separate me from Byron," Kyle growled.

Kyle's resolve surprised Logan. His first impression of the city boy had been someone who had led a pampered life. Had a week in the enclaves toughened him up? Doubtful. He had probably been this spirited all along. After all, they were counterparts.

This reminded him of the twin aspect of their fractured worlds. "So is everything phasing back into one world?"

"Yes," Abe said simply.

"And we're not going to merge or anything?"

Abe grinned. "No, and the wink-outs should stop. Time will tell with that one, though."

"Then let's get this done with," Logan said.

"Hold on," Abe said. "Do you boys know what you're getting yourself into?"

Kyle remarked, "Yeah, we go back, take out the inhibitors, and deal with the Guardians."

"Yes, but know that your spirits cannot follow you into the city because of that inhibitor. You won't have help."

"It doesn't work underground." Kyle said. "I can bring my spirits with me."

"That's true, but access to the bunker is aboveground. You will not have your spirits."

Kyle thought for a moment. "Neither will the Guardian, then. Sort of levels the playing field, doesn't it?"

Abe nodded slowly. "Perhaps so, but the Guardian you will face, Kyle, has Forerunners at her disposal regardless of the inhibitor. Yando's been bringing her regular deliveries of spores so she can keep them somewhat solid, though I'm uncertain why the inhibitor doesn't repel them."

Logan cut in. "Why were the Seekers helping the Guardian? Wouldn't they want the inhibitor to go away? I don't understand why Yando brings her spores."

Abe sighed and relaxed his shoulders. "It's an age-old tradition passed down through generations. Some think of it like appeasing the gods, and that's not far from the truth. The Guardian's bunker is an innocuous, two-story building located in a rundown part of the city. There's nothing special about it except that the Wiscuppa River flows directly underneath from the east. The Guardian poisons the water every time her monthly delivery of spores is late. One simple spell and virtually our entire free-flowing water supply is tainted for weeks."

He paused to let that sink in.

Logan tried to imagine Seekers falling sick, perhaps dying from the poison. Would it be instant, like choking on deadly jekka berries? Or would they be blissfully unaware of the danger until far too late, their bodies already fatally weakened before they noticed anything was wrong?

He shuddered.

"It's an awful irony," Abe went on, worry lining his face. "We can kill the Guardian simply by refusing to make a delivery. But it wouldn't be a quick death. The spores prolong her life span. Without the spores, her magic would falter, and she would begin aging again, finally gasping her last breath several weeks later, giving her plenty of time to give us a concentrated dose of poison for as long as she can. Tainting the river won't just spoil our water supply. It will kill all the fish too, about thirty percent of our food supply in this subterranean world. And sustained poisoning will kill our already endangered Swimmers, which would be a travesty." Abe paused. "So you see, spore deliveries must continue until we're able to take down the Guardian in one unexpected, decisive attack."

Satisfied with Abe's answer, Logan asked, "And is that what I should expect at my end? Will the enclaves' Guardian be wielding tech?"

"Likely, but I'm not sure to what extent. Whatever tech he does have will be used with ruthless precision. But ending him is just part of the deal," Abe said.

"Then let's fetch Kiff and Byron and go," Logan said.

Abe clapped his hands together. "Well then, all that's left is to say your goodbyes."

"But only for now. We can visit each other very soon," Kyle said. "The city and enclaves will be able to interact again."

"Yes, but it will take time, diplomacy, and trust." Abe grinned, the wrinkles at the corners of his eyes crinkling pleasantly. The old man no longer seemed as burdened by the world. "With your governments and people more receptive to change thanks to each of you and what you brought to your worlds, we are at a tipping point. No better time for Apparatum to return than now. It will be a long road, but one worth traveling."

Logan thought for a moment. "Won't anyone be scared of the Forerunners, especially city dwellers like you just said?"

"The spores are bringing not only the world back into balance, but also the lost and fractured spirits your people tamed. They will mend, become whole once more," Abe said. "And they will converse, establishing themselves once again on equal footing with humans."

Kyle asked, "But aren't there going to be people who won't accept them even if they are truly kind and good?"

Abe winked. "Then maybe that is for you and Logan to remedy. Maybe your duties extend beyond just destroying the inhibitors. You two are catalysts, and I see no reason why that will change in the near future. You will continue to be forces of change. But enough discussion, there will be time to talk later. Now, action is required of the two of you." Abe's eyes went to the useless skip pack. "With the skip pack dead, we'll need to use the access tunnel to return to the shaft. Then it's going to be a long, slow climb down. I have some rope stashed nearby for such an eventuality."

Kyle smiled. "We might not need the rope if my Glider's still hanging around down there. I can take both of you, just not at the same time."

Abe brightened. "That would be marvelous. Wouldn't it, Logan?"

Logan nodded, eager to experience the brief flight in the Well even if it was only as a passenger.

Chapter 30
Kyle

Abe led Kyle and Logan to a tunnel entrance hidden under a clump of long grass some forty feet from the Well. "It's steep," he said, gesturing down into it, "but it'll get us started." He looked at Kyle. "I do hope your Glider is waiting, otherwise we'll have a very slow and dangerous climb down to the bottom. Perhaps I should fetch the ropes I put aside . . ."

"I'm sure my friends are waiting," Kyle said. "Let's go."

Logan had already stepped inside to lead the way, but he paused to wait as Abe turned back and gazed at the twisted metal glinting in the light of the three moons. "That Tower was very special to me," the old man said. "But we don't need it anymore. And I don't need my collar either."

He fingered the metal cowl around the back of his head and reached up to unfasten it. It came off with an electronic buzz and click. Abe tossed it aside, and it hit the ground with a clang.

"If everything works out the way I expect," he went on, "soon Apparatum will be fully in sync, completely restored, and I won't need a portable phasing device to help me visit one place or another."

Looking west, Kyle thought he could see a distant pinprick of light. Maybe two or three. Or was he imagining things?

Seeing where he was looking, Logan said, "There's nothing there. I mean *nothing*. I was just at the city yesterday, and now I can't see it at all. I wonder if Kiff and I will see the enclaves when we get there?"

The old man exhaled slowly, and another faint plume of light lit up his face. "We have to wait for the spores to spread across the land and bring everything back into sync with us and the underground. *Then* we'll see the city and the enclaves. It will take time, perhaps a day. We'll know when normality is restored when we can touch walls and bump into people. Before that, citizens should start to see their own breath glow."

Kyle shot Logan a glance. He found it hard to imagine how the high-tech people of the city would take to such a thing. Fiery breath at night? Was that something the ancient civilization of Apparatum had been used to?

But that small, newly restored phenomenon would be nothing to the return of tech to the enclaves and tethering in the city once those inhibitors were down. Everything was about to change.

They all headed down the sharp slope into the ground. After a few minutes of slipping and tumbling, the tunnel leveled off, and they found the Glider and Weaver spirits waiting for them, surprisingly ethereal in the blackness. Kyle felt a sense of satisfaction tinged with pride. He'd hoped they would be here, but he'd also feared they would be solid by now, unwilling or unable to tether with him again. Yet here they were, waiting patiently.

Without hesitation, they ducked and walked into him, *through* him. It felt like icy hands grasping his internal organs, and he shuddered. But at least he had them back.

At the far end of the tunnel, the three of them looked down into the Well. All was quiet now, but it wouldn't be for long. "Who's first?" Kyle asked.

Logan nodded toward Abe. "Age before beauty."

Kyle called on his Glider, and the spirit went to work.

The Glider's wings seemed far more prominent now as he lifted them wide, glowing blue in their usual spiritlike fashion but more leathery. He still felt light, able to lift off the ground without effort, but he worried the Glider would eventually have to resort to a physical transformation into solid form in order to get off the ground.

It was a two-hundred-foot descent from their tunnel to the two lower access points halfway down the Well, a fast and easy ride except for the pressure in his ears that forced him to slow a little. He deposited Abe at the entrance to one of the tunnels and said, "I'll be right back." With that, he shot off upward, feeling much lighter.

Logan was sitting on a fat vein with his legs hanging over the side. "My turn," he said, sounding nervous.

The ride down was uneventful, and when Kyle landed once more in the lower access tunnel, he found Abe chatting amiably with Byron, whose orbs glowed brightly in the darkness. Behind him stood Kiff.

"You did it," Kiff said, looking at Logan with obvious pride.

"We did it," Logan said. He banged Kyle on the shoulder with enough force to make him stumble. "Kyle's the man. Ate all that wreckage in no time and freed the sporecore."

Kyle shook his head. "Logan practically threw that giant Sentry down the shaft at me. It was like a giant robot spider. Logan twisted its legs off and tossed them down."

They all grinned at the idea.

"Where's Makow?" Kyle asked. "Why are you here? You were all supposed to wait back at the campfires where it's safe."

"Yeah, but then we heard the explosions," Byron said. "We figured it was all over and came to find you."

"But not Makow?" Kyle growled, suddenly annoyed with the man.

"He brought us here, but he didn't wait. He saw the Well was open and started laughing. He said he was heading back to the settlement to let everyone know. He said they'd be impatient to get started."

Abe nodded and grunted, "Good, good. The sooner the better."

"Get started with what?" Logan asked with a frown.

The gentle draft suddenly changed directions and started sucking downward. "It's been half an hour already?" Kyle said, amazed. "The sporecore's about to erupt again. Let's go."

The dull boom from below came quicker this time, followed by the sudden blast of wind and a spectacular shower of glowing spores shooting up the Well. There seemed to be more, the air thick with them as though the sporecore was ramping up its output and trying to make up for hundreds of years of frustration. Kyle didn't think the fungal cannon's lightshow would ever get old. He almost wished he was back on the surface right now.

The group hurried away down the tunnel.

Back at the intersection where the pile of remaining tech levitated on the floatpad, Kyle knew it was time to say their goodbyes. From this point forward, he would be traveling west with Byron while Logan and Kiff headed east. Abe said he would walk with Kyle and show him the way to go. "You can't go upstream. I'll have to show you the alternate route."

"Nice of Makow to wait for me," Kyle grumbled.

Abe looked at him with a twinkle in his eye. "As young and healthy as you are, young Kyle, I very much doubt you'd be able to keep up with Makow. You'd only hold him back. It's best that he heads off alone. By the time you reach the settlement, he'll have got things organized as well as had a meal and rested."

They all looked at one another in the glows of their combined puffs of breath.

"Hey," Kyle said to Logan, "make sure Kiff doesn't go running off ahead of you. Watch your step in the cavern with the mist. Kiff'll tell you all about it. There's a cavern with a vac-train station and tunnel. Be careful. Hunters might be waiting there. Someone called Grib?"

Logan's eyebrows shot up. "I know him. He thinks an awful lot of himself."

"If you can get past them, follow the metal vac-train tunnel. It's quite a walk. Look for a hole in the wall on your left leading to the Fixer Enclave. Or just carry on. I'm pretty sure the tunnel leads all the way to the Hallowed Spires, and—"

"I'll figure it out," Logan said with a grin. "I would give you a few tips as well, but you'll be taking a different route. Keep that robot boy away from the water, okay? But be careful with the clackers, too." He frowned. "Wouldn't it be safer if we traveled across land?"

"And meet kalibacks and orb scavengers and gangs of deadbeats?" Kyle grimaced. It occurred to him that he had a Glider at his disposal, but it was useless aboveground with the spirit inhibitor still in place. And the tech inhibitor would be a problem for Byron, too. As for Logan and Kiff, they would be on foot the whole way, and the underground route heading east was pretty safe for the most part.

"Let's get to it," Abe said, patting both Kyle and Logan on the shoulders. "You boys each have a journey ahead of you, and being underground among these thick spores will facilitate the syncing process as you approach your destinations. I suggest you travel as far as you can, then get a good rest before tackling the Guardians. You'll need your wits about you."

Chapter 31
Logan

Despite Logan's protests, Kiff led the way. It was good to see him so healthy and spry, and he didn't have the heart to tell him to exercise more caution.

His little brother ran ahead, easily hopping and ducking through the purple roots sticking out of the tunnel walls. It was amazing to see the sporecore had extended its reach this far in.

Kiff called back to him, "Don't worry. Not much danger in this part. The chasm's the big problem. We've got at least two caverns of fungus to wade through before we get to that."

He caught up to Kiff and insisted they catch their breath. They hadn't traveled far, but going up and down the Well with his heavy load had taken its toll. The gear he carried with him was weighing him down, but he was unwilling to part with any of it or offer his little brother a chance to carry a weapon.

The breach wand and the grenades could be used by anyone, while everything else required tech abilities to unlock their security safeties via an implant or in Logan's case directly with his talent. As impulsive as Kiff was, no way he'd let him handle either of the free-use devices. Especially since both could bring down the tunnel with ease in the wrong hands. And Kiff's grabby paws were just that. How often had he gotten himself and Logan in trouble in the enclaves? Too many times to count.

Kiff frowned. "I'm hungry."

"Not much I can do." He couldn't recall which mushrooms were safe to eat and honestly hadn't been that enamored with the ones he had tasted in the wild. "Are Mom and Dad okay?"

"They're fine. They took good care of Kyle." Kiff smiled wider, his dimples appearing to full effect. "Nomi did, too."

"What do you mean?" Logan said with suspicion.

"Relax. She was sweet on him, but I think she's going to be more excited to see you again."

Logan tried to sound laidback in his response, but it still came out too eager. "Really?" He changed the topic. "And who's the sovereign now?"

"Durant. Kyle kind of got in trouble with him."

"How so?" Was he coming back to another government official who was already closed to the idea of reuniting the city and enclaves?

"Kyle took a bunch of Breakers. You should've seen how many. Lots and lots of them. And he broke through to a tunnel. That's how he knew stuff was down here."

"And Durant didn't like it?"

"Not at all." He frowned. "You think he'll send us to the Pens for blowing up the Tower and everything?"

"I don't know, but I'll do all I can to prevent that." And he knew he would. He had a voice and would use it. Maybe his people would be so impressed with the tech he could wield that they'd be eager to welcome it back into their lives.

Logan stood and reached out to help Kiff to his feet. "We need to get back as fast as we can before everyone goes crazy. If I can tell them what's happening, maybe things won't fall apart so bad."

His brother ignored his extended hand and popped up on his own. "C'mon. Just a little farther and it really opens up."

Kiff hopped about on his mended leg. Kyle had done excellent work. What was it like to be able to weave, glide, fix, and do all the other feats capable with tethered spirits? And Logan was especially curious about the attributes of the two new spirits. Wait, *Forerunners*. They were no longer phantoms. Or at least, they soon wouldn't be. Was that change happening as they trekked back to the enclaves? What would his mother and father make of their spirits slipping free and standing before them whole and complete? And when the Forerunners spoke, he really wanted to be there to see his father's reaction to that.

It sounded intimidating. How was he supposed to help all of the enclaves adjust to having their spirits step out and declare their independence? Would it be gradual? Abe had said the spirits were damaged, their intelligence dulled by the phantom state they had been in for so long. Would their intellect come rushing back all at once, or would it be a slow process?

Ahead, Kiff stood at the edge of a sizeable flat area covered in large mushrooms, many of their dull-grey caps ten feet in diameter. He recognized them as the same fungus he had ridden in on the river. Their caps were wider across but far shallower than the grubberming he had ridden. Once their gills were scooped out, Logan doubted there would be a large enough cavity to ride in. His boat, with its more bowl-like cap, had to be a much younger one or perhaps a slightly different species.

Kiff climbed onto the first one with surprising restraint. He stepped softly across it and motioned for Logan to follow. He pointed at the sunken footprints that trailed behind him. "It's real easy to break through. And they give off a nasty cloud of dust."

Logan stepped onto the wide surface and felt how fragile the cap was. Yeah, definitely the mushroom boat had been sturdier. These must be older. That would explain their large size and weak exteriors.

Three steps in, Logan's boot broke through. A puff of dust sprang free, and he coughed and coughed. He stepped lively but cautiously away from the rupture and was pleased to leave the cloying cloud behind.

Kiff was three caps ahead of him when Logan spotted two vulpers eyeing them off to the right. He trusted Yando was being truthful, that the predators would leave them alone as long as they stayed out of any minquin manure. Logan searched the air, fearful a swarm of the winged creatures would appear and drop their excrement on them. Only a few blue-and-red birds fluttered by.

"Did you and Kyle come across any creatures that tried to attack you?"

"No, but Makow made us be careful around the mindsapper. It was a funny-looking mushroom, like someone had painted a huge durgle egg bright orange."

Logan didn't know how an egg-shaped fungus could be that much trouble, but he didn't like the name. He'd be sure to steer clear of it.

With so much fungi around them, bright breath wasn't really needed. How soon would the spores drift into the enclaves? Would suddenly breathing light cause a panic?

They hopped off the last grubberming mushroom. The vulpers milled around, striding back and forth in a clearing less than a hundred feet away. Luckily, Kiff hadn't seen them. He was too occupied with being a trailblazer. That was fortunate. His brother would be too tempted to go pet the carnivores.

The ceiling of the cavern dropped closer to them. Making it feel even lower was the fact that long strands of glowing tendrils drooped, some almost touching the ground while others terminated a few feet above his head.

Kiff expressed his insights with glee. "Don't brush up against any. They sting."

"Did one sting you?" Logan asked as he ducked under a thick patch of the tendrils.

"Nope." Kiff, thanks to his smaller stature, weaved through the tendrils far faster than Logan.

A wider variety of fungi presented itself in the next section of the cavern. Logan recognized the tall fungal mounds as identical to the ones in the Seekers' cavern. These were not as impressive in height, but they still towered over them.

Kiff kept a respectful distance from the plentiful red-and-white fungus. "Those are poisonous."

"Got it."

A few minutes later, they left the cavern, entering a large tunnel where darkness once more pressed in. "Is the chasm coming up soon?" Logan asked.

"Nope. Gotta go through the mindsapper part first." Kiff slowed, allowing Logan to catch up.

In the glow from his breath, Logan could tell the darkness unnerved his brother. He clamped his hand on Kiff's right shoulder and said, "You're doing great. I'm glad you can remember so much. I probably would've tripped and landed right in the thick of some of those poisonous ones if you hadn't warned me."

Kiff grinned and asked, "Is tech fun?" His eyes fell on the tremble gun in its holster.

Logan used his mind to make sure the safety was on and pulled the weapon out. He handed it gingerly to Kiff. "Go ahead, hold it. I have the safety on so it won't fire."

Kiff grabbed it by its hilt and pointed it forward. "What's it do?"

"It's a tremble gun."

"So it gives you the jitters? That doesn't sound so bad."

"No, it turns your nervous system against you." He pointed at the muzzle. "It shoots an electrical charge out of here, enough to make you lose all control of your arms and legs. You fall to the ground and twitch for about ten minutes. That's on the medium setting, though."

"What if you hit somebody full blast?"

Logan answered, "The effects last twice as long, and the victim is twice as sore afterward."

"You've used one before?"

"No, but—"

Kiff interrupted him. "Then how do you know what it does? Did you read about it, or did a Hunter show you?" Kiff's eyes widened. "Nobody shot you with it, did they?"

Ahead, several clusters of the yellow mushrooms with the blue gills glowed, returning them to proper lighting. Logan could see another cavern, this one twice as big as the last, opening up before them.

"No, nobody pegged me with one. I'm too fast." He winked at his brother. "And they have soldiers, not Hunters." He slipped the gun out of his brother's hands and back into its holster. "I can put my mind into most tech and figure out what it does."

"Does it talk to you?"

"No, nothing like that. I suspect it's a little like how Mom and Dad tether with their spirits."

"That's wild," Kiff said. He stepped into the cavern and held his hand out to Logan, who took it graciously. "I'm glad you're back."

"Me too, Kiff."

His little brother didn't hold his gaze long. He tugged at Logan, pulling him down the slope toward the wide array of mushrooms.

Kiff pointed at the largest mushroom in the entire chamber. "That's the mindsapper. It's definitely bigger than before, and it's opened up now. We have to be careful."

Logan stared at the immense fungus. Even with it being several hundred feet away, it was impressive, at least thirty feet tall, bright orange with yellow blotches. The top half of the egg cap had peeled back, exposing a cluster of upright purple growths that reminded Logan of the Hallowed Spires.

He exhaled and saw, mixed in with the bright green spores, several others which flared orange. This alarmed him. Had they come from the mindsapper?

"Kiff, I don't know if we should . . ." His head throbbed.

His brother slipped free and raced forward, amused that his breath was changing color. "Look at all the orange. It's like I'm breathing fire." He danced around and exhaled three or four times. "I'm an orb scavenger."

Logan took in a shallow breath, and his vision swam. He reached a hand out. “Kiff, I don’t think we should breathe any—”

Kiff suddenly crumpled to the ground, like a puppet whose strings had been cut.

Logan stumbled toward his fallen brother, stars appearing momentarily in his field of view before everything went black.

Chapter 32
Kyle

Kyle, Byron, and Abe emerged into Makow's familiar cavern, but of course Makow was long gone by now. The smell of leftover vulper meat caught in Kyle's nostrils, and he spotted a grey-furred rodent with a black-and-white stripy tail making off with the remains of the carcass.

Abe led them past the campfires to the chasm where the Wiscuppa flowed ten feet down. He headed upstream, around a bend, and into a narrow, echoing passage. The river roared here, but the walls soon widened again, and shallow rocky banks came into view. Moored there was what looked liked a huge mushroom boat.

"That's what Logan and I came in," Byron whispered, and Kyle almost detected a grimace on his smooth faceplate.

Over their heads on the glistening, rounded ceiling hung a collection of bright orange mushrooms. They looked like they'd been put there as some sort of marker.

"This is the Wiscuppa," Abe said, leaning on his staff as spray from the river splashed up over his robes. "Yes, Logan and Kiff came down this way, about a two-hour journey. Unfortunately, it's a one-way route. Unless . . ."

Kyle glanced at him. "Unless what?"

"Unless you can hitch a ride with a Swimmer."

"Is that a possibility?"

Abe smiled. "For you, absolutely. You tamed a Digger. A Swimmer will, I'm sure, be child's play." His smile faded, and he frowned. "The problem is finding one."

Sighing, Kyle looked around and spotted another tunnel leading off roughly parallel to the fast-flowing Wiscuppa. "What's up that way?"

"It's the way we normally travel from here back to the settlement. It takes much longer, though, and there's always a chance of running into canyon clackers along the way. Makow is a long way ahead by now. When you arrive at the settlement, get something to eat and a decent rest before continuing on to the city."

Kyle looked at Byron. "What do you think, Byron? Clackers or Swimmer?"

Byron's eyes flashed, and he tilted his head. "You want me to go underwater? Sitting in a giant mushroom boat was bad enough for someone like me."

"Someone like you?" Kyle feigned surprise. He missed teasing his brother. "What do you mean? I thought you were a good swimmer?"

"I think you mean I'm a good *sinker*. And I can short circuit really well with the right amount of water. One trip down this river was enough for me, thanks."

Kyle laughed. He looked at Abe. "I think we're going to take our chances with the clackers."

Abe shook his head. "Well, no dilly-dallying, then. I wish there was room for you to fly, but this tunnel is low and narrow much of the way. When it opens up, beware of the clackers. You'll probably reach them in half a day or so."

Half a day, Kyle thought, cringing inside and instantly regretting his decision. "I really have to use this tunnel? There's no other way?" He shrugged. "Well, I guess we'll head off, then. We'll see you again soon, won't we?"

Abe nodded. "I'm going to stay awhile and monitor the sporecore, then return to the surface and catalog the progress of the syncing." When Kyle raised an eyebrow at him, Abe shrugged. "These things are important to old scholars like me. Now be off with you both. And good luck."

He abruptly turned and headed back up the tunnel toward the Well, leaving Kyle and Byron alone.

“Well,” Kyle said, “just you and me again. You and me against the world. Or something like that.”

He stared into the darkness of the clacker tunnel. Exhaling hard, he was pleased to see a strong glow before his eyes. At least he wouldn’t be scraping around in complete darkness. Besides, Byron had a built-in chest lamp.

And he still had two dormant spirits if he needed their assistance.

Should he release them yet? They wouldn’t be any help aboveground with the inhibitor still working, but perhaps they would be an advantage underground, especially if he could enter the Guardian’s bunker from below. Plus, there were plenty of situations he could think of along the way that might require the help of spirits, especially the Glider. What if he came across a pit of fire too wide to jump, or perhaps a deadly subterranean jungle that would be much easier to fly over instead of plowing through?

It occurred to him that Logan was soon to run into a similar problem—the cavern where the misty chasm masked a boiling spring. Kyle grimaced, thinking he hadn’t properly warned Logan about that, only mentioned it in passing. Kiff would guide him, of course. He wasn’t likely to forget!

Logan needed a Glider to fly him across, or a Weaver to build him a bridge, both of which Kyle could supply. A Weaver would soon have a tough structure spanning that chasm as long as suitable materials could be found nearby . . .

But if there were no suitable materials, then a Glider would probably be easier.

Kyle sighed. It was time to let go of an old friend.

Chapter 33
Logan

Logan sat up, surrounded by complete darkness. His mouth was dry. He coughed out a breath, but no spores lit up. Where was Kiff? Had he been taken?

Kyle had warned them that Grib and other Hunters were down here. Had Logan blacked out, and they had come along and taken him prisoner? Or had they gassed him? An explanation felt just out of reach, intangible like a spirit.

He felt around as he faintly called out, "Kiff, you there?"

No response.

The ground was solid rock with a light dusting of grit. He was still in a cavern. He probed about for at least ten feet in all directions. Nothing but rock. His voice cracked as he dared to shout, "Kiff!"

Nothing, not even an echo. Where was he? He stood, casting his hands upward in case there was a low ceiling. There wasn't.

Stretching out, he staggered. His head hurt, and his balance was off.

The ground began to shake, and he dropped to all fours. A roar sounded from above, at first muted and distant but then quickly growing in volume.

Suddenly, the air was filled with orange glowing spores. Something was off about that, too, but his mind couldn't latch onto what. The sporecore produced the light-bringing spores. Was he in a chamber near the massive fungal cannon?

With light coming from all around, he saw he was indeed in a large chamber, one that dwarfed even the settlement cavern. The rock he found himself on was thirty feet across. Twenty feet in front of him, it dropped off. He crawled toward that drop-off.

The roaring no longer came from above but originated somewhere out of view below. If he could make it to the lip of the rock, maybe he could see what called out.

The ground shook. His gut told him whatever made the roar had to be causing the seismic disturbance. He was not in a hurry to stand up given the lurching nature of the rock underneath. How the rock had not split into pieces from the shaking, he had no clue.

The roaring stopped along with any signs of movement.

The orange spores dimmed, the darkness returning.

A huge plume of bright orange shot up from below. Logan dropped back from the edge. Whatever was down there had to be gigantic to create such a daunting glowing cloud.

The creature in question flew up into the air, casting several jets of spores outward, reminding Logan of the flames orb scavengers belched from their tiny mouths.

It was immense, appearing even bigger thanks to its large leathery wings. Its body was thick and muscular, easily the size of three clackers. Its neck brimmed with impressive quills and snaked out almost fifty feet in length while its tail was twice as long and adorned with what looked like blue, translucent fins. Its body slipped back and forth between solid and ethereal.

Four arms ending in claws extended out from the upper torso, each wrapped in brown fur. Its legs were equally fur-covered and ended in three-clawed feet. The head was hammer-shaped with its solitary eye blinking at him from the center. The downcast mouth dropped open, revealing rows of sharp teeth.

It circled about in the air, lighting its way with its breath, the whole time its eye unwavering in its attention to Logan. A symmetrical pattern of green framed the eye and meandered down the creature's pronounced cheeks, a sinister mask.

His vision swam, unsteadiness again afflicting him. Was it the creature's breath that made him lightheaded? *Orange spores, something about them.*

Logan didn't know why, but he spoke to the creature. "What are you?"

"All things and none." Its voice rumbled, sending vibrations throughout the cavern.

"Are you a Forerunner?"

The creature froze in mid-air. Not even its wings moved. How was that possible?

"Doom seeps in."

It wasn't making sense. Logan breathed in, almost gagging on the sheer number of spores present. "Where's my brother?"

No reply.

Logan's heart raced. Something was happening. While he could move, all around him stood still, even the plumes the creature had previously expelled. They hung in the air, no longer dispersing, their orange even brighter than before.

Something about the spores, their color. Logan stiffened and tried to gather his thoughts. The orange spores weren't right. They should be green. Why were they orange? There was an important difference.

Abruptly, the scene plunged into darkness, and he felt his body lift off the ground. A gentle breeze swept over him, gaining in intensity. He was on the move. But how? He didn't have on a skip pack.

He looked down, suddenly aware he wore simple enclave clothes, a light-brown shirt and pants. His city boots were gone and, in their place, simple moccasins like the ones Kyle had been wearing in the Well. Had they switched clothes for some reason?

The temperature dropped, and the air he now breathed held a slight moistness.

A strange fluty voice intruded on the darkness. "You must free yourself. Stir, young one. Lift yourself free."

Logan exhaled, producing glowing green spores. Their color gave him comfort, put him at ease.

He took in several more breaths, his mind rising out of whatever fog had held it.

He closed his eyes and willed the darkness away. When he opened them, there was enough light for him to see he was in a small cavern. Tiny curls of mist filled the air. He puffed out a large glowing cloud to see Kiff standing over him with a Glider spirit hanging back behind his brother, its appearance oscillating from solid to immaterial.

The Forerunner smiled and draped its wings protectively around Kiff. "You are awake. That is good."

"What happened?" Logan rose to his knees and rubbed at his brow. He was once again wearing his city clothes.

"The mindsapper." Kiff slipped out from under the Glider's wings. "It got both of us."

"What?"

"Its spores cause most to slumber and dream until their bodies fail." The Glider's words were pleasant despite the grim topic. "Then it uses the nutrients from your body to manifest offspring."

The orange spores. He suddenly recalled they had been all over the place just before Kiff had collapsed, and he himself had slipped into unconsciousness. "Then how did we get out?"

"I came and pulled Kiff into me. We then grabbed you and took flight."

The escalating breeze in my nightmare. "You tethered with a Glider?"

Kiff smiled. "It was wild! I only recall part of the ride, but flying is amazing!"

Logan stood and faced the Forerunner, looking deep into its amber eyes. "Thank you."

"It is you that should receive my gratitude. You freed me, lifted the veil that made me little more than an animal for so long."

"Are you from above?"

"Yes. I spent time within your counterpart until he released me with the understanding that I perform one more task."

"Rescue us from a mindsapper?"

"No, that was unexpected. My duty is to help you cross a chasm here in the mists." He waved his left arm up and outward, sweeping his wings open and closed to dispel some of the mist.

"Thank you," Logan said.

The Glider spun about and walked off. "Come. Let's get you moving onward. There is still much to accomplish."

Agreed, thought Logan.

His head clear once more, he scrambled after the Forerunner, sending Kiff a smile. His brother grinned widely, his eyes dancing. Logan knew he was bursting to tell him more of his time within the Glider, and Logan realized he was eager to hear it all. He was back with his brother, and all that stood between them and their parents was a crazed Guardian.

He patted the tremble gun in its holster. To believe Abe, his mastery of tech would only get him so far in the battle. Shutting down the inhibitor could prove tricky if he couldn't use his tech abilities. Could he defeat the Guardian before reaching the surface and its no-tech zone? He was certainly willing to try.

Chapter 34

Kyle

Kyle was sick of tunnels. He and Byron had been walking for several hours now, and his feet were sore. The walls closed in on them and opened up again, over and over. He peered at every fungal growth hoping something would interest him. The sheer monotony of it all got to him. One foot in front of the other, trudging along, mile after endless mile . . .

It had been hard to say goodbye to his Glider, but Abe was right: these tunnels were far too narrow and low to fly without careening off the walls.

"How long now?" he asked Byron, who seemed to relish keeping up with his older brother for a change and had recently taken the lead. His new body had a longer stride, and he didn't have to worry about fatigue. Right now, Kyle wished he were a robot himself.

"Six hours and twenty-two minutes," Byron said.

"You're a walking clock," Kyle muttered. "Are we still headed west?"

"Southwest at the moment."

"How far do we have to go?"

At this, Byron balked. "I don't have a built-in map."

"Really? So you can bore me with the precise lunar cycles of our three moons, give me horrible statistics about the number of people who were repurposed last year, and list every official member of the Hub including the names of their spouses, but you don't have anything useful like a map?"

"I can only download what's available!" Byron protested. "There's no map of the underground anywhere on record."

Kyle grinned to himself. His brother's upgrade had somehow matured him beyond his eight years and made him talk like an old professor on occasion, but he was still easy to tease.

Although Kyle's breath vapor was consistently bright, and his single remaining spirit—his Weaver—offered a green glow to his skin, by far the brightest light was Byron's chest lamp, which shone ahead and lit up the tunnel in stark contrast. Brightly colored fungal growths smothered the ceilings and walls, but they looked kind of ugly when doused in bright white light, the same way that the nighttime razzle-dazzle of the city's casinos looked dead and cold in the daytime.

"When Abe said half a day to reach the clackers," Kyle said, "did he mean half a *daytime* or half a full round-the-clock day?"

"I don't know," Byron replied.

"If he meant half a *daytime*, from dawn until dusk, say about twelve hours, then we should be there by now. But if he meant—"

"You sound like you *want* to run into clackers."

"Anything's better than this endless walking."

"Do you need another rest?" Byron asked.

"No. I'm beyond rest. I'm pretty much sleepwalking right now. If we stop again, my legs will seize up. All I want to do is get there and eat something, then go to bed for a week."

They fell silent again. Kyle knew he was acting like a complaining child, but he didn't mind around Byron. He felt relaxed with him, far more relaxed than he ever had with Kiff.

The journey had started out brisk and pleasant. They'd chatted nonstop, catching up with events over the past week or more. Kyle felt vindicated that their dad had repeatedly lamented his decision to send their son for repurposing instead of giving him a chance in the Ruins. Clearly Kyle had proved him wrong on that count. A determined fourteen-year-old boy could survive anywhere with a bit of luck on his side.

Their dad saw that now. Moreover, he'd vowed to never again let the city's overbearing presence trump his sense of right and wrong. If the lack of an implant made his son a "deadbeat" in society's hypercritical eyes, then so be it, he'd fight for his son's life every step of the way instead of complying with the "recommended course of action for the good of the city."

Kyle was delighted his dad had seen the error of his ways. He unreservedly forgave him and couldn't wait to see him again.

He found it hard to blame his mom for anything even though outsiders might argue she was equally guilty. She'd gone along with the decision to have him repurposed instead of standing up for him, but Kyle knew how tough the government was. His dad had complained about it enough times. He almost remembered the speech word for word: "Anyone who doesn't comply, who complains and makes waves, runs the risk of social rejection. Corporations err on the side of caution and replace unpalatable employees, and those shunned workers face zero chance of reemployment, meaning less household income and ultimately a backslide to less favorable dwellings farther outside the center . . . a slippery slope that I've fought tooth and nail to avoid!"

But all that was changing. Mayor Baynor was gone, as was the nasty General Mortimer, and the citizens of the city had been enlightened to a world beyond the Wall. Still, according to Logan, the current mayor wasn't much better. It might take several replacements to filter out generations of corruption. Hopefully, destroying the inhibitor and somehow uprooting the Guardian would give the city a real chance to start anew.

Uprooting the Guardian. The mysterious character sounded like a tenacious weed choking the life out of everything around it. Maybe that wasn't far from the truth.

"Give me everything you have about the Guardian," Kyle said, deciding it was time to start putting some sort of plan together. "What does the datahub say about him?"

"Her," Byron corrected.

Kyle blinked. "Oh, yeah."

"The Guardian in the enclaves is a man, but the city Guardian is a woman. Logan and I started researching a few days ago. Didn't find much, though. Want to know what Logan said?" Byron's voice suddenly switched to Logan's as he played back an actual recording. "*Really? That's it? Huh. This is one subject my own people back home know more about. They speak of the Guardian in the Capitol as an ancient man who cannot ever leave the Hallowed Spires, whose life is devoted to protecting the enclaves against the evils of the Broken Lands. He has seven hooded servants by his side who have given their lives to him and his cause.*"

"Yeah, that's pretty much what Logan's mom told me, too," Kyle muttered. "Since when have you been recording things people say?"

Byron's mechanical step faltered. "Um, well, since I was upgraded. But the recordings get wiped after three days. I only have so much disk space."

"So you have recordings of Logan talking to Rissa?"

"No, I was never around when they were together."

Kyle nodded to himself as he traipsed along. "Okay, but did Logan talk to you about her? I know he studied with her, something I never got the chance to do."

Now Byron was quiet.

Kyle reached forward and tapped Byron's hard shoulder. "Little brother?"

"He said something the last time he studied with her. Not sure you'd want to hear it, though."

"Try me."

Byron's voice changed again. ". . . *Don't know what Kyle sees in her. She's full of herself. I mean, she's smart and looks nice enough, actually pretty stunning until she opens her mouth and starts talking. Kyle could do better. Someone like Nomi back home. Now, there's a girl worth talking about. Really nice, a heart of gold, and pretty as well. Rissa is . . . well, I can't stand being around her. I really think Kyle could—*"

"Enough," Kyle said, and the playback cut off.

Another silence ensued. So Rissa wasn't good enough for Logan? Well, it figured. Logan was from a backward village with dirt streets and hustle-drawn carts. The fastest way to get a message to another enclave was via Glider—if one could be found at such short notice. The closest they had to a stream screen was an unravelled scroll pinned to the wall. Logan probably found Rissa way too sophisticated. She intimidated him. It was true that she had a sharp tongue, but Kyle had always seen through her tough facade.

"He doesn't know her well enough," he said eventually.

"He knows her better than you do," Byron said. "He *studied* with her a few times. She agreed to join him because . . . well, he's Logan, the boy from another land. Logan Orm from the Wild." His voice took on a playful tone. "She might even find *you* interesting when you see her next."

"Hey, watch it."

But inside, Kyle felt a thrill. The idea of Rissa finding him interesting and maybe even wanting to spend time with him . . . well, he was game even if Logan wasn't. His counterpart could keep Nomi. The girl from the enclaves was certainly nice enough, pretty and pleasant, but Rissa was something else entirely.

"I think Abe meant half a daytime," Byron said in a low voice.

"What?"

"He said it was half a day to the clackers. We've been walking for six hours and forty-eight minutes now, about half a daytime, and there's a giant cavern ahead."

A shudder of excitement shot through Kyle. "So we need to be on the lookout for clackers."

"You say that like you're looking forward to seeing them."

Kyle patted Byron on the shoulder. "After seven hours in this tunnel, I'm ready for anything."

Chapter 35
Logan

It was a short walk to the cavern containing the chasm. The air was thick, and a heavy mist filled every open space. The Glider's blue glow, along with Kiff and Logan huffing and puffing, gave them ample light, allowing them to quicken their pace. Kiff even held out one of the yellow mushrooms with the glowing blue gills underneath like a torch. They soon came across the chasm with little difficulty.

The Glider eyed Logan before slipping closer to Kiff. "This young one has more affinity to me. He will carry you across."

Thinking back to Kiff's possession by an unruly Breaker, Logan was wary of trusting the Glider. While this Forerunner had the intellect, he was still skeptical of its intent. Logan tensed. "You won't hurt him?"

"Not in the least. I will help the two of you and maybe later, if our paths cross, you will assist me." The Glider moved in front of his brother.

"Wait, how can you go from being some animal spirit to a free-thinking creature so quickly? I don't understand."

The Forerunner smiled, revealing flat grinding teeth. *Thank goodness, it's a plant eater.* That settled Logan a little.

The Glider's wings flapped slowly back and forth, stirring up the mist around it. "My people have an ancestral memory. Mine was suppressed while I was topside. In my sleep, I sometimes caught snatches of my former life, but always my more instinctual side took hold when I awakened."

His memories had been rerouted. Logan thought of how data could still be inherent in tech, but sealed off from access through firewalls or other security protocols. "So the spores rebooted you?"

"I know that I am myself once again with access to my life before."

Kiff asked the next question, "How old are you?"

"Our lifespans are measured in hundreds of years. I was here before the blue mist that some of your people saw fit to blanket the world with."

Logan was happy he had qualified his comment with the word *some*.

"But my people can't tap into any ancient memories," Logan said. "They have no idea what to do with your kind."

He realized that was only partially true. There were records in the city, files that had been hidden away that contained pieces of the past. They hadn't been enough for him to paint a complete picture of past events, but Abe had supplied the rest.

"Then much work will be required of all of us to share in the knowing. Once something is learned, it is hard to stop it from taking root and growing." The Glider's eyes were warm and radiated a sense of calm. "Our hope lies in how easily new ideas can be introduced and cultivated. Change will spread much like the spores do."

The Forerunners, at least this one, were incredibly optimistic. Maybe it was being so close to one reveling in its rebirth, or the numerous experiences he had endured above and below ground, but Logan shared in the hopefulness. He wanted to see the world brought back together. Both above and below had been fractured for too long.

Kiff said, "When a puzzle breaks apart, you have to find all the pieces and put them back together."

Logan looked at his brother, surprised at his insight.

The Glider slipped into Kiff, allowing his wings and the pointed tip of his head to stick out of the small boy. Kiff giggled and waved at Logan. "Time to fly."

His little brother squeezed him tight with his small arms around his midsection, while the long, slender arms of the Glider emerged from Kiff's waist to also tighten around Logan's lower half. He faced forward, affording him a better view than when he'd had to stare awkwardly at Kyle's chin earlier.

Having Logan snugly tucked in, Kiff flapped the wings and crowed, "It's amazing! I can feel him in my head. He's showing me how to fly. The wings aren't really needed except to steer. Gliders float."

They lifted off the ground and swept across the chasm with ease. There was very little to see of the cave floor as the waist-high mist filled nearly all of the chamber. The Glider allowed Kiff to take one circle around this half of the small chamber before depositing them both on a large, moss-covered rock. It disengaged from Kiff, who looked at the separated Forerunner as if he had to let go of a fond pet.

Kiff said, "Thank you, Glider."

"Langune is my name."

"Well, thank you, Langune," Logan said.

"Where will you go now?" Kiff asked, staring up at Langune in sheer fascination.

The Forerunner, looking solid now, nodded to the ceiling. "Above."

Logan put a hand out. "Not yet. Wait a little. Kyle and I have to shut down the inhibitors. Going topside now won't be good for you."

Langune nodded slowly. "I will bide my time." The Glider took off and disappeared in the mist, the moist air swirling about to fill in where the flying creature had just been.

Would Langune wait a day or a week? Logan hoped the latter, just to be on the safe side.

"Where to now, Kiff?" Logan said.

His brother slid down off the rock. "There's another tunnel somewhere over here. Just have to find it."

Logan skidded off the rock and hastened after his brother. They continued through the mist, eventually coming across the exit. Above, dagger-like stalactites hung from the ceiling. *A good thing Kiff hadn't glided into any of them.*

They traveled through the tunnel, the grooves and ridges along the walls revealing it had been gouged out by Breakers. If they encountered the Guardian or his Hunters in this narrow tunnel, how would Logan fight back? Many of the weapons he'd brought with him could all produce cave-ins. Maybe he could get away with firing off his tremble gun on a low setting, but against Hunters, would that even slow them down? And no telling the powers the Guardian had at his disposal.

Kiff sprinted ahead, toward the recognizable blue glow of a colony of the light-bringing yellow mushrooms. They entered a small cavern covered in these toadstools, a healthy amount gathered at the center of the ceiling, hanging down in clusters and reminding him of the overwrought chandeliers in the mayor's office.

Logan grabbed his brother by the wrist and said, "Kiff, we have to go forward with caution. No telling if anyone's set up an ambush for us. If they're tethered and not using tech, I won't be able to sense them ahead of time." He sent his mind forward, encountered no signs of tech.

Kiff tensed. "Okay."

Realizing his firm demeanor frightened his brother, he jokingly said, "You'll have to use your dimples to get me in good with Nomi when we get back."

Kiff grinned and pulled him forward, once again, brimming with exploratory enthusiasm.

Chapter 36
Kyle

Wary of running into clackers, Kyle gently pushed past his brother and led the way out of the tunnel into a cavern. Although he stepped in front of the dazzling beam from Byron's chest lamp and cast long shadows, there appeared to be some natural illumination all around—numerous ten-foot-wide shafts of daylight pouring through the low ceiling.

The last time he'd been aboveground had been back at the Well, and it had been dark. The middle of the night? Early morning just before sunrise? He had no idea. Add an hour of chitchat and then seven hours of monotonous walking, right now it couldn't be later than mid-afternoon.

"Switch your lamp off," he told Byron.

The boys moved slowly now, edging out into the cavern until they could see they were alone. The vast space widened to at least three hundred feet and stretched into the distance as far as he could see. The floor was mostly flat, the ceiling only seven feet high and seemingly supported by dozens of lumpy columns where stalagmites had risen to join with stalactites.

The shafts of light fascinated Kyle. "Are those clacker holes?" he said, walking over to the nearest and peering up. The ten-foot-wide tunnel was angled at about forty-five degrees and cut through at least sixty or seventy feet of solid rock over their heads. "We're pretty close to the surface here. But no, these can't be clacker tunnels. Clackers can blast their way through rocks if they need to, but they wouldn't go to this amount of trouble. And these tunnels are much wider than clackers. A Digger must have made these."

"Well, maybe clackers use them because they're an easy way to get underground," Byron said.

Kyle had to agree. Canyon clackers were half the size of Diggers and typically moved about near the surface during rain when the soil was moist. This region seemed to be all rock, and they surely wouldn't pass up ready-built entryways to the underground.

"I'm going to take a look," Kyle said, wondering how to climb up into the shaft in the ceiling. Clackers, with the girth of ordinary passenger cars and probably a bit longer, could easily reach up and climb with their horrible, muscled, wormlike bodies. Before he went clambering up any tunnels, though, he looked inward at his Weaver and said, "You need to step out for a moment. You won't desert me, will you?"

His Weaver grunted noncommittally.

"I just want to take a look. I'll be right back. Stick around, okay?" He hardened his voice a little. "Remember you're still tethered to me."

At his command, the Weaver eased out of his body and stood there looking lost. Tall and slim with taut, muscular arms and surprisingly nimble fingers, it moved slowly away as if unsteady on its legs. The strange tethering strand quickly stretched, barely perceptible, more of an unspoken rule than an actual limitation. Kyle hoped he hadn't just given up his last spirit for good. He *really* needed to deactivate the inhibitor in the bunker.

He turned back to the open shaft overhead. "Give me a boost," he told Byron.

"Why not just use that tunnel over there?" Byron suggested, pointing to one that emerged from a distant cavern wall to their right. It looked far easier to traverse.

They hurried over to it. Byron hung back as Kyle began the steep climb. Somehow, his orbs looked mournful. "Yes, I know," Kyle said, "you need to stay below as well."

Byron had never stepped into the wastelands before, certainly not beyond the ridge near the city. The enclaves' tech inhibitor would shut him down, and with not an ounce of residual power, his cranial monitors would switch off. If they failed to reboot, his brain would die. Luckily, Byron wasn't as blissfully reckless as Kiff and knew the danger all too well.

"I won't be long," Kyle added. "Just keep your sensors peeled for clackers."

He began his climb up the steep slope, finding plenty of ridges to grab hold of. Above, the circle of daylight beckoned. At last he reached the top and stuck his head out into bright sunlight.

There, he gaped at a stunning view—the city of Apparati in the west, exactly how Kyle remembered it but only just visible, with the distant horizon visible through the transparent buildings. *It's phasing in*, Kyle thought with excitement. Like a city made of glass, it struck an eerie chord as though inhabited by ghosts. Kyle imagined thousands of people milling about in the streets in absolute silence, blissfully ignorant of their insubstantial state.

Kyle scanned the barren wastelands that lay in front of the city. He saw clusters of old buildings here and there, many of the closer ones strangely dark and real compared to the ethereal city beyond, slightly more phased in. The jagged tech ridge, endless vehicles and small machines that had shut down at the inhibitor's outer reaches, stretched from north to south, parallel to the thirty-foot Wall where the wastelands ended and the city began.

A low, rumbling sound brought his attention to the foreground. A dreaded canyon clacker reared up some five hundred feet away just where he'd been focused on the city beyond. Lying still, it had blended with some of the rocks around it. Now it was plain to see. Kyle hurriedly ducked down into his sloping tunnel, then peered out again to watch.

The wormlike creature, a loathsome thing as thick around the middle as a car but maybe twice the length, lurched forward using endless muscles along its flanks. Before Kyle could get a better look, it dipped its head into the ground and began to slide down into it. It had to be using an existing Digger shaft similar to the one Kyle hunkered in, sixty or seventy feet of displaced rock.

Dismayed, Kyle realized the clacker was descending into the cavern below right between him and his destination.

"Great," he mumbled.

Chapter 37

Logan

Logan found Kiff waiting by a large fissure in the wall to their left. His little brother cast his bright breath at the opening and said, "I saw some bugs crawling into that. Looks like they're gone now."

Logan glanced around the tunnel, seeing no evidence of insects.

They continued through the narrow tunnels. Kiff could stand, but Logan had to crawl on all-fours at times. The journey was much more up and down than his trek from the city to the Seeker settlement. Their progress was made even trickier by the green and spongy mosslike growths covering the floor and a good portion of the walls. Logan slid on his rump several times. Kiff did too, but he enjoyed the slick form of travel more.

Eventually, the passage widened and the moss thinned out, so that they were both able to walk relatively upright.

Kiff blasted out a large glowing cloud. "I think up ahead is where Grib and his men sent me after you. You think they're still down here?"

"Probably." Logan stepped in front of his brother. "Let me go first." He scanned for any tech and was surprised to encounter a good deal. Thankfully, no weapons.

He registered a large vehicle, a driller, and a system of hanging lights. He probed further and latched onto a large access door and a train that differed from the maglev back in Apparati.

Kiff elbowed him gently in the side to get his attention and said, "I hear something." He nodded in the direction of the tech.

Logan whispered, "Like what?"

"Voices, I think." Kiff held his breath.

Someone waited for them around the next bend. Since he could detect the driller, it had to be within a hundred feet. The train was harder to pick up on. *Shielded by the metal walls of the tunnel*, Logan realized.

"Well, they aren't carrying any tech," Logan whispered.

Since the cavern ahead would be larger than the tunnel they were in now, he drew his tremble gun and set it to medium power. He could risk using it. The breach wand was great for disrupting force fields but not much else. He had grabbed it thinking it might be effective against the inhibitor. Against a squad of Hunters, it wouldn't help. That left the grenades and the sonic scrambler. They would be weapons of last resort.

Logan indicated for Kiff to hang back. "Stay until I come for you."

He nodded, his wide eyes filled with fear.

If the squad of Hunters had brought in reinforcements and one of them was a Creeper, no amount of stealth on Logan's part would matter. He'd be spotted right away.

He padded forward on the balls of his feet, disturbing very little of the loose gravel. He peered around a rough abutment of rock to see that the tunnel spilled into a large chamber.

A square, metal-walled building stood on the far side next to a long, octagonal structure some twelve feet high that disappeared into the cavern wall.

Logan fiddled around in the building's systems, skimming through maintenance tutorials and protocols to find that it was a boarding station adjoining a vac-train tunnel. The place still had power and was fully functioning. A recent diagnostics test reported a breach, though. The hole in the wall that Kyle and his Breakers had made?

Logan brought to life several dormant cameras and panned around inside the small building. He saw a pair of sliding glass doors used for boarding the train, and a smaller door that seemed to be a service hatch leading into the metal-walled train tunnel itself. The log showed that it had been opened recently. Kyle must have arrived that way.

He couldn't detect much beyond that but assumed there would be plenty of tech running along the train conduit.

The metal of the station's exterior reflected the harsh light from a makeshift campfire nearby. The driller, a good distance from the fire and shrouded in darkness, sat parked about thirty feet from the hole it had obviously drilled.

Four Hunters, their spirits drifting in and out of their bodies at their shoulders, stood around the fire, eating durgle.

Logan exhaled softly. The spores lit up but were not as prevalent this far from the Well. Had the Forerunners here gained any of their former intelligence? He more closely examined the spirits, searching for signs they were remaining solid for any period of time. The one submerged in the tallest Hunter, who he recognized as Grib Lottle, flashed solid once or twice, but it could be a trick of the flickering fire. He didn't know the others. Perhaps they had been deployed from the Hunter Enclave.

The shortest, a red-bearded man who seemed to like letting the upturned horn of his Hunter emerge quite often, barked at the others, "I don't like being down here. My spirit is acting up."

Grib chewed on his durgle leg. Before he spoke, his spirit completely dropped back within. "Not sure what you mean. I've got total control."

Grib liked to talk about his accomplishments.

From the shorter man's reaction, he'd had his fill of Grib's comments. "Is everyone in your enclave such nattering jergas?"

A Hunter with a slender frame stepped in. "Easy, Rabel, we need to perform our duties. You don't want the Guardian to hear we caused trouble on this mission, do you?"

"Mind yourself, Lantil. I'll speak my piece if I want to," the bearded man said. Rabel looked at the fourth Hunter. "How much longer does Nailor want us to wait it out down here, Trimbor?"

The short stocky man shrugged his shoulders and made a show of swallowing his food.

Definitely the men who had brought Kiff below. Logan tuned out their trivial conversation and studied his surroundings. He and Kiff needed to get by these men with a minimum of trouble.

The tech was operational in just about everything, including the hanging lights. One or two blown lights, but otherwise fine. He could switch them off and disable the vocal activation system with ease, leaving the campfire as the only light source. Not the best distraction given he was facing Hunters, but every advantage counted.

He turned his attention to the driller next. It was impressive that such old tech was still in working order. Being kept out of the elements helped. Despite its exterior being covered in fungus, it would fire up. While he could activate the large drill bit, he'd need to be in the cockpit to have any hope of steering it. Still, the sudden firing up of the spinning metal cone could serve as another diversion.

That left the vac-train. Could he and Kiff race into the station, pile into the train, and zoom out of harm's way? He spent a few minutes exploring the air evac system, the door access rigging, and the basic mechanics of the train itself. The glass doors he could cycle open with little problem. The amount of time required to empty the tunnel of air, if it could even be emptied with the breach Kyle had mentioned, and get the train up and running seemed too long. It would give the Hunters plenty of opportunity to hack away at the train. Their spirits would shatter the front windows with a little determination. While not as destructive as Breakers, Hunters still packed a punch. And while he was uncertain of the exact thickness of the window glass in the train, he wasn't willing to risk it.

The sudden shifting of gravel behind him pulled Logan immediately out of the tech. He spun around and glared at Kiff.

His brother smiled sheepishly. "Sorry, I got worried."

Logan nodded and silently pointed at the Hunters.

Kiff whispered, "This is where they brought me in. Grib wasn't very nice." He glared at the Fixer Enclave native.

Logan moved the two of them farther back in the tunnel. He kneeled and whispered, "Here's what we're going to do."

* * *

Logan stepped into the chamber and barked at the Hunters, "Nobody move!" He switched off the lights, placing an impeder loop in the light system's simplistic program so the Hunters couldn't just trigger them back via voice command.

The guards froze, except for Grib who started toward him.

Grib said, "Look who's come back. Little Kiff and his brother."

Even in the dim light, Logan could tell Grib didn't recognize him, that the man thought he was Kyle.

Logan said, "Back off! Stop!" He aimed his tremble gun at the approaching Grib while he snaked his mind into the driller's mainframe and worked on getting the drill bit spinning at maximum speed. After stuttering and blowing out dust and truggle rat nests, it roared to life.

The second the driller flared into action, he shot Grib.

Rabel spotted Logan and raced toward him, his Hunter projecting several feet in advance of him, spite painted all over its transparent face. He yelled, "Lights! Lights!"

Logan relished the man's frustrated look at no longer having added light at his beck and call. He grabbed Kiff's hand, and they ran toward the station door.

He fired at the rapidly approaching Hunter and missed. The other two, Lantil and Trimbor, were easing the convulsing Grib to the ground.

Rabel snapped at his fellow guards, "Leave him! Get over here and flank them!"

With the size of the cavern, Logan risked tossing a grenade. Only he did it a good number of yards in front of the twitching Grib and the two men scrambling to their feet. He didn't want blood on his hands.

The grenade exploded, showering the men in dirt and rock. They cowered briefly, but, after checking they were both still intact, they sprinted toward Logan.

"Get to the station, Kiff!" he shouted.

His brother veered right and bolted toward the open door, keeping close to the cavern walls.

Rabel, his spirit eagerly extending itself a few feet ahead, hurled himself at Logan.

He ducked and jammed his tremble gun up and fired, missing both the spirit and its host. The aggressive Hunter skittered to a stop and lunged at Logan again. This time, he tackled him, driving Logan's right shoulder hard into the ground.

The tremble gun fell out of his hand, and he scrambled to slide free.

The man's spirit emerged and wrapped its arms around Logan.

Logan managed to pull his left arm free and snatched the breach wand from his belt. Doubting it would have any effect, he activated it and plunged it deep into the Hunter's ethereal head.

The cavern was soaked in a brilliant orange flash, and Logan felt the bearded man and his Hunter fly into the air. They landed almost ten feet away. Rabel scrambled to his feet and stared at his spirit, which had been separated from his body thanks to the wand.

Logan also stared at the spirit, mystified that tech would have any effect on it.

The freed Hunter shuddered and grew solid. It twitched about, a stunned expression at its new mobility playing across its contorted face.

Rabel moved toward it. He reached his arms outward and said, “Get in!”

The Hunter cocked its head and then rushed past its former host, knocking him over.

Lantil and Trimbor, the two Logan had tried to contain with the grenade, watched the drama unfold as the spiritless man charged after his divorced Hunter.

The Hunter, now a fully fleshed Forerunner, easily evaded Rabel. Crouching on all fours, it opened its mouth. “No more. Cruelty flows within. I will not tether to you again.”

The men stared at the spirit in surprise. Even Grib, despite shaking and rolling all over the ground, craned his head toward the freed spirit and gawked.

“What’s going on?” Rabel shouted.

The corporeal Hunter bounded toward the tunnel leading to the Well. Did it sense it owed its new intact status to whatever lay in that direction? Logan was unsure if the Forerunners could be that sensitive to the spores and the Well, but maybe they could.

Grib stood, trembling.

Rabel yelled, “Help me grab it!”

Lantil came running. When he arrived at the tunnel entrance, Logan saw the man’s breath light up the spores all around him. The Hunter within Lantil pulled free and escaped down the same tunnel. It didn’t linger to show off its new form.

Logan tore off to join Kiff.

His brother hovered in the open station door, waving at him furiously. “Hurry, Logan!”

Logan ducked inside the station and yanked Kiff along with him, racing at full speed. He shouted, “Lights!” The station lit up. He cycled open the smaller service door on the opposite wall and motioned for Kiff to enter the train tunnel. "Time to go."

Grib, now inside the station and barrelling toward them, yelled, "Stop!"

The other man with his Hunter still tethered, Trimbor, entered the station.

Logan vaulted through the doorway and landed awkwardly. He steadied himself and tore off after Kiff. The Hunters were going to make it in, he thought as he ordered the service door to close and locked it tight. What little light that had encroached into the tunnel from the station winked out as the door hissed shut. He didn't have another plan in mind. He'd be lucky to use the wand a second time if one of them got close enough for hand-to-hand combat.

Red lights had flickered on farther along the tunnel, but the first fifty feet or so remained dark. *Worn circuits*, he thought absently. *Nothing I can do about that.* Kiff was well into the lit area.

Logan approached the start of the red running lights. Inside the vac-tunnel, his breath triggered very few spores. Probably because the service door hadn't been opened much if at all in the last couple hundred years. He was thankful for the lights. While not bright, they would help them find their way. That was, of course, if there were no other sections that were out.

Heavy footfalls rang out behind him, cutting through the silence. Someone had made it in. At the same time, he heard a second person slam into the service door from outside. He accelerated toward his brother.

Should I turn off the running lights?

Kiff wheezed ahead of him, his pace rapidly declining. Logan caught up and said, "We have to keep moving." He looked at the shiny metal walls lining the vac-tunnel. Could he employ the sonic scrambler safely in here? *Maybe.*

His brother stumbled and caught his right knee against the single alignment rail. Logan stopped to lift him back up.

Kiff howled in pain at being jerked to his feet. He favored the injured knee and sent Logan a sad look. "I'm sorry. It hurts."

Logan slid his arm under Kiff's and propped him up so very little weight would fall on the knee. "We have to keep going. Find somewhere to hide."

He glanced ahead. In the dim red light of the running lights, he saw no such place, just endless metal panels almost seamlessly joined together every thirty feet or so. Any second now, their pursuers would be all over them.

Suddenly, a furious yell echoed from behind them. Logan shoved his brother out of the way just as Grib came hurtling out of the darkness and pounced. Logan went down hard.

The man drove his fists into Logan's face, each blow more severe because of the added power of his Hunter being channeled into the attack.

Logan lost consciousness.

Chapter 38
Kyle

Kyle hurried back down the tunnel to where Byron waited. "Trouble," he said, panting as he looked toward the cavern ahead. "Saw a clacker come down here."

He saw no sign of the giant worm, but much of the place was shrouded in darkness at the far western end. There could be a dozen of them waiting in the shadows for all he knew. But right now he was safe, at least five hundred feet away.

Remembering his Weaver, he turned about and found the spirit standing nearby on firm footing, already losing its glow and becoming more solid. "To me?" he said, unsure if he would still be able to tether with it.

To his surprise, the Weaver strode toward him with its head tilted to one side, its eyes larger than Kyle's palms and darker than night. "You still require my service?" it whispered.

Kyle jumped. The voice had been low and rumbling, reverberating deep in its throat. More to the point, it had *spoken aloud*. "Uh, yeah, if you, uh . . ."

The Weaver eased closer, looming over Kyle and suddenly seeming much more solid than it had a few seconds before. Its green aura was almost gone, though its yellowish-brown skin had taken on an oddly luminescent quality of its own. Having been a spirit for so long, naturally it was naked, an issue that hadn't even occurred to Kyle until now. He was used to them being ethereal and glowing, a little fuzzy around the edges. Now he faced a real, live, flesh-and-blood creature.

This particular Forerunner looked like a very tall, slim man with bulky shoulders and arms but unusually long fingers, ugly folds of skin all over, and an entirely inhuman face with dark eyes and a small, lipless mouth. Despite its ugly appearance, there was something gentle and graceful about this race of builders and creators.

"Know that I'm no longer beholden to you," it said. "I agree to this continued tethering because my kind are loyal." It frowned. "And because there's something compelling about you that piques my curiosity and encourages me to linger."

Kyle nodded. "So you're still with me, then?"

"For now."

Checking for clackers, Kyle saw and heard nothing. Satisfied, he returned his attention to the Weaver. "And do you have a name?"

The Weaver frowned deeply, adding to the wrinkles on its forehead. "My past is unclear. I recall the smell of the underground and have vague memories of some of the places we've journeyed the past day or so, but it feels like a distant dream. I've been aboveground too long. My mind is addled."

"How *did* you end up aboveground?" Kyle asked.

"The lure of freedom was strong. It always has been. In the early days, when the sporecore was blocked, it's said that our people rose to the surface and enjoyed a full day of glory, standing firm under the sun and the moons and feeling the wind and rain on their faces. Unfortunately, without spores in their lungs, they quickly became phantoms, their faculties deserting them. They became lost, seeking out solid forms to tether with so that they might feel whole again. This went on until the city installed the inhibitor, and then all those lost spirits were flung violently to the east."

"But the ones who stayed underground . . ."

The Weaver held up its strong hands and flexed its slender fingers. "Surrounded by spores, they remained normal. I have been on the surface most of my life, and I'm old . . . and yet even now my mind is sharpening, my body strengthening. I feel whole after just one day underground."

Kyle glanced at Byron, but his brother's glowing orbs gave no hint of expression. He returned his attention to the Weaver and said, "So with the Well unblocked and the spores in the atmosphere again, you should be able to walk on the surface like a normal person, right?"

"Correct."

"Except for the inhibitor?"

The Weaver dipped his head in agreement.

"But it's a *spirit* inhibitor," Kyle said. "Sorry, I'm just trying to work this through. The inhibitor repels your *spirit* forms, not your solid forms, so surely that means—"

"It repels both our forms indiscriminately."

Kyle tried to imagine a solid Weaver being whisked through the air, repelled by the inhibitor and flung east all the way to the river. The Fixer and Skimmer had been yanked from his body and tossed like leaves in a gale.

The Weaver spoke softly. "I would not fly through the air the way my brethren did. It would be much more painful for me now, probably fatal. The spell is powerful no matter what our form."

Now Kyle tried to imagine the solid Weaver bouncing and scraping across the land at great speed, getting torn to shreds on whatever bushes and old buildings stood in the way, possibly being flattened against unyielding walls . . .

"Okay, I get it," he said with a sigh. "The inhibitor's still a major problem. Both of them are." He sighed. "Look, is there something I can call you? A temporary name while you try to remember it?"

The Weaver shook its head. "My name will return to me in due course. Until then, please do not confuse my already muddled thoughts."

"Fine. Do you, uh . . . want my shirt or anything?"

The Weaver frowned. "Excuse me?"

Kyle gestured. "To cover yourself."

"Why?"

The Forerunner looked so perplexed that Kyle rolled his eyes and said, "Look, if I ever disable that inhibitor, you won't get to walk around like that in the city. Trust me."

The Weaver's mouth stretched into a smile. "If I find a suitable grubberming to peel, I will wrap it around myself."

"Good. Okay, stay with me, Weaver. I think there are clackers ahead."

Kyle brushed past and headed off across the cavern, wary for signs of movement in the darkness at the far end. Byron's servos started hissing as he hurried to keep up. Casting a quick glance over his shoulder, Kyle saw the Weaver lurching along behind.

So much for my spectacular tethering powers, he thought. *It's following me because it wants to, not because I'm ordering it around. It's a person now, not a thing.*

And with that, he realized the Weaver was a "he" rather than an "it."

When Apparatum was fully back in sync and all the spirits were solid, flesh-and-blood creatures, Kyle knew he wouldn't have as much power over them as he had before. They wouldn't need him. On the other hand, he'd forcibly tethered with a Digger, something very few could do. The solid-form Forerunners might not desire tethering the way spirits did, but Kyle could probably wield great power over them if he tried.

Then again, why would he? In solid form, most of the Forerunners were intelligent *people*, not mindless animals. And if they had no desire to tether, who was he to force them even if he could? In a funny way, reopening the Well had diminished his standout tethering power and rendered him normal.

Only because I'm a good guy, he thought.

That was the big difference. He would always have more tethering power than any other. Unlike some people, he would not abuse that power.

Shafts of light from numerous Digger tunnels lit their way across the cavern, but eventually they petered out. The rocky columns grew thicker and more plentiful, further darkening their route. In the fading light, Byron switched on his chest lamp.

Kyle immediately batted at him. "Turn it off!" he whispered.

"But then we won't see the clackers leaping out at us."

"They don't leap. They screech and slide." Still, he had to concede the beam of light made him feel better. Plus, now that he thought about it, clackers didn't have eyes anyway. They hunted by scent and sound; they would be aware of approaching travelers regardless of Byron's dazzling lamp. "Keep your noise down, then," he warned.

Only then did Byron's servos suddenly seem very loud, echoing around the cavern as they picked their way across the smooth, rocky floor.

They were by now close to the cavern's end. An exit tunnel awaited them somewhere in the shadows, but it was impossible to see. Perhaps when they got close enough for Byron's lamp to penetrate the gloom, then they'd be able to—

An earsplitting screech halted them in their tracks. Kyle paused with Byron and the Weaver as a canyon clacker lurched out of the shadows just thirty feet ahead.

With another screech, it slid halfway into the subdued light. Clackers were ugly things with huge open mouths that dripped thick, stringy saliva. This one paused, sniffing the air and fixing on what it probably saw as intruders in its den.

Kyle thought he'd been ready to face them again, but now he recalled his first encounter in the rain on his way across the wastelands. He had barely escaped with his life.

He turned and pushed Byron and the Weaver behind the nearest thick, lumpy column. About as wide as his waist, it barely concealed the three of them. "We need to—" he began.

The clacker let out a piercing screech, and the column promptly shattered, sending chunks flying in all directions and pummeling Kyle as he turned away and threw himself down. He heard bits *ping* and *clang* off Byron's body, but the boy quickly ducked and laid himself out flat. The Weaver spread himself on the rocky floor also, grunting in surprise.

The sonic blast faded with the last of the debris shower.

"Stay here until I call you," the Weaver hissed, and without waiting for an answer began to shuffle across the floor on all-fours.

The clacker again let out a shriek while advancing another half-dozen feet, its entire body rippling and pulsing as muscles pushed it along in a way Kyle found repulsive. This shriek was different than the last one, merely a warning rather than a sonic blast. Kyle clapped his hand to his ears.

If Byron was frightened, his robot body failed to show it. Maybe his brain was quivering with fear inside its cranial casing, but externally he just lay quite still on his metal belly with his head turned toward Kyle and his orbs glowing brightly.

"Can you throw that noise back at it?" Kyle asked him.

The tiniest flicker in his eyes suggested he understood. As the clacker rumbled incessantly, Byron twisted around and directed his face toward it. From his chrome-lined mouth came a playback of the clacker's sonic blast, and it hurt Kyle's ears. Yet the recording wasn't nearly loud enough to do any damage.

It surprised the clacker, though. The creature jerked backward and swung its ugly head from side to side, grunting and moaning. It kept on doing this for several minutes.

Kyle shook his head in disgust. "There's no way we're getting past it. Typical! I'll bet Abe and Makow and all the others pass this way all the time and hardly ever have any clacker trouble."

The Weaver let out a shout, and the clacker swiftly looked his way. *Except they don't have eyes*, Kyle remembered. *It's not looking, just sniffing the air.*

The clacker lunged a dozen feet, emerging completely from the shadows to where the Weaver was jumping about, obviously trying to draw the monster toward him.

But to what end?

Chapter 39
Logan

Water slapped Logan in the face, rousing him quickly. From the corner of his eye, he saw Grib standing over him, swinging back a canteen to deliver another dousing.

Logan shook his head and reached up to block the next deluge. "I'm awake."

The Hunter froze then sneered at him. "No weird stuff out of you." He pointed at Kiff who sported a bruise on his right cheek, evidence that Grib played rough. "He told me what you can do with *tech*." He said the last word with fear and uncertainty.

Logan sat up. They were back at the service entrance to the station. It was torn open, allowing light to stream into the dark tunnel. Most likely the Hunters had destroyed the door while he was unconscious.

The man smirked and kicked free a twisted section of the door still lodged in its frame. "We did that. You didn't. Flimsy door didn't stand a chance. You should've closed the other one on us. It's much stronger."

Grib squatted on his haunches and drew up close to Logan, his Hunter's muzzle poking out and almost touching Logan's forehead. "Why'd they lose their spirits? Did Kyle take them?"

The Hunter thought Kyle was nearby, yanking spirits out of their hosts. He almost wanted to lie and say it was true. That would unsettle the man even more.

"No, he's going back to the city. He's needed there."

"And you came crawling back with your brother, huh? You think Durant will let you return from exile just because you can make some machines work?"

Logan didn't answer.

The Hunter exhaled, igniting a few spores. He looked at the glowing vapor. "Why does our breath glow?"

Logan said, "The spores in the tunnel. They're getting in, even this far from the Well."

Grib crossed his arms and shot him a skeptical look. "So all they do is make your breath brighten up a room?"

"They also make your spirits solid and make them smart again. The spirits are called Forerunners, and our people used to live alongside them and not just jerk them around to do our bidding." Logan didn't know why he was dumping all this info on the Hunter. Maybe practice for when he really had to reveal all to the rest of the enclaves. Or maybe he wanted to overwhelm Grib, making it more likely the man would lower his guard, and they could escape.

Grib scoffed. "Nonsense. I'll get you to a Skimmer, and we'll find out what's true and what's utter gibberish." He glared at Kiff, who drew back from him.

"Leave my brother out of this. I'm just bringing him back home after you tossed him into this dangerous place to track me down."

Grib wagged a finger. "Actually, we were after the other one, but you'll have to do." He pulled a small black tool from his pocket. "What did you do with the tracker Nailor put on him?" He pointed at Kiff.

"I dealt with it." Logan glared at Grib. Did the man know the device had contained explosives?

Grib shrugged and tossed the useless tool on the ground. "Knew Nailor was putting too much faith in his little gadgets." He looked at the station door and then at Kiff, raising his hand as if intending to deliver a backhand to anyone nearby. Not an idle threat from how his brother cowered. "Now get up and walk. We're breaking camp and heading home." He pointed to Logan's weapons stacked off to the side, well out of reach. "You do anything with that and you're looking at a spear through the gut."

Logan stood and entered the station.

The three other Hunters, two still missing their spirits, stood in the station, eyeing Logan with apprehension. Grib addressed them, grandly updating them on what he had accomplished alone. Logan detested how hard the man sold himself. Rabel rolled his eyes when Grib wasn't looking, clearly annoyed at his boasting.

Logan and Kiff needed to ditch these men.

Grib turned his attention to Logan again. "We just have to scavenge some tech from that driller. Nailor wants to bring back gifts for the Guardian. Not your weapons, though. They stay here. No sense toting them along and letting you get close to them." Logan noted his spirit was restless and pulled itself out of the man's body with more rebellion than before. It wouldn't be long before he lost it. The sporecore must be really pumping out the spores. And with the driller hole letting in a healthy amount of spores, it made sense these men were suddenly facing their spirits breaking free.

Unnerved by his stirring spirit, Grib barked orders at the men. As he roughly pushed Kiff and Logan through the station and out to the cavern, his men took Logan's weapons and, swinging as wide away from him as they could, marched toward the driller. Grib deliberately shoved Kiff far from the flames, a show of unnecessary force for Logan's benefit, and then turned to glower at Logan. At least Kiff's knee no longer appeared to be bothering him.

Kiff looked on the verge of tears. His head slumped.

Logan had to get them out of here. But what could he do?

Trimbor, Lantil, and Rabel dumped Logan's weapons well away from the fire, at the edge of the darkness. Smart thinking to move them to where they thought was out of range. Holding torches, they trekked over to the driller. Trimbor and Lantil disappeared inside the machine to retrieve the Guardian's tech offerings. Logan wondered what they could possibly think was fitting tribute for the Guardian. Just yanking off parts and incomplete systems from the driller made little sense to him. He almost felt sorry for the machine, being cannibalized by such ignorant people. Rabel had his back turned to them, waiting for his colleagues to toss down whatever tech they managed to rip loose. He had to act now, but a plan had still not formed in his head.

Grib hung close to Logan. Unattended, Kiff began to crawl toward the fire.

". . . can't stomach being underground," Grib was saying. "If the Guardian didn't want us here, there's no way I'd be slumming it in this place." He eyed the station nervously. "Tech isn't natural. Nailor's going to owe me . . ."

Kiff kept low, sliding forward on his belly as if he were tethered to a Creeper. The fire was only feet away from him now.

Grib said, "You're as much trouble as your father."

Behind the loud man, Kiff skirted around the fire, eyeing a small pile of gathered wood off to the side.

What was he doing?

The boy shot a look at the other three Hunters occupied at the far end of the cavern, detectable in the darkness thanks to the torches they held, and slipped his hand around the end of a piece of wood. He poked it into the fire, which sputtered to life.

Luckily, Grib didn't notice.

Kiff held it in the flames for what felt like an excruciatingly long time, all the while keeping his eyes locked on Grib's back.

The man was still talking. ". . . waltzing around the enclave with the biggest Breaker and demanding respect . . ."

Logan's father wasn't like that at all. What a warped view of the world this man had.

Kiff had succeeded in lighting the end of his crude torch and was rising slowly. Logan wanted to wring the man's neck but decided letting him rant would keep him distracted.

"... And then you come along with your twin and cause even more unrest. I don't like it and neither does the Guardian."

It was a miracle no one by the driller had looked back. But, then again, they could hear Grib's blathering echoing throughout the cavern so they knew there was no trouble as long as he spouted off at the mouth. *Probably don't want to pay him anymore attention than they have to*, Logan thought.

He risked feeding the man's ego. "You've met the Guardian? He's spoken to you?"

The Hunters were almost done with salvaging the driller tech.

"Not directly, but his servant comes to me, gives me critical instructions and duties."

Kiff sprang on Grib, stabbing at him with his torch.

Grib shrieked and rolled to the ground, his tunic on fire.

The Hunter within the man did more than just emerge. It slipped free and blinked in surprise at what had transpired, shocked at its freedom.

Kiff ran toward the station entrance. Logan did the same.

The man continued to roll around in his attempt to extinguish the flames.

The emancipated spirit lingered, watching its host's desperate actions. It stared briefly at Logan and then raced toward the tunnel leading to the Well.

With the flames extinguished, Grib sprang to his feet and pursued the near-tangible spirit.

Logan hovered outside the station doorway so he could keep an eye on the panicstricken Grib. The Hunter valued retrieving his emancipated spirit over corralling Logan and Kiff.

Kiff was already through the station and waving for him to follow. Logan reached his mind out to close the large door leading into the station—the one Grib had taunted him about not sealing shut.

Grib, seeming to realize where his duty rested, abruptly spun about. He shot Logan a deathly look and charged at the station entrance, abandoning his spirit for now. The man wailed, "Stop!"

Logan jumped through the doorway and triggered the door without looking back. It slid shut behind him in a matter of seconds. He futzed with the locking mechanism, adding an impeder and chaos subroutine to make it impossible to open.

Kiff asked, "You think he'll get his spirit back?"

"No way that Hunter will tether with him now." The Forerunner's awakening wouldn't let it be subjugated by the likes of such a cruel man again.

Weaponless, except for Kiff's very non-tech torch, they exited the station through the hopelessly damaged service exit and down the long, empty tunnel.

* * *

They walked for two hours before coming across the breach in the tunnel Kyle had told them to look for. In that time, Logan had tried to satisfy the million questions Kiff had about tech. At least he now knew of one person in the enclaves eager to see the machines reintroduced into their world.

"I need to get you home," Logan said, knowing what Kiff would try to pull next.

Kiff puffed out his chest. "I want to go with you. I can help you stop the Guardian. I helped us escape back there."

Logan admired his verve. His little brother didn't back down from anyone or anything. He smiled and said, "I know you can, but we need to make sure everything is safe topside. What if the Guardian's sent trouble our parents' way? I need you to get to them and make sure they're safe. Can you do that for me?"

Kiff nodded. "I can."

"How far away is the surface?"

Kiff shrugged. "We're close, but there may be more Hunters."

He expelled a breath, igniting very few spores. If the spores hadn't reached the enclaves yet, would he and Kiff be out of sync, no more than spirits to the people up top? Abe had said it would take time for the spores to spread their influence.

He took his brother's torch and crawled through the breach.

I guess we'll find out soon enough.

Chapter 40

Kyle

The enraged clacker opened its mouth and screeched.

The Weaver threw himself sideways, and the ceiling overhead cracked, leaving a precarious hole that might easily crumble apart and bring many more tons of rock crashing down. Undaunted, the Weaver picked himself up and began hopping around again, surprisingly agile considering his age. He hollered at the clacker, clearly trying to provoke another sonic blast.

The next screech brought down the roof with a tremendous racket. Through clouds of dust, the pile of rubble looked like a miniature hill growing up through a void in the ceiling—a void that let in cracks of daylight.

While the clacker continued sniffing at the air and salivating heavily, the dust billowed slowly outward and rolled over Kyle and Byron where they lay flat and still. Kyle couldn't believe how much damage had occurred in the space of a few seconds.

Barely visible in the gloom now, the Weaver dashed about, effortlessly picking up chunks of rock and flinging them into specific positions, though for what reason Kyle couldn't see. The Weaver seemed to be building something, moving fast as though he had done this same thing a thousand times.

A wall, Kyle realized, seeing the low, chest-high structure quickly taking shape. Out of the dust, built among and on top of the rubble, a surprisingly neat wall began to emerge, stretching slowly and steadily toward the shadows at the end of the cavern not too far from where the clacker waited.

The clacker sent another sonic blast, and part of the wall shattered—but the Weaver had already moved on past that spot, and he ignored the damage, continuing his work uninterrupted.

Clearly confused, the clacker swung from side to side, sniffing the air, its mouth wide open. It slid forward and a little to the side until it came upon the wall, where it stopped and sniffed at it before turning away again. Kyle imagined the wall itself held no interest, and perhaps it masked the scent of anyone hiding behind it.

The Weaver wasn't just hiding, though. He was darting back and forth, keeping low, collecting more chunks of rock in his large but nimble hands to continue building his wall. He kept this up while the clacker sniffed around and sent warning shrieks now and again.

Then the Weaver went quiet, apparently done with his job.

In the silence that followed, Kyle became aware of another clacker in the shadows. And another. He sucked in a breath. How had Makow avoided these monsters? Maybe they hadn't been here at the time. Or maybe Makow had simply darted past. Kyle wasn't sure if great haste was a good thing or not where clackers were concerned. They were pretty speedy themselves once they caught a scent.

"This way," Kyle whispered to Byron. "And turn your lamp off."

Byron's chest lamp was pointing directly upward at the cavern ceiling. Kyle knew in his heart that the clackers couldn't see the beam, but at this point he felt safer smothered by shadows. When the lamp winked out, Kyle nodded and steeled himself.

As he started to wriggle across the floor toward the enormous mound of rubble, the clacker jerked its head around and rumbled at him. At that moment, the Weaver must have thrown a rock because one went skittering across the floor, a timely distraction. The clacker jerked again, turning that way.

"Run," Kyle said.

He and Byron got up and sprinted the remaining twenty feet to the rubble. The two hidden clackers screeched briefly from the shadows, but Kyle was already throwing himself down behind the new wall, Byron right behind. They lay still a moment, aware that the first clacker lurked not five feet away on the other side of the makeshift barrier. The stench was terrible, a bit like rotting vegetables.

Amazed at the Weaver's fast work, Kyle began crawling over loose rubble, following the low wall as it curved into the darkness at the far end of the cavern. He passed the shattered section of wall and was, for a few seconds, vulnerable if the clacker happened to see or hear him—but he shuffled safely past and waited for Byron to catch up.

At least he has no scent, Kyle thought with relief.

The wall stretched about fifty feet in all, and Kyle couldn't help marveling at the workmanship for such a hasty, haphazard job, each chunk of rock somehow placed in the perfect position alongside the next, and all bonded together in a way Kyle couldn't fathom. He'd built a wall of his own back at the rock quarry in the Fixer Enclave, and while he could understand the careful placement of pieces, he had no idea how the bonding worked. It was like the rocks melted around the edges and turned to glue, hardening a few seconds later.

The Weaver waited patiently in the darkness, glowing a dull yellowish-brown. The chest-high rocky barrier ended at the cavern wall next to the exit tunnel. Somewhere on the other side of the barrier, two clackers huffed and rumbled, apparently confused that a wall had appeared out of nowhere.

Kyle, Byron, and the Weaver slipped into the dark tunnel and hurried away, leaving the clackers behind. Byron switched on his chest lamp again so they could see.

"We're not safe yet," the Weaver warned. "There might be others ahead."

The idea of running into more clackers within the confines of the tunnel struck Kyle as horrifying. But the Weaver turned out to be right about the danger. They passed what was obviously a crude clacker hole in the ceiling where the creatures had burrowed in at some point in the past.

Luckily, this tunnel was short. The group emerged into what appeared to be a sunken city landscape, hundreds of thin sandstone columns standing tall and proud like high rise apartment blocks corroded by an ocean. Looking all around and upward, he saw a domed ceiling smothered with bioluminescent fungus that gave off an ambient blue light. *I'm underwater*, Kyle thought in amazement. Of course, the three of them weren't really underwater, but the effect was hard to shake, especially since Kyle thought he could hear the dull roar of water in the distance.

He followed the sound of the water. It meant meandering around dozens of the curious sandstone stacks and pausing while Byron shone his lamp on the floor ahead. The light never quite picked out the critters that lived here; they instantly scuttled away, leaving Kyle with the feeling they were toying with him. He heard clicks and taps and occasional warbles.

Something flew by his head, and he yelped and ducked. To his surprise, the Weaver laughed long and deep. "It's just a minquin," he eventually said.

Kyle scowled. "I thought minquins were supposed to be dangerous."

"Only when you walk into their nest. And even then they're a mere nuisance." The Weaver grabbed his arm and pointed ahead. "Don't touch those things in front of you, though. Stinger vines aren't pleasant."

Kyle jerked backward, realizing he'd nearly swept aside some of those long, trailing tendrils that hung from the ceiling. Slightly translucent and glistening, they repulsed him.

"Ah," the Weaver said, suddenly distracted. "Grubbermings."

He strode over to a clump of massive mushrooms and selected one, then carefully dug his fingers into the cap and began to peel back a skinlike layer. He wrapped this twice around his midsection. "Better, young Kyle?" the Forerunner said, deftly securing it.

"Much," Kyle muttered.

The sound of rushing water increased as they moved farther into the dome. The floor seemed to be a mixture of sand and loose dirt with mounds of that sand-colored rock, and Kyle came across a crack about twelve feet long and two feet wide. He peered down, hearing a raging river but seeing very little even with Byron's beam of light.

"Don't fall down there," the Weaver said, "or you'll end up back at the Well where we started. That's the Wiscuppa passing below us."

Byron visibly shuddered. "My joints are getting stiff just thinking about it. I need some oil."

Kyle absently patted his pockets where he normally kept a tiny bottle of high-grade joint lubricant. Of course he didn't have one on him now, not with these foreign enclave clothes.

"We still have a long walk ahead," the Weaver said, frowning heavily. "I remember this place. I remember making this journey and peering down at the river below. We're perhaps halfway to the settlement."

"Halfway!" Kyle exclaimed. He sighed heavily and slumped down on the soft floor. "So what's ahead of us? I'm so fed up with this. Why isn't there a faster way to travel?"

"Faster than what our bodies are equipped with?" The Weaver snorted. "I pity you and your kind, always bemoaning the limits of your being. Have you thought about breaking into a run instead of walking the entire way?"

Kyle's mouth dropped open. "Run? Are you serious? I'm not Makow. I could run for maybe a few minutes, but then I'd need to stop and get my breath back. It takes a lot of training to just run and run without stopping." Remembering how fast the Weaver had moved back in the previous cavern, an idea popped into his head. "What about you? Can you run and run?"

"I can," the Weaver rumbled with pride. "This old body may be out of shape through such a long period of disuse, but I am confident I could, ahem, *run and run* all the way."

Kyle jumped to his feet. "Then can't you carry us or something?"

"*Carry* you?" The Weaver looked at Kyle, then at Byron. "Perhaps one of you. Not both."

"I can keep walking," Byron suggested. "I'm not tired, just a bit squeaky."

Shaking his head, Kyle took a step toward the Weaver. "What if we tether? Will that help?"

The Weaver stood silent and thoughtful. "If I recall, tethering in this solid form is greatly different to tethering in spirit form. I will be much stronger than you. I will be in control of your body rather than simply aiding you. You will become part of *me*."

"Well, whatever," Kyle said. "If it helps us get to the city quicker, I don't mind you being in control. Heck, I'll be happy to fall asleep while you run. C'mon, what do you say?"

Chapter 41
Logan

A few yards into the exit tunnel, Logan came to a very thick wall with an opening he could crawl through. He recognized a Weaver's handiwork. He peered through the six-foot-deep hole and could see another half-demolished wall before the tunnel led to the quarry outside.

Kiff scrambled over the first wall. Logan followed, worming his way through the lengthy hole far slower than his brother. They crept forward, absolutely quiet. Both slipped over the second wall with little trouble.

When Logan stepped out into the quarry proper, he ducked down. Two archers stood at the top of the path that wound down into the quarry, facing in. He slid up against a large rock and motioned Kiff over.

He whispered to his brother, "There are archers posted. I think they saw me."

Kiff shuffled to the edge of the rock and peered around. His head darted back quickly. "I see them, but they're just standing there."

"I know they saw me. Why aren't they coming after us?"

Kiff shrugged. "Well, it is still dark out. Maybe we're too much in shadow down here." He puffed out a breath. Only a trickle of spores lit up.

Logan pointed to the disappearing haze. "So some spores have made it this far."

"What if we just run up and try to pass them?" Kiff said.

"They have arrows, Kiff." He shook his head. "That's not going to work."

There was no tech lying around this time to provide a distraction. Logan picked up a small rock. "Maybe we just try the simple approach." He flung the rock off to the right, deeper into the quarry. It ricocheted off a squat boulder and disappeared behind a makeshift storage shed.

Logan pressed himself against their hiding place and waited to hear the approaching footfalls of the guards, perhaps a shout of warning from one or both of the archers.

None of that happened.

He slipped around to see if he could locate the archers. They ran down the path, their weapons drawn, shouting but making no sound. What was going on?

Kiff said, "Look. They're see-through, like spirits."

It was true. Closer now, he could see they were insubstantial. The archers barreled past their hiding place, paying no attention to Logan and Kiff. *How did they not see us?*

Logan's head hurt. If the archers were spirits, would they in turn see Logan and Kiff as insubstantial, too? Did that mean their arrows would pass safely through their ghostly forms? He wasn't willing to test the theory after flinging a rock just now; the stone-tipped arrow heads would be just as substantial.

Or would they? What if the arrows were more attuned to the ghostly archers than they were to the rocks on the ground? A second glance at the shed told him it was also ghostly, although not as see-through as the arrow. There had to be a strange logic to all this, but it eluded him for now.

"Why didn't they make any noise?" Kiff said. "They were shouting and came thudding past us. I didn't hear any of that. And they looked like spirits."

"And I'm sure that's how we'll look to them."

"Why?"

"Because we're out of sync."

Kiff frowned. "Then that means Mom and Dad can't hear us either."

"But that's a good thing." Logan knew his brother was upset. "Not for Mom and Dad, but if others can't hear us or see us clearly, we can sneak around much easier."

“But when will everything be all put back together?”

“Once more spores come to the enclaves.” He put a reassuring hand on his brother’s shoulder. “And that’ll happen faster than you think. The Well is pumping out spores like mad right now. Maybe a day or two if that.”

The archers disappeared behind the shed. Kiff looked flustered.

Logan knew he needed to keep his little brother moving, his mind occupied, or he would fall apart. He grabbed his hand, thankful it was solid to him. “C’mon, while they can’t see us.”

They ran up the slope and out of the quarry without raising any alarms. Not that he or Kiff could hear any if they were raised.

Once out of the quarry, Logan guided them into the woods, heading toward their home. While it wouldn’t be a perfect reunion, Kiff needed to see their mom and dad.

And Logan realized, with growing urgency, he needed to see them, too.

* * *

Their route took them close to the edge of the woods leading to the Broken Lands. Despite it being late, many people streamed through the forest. All were pale and ethereal, their voices non-existent. It was weird watching their mouths move and hearing no words. Every group they hid from looked excited about what was happening out in the Broken Lands.

Logan knew why they were out at this late hour: the sporecore eruptions. It pleased him to see most were not frightened by the light show. Maybe they sensed that the event was a boon. A part of him wanted to race alongside them, partaking of the wonder.

But he also spotted quite a few Hunters and Creepers. Thankfully, none of the extra-sensitive spirits had detected him or Kiff. One man with a Creeper had crossed right by their hiding place in a thick lyga bush and not been alerted to their presence.

Logan and Kiff trailed one ghostly family as they dashed through the woods, ending up at a secluded rock formation that offered one of the best views of the wastelands. The father, his Fixer spirit hopping about on his shoulders, helped his three children, all too young to tether, onto the large rock. He spoke to them with such animation that Logan wished he could've heard the story he was spinning. The man's eyes were alive with curiosity and wonder and, judging from the wide smiles of his children's faces, his words must've been comforting and hopeful.

Kiff grinned and whispered, "Looks like everybody's happy. They see new magic being born out there, don't they?"

Logan said nothing. Not all were happy at the changes. The Guardian and Durant surely weren't. The public might greet the eruptions as a natural wonder tonight, but the government would soon weigh in on the subject and surely skew it as something to be mistrusted. He decided to spare Kiff his sour outlook.

"You think Mom and Dad might be out here?" Kiff poked his head out of the mess of tall grasses they now lurked in. He scanned the people coming and going.

"Maybe." Logan looked as well. After a minute, he said, "Let's try home first. If they're not there, we'll come back and check again. Dad isn't the type to get out of bed in the middle of night just because there's some extra twinkle to the night sky."

Despite the sheer number of people out and about, they worked their way home without incident, experiencing only one sporecore eruption during their time in the woods. Sadly, neither could see much with the thick canopy blocking out most of the lights. Logan did find it encouraging that their breath seemed to light up more than when they had first fled the quarry.

The streets were mostly empty. Anyone up was at the Broken Lands. The buildings appeared more present than the shed in the quarry. As Logan yanked Kiff down yet another side alley, his brother pulled up short and crossed his arms.

"We have to do something, tell somebody."

"That's not smart." Logan headed down the alley and motioned for Kiff to follow. "C'mon, I bet Mom and Dad are home."

"You need help." His brother reluctantly followed. "What are we going to do at home?"

"I leave you with them while I go back down underground."

Kiff said, "But you should stay. Let's wait until everyone's in phase, and then Dad and some of his friends can come along. Maybe you can even persuade Sovereign Durant to help you."

Logan felt his patience eroding. He couldn't wait around for that. And there was no way Durant would be on his side, at least not based on how he had treated Kyle. "Let's just go see them. They can keep you safe."

"But won't we scare them with how we look?"

Logan slipped across the open market area and past the first three houses. No torches were lit. Kiff bumped into him as he drew to a stop behind a short lyga bush. "We'll explain what's happening. It'll be okay."

"But how?" Kiff's tone was frantic. It had been a long time since one of his panic attacks.

Logan knelt and put his hands on his brother's shoulders. "It's okay. We'll write them a note. Explain everything on it. We can interact with things here. We're not helpless." He plucked a ripe berry from the lyga bush, plopped it in his mouth and bit down on it, allowing the sweet juices to coat his tongue. He made a show of mashing it to a pulp and stuck out his now purple tongue. "See, we have an effect. Taking scrolling pen to parchment will be a breeze."

"Okay," Kiff said softly.

Logan escorted him to the front door. He went to knock, but his hand slipped slightly into the door, making not a sound.

He withdrew it, surprised at the brief stab of pain caused by passing through the structure. No walking through walls for either of them now. The buildings were growing more in sync with every passing minute. He knocked on their front door using a large staunch branch instead. Strange how it worked fine.

It opened, and their mother, pale and ghostly, stared back at them, her eyes widening in surprise. Words spilled out of her mouth, but neither Kiff nor Logan could hear them. It was clear from her shocked expression she saw them as apparitions. Her Fixer hopped about on her shoulder, in near panic mode.

Logan tried to slip inside without running into his mom, but his shoulder passed through her, and they both reacted with more shock. It tingled to slip through her. He didn't want to do that again and risk injury to either of them.

Partly fearing his mother would try to hug him, he needed to communicate the danger of contact to her. He moved quickly into the kitchen and reached for the pen tucked in the large alcove next to the drying stand. His fingers disappeared into the pen and partly into the wooden alcove, the tingling almost a sharper burning sensation this time.

His father entered the kitchen, looking half asleep. When he spotted Logan, his Breaker emerged and swiped aggressively at the air. He tamped the spirit back down and grinned warmly at his long-lost son. He spoke, and surprisingly Logan could faintly hear him. While he couldn't make out the words, speaking louder might do the trick.

He cupped his hands around his mouth and shouted, "Don't panic! We're both okay! Just out of sync. Don't touch us. You might hurt yourself."

Though his parents nodded in understanding, clearly they were straining to hear what he was saying.

His mother's lips moved, her words faint and indecipherable.

He again shouted, "You have to speak up! We're not in the same zone yet, but you can hear me if I yell, right?"

She nodded as Logan stepped aside to let Kiff enter.

His father made a great effort to project his voice. It still came out as a whisper. "What's going on? How are you back, Logan?"

Logan was pleased to see tears forming in his father's eyes. He replied, "We blew up the Tower and unearthed the sporecore. It's the light show you might have seen out in the Broken Lands. The spores in the air are bringing everything back to one reality. The more spores in the air, the less like ghosts we'll be to each other."

He looked at his mother. She appeared more see-through than his father.

Panic played over his father's face. "It's not safe for either of you. The Guardian is looking for you. You must go, hide. If he finds you here, I don't know what he'll do. I'm surprised no one spotted you coming."

"Some people were out, but no one noticed us. They were too caught up in what's happening in the Broken Lands. I didn't see anyone spying on our home." Not that he had been looking. Hopefully, the Guardian hadn't appointed any Creepers to watch their house.

"Still, you need to leave. Go out the back," his father said.

Logan saw the pain in the man's eyes. He shouted, but not as loudly as before, "I'll find someplace safe for Kiff, and then I have to go stop the Guardian and his inhibitor! It's the only way to bring everyone together."

His father looked ready to respond, but their mother held him back. She spoke calmly to him and nodded with confidence toward Logan. She mimed hugging both Logan and Kiff then sent them toward the back door.

Kiff said nothing, attempting to put up a brave front. Logan took one last look at his mother and then guided his brother out the back, trying and failing to ignore Kiff's sobbing.

Chapter 42
Kyle

Tethering to a Forerunner was again a strange experience. When Kyle pressed the palm of his hand to the Weaver's, whatever faint aura still existed within the creature flared slightly and spread up Kyle's arm. At that point, the Weaver moved closer, turning and edging sideways until the two of them were shoulder to shoulder. Then they began to merge.

Linking for the first time with a spirit out in the Broken Lands had been weird enough. It had been even stranger with the Digger, actually sinking down into the creature's flesh. Now Kyle found himself sharing the same space as this man-shaped creature that stood much taller than him. He knew one of them was now slightly out of sync with the other—the tethering process required it—but he had no idea how it happened.

He felt buoyant as though floating in water. He couldn't feel the floor anymore, suspended as he was within the Weaver's larger frame. It seemed he was peering out from the other's chest. When he lifted his hand to find some semblance of himself, he stared at the much larger digits as if they were his own.

He tried a few steps. Apart from a longer stride, all his weariness was gone, and he felt ready to leap around. He did so, whooping with delight at the incredible strength coiled within his legs. "This is nuts!" he yelled. "Okay, I'm ready to run. Can we run? Let's run. Come here, Byron, I'll give you a piggyback ride."

Hoisting his heavy robotic brother onto his back took no effort. Once Byron's arms were securely clamped around the Weaver's neck, he took off at a run, straining to see in the darkness and occasionally bumping into sandstone towers.

The domed cavern gave way to spectacularly illuminated passages filled with fludda mushrooms, bright orange and cramming the floor, walls, and ceiling so that barely a square inch of rock could be seen. He stomped his way along, aware that the fungal floor had been trodden flat many times before. It seemed the mushrooms kept trying to repair themselves but always ended up getting squashed again.

"This is great!" Kyle yelled.

His voice came out much deeper than normal, and he realized he was actually using the Weaver's vocal chords instead of his own.

"Wait," he said, continuing to jog with long strides. "Who's in control here? Me or you?"

"Are you talking to me?" Byron asked from behind him.

"No, I'm talking to Weaver. Hey, Weaver, this kind of feels like it's *me* running, not you. Like *I'm* the one in control."

A voice somewhere at the back of his mind said, "You are. I'm . . . I'm simply observing. The weight of your presence is quite staggering. I should have realized. We all felt your overwhelming presence from the moment we came across you near the spirit barrier. We all felt drawn to you like no other. And now I realize how immensely powerful your hold is over me, like a giant cradling an infant."

Kyle slowed to a stop. "Should we separate? I'm not *trying* to take over or anything."

"No, continue on. I shall rest in this dream state while you take us to our destination." After a pause, the Weaver added, "I've been with you long enough to trust you."

With that, the Weaver seemed to slip away, receding inward. It felt just like when he had been a spirit creature, only now his physical body was somehow wrapped around Kyle's like a super-advanced skip pack.

He started running again, relishing the freedom it gave him and looking forward to leaving these tunnels forever.

* * *

An hour or so later, Kyle trudged out of the narrow tunnel and looked down over a ridge within a long, dark chamber. The sound of rushing water had been growing steadily for a while now, and finally here it was, the Wiscuppa river where a traveler made the choice between sailing downriver or walking for a day and run the risk of bumping into clackers. To Kyle's mind, the choice was very simple.

"You and Logan had it easy getting to the Well," he said over the roar, watching the river churn and tumble away down a sloping crevice into darkness. The water came from a calmer stretch higher up, a mere trickle in comparison. There, several huge mushroom caps lay waiting, already scooped out and ready to be used as boats.

Still firmly attached to Kyle's back—or the Weaver's back—Byron let out a whirr and click, something he did on occasion to emulate displeasure. "It wasn't fun. It was pretty smooth and fast most of the way, but there were some bumpy rapids as well. Horrible."

"How are you doing, Weaver?" Kyle asked.

A voice floated from the recesses of his mind. "Well rested, thank you. At least my mind is. I sense that you need to rest yourself. Your thoughts are becoming muddled."

"I know," Kyle agreed. "But if I stop now, I'll never get back up."

They continued their journey, walking alongside the river on an elevated ledge. It wasn't long before they arrived at what Byron told him was Makow and Yando's settlement. Kyle hadn't met Yando, but he thought about Makow with renewed respect. "Do these guys often make this journey to the Well and back? Like I said, getting there from here is easy downriver, but coming back . . . Man, it would bore me to tears."

"And Abe," Byron reminded him. "He's just an old man."

"Abe, too, yeah."

The idea of the man walking so far underground bothered him for some reason. He remembered the time Abe had shown up outside the Repurposing Factory in the city just as Kyle was trying to escape. He'd unlocked the door and promptly vanished. He'd also shown up in the wastelands, syncing in to visit Kyle and Logan separately, and then showing up again at the Tower. The old man could get around! Maybe he rode hustles on the surface. He'd already displayed a competent experience in that respect. And, unlike Kyle and Logan, he had a device on his neck to enable instant syncing.

Not anymore, Kyle remembered.

The settlement was small but bustling, a curious mixture of fungi, timber, and stone. Kyle counted twelve buildings, some of them two stories high. Still in his Weaver's body, Kyle paused to watch men and women hurry about with children in tow. There were Forerunners, too, solid and real. A Breaker here, a Creeper there, even a Fixer, one of those furry little critters on stalklike legs.

"What are they doing?" Kyle asked aloud, noticing that a dozen adults, men and women alike, carried supply sacks as they waved goodbye to others in the background. Evidently several groups were intent on leaving. *Probably those expeditions to the surface Makow said he was going to arrange*, Kyle thought.

"Hey," Byron said suddenly, his metal arm whipping up to point. "There's Makow."

Kyle smiled. *Right on cue.*

He decided now was probably a good time to extract himself from his Weaver's body while he went to speak with his former guide. He thought for a moment, then began to edge sideways while willing himself to let go of his host. It felt like climbing out of a massive party costume. He leaned to the left and took a deep breath as his head emerged from the Weaver's frame. Then he stepped down and planted his left foot on the ground. He set about wiggling his other foot free, but this one caught up in the flesh of the Weaver's leg. Suddenly panicked, he wrenched himself free and stumbled clear with a gasp.

Upon separation, the Weaver groaned and stretched as if waking from a deep sleep.

"Will you still help me?" Kyle said, now feeling intensely exhausted. "Once we're done here, will you come with me to the Guardian's bunker?"

"As far as I am able," the Weaver agreed. "But for a moment, I would like to walk around this settlement. It's very familiar to me. I've been here before, long ago. Perhaps this place will help restore some hidden memories."

The Weaver strode away, still wearing the flap of grubberming skin around his waist. Glancing around, Kyle winced at the sight of other Forerunners walking about quite unabashed at their nakedness. His Weaver looked foolishly modest now.

"Makow!" Kyle called, hurrying over to the man.

"Ah, there you are, Kyle Jaxx of the City. Quite a trek, eh?"

Kyle shook his head. "Never again. How long have you been here?"

"I arrived four hours ago."

Staggered, Kyle shook his head. "But you left just before I did!"

Makow laughed. "I've heard about you lazy city folk. With relatively little practice, you can learn to jog and run for hours on end without resting. I got here in less than half the time it took you. I'm well rested and ready to go topside."

Kyle looked again at the groups preparing to leave.

Gesturing vaguely, Makow said, "We're escorting our Forerunner friends to the surface. They haven't been up there for a very long time. They're ready."

"But the inhibitors—"

"Will be disabled shortly," Makow said with a grin.

Now Kyle was confused. "Disabled by who?"

"Why, *you*, of course! Did you forget?"

"No, it just sounded for a second like someone else was going to—"

Makow slapped him hard across the back. "We're all counting on you, Kyle. And we're ready. There's a place north of here, a sort of miniature settlement, an outpost if you like. An ancient Digger tunnel leads up into the wastelands. That's where, from time to time, Forerunners step out into the sunlight and challenge the inhibitor's influence. We beg them not to, and sure enough, it's the last thing they do before they're beaten to death on their fast and violent journey across the land to the east." Makow slapped Kyle on the back again. "But this time it will be different. This time the spirit inhibitor will be disabled."

"But . . . but . . ." Kyle hardly knew where to start with his protests. "Why are you in such a rush? I'm not even at the city yet! I have to get in and past the Guardian before I can switch that inhibitor off. What if I fail? And even if I manage it, how will you know?"

With a smile, Makow said, "We'll know. We'll be watching the city. And we have one or two volunteer Breakers who will ascend partway to the surface and test the inhibitor from time to time. When they no longer feel its magic, then we'll know the time is right."

Kyle watched the dozen-or-so human settlers as they separated into three teams. With the Breakers, Creepers, Hunters, and other Forerunners that joined them, the entire mass probably numbered thirty in all. The settlers were jovial and excited, but the various Forerunners remained stoic, perhaps nervous. And understandably so. The inhibitor's power was terrible and unrelenting.

Kyle shuddered. "Why's everyone relying on *me*?" he grumbled.

Makow heard him and turned serious for a change. "To be honest, everyone was expecting Logan to gather a force of tech weaponry and break into that bunker in a way our people could not. But the Guardian wields powerful tethering magic, so you're an equally good choice for this mission—if you can get inside."

"I'll try," Kyle said.

"And you have Byron by your side. You make an unbeatable team."

Byron seemed to puff up with pride at this comment, and he whirred softly.

Makow studied Kyle for a moment. "Well, good luck, Kyle Jaxx of the City. The Guardian's bunker is only a few hours away. You might find it wise to rest and eat. You look worn out." He pointed. "Look, there's young Milene. Ask her to take you to Gracil. She will welcome you into her home."

"And you're all leaving right now?" Byron said, gesturing to the restless teams.

"Well, these teams need to spread the word among other settlements and eventually meet at that clacker tunnel I told you about. I expect we'll be there, waiting, in ten to twelve hours from now. Perhaps you will be victorious by then."

Kyle felt like he was in a dream as he shuffled away. How many Forerunners would soon be heading to the surface for the first time in hundreds of years? How many were relying on him to take out this ancient Guardian so many found fearsome?

His stomach flip-flopped. *Too much pressure*, he thought.

Though very, very tired, Kyle knew he wouldn't sleep a wink.

Chapter 43

Logan

Logan didn't like leaving Kiff in the small barn near the outskirts of the enclave, but he didn't have a choice. He scavenged some fruit from the nearby woods and left his canteen for his brother, but it still felt like he was abandoning him.

Kiff seemed to take it in stride, his previous panic stifled for now.

Logan finished arranging the small bales of junny grass in the upper loft and pointed to the window at the front of the building. "You can see the main road leading into the square. Be careful when you look out. The window's pretty small, but someone could still see you. Anyway, I hope to be back in a day or two."

Kiff smiled. "Maybe by then everything will match up, and nobody'll be a ghost." He tapped his foot against the wooden floor. "You sure I won't pass through the floor?"

"I think so." Logan thumped his own boots against the now solid floor. The barn appeared more present than any structure they had been around so far. Was that because more spores were in the air or that their current location was a mile or two closer to the sporecore's expulsions? Either way, he didn't think Kiff was in any danger of slipping through the wood. He squeezed his brother tight. "Be careful. They may not be able to hurt you now, but that's going to change."

I will," Kiff grinned.

"When you run out of food and water and get hungry, go back to Mom and Dad. I don't care if the Guardian catches you. I don't want you to stay up here and starve. Besides, it's me he really wants."

Kiff looked up at him, the thrill of adventure wiped clean from his expression, replaced by a weariness. He settled into the makeshift bed and shot Logan a plaintive look. "Could you at least stay until I fall asleep?"

Logan nodded and drew up next to his brother, protectively wrapping his arms around him. He whispered, "When you wake up, it'll be to a better world."

Kiff smiled with his eyes closed and muttered, "I know it will because you'll be back by my side again."

Logan was tired himself. Maybe a short nap would be okay in this instance. He needed to be at his best against the Guardian. Just a few hours. He closed his eyes and drew in several slow breaths.

What could it hurt?

* * *

The buzzing of liffa flies stirred him awake. He slipped free of his brother. Light streamed in from the window, and he went over to look out.

People were walking down the road leading to the enclave. They looked more solid and less like ghosts. Logan didn't know if that was because he was seeing them in the daytime or they had grown more substantial. He thought their breath glowed but couldn't be sure in the full light of day.

A troop of eight Hunters moved in formation toward the path leading to the quarry. Relief for the night shift? If so, Logan needed to get to the quarry ahead of them. He stood and padded over to the trapdoor, opening it with enough finesse to produce only a faint squeak. Kiff didn't stir. He gave his brother a quick look and then dropped down the ladder.

He exited out the back of the barn and through a well-tended pasture. If he cut through the woods, he might pull ahead of the Hunters.

Logan crashed through the thick vegetation, not caring about the noise he made.

He came across an open path, one he knew well. It led to Nomi's house. He paused and looked down it, thankful he hadn't startled any of Nomi's family on their way to the market. He continued and, a few minutes later, emerged at the edge of the quarry. He didn't see any archers at the entrance, so he hustled down the incline toward the bottom of the quarry.

He had arrived ahead of the Hunters, and the archers were somewhere else. Pleased with his luck, he raced across the open expanse, eyeing the storage shed. Were the archers inside taking a break? It didn't matter. All he needed to do was get back down into the tunnel and head southeast toward the Hunter Enclave. Kyle had told him the metal-lined tunnel led to the Guardian's underground shelter beneath the Hallowed Spires.

He scrambled down into the semi-tunnel. As he approached what was left of Kyle's rough-and-ready wall, he heard faint voices ahead.

Logan ducked below the wall and listened. It wasn't easy. The people talking were barely audible.

". . . not liking this. No one said anything about this place being haunted." The voice was weak and muffled, as if its owner had a thick cloth over his mouth.

Another answered, "It was the boy, Logan Orm. The one who ran off to the city."

"You sure it wasn't that Kyle kid? They look a lot alike."

He thought of the area ahead. About ten feet of tunnel before the better-built Weaver barricade. The archers didn't have much room to maneuver, much less fire their weapons. Maybe he could get past them as they tried to draw their bows in the tight space.

"You ask me, we just close this hole up. No one'll want to come down here if word gets out that spirits of exiles are turning up in the quarry."

While it was a good thing he could hear their voices—it meant the enclaves were almost in sync with Apparatum—it might also mean the archers could do him harm. He exhaled, noting the spore cloud was almost as strong as when he had first entered the Seeker settlement.

A puff of light filled the air, one Logan hadn't breathed. They were right on top of him. Had they seen his plume of glowing spores? He sucked in a breath and held it.

The archer with the deeper voice said, "Shouldn't we be worrying about our breath suddenly setting fire to the air?"

The other, his voice lighter and more capricious, said, "I know it has something to do with those fireworks out in the Broken Lands. You know they went on all last night?"

"I was with you, Wrink. I saw." He paused. "I bet our relief will have something to say about that. Maybe they'll fill us in."

"Maybe."

Logan hissed out a slight breath, furious at the curling trail of glowing vapor he produced. He watched it work its way up past the threshold of the partial wall.

The conversation stopped, and he heard the men move back. Swift whispering followed.

He'd been found out.

At that moment, he heard the Hunters outside at the quarry entrance, shouting down to the archers, their voices very audible. Logan was certain they had to be completely solid, nearly aligned with him.

He couldn't go up. He braced himself, drew in a deep breath, and expelled it swiftly, directing the glowing blast downward into the ground. He leapt over the wall and launched himself at the archers, waving his arms about and shouting up a storm.

They slipped back into defensive positions as best they could. Neither went for their bows. Instead, they drew their short blades.

Logan hadn't thought of that. He dropped lower, sped up, and crashed into the larger man. The archer screamed in pain and pawed at him but couldn't move fast enough to drive his blade into Logan's back. He understood why. The pain of coming in contact with each other was jarring. As much as he had bounced off the man, some of him had sunk into the archer's chest, at least Logan's left forearm. It had hurt. He could only imagine how the archer felt, experiencing the pain not in his arm but in his chest.

The man howled, and his Hunter slipped free. This saved Logan from the other archer. At seeing his partner's spirit dislodged, the man's eyes widened, his knife-wielding arm going slack.

Logan blessed his luck. He shouted, "Leave me alone! I wish only to disappear!"

While the men looked solid to him, he hoped he appeared just a little bit like a ghost to them. He scrambled into the narrow opening in the Weaver barricade, expecting a knife or arrow in his back any second as he wormed his way through all six feet of it in record time.

Nothing.

He entered the small cavern, found the vac-tunnel breach, and entered the manmade passage. Behind him, he heard a flurry of activity and the archers calling out to the Hunters. Would they follow him? He didn't have time to worry. At his command, the running lights flickered to life.

He looked northwest, in the direction of the vac-tunnel station. He would go southeast. Maybe his pursuers would go the other way. Some sensation was returning to the arm that had slipped into the archer's chest. He was happy that the same was probably true of the man. He couldn't live with the idea of springing a heart attack on someone.

He raced down the tunnel, determined to run all the way to the Hallowed Spires.

After five minutes, he slowed to catch his breath. Not detecting any pursuit, he resumed moving but at more of a brisk walk.

About ten minutes later, he came to a large door. He accessed the tech and registered that this was a security checkpoint. Only those with the right clearances could open it and head onto the Hallowed Spires. Logan smiled. He had clearance. He weaved through the firewalls with ease and unlocked the door. It slid upward silently, taking almost a minute to disappear into the ceiling.

He stepped into the tunnel and again verbally activated the running lights along this segment.

Without looking back, he ordered the door to close behind him, eliminating any chance of his pursuers getting in.

He drew in a breath and exhaled, producing only a little light.

There were not enough spores in this part of the tunnel to make a difference.

With renewed resolve, he moved at a quick jog.

His Guardian showdown awaited.

Chapter 44
Kyle

Despite his anxiety of the mission ahead, Kyle slept hard.

He woke to the sound of a small fire crackling in the hearth at the foot of the surprisingly comfortable bed he lay upon. He hadn't bothered undressing or washing, and he was afraid to look at how dirty he'd gotten the sheets.

Groaning, he sat up and composed his thoughts. It seemed a lifetime ago that he'd thrown himself down onto the bed and fallen asleep. Byron had approached a girl he knew, a lively young thing named Milene, who had promptly jumped on the robot boy's back and acted like he was an old friend. She had led them to her mother, a thin-faced, black-haired lady. Stern yet welcoming, she had ushered Kyle and Byron into her modest house. "Sleep," she'd said, and as though hypnotized by her voice, Kyle had floated into this room and been asleep before his head hit the pillow.

Or so it had seemed at the time. It was all a blur. But certainly Kyle felt refreshed now. And ravenous.

He padded across the floor and ventured into what looked like a living room. Everything smelled old, but the place looked clean and well organized, if cluttered and oppressively dark.

We're underground, he told himself. *It's surprisingly light in here, all things considered.*

What light there was came from several lanterns around the room as well as patches of bioluminescent fungi clinging to the walls. Kyle sidled up behind a rocking chair, which moved silently back and forth, the top of someone's head just visible. He remembered she was Gracil, the leader of the Seekers. "Hello?" he said softly.

The black-haired woman climbed to her feet and faced him with a smile. “Well, you’re awake at last. I trust you slept well?”

“I did, thanks. I, uh . . . I guess I need to go. I feel like I’ve been asleep forever.”

She looked him up and down. “I can’t let you leave this place without a change of clothes. You poor boy. Normally I would have insisted you bathe before falling asleep, but you were dead on your feet. Please, take a bath. I’ll bring you hot water and fresh clothes—”

“I just need to eat,” Kyle said. “You’ve been really nice, but I have to leave soon. If I can eat something, then I can head out.”

But Gracil wouldn’t take no for an answer. Kyle found himself bustled into the bathroom, where he was appalled to find an ancient, metal tub with no faucets. It was already half filled with fresh cold water just for his benefit, and as promised, Gracil personally delivered one pail of hot water after another while Kyle huddled in a corner slowly stripping away his filthy clothes. He decided he was as disgusted with himself as Gracil must be. Most of the grime had come from his time in the Well with the Digger, but he guessed endless exploding mushrooms had something to do with it, too.

Once washed and dressed in the oddly simple and slightly scratchy clothes of the underground world, he migrated to the cluttered kitchen and ate without saying a word for a full ten minutes. Gracil’s meal was a blend of raw mushrooms and unknown leafy vegetables along with the main course, a fabulous fish of some kind. She also poured him a steaming mug of something that smelled of . . . durgle? Some sort of soup? He wasn’t sure. Part of him wanted to know what everything was called, but mostly he didn’t care. He was more interested in learning how these people lived in such quaint conditions, a sort of cross between the enclaves and the poor, outer suburbs of the city.

While eating, he wondered what time it was. How did these Seekers measure time anyway? Did they even have a regular day and night like people on the surface?

Byron showed up with a younger boy and girl hanging off his arms. The girl was Milene and the boy Bront, and they adored Byron and his mechanical body. Kyle grinned at him as he finished his meal—breakfast, lunch, or whatever.

Then it was time to leave.

Gracil's husband, the man named Yando that Abe, Byron, and Makow had mentioned in passing, had already left with the expedition. "How long have they been gone?" Kyle asked. "How long was I asleep?"

"Nine or ten hours," Gracil said.

"Actually nine hours and thirteen minutes," Byron said, causing Milene to giggle. "Well, a bit less. I stopped my counter when I came in and saw you finishing your breakfast."

Kyle shook his head, amazed at how well he'd slept. Feeling refreshed and warm inside, he smiled at Gracil and held out his hand. "Thank you."

"No, thank *you*," she said. "Makow will guide you the rest of the way. It'll only take an hour."

"I thought it was at least two hours to the bunker," Kyle said with surprise.

"Not with a couple of friends to carry you."

* * *

The 'couple of friends' Gracil had mentioned turned out to be Kyle's Weaver along with a scaly, tusked Breaker. Makow was there to see them off. He helped Byron climb onto the back of the brutish Breaker, where he clung to a specially designed harness that enveloped the creature's chest. It meant Byron could insert his feet into what looked like stirrups and hang onto handles without throttling the poor Breaker.

Makow laughed at Kyle. "Don't worry, she's happy to assist."

"*She*?" Kyle blurted.

Makow formally introduced the Breaker as Vimara, but Kyle was distracted by the fact that she was female. He didn't ever remember wondering about the gender of spirits while at the enclaves. He'd always referred to them as "it." She was just as naked as the rest of the Forerunners, yet her form was somewhat nondescript from his perspective, all scales and great bulky muscles with huge arms and three-toed feet. Tusks jutted from her cheeks, and her heavy brow suggested she was either annoyed about something or just naturally grumpy.

Kyle tethered with his Weaver the same way he had before, and then they were ready. As they bade farewell to Makow and took off running, the Weaver whispered, "I have remembered my name. It is Shailen. I recalled a great deal as I wandered around the settlement. However, this is not *my* settlement, just one of many that I visited in the distant past."

"How long ago?" Kyle asked aloud, unconsciously using the Weaver's own vocal chords.

"What?" Byron asked from the back of his Breaker just ahead.

"Not talking to you, little brother. I was talking to Shailen here."

The Weaver answered the question, again speaking directly into Kyle's mind. "It was at least two hundred years ago that I left my family and friends and headed to the surface. I was a fool. Young and brash, no more than eighty years old, I believed I would be unaffected by the inhibitor."

"Eighty!"

"Like others before me, I made sure to emerge on the surface as near to the spirit barrier as possible in case the inhibitor repelled me. And of course it did. I was just a little to the west of the barrier, the same place we lost two of our friends earlier on our journey, and the moment I stepped out of the tunnel, I bounced and scraped my way down to the river and was ejected onto its banks on the far side. For a while, I existed as flesh and blood among dozens of my ghostly peers. I tried to find a way back underground, but there are no entrance tunnels east of the river. I faded fast and quickly forgot what I was doing. After that . . . well, I had nothing but an urge to tether with a human, though I didn't understand why until now. I needed to be *real* again."

Kyle digested that as they sped through a cavern, leaving the settlement far behind and heading up a slope. Small flying creatures screeched out of nowhere, but the Breaker roared and swiped at them, and they veered away, leaving clouds of swirling, glowing spores. The Weaver actually knocked one from the air so that it spun and hit the wall.

"Ugly thing," Kyle commented.

"Minquins," the Weaver said with disgust. "I wouldn't care if I never saw one again. I haven't been to this area before, but Vimara told me these tunnels are rife with them. Never fear, though, we are making haste through this foul place."

They certainly were. Kyle felt a little less like he was in the driving seat this time. The Weaver seemed to be in control, stampeding after the Breaker under low overhangs and around spiky fungal growths that looked like those jagged kilbatoo bushes orb scavengers liked to nest under. Taking turns suited Kyle just fine. The Breaker knew the route, and the Weaver knew perfectly well how to avoid natural dangers.

The tunnels narrowed and sloped sharply upward and around bends. Byron's Breaker didn't once hesitate despite numerous intersections. Kyle quickly grew confused at the number of forks they navigated and was glad to be along for the ride for this final stretch of the underground.

Finally, they arrived. Daylight flooded the tunnel ahead, and just a single metal grate blocked the way to the great outside.

The Breaker and Weaver stopped the moment they saw daylight, pausing thirty feet back along the sloping tunnel. "We go no farther," the Breaker said quietly. It was the first thing she'd said throughout the entire journey, and she spoke in a strangely soft yet deep voice.

Kyle could sense the anxiety deep within the gut of his Weaver and could actually feel the physical push of the inhibitor somewhere beyond that grate. Though they were only thirty feet away, the tunnel sloped downward enough that the inhibitor's power skimmed over their heads. He hadn't felt it at all when tethered to intangible spirits, but he could now, a pressure on his left-hand side pushing him toward the wall on his right.

"You'd better wait here," he told his Weaver.

A shame, he thought as he disengaged and stepped down onto his own two feet, becoming corporeal within seconds. The inhibitor's power faded as he became himself again. *I could really use the Breaker and Weaver when I get inside the bunker and deal with the Guardian.*

Though he planned to send Byron home, he had a feeling his brother's electronics might be able to get him inside the bunker. With that in mind, he slapped him on his shoulder and said, "Just you and me, pal. Ready?"

Chapter 45
Logan

Logan stared at the green access panel. All he needed to do was place his palm on it, and the door in front of him would open. He had encountered roadblocks in the door tech numerous times until stumbling onto two well-concealed backdoor entry points, something any normal tech-savvy person would never have found. They had allowed him entry, and he had easily cycled through the security protocols and inserted his identity as one the program would accept. Now all he had to do was open the door and face the Guardian beyond.

Why was he hesitating? Looking at his deed from his little brother's perspective, it was the last piece in the puzzle, the final obstacle to uniting their worlds. Well, he did have to tear down the inhibitor, but that was more of an afterthought. Facing a flesh-and-blood person would be much harder than confronting a machine.

Was Kyle at the city now, facing uncertainty of his own?

The trek along the metal-walled vac-tunnel to the Hallowed Spires had taken almost two hours. In that time he had played out his confrontation with the Guardian dozens of ways. He needed to get the upper hand fast. The Guardian would be adept at manipulating tech, maybe even at a level beyond his own impressive abilities. After all, someone locked away in the tech haven of the Spires would have had many years to perfect his abilities.

He grunted and slapped his hand down on the panel. The door opened, rumbling far louder than he liked.

He stepped into a small chamber that led to a hallway. Lights came on upon his entrance. Casting his mind forward, he registered several alarm systems. Deciding it best not to disable them as that might attract attention, he moved forward. He'd take his chances with being recorded on video. Maybe the Guardian didn't check his monitors that often. When was the last time anyone had entered the Spires from below? Of course, that could also paint a big target on him. A door cycling open that had remained closed for hundreds of years was bound to rile up the Guardian.

He sped up, searching for any hint of tech he could use as a weapon. He encountered none—just a lighting network, a rather sophisticated plumbing and filtration conduit, and a ventilation system. He passed three cameras but didn't try to duck out of sight. After two hundred feet, the hallway ended at another door, this one far more ordinary and tailored for human dimensions as opposed to the past two which had been gaping and vaultlike.

The room beyond held very little tech. He decided to access it just the same. The door slid into the wall as he triggered its proximity sensors. Ahead was a decent-sized atrium with two identical doors spaced ten feet apart on the far wall.

He breathed out, expelling a faint glowing cloud, a good sign that air was cycled from outside, and that the spores had made it as far as the Hunter Enclave.

He approached the door on the left, and it opened when he got within five feet of it. Inside was a simple bedroom. He entered. To the left a bed along with a nightstand were mounted to the wall. A journal and pencil sat on a metal desk opposite the bed. Logan reached for the journal.

As his hands grazed the surface of the red cloth cover, a raspy voice cut through the air behind him. "Please refrain from looking at my private ruminations, young man."

Logan froze.

The man continued, "You are my guest, but there are boundaries to what you should be exploring and limits to my patience. Please turn around and acknowledge me."

Logan turned about slowly and stared at the Guardian. He stiffened, shocked by the man's appearance.

Very little of the Guardian was human. His body was mostly tech, but cobbled together and jury-rigged. Nothing like Byron's streamlined robotic housing. While the right half and lower jaw of the man's face was flesh and blood, everything else was machine. A steel mask covered the left side, a red glowing eye deep in a socket. The man was hairless except for a gray patch of wild stubble on his chin.

The Guardian smiled. "Don't worry. I know my appearance isn't conventional."

He extended his right arm, a massive array of servos and gonzo-mechanized musculature ending with a gloved hand. Logan shook it, aware of the strong grip that could crush him. The Guardian's left arm branched into three extensions. The top one was clearly a weapon, ending in a large muzzle. The other two looked like they were used to link up with tech in some manner. His legs were comprised of a darker metal. Poking out of his back a good several feet were various tools and apparatus, their functions surely offensive and defensive.

Logan resisted probing the tech, fearful it would upset the Guardian. He didn't want to be blown to pieces. Not that this man would do so in his living quarters. *He probably has a much better place to do me in.*

The Guardian chuckled and spun about. "Come along. I really want to know why you're here. You can start by telling me how you gained access to my home from underground."

Logan followed, unsure of his next move but knowing the Guardian was playing with him.

The door closed behind him, and they entered the other doorway to the left. They walked down the much wider hall in silence. At the end of it, the Guardian waved a hand at the access panel, and Logan dared to cast his mind outward. The Guardian was interacting with the tech much like Logan did. He didn't need to palm the door open but could trigger it with his mind.

The Guardian paused and sent him a suspicious look. "Is that you I feel tickling at the edges of my precious tech?" He shook his head. He said with slight menace, "Where are your manners?"

The man entered the large chamber beyond and Logan did the same, making every attempt to retreat as far back within himself as he could.

* * *

It was clear they were in the main chamber of the Hallowed Spires. Above, he spied the inner reaches of the three distinctive towers that rose up beyond any dwellings in the Hunter Enclave. The area would be large and inviting if it wasn't for the piles of tech that ranged all over the space.

The Guardian waved majestically around, eyeing the machinery with pride. "My collection."

Logan knew better than to try and link with any of the tech. Some he recognized, while others were harder to comprehend. All looked ancient. He spied several spy-eyes and air vehicles as well as some land transports. All looked picked through and fairly dismantled. Ordinary household appliances also littered the floor.

"Where'd you get all this?"

The Guardian moved away from him, placing his gloved hand against his collar and rubbing at his metal neck, a massaging gesture that did nothing for the rigid, coiled musculature, merely a hold-over gesture from when the man had been flesh and blood. "My servants went out to the Broken Lands as soon as the inhibitors were brought online. Early on there was much tech left behind when the city dwellers retreated. They delivered this all back for my use. It has helped me maintain myself."

Logan wondered about the man's mental capacity. How much of his brain was still intact and how much had been replaced by tech? Byron's brain was fully functioning, but with as long as this Guardian had been here, subsisting on scraps of outdated tech, there was no telling just how rational he was. "How long have you been here?"

"Since the inhibitor was built." His cheek twitched, and he swatted at his face as if waving off an invisible gew fly. An idea seized him, and he addressed Logan with a manic tone. "How did you arrive here underground? Is the Sentry still down there? Part of me thinks it is, but its signal disappeared so long ago."

"It was, but it's gone now."

The Guardian glared. "Gone? How?"

"I took it out." Logan didn't like how the man was looking at him.

The man laughed. "Little you took it out? Impossible!" The Guardian's voice was uneven. "Did it eliminate the sporecore? No one wants that thing spewing its foul offspring back on the surface again. That's why the Sentry was sent there in the first place."

Logan responded, hating how defensive he was being. "Abe does and so do Kyle and I. We blew up the Tower and we got rid of all the debris plugging up the Well. The sporecore's been shooting out spores for almost a day now."

The various tech sprouting from the Guardian's back quivered and snaked about. The man was becoming unhinged. "And so you strolled into my domain intent on what? Ending my days as Guardian?"

Logan sputtered out his answer. "I don't want to hurt you, no."

The man grimaced and then fumed. "I know why you've come. Torren sent you to destroy my inhibitor." He swept his arms around and looked lovingly at the walls of the Hallowed Spires. "Nestled within this sanctuary, tech works for me. It's the only place in all the enclaves where that is so. A thin layer of durilium throughout the structure keeps it that way. No one else should be given my gift. No one!"

Logan kept scanning the junk, hoping to spy any sort of weapon.

The Guardian stared at him, studying his intent. "Nothing in there will help you."

He decided to play dumb. "What do you mean?"

"Come now. I know you think your abilities beyond my own, but you're only fooling yourself. You're nothing. I am not a Sentry with limited defensive measures." All around Logan, several different items of tech hummed to life amid the piles of junk.

Logan sighed. No reason to keep up his innocent pretense. "The worlds are coming back together. The inhibitors have to be shut down so everyone can access tech and work alongside the Forerunners."

The Guardian's voice quaked. "Never! Tech should be handled by those who revere it. It's not for all! You should know this!" His eye danced madly. "Don't you sense that when you link up? Yours is a bond that runs deep. It's not something to be offered to everyone." Several of the extensions on his back started squirming as if desiring to break free. One snakelike mechanical appendage festooned with foot-long barbs along its sides curled up and over the Guardian's head, looking for all practical purposes as if it was a kaliback's tail poised to strike. "And now I think you are no longer deserving of it yourself."

Even if there was time to root through the junk all around him and stumble across a weapon, he was facing someone bristling with lethal tools. It didn't take nosing around in the man's tech to see that he was a walking arsenal. It made perfect sense. Why leave weapons around for others to use when you can keep everything linked to you?

"Torren sent you to your death, young man. A pity to snuff someone so gifted." He brought his left arm up, and the weapon mounted at its end whined to life. “I will make it quick if you allow me.”

Insane. The guy is stark raving mad. Logan bolted into the sprawling piles of junk, narrowly avoiding a beam of white energy. It vaporized a drifter blimp’s undercarriage. Logan didn’t know how long it would take for the man to target him again. He ran, putting as much useless tech between him and the unhinged Guardian as he could.

Chapter 46
Kyle

Bright daylight beckoned. When Kyle approached the old, rusted grate at the top end of the tunnel and studied the chain looped around its bars, he noticed that the padlock was broken, just hooked over one of the links. He pulled it off and yanked the chain loose.

"Logan broke it," Byron explained.

"Ah." Kyle braced himself and pushed. Hinges groaned as the ancient grate swung open. "We're in business."

He took a moment to glance back at the Breaker and Weaver waiting in the darkness of the tunnel, their breath glowing faintly. Then he stepped out into the sunlight.

He climbed up a short but steep bank thick with long grass, then turned to see if Byron needed help extracting himself from the ditch. He didn't. The robot boy had become remarkably agile since gaining a new body.

They stood together, looking around. Kyle noticed that his breath gave off the faintest of glows, and he smiled. Everything around him was clearly in sync.

"We're in Sector Six of the Eastern Quadrant," Byron said. "Dobermill Park, about half a mile from the Wall. I followed Logan here."

"From where?"

Byron pointed. "That way. Out of the park and then about half an hour's walk through the backstreets of Graysdurn." He paused, then pointed and said, "Uncle Jeremiah lives eleven-point-two miles in *that* direction, over in East Morley."

Now that Kyle had a better sense of where he was, he nodded and started walking. "Half an hour's walk through the backstreets? Do you remember the way?"

"Of course!" Byron sounded indignant. "There are five left turns, three rights, and we cross eight intersections, a total of nine thousand, four hundred and twenty-three feet from the gate at the end of this park to the only door of the Guardian's building. We'll pass seventeen stores, or eighteen if you count the one that's closed on the corner of Marble and—"

"All right, all right." Kyle gave his brother a gentle push. "Show off."

They walked in silence. The city loomed over the treetops, the high-rise apartments dulled by the smog. Small, dark machines scudded across the sky. Distant police sirens wailed in the air. And as they neared the edge of the overgrown park, the familiar smells of outer city carbon monoxide wafted over them as old-style road rumblers belched along the road.

Suddenly, Kyle wasn't so eager to be back in the city anymore.

* * *

"There's no handle, no lock, nothing," Byron said in the lowest voice he could manage. "It's more like a wall."

Kyle shook his head and stepped back from the massive steel door that marked the one and only entrance to the two-story Guardian building. "I expected an electronic pad. I thought you'd be able to get me in."

"Sorry. I don't sense any tech here at all except for the spy pylon forty-three feet directly behind me. It's watching us."

Kyle ignored it. He knew from stream screen footage that those tiny cameras could zoom in and pick out the color of his eyeballs if he looked its way. It could also run a scan on his implant—if he had one. The fact that he didn't was a red flag. He was a deadbeat wandering the streets, sure to attract attention. Even as he stood there waiting, he thought he heard the dull whine of a police cruiser as it altered course and headed his way.

"What are you going to do?" Byron whispered.

Kyle glared at the steel door. No handle, no lock. How did the Guardian get in and out? What happened when Yando delivered a sack of spores to her? She had to have some way of retrieving the sack from the doorstep.

A police cruiser appeared over the rooftop, its whine increasing tenfold. "You there," a reverberating voice blasted out. "Remain where you are. You're under arrest."

When Kyle placed his hands flat on the cold metal of the door and stood there as though preparing to be frisked and arrested, Byron whispered, "That's it? You're surrendering?"

"What? No! I'm just trying to figure out how to get in."

As it happened, his submissive posture probably lulled the police into thinking he had indeed given up. The cruiser eased lower, and Kyle shut it out, leaning harder on the door and trying to concentrate on what was inside the bunker.

He could sense spirits. Their addled thoughts flitted through his mind, though he couldn't grasp anything coherent. They were there, tethered and subdued. The Guardian kept them locked up within her, reigning with an iron fist and a cold heart.

Only they weren't spirits. They were tangible, solid. Fully-fleshed Forerunners who for some reason remained under the Guardian's spell. She was powerful indeed!

Kyle closed his eyes and whispered, "To me."

Whether because of the steel door or the Guardian's will, Kyle couldn't quite take control of the creatures. He gritted his teeth, trying to get an image of something, *anything*, behind the steel door. He caught a glimpse as seen through the eyes of a Forerunner—a Hunter?—but it wasn't particularly interesting nor helpful, just a dark room full of clutter. Still, the brief vision revealed that the Guardian, along with her tethers, knew he was out here. She was even now turning toward the hallway, facing the immoveable entrance door that Kyle stood behind. She had caught him intruding.

Dimly aware of the cruiser's flickering blue lights as it descended behind him, Kyle drove his mind deeper into the Hunter's. It snapped at him, and he flinched. But he became aware of another Forerunner more susceptible to his will. Or perhaps one less hostile.

Confused, he scoured the ancient mind, trying to figure out what kind of Forerunner this was. He didn't recognize it. When he managed to look out through the creature's eyes, he found himself even more befuddled. He seemed to be submerged in murky water, floating around in some sort of rectangular room the length and breadth of the building.

Settling deeper into the Forerunner's mind, snatches of information came to him—visions, senses, memories, all swirling around, each giving him new glimmers of understanding. He was underwater in a vast sublevel. The so-called Guardian's bunker was completely flooded.

Kyle frowned. No, not flooded. The bunker was a specially constructed chamber to hold thousands of gallons of ordinary rainwater, the same water that gushed along the Wiscuppa and throughout the underground world. Though the floor and walls were thick with fungus and algae, making the place look organic, beneath was a lining of non-ferrous metal sheeting—probably durilium, which Kyle knew was used for most underwater structures. Set into a wall at one end was a huge, circular door about ten feet across, sealed shut through disuse, its hinges and joints smothered in grey and green lumps. The Forerunner had entered that way long, long ago, but now it was trapped.

"What *are* you?" Kyle whispered.

To his surprise, the answer popped into his head. This was the ninth and final Forerunner, the only one he had not yet tethered with—the Swimmer.

In his dreamlike view through the Swimmer's eyes, Kyle moved slowly about the bunker, an efficient water filtering system his only source of comfort. He was alone except for dozens of small fish that swam in and out through grates low on the walls. For just a moment he wished he had a mirror to look into . . . but even as he thought about it, he received a vivid image of himself: deep-red in color, longer but more slender than a Digger, a spectacular array of long, extravagant fins, a blunt nose and small mouth, two bulbous eyes, and a thick tail that split into three.

He sensed movement. Looking up, he noticed that a metal grid formed part of the ceiling, a single, narrow stretch from one end to about halfway across. The shadow of the Guardian moved above, one footstep clanging noisily on the grid, the other dragging.

Kyle watched and listened, fascinated, as she headed along a hallway toward the steel external door that his physical body stood outside. She mumbled something.

A second later, Byron's familiar voice cut sharply through his dreamlike state, "Kyle! Wake up!"

He blinked awake. Dimly aware that the police cruiser had touched down behind him and doors were hissing open, he stared in amazement at the steel door he leaned on. His hands were still planted firmly on the cold surface, only now the door had vanished, replaced by some sort of hazy glasslike sheet. Daylight flooded the hallway beyond.

No more than a yard away, glaring out through the glass at him, was the hideous face of the Guardian—elderly and thin with an enormous hump to one side that protruded higher than her head and stuck out twice the width of her shoulder. She wore a raggedy black robe, and her hair hung in white, straggly wisps. Her mouth was toothless, her eyes milky-white and staring.

Before Kyle had a chance to pull back, the glasslike door rippled and dissolved, and he toppled forward. A coldness passed through his body, and then he was inside the building, gaping as the outside noise shut off.

The Guardian stumbled backward, her eyes widening.

She composed herself quickly. With a gesture of one gnarled hand, the hallway darkened. Kyle spun around in time to see the rippling glass surface turn opaque, blocking out the sunlight, the startled policemen, and Byron. The steel door was back—hard and cold, immoveable.

At the back of his mind, he thought about the police and hoped Byron would skedaddle. There was no reason for him to stick around in the street and be arrested.

A silence ensued, broken only by the oddly soft noise of cops hammering on the door, their voices muffled, distant.

It took a moment or two for Kyle's eyes to adjust to the darkness. Torches flickered on the walls, revealing the bizarre, twisted woman staring at him with obvious shock.

"How did—how did you *do* that?" she demanded. "I didn't—" She screwed up her face, then cast her eyes downward at the glistening metal grid flooring. "Traitor!" she hissed. Her breath lit up bright, and Kyle saw spores swirling in the air.

She turned and hobbled off along the empty hallway toward the single door at the end, which stood ajar.

Kyle tore after her, his shoes clanging on metal. He glanced down, realizing he'd seen this stretch of grid flooring from below. The Swimmer was right below his feet.

The Guardian turned back to face him, and though now shrouded in darkness, he could see her hand lift and move about in what looked like a vague, meaningless gesture. She had to be invoking magic again, but what—?

A torrent of water shot up through the grid flooring directly in front of Kyle. Skidding to a stop, he watched in amazement as, through the foamy spray, a wall formed and began to solidify. It rippled like the surface of a pool, then froze and darkened, accompanied by the deep groaning of rending metal. Kyle backed up and saw that the wall was now complete, floor to ceiling and spanning the hallway.

Kyle sensed anguish, and he glanced down through the metal-grid flooring where, below, he could see the huge shape of the Swimmer in the murky water. He understood immediately that the trapped Forerunner had created the wall, but he also realized it had merely been obeying the Guardian's command.

"Let me through," Kyle said.

The Swimmer sent him a pang of regret, a reluctant denial.

He tried again. "I can help you escape from this place. Take down this wall and let me through, and I'll see to it you're freed. I'm your only chance."

After a pause, the wall reverted to its glistening, rippling state and promptly collapsed, drenching Kyle's pants before the deluge poured back through the floor to the tank below.

Ahead, the Guardian had made it to the room at the end. She swung to face him again, her mouth dropping open.

He charged toward her before she had time to create another wall.

Rather than attack, he veered around her and shot through the open doorway. She was slow. Perhaps he could disable the inhibitor quickly before she caught up to him. All he had to do was find it.

He stopped and took in his surroundings as the woman, huffing and panting, hobbled in after him. The floor in here was solid concrete. There would be no watery wall magic now. Besides, surely not even this crazy woman would want to flood her home and all her belongings!

Maybe that's why there's no tech, he thought. *Electricity and water don't mix.*

Or it could just be that she despised tech the way all her ancient people had.

The enormous room was cluttered with junk piled up against all four walls and partway up the wide, circular staircase in one corner. No windows anywhere, just a dank, dark room lit by torches and candles, wisps of black smoke rolling across the ceiling and out of a flue.

An armchair in the center of the room faced a simple roll-down projector screen complete with a silent, blurry, moving image. He watched in fascination, recognizing the outside of the building where two cops pounded silently on the bunker door, their mouths moving as they yelled. The image, streamed directly from the spy pylon, showed Byron still there in the foreground, backing away slowly as two more cruisers descended.

Except there was no sign of a projector in the room. No tech whatsoever. So how—?

"Get out," the woman said hoarsely, still standing in the open doorway.

"Where's this picture coming from?" he asked, and as he spoke, he realized his own breath was pluming in bright green before his face. The room was thick with spores. *Yando's deliveries*, he thought.

The Guardian didn't answer, but she absently waved her hand and the picture cut off.

Kyle gasped. This woman had to be some kind of witch, somehow snatching tech images out of the air.

He tore his gaze from her and looked around, amazed by all the junk. One wall was piled up with books and wooden boxes, precariously stacked. Old clothes, drapes, and sheets smothered the floor in one corner, a mountain of filth that Kyle knew had to be infested with truggle rats. He could smell their foul scent. The floor under his feet was littered with tiny, telltale pellets, at their thickest under some stacked metal tables that clearly hadn't been used in a few lifetimes.

He saw odd sacks, too. Piles of them, all empty. They were stacked near a vent in the wall where a draft blew in from outside. *Probably Yando's. This woman must dump the spores out and fill the building with them.*

"So you're the Guardian?" Kyle asked her, wishing he could get the stink of truggle rats and mold and other smells out of his nostrils.

The woman glared at him, hunched sideways with one arm dangling. She held her other arm across her oddly barrel-shaped chest, and Kyle saw that her forearm was thick and gnarled, *scaly*. Her fingers, long and slender, could easily wrap around his entire skull if he let her get close enough.

"How did you force the Swimmer to open the door?" she rasped, pointing at him. "Answer me!"

The hump on her shoulder turned out not to be a hump at all. It was another head. Long tusks curled from its cheeks, and its eyes darted from side to side.

Suddenly Kyle understood. He pointed to the sacks piled by the vent. "That's why you have spores delivered here—because you have Forerunners with you. They'd be like ghosts otherwise. And the Swimmer down below somehow manipulates water? You're not tethered to it, but you have some kind of control over it. You have it trapped, so you can easily threaten to starve it or poison its water. Or harm it in some other way." He tightened his jaw at the thought of how vulnerable and helpless such a creature was. "So you use it. You order it to build a steel entrance door and walls, and to act as some kind of security guard."

"Not *steel*," the Guardian scoffed. "The door at the front is made to *look* like steel."

Kyle paused, then nodded. "And the Swimmer can make it dissolve again so you can step outside and pick up Yando's deliveries."

The Guardian took a few steps closer. "That's not all it can do," she growled. "Swimmers are the source of all magic, and some people—like me—can harness the power of that blessed water." She drew herself as straight as her twisted body would allow. "I'm the most powerful conjurer who ever lived." Now she paused, narrowing her eyes. "Except that you overrode me. Tell me how you did that. Tell me how you took control of my Swimmer."

Kyle shrugged. "I didn't. It helped me. Maybe it's fed up with being trapped down below." He leaned closer. "How many others do you have with you? I see a Weaver, but there's something around your waist under your robe . . ."

She moved suddenly, sliding sideways, trying to dart closer and take him by surprise. He jerked away, shocked by her motion. She was fast but sporadic, and her grasping Weaver fingers missed him as he backpedalled to a safe distance near the staircase.

"That's a Creeper," he said, trying not to show how rattled he felt. "What else do you have?"

She stood silently, glowering at him.

"What's upstairs?" Kyle asked. He looked up the stairwell. Faint daylight shone in through a window somewhere.

He wanted to run up the staircase and look, but the first nine or ten steps were crammed with things—an electric lamp with the bulb missing, a wooden bust of the well-regarded Mayor Liggerman from the distant past, random bits of gnarled wooden furniture, picture frames, half-empty bottles of ancient liquor, stacks of files, a stream screen on its side with a crack across the glass . . .

Kyle lifted a foot to place it amid the junk, but at that moment the Guardian screamed and lurched toward him. As he fell back on top of a stack of files, spilling them everywhere, she swiped her Weaver's hand at him. Its reptilian claws were surprisingly sharp, and they raked across his face.

He lifted his feet to her broad Weaver chest and kicked. She flew backward, stumbling, as he snatched at something from the surrounding junk—the electric lamp—and brandished it. "Stay away from me," he warned.

He felt blood ooze down his face, tickling his chin. His breath puffed out in short, bright bursts, giving away his rattled state. Hers was somewhat more controlled as she approached him again.

A small creature crawled out from the neckline of her robe and up onto her head. A Fixer! While its six stalklike legs remained deeply embedded in her flesh as it climbed, its three tails stuck up straight behind, and its long ears twitched. The plump, furry healer had sensed Kyle's injury.

He remained still, gazing into its large, dark-brown eyes. They were moist and shiny in the light of its own quick breaths.

"To me," Kyle said.

As it reared up, the Guardian turned her head sideways and hissed with sudden fury, "Not him, you idiot! Leave him alone! Let him bleed!"

The Fixer leapt off her head toward Kyle—and promptly flew across the room as though swiped by a giant, invisible hand. The creature smacked hard against the wall.

Stunned, Kyle gasped as the Guardian screamed in anguish.

Chapter 47

Logan

The Guardian howled, furious he had missed his target once again. Logan rolled to his left and scampered up the side of an impressive mountain of tech, putting more distance between him and his insane stalker.

"Fool! Accept your fate!"

The man was unhinged, as if a mob of Breakers had possessed him, driving out all rational thought and leaving only savagery behind.

Logan searched through the tech with his mind, desperate to latch onto anything that could be used to his advantage.

"Come out now! Don't make me climb in there to get you."

Having infiltrated a large raised section of tech, the area most stacked and claustrophobic with machinery poking out at every possible angle, Logan had snagged his clothes on two mechanical outcroppings already. With the Guardian being twice as big as him, entering the narrow paths through this section of junk would be foolhardy.

A large upended skimmer at the bottom of a pile to his left thrummed to life. It lifted up on four concentrated jets of air, causing tech to topple over in Logan's direction. He jumped away, barely avoiding being crushed. *He's just taking random shots at me. He doesn't know where I am.*

The Guardian laughed. "I'll upend everything all around you until you come out or I get lucky and pulverize you."

Another vehicle Logan didn't recognize roared to life and rolled down the side of a pile, slamming into an inert vehicle. *Not even close.*

"You're outclassed in here. I know everything inside and out. There's no way you can sift through all this and find anything to use against me."

He was right. So much of the tech was non-functioning, having been stripped for parts or damaged in other ways. Logan could poke and prod here and there and maybe luck out, but the Guardian had a distinct advantage as long as they fought within the Spires where tech functioned normally.

But outside was another matter entirely.

How to get the Guardian to open a door? Logan reached out, latching his mind onto a large door to his right. Its security protocols were intricate. No hope there. Noticing a series of windows twenty feet above, each inaccessible thanks to a reinforced roll-down barrier, he probed their protocols and found the shuttering mechanism easier to unravel.

Several projectiles launched into the air from the general direction of the Guardian's last outburst. They arced over a large junk pile and landed at the base of another, their upturned ends flashing bright red. *Grenades of some sort.*

Logan vaulted up the pile closest to the bank of windows, hoping to escape the blast.

The grenades went off, their blast hurling Logan with even more force toward the window. Luckily, his back didn't wind up with any shrapnel. He landed on the narrow ledge along the three windows and made short work of the first two shutters. They rolled up and out of the way, sending rays of bright light into the large room, probably for the first time in many years.

Thick glass separated him from the outside. He needed something heavy to knock against it. On the opposite wall, a reinforced catwalk led to a ladder ascending toward the smallest of the spires. *No help there.* He couldn't latch onto it and direct it to swing over and bash into the wall. It was not tech, just a well-constructed framework.

The Guardian looked up at him and laughed. "Suit yourself. I'll allow one last glimpse of your home before your demise."

Logan was trapped. The windows were fixed panes. He looked through the thick glass to the outside world. Below, citizens went about their day, running errands, oblivious to the battle unfolding within the Hallowed Spires. They were quite solid in appearance.

"Come down from there, boy!"

Could he goad the Guardian into blasting open a window? To what end? So he could escape? But then what? Be captured by Durant and brought back to the Guardian in chains? He couldn't stay locked in here. The Guardian had the advantage in every way.

If he could get him to step out, however—

He needed to get at the man, unsettle him. Having lived so long with such little human interaction other than to boss around a few select servants, the man had to be lacking some in the mental faculties.

A small drone smashed into the wall near Logan's head, raining parts onto him. He stiffened and glared at the Guardian.

"I'm not coming to you and making it easy. Take me out from down there if you can."

The Guardian roared and, with a wave of his larger arm, sent a moderate-sized lift washer—the kind that hovered on the outside of buildings in the city to clean windows—rocketing toward Logan.

He ducked, letting the machine smash into the window. A stiff metal extension rod shot out and skewered him in the side. Logan staggered backward as pain flared. The lift washer fell toward him, and he shoved its falling bulk to the side. He gulped in panicked breaths. His side was on fire. He touched the half-inch-thick rod. It stuck out from him by a good ten inches in the front. His other hand felt around his lower back. The other end of the rod protruded by only three inches at most. His hands were sticky with blood.

He needed a Fixer to remove it and heal him. Then he could think about coming after the Guardian again. Was Kyle screwing up as badly as he was?

A quick inspection of the window revealed the glass had a thin crack running up and down but looked otherwise unaffected.

Logan saw a larger vehicle, a grav tank, floating up out of a pile of junk. He reached out and wrestled with the tech, hoping to take control of the vehicle from the Guardian. He felt a flicker of the man's presence in the tech but pressed on nonetheless.

The tank wobbled toward Logan as he strived to override the Guardian's programmed directives.

The Guardian shrieked, "How dare you! Don't tamper with it."

Doing his best to ignore the throbbing pain in his side, he slipped deeper into the tech. The Guardian looked flustered and outraged.

Logan felt the man's mind swamp his own meager tinkering and seek to send the tank at him full force. His injury was hampering his ability to focus on the tech properly, but he still kept at it, thrusting himself deeper into the machine's coding matrix.

Outraged, the Guardian guided the tank to hit him at full speed.

Logan sprang onto the hood of the tank and pushed off it a second before it crashed against the large window behind him.

Dropping off the side, he landed hard against a defunct vacuum robot, amazed he hadn't ended up flattened. His side felt like it was on fire.

The Guardian howled yet again, his anguish reaching out into the open air of the Hunter Enclave.

Eyeing the old man, there was a weariness heaped atop his insane bluster. The Guardian gulped in several breaths, indicating that while his torso was all tech and armor on the outside, lungs survived within to some extent.

Logan scaled the tank now wedged into the frame of the window and slipped out the jagged opening onto a ledge, his vision swimming. He needed to get away, get help.

The Guardian raged within, but his curses were distant, replaced by the strong winds buffeting Logan. Nearly forty feet below, two men tethered to Creepers looked up at Logan with fear.

The tank slipped back into the Spires. He looked within. The Guardian stood atop a lift platform, hovering only ten feet away from the exposed window. He sneered at Logan. "Do you take me for a fool? Run, flee. I'll not follow you, but I will set Hunters onto your trail. You will be caught and brought to me."

Logan saw the grav tank still aloft behind the man. He was going to fling it at him once more. It was only a few feet from the catwalk on the opposite wall. A risky idea entered his head. He slipped into the grav tank propulsion array and shoved it backward, ramming its bumper repeatedly against the catwalk.

The Guardian laughed and wrestled control from him. "You're no match for me. You can't stop me."

Logan shoved the vehicle back a final time and watched the mashed-up right end of the bumper hook onto the lower section of the catwalk ladder.

Ten feet below him and to his right was another ledge, much wider than his current perch. He needed to time it just right. He released his limited hold on the tank, and, once more wholly commandeered by the Guardian, it lurched forward. Hooked to the bumper, the catwalk tore free and dragged behind it. It only took seconds. The grav tank shot harmlessly past the Guardian, but the main bulk of the dislodged catwalk slammed into him as Logan jumped.

The Guardian screamed.

Logan landed on the wider perch, grunting in pain from the rod.

A second later, the grav tank broke through the side of the Spires, sending hunks of stone and plaster to the ground. Trailing behind it was the bulk of the catwalk, now twisted and hopelessly wound around the Guardian. In the bright light of day, the man's metal housing shone bright. The tank flew across the sky and plunged into the side of a squat building. The catwalk, meanwhile, separated and landed atop another building, taking the struggling Guardian with it.

Realization played across what little flesh and blood remained of his face.

He knows he's at the mercy of the inhibitor.

The man gasped, and his one good eye widened as his arms and legs locked into place. The red light of his artificial eye dimmed, and an exhaust port extending from his lower back expelled a dark cloud. No longer safely shielded from the effects of the inhibitor, all his tech systems were shutting down.

He teetered on the small roof, staring at Logan with regret and a hint of resignation.

Suddenly, the inadequate roof trusses underfoot gave out, and the Guardian came crashing down into the small building.

Gritting his teeth against the pain in his side, Logan staggered left and scaled down a drainage spout, jumping down the last dozen feet or so to land on all fours, tamping down the pangs of guilt. He had killed the man.

He fought back his tears. He was not done yet.

Two Hunters ran up to Logan and grabbed him by the wrists. The taller one said, "What have you done?"

Logan knew he couldn't stop now. He had to block out the pain, escape these men, and shut down the inhibitor for good. He lurched forward and wrested himself free, the rod in his side lodging a harsh protest at his sudden action.

Casting his mind outward, he zeroed in on the main door to the Spires. Without the Guardian to worry about, he could take the time to unlock the door.

"Stop! Someone grab him!" shouted the Hunter he had just slipped past. The man's spirit tugged to be free, eager to pursue Logan.

He limped past several surprised merchants and into a large crowd, hoping no one would snag him, all the while mentally working through the door's lock.

A man tethered to a Skimmer latched onto his right arm and pulled him back. "Young man, stop this nonsense! What are you doing? Was that the Guardian up on the roof?"

Logan squirmed free, but not before the man read some of what was on his mind. The man's face contorted in shock, and he pointed at Logan with a mix of fear and awe. "You're the boy who fled to the city." He shook his head, clearly astounded by the info he had managed to snag. "You came back. The sporecore? What's going on?"

Logan broke free and scrambled through the throng of people. He kept at the lock even though it divided his attention. If someone else decided to heed the Hunter's command, he'd be caught. How many times could he hope to snake free?

He darted out of the crowd and approached the large double doors. Two more security protocols remained to be unraveled.

A man with fiery red hair and waving a pick over his head ran at him, his Breaker leering at Logan from the man's shoulder. "Stop this now!"

Logan had the door completely unfettered. Several loud thunks sounded within, and it opened slowly outward with great ceremony.

Everyone around him turned and stared with disbelief at the unveiling. Logan knew only the servants were in contact with their Guardian. The man never came out. Having the Spires suddenly open up was just something that didn't happen. The shock of the event froze everyone, including the man with the lustful Breaker.

Logan didn't wait. He darted inside and raced toward the center of the tech-filled room. The surprise would soon wear off, and guards would pour in after him. He had to locate the inhibitor. He searched in the upper reaches, convinced it would need to be elevated to perform its job. He latched onto the inhibitor quickly. It was tucked away in the framework of the tallest spire. While he could turn it off from here, he needed to make sure it could never become operational again. He needed to destroy it.

A pair of guards slunk into the chamber and glared at him. Logan raced into the thick of the tech and searched for the means to get himself airborne. The rod in his side still worried him, but there was a spreading numbness around it that almost made him forget he was injured. Almost.

An arrow flew past his head, missing his left ear by inches.

He activated a bulky river rover, coaxing it to roll forward on its ramshackle treads toward the two men. This unnerved his attackers, and they slipped back behind the doorway. Logan weaved through the piles of tech, knowing the deeper he went would keep him out of range from any further arrows.

He prodded various tech with his mind. A quad leaper captured his attention, but its burnt power core rendered it useless. He managed to fire up a two-person Bounder but wrote it off after scanning its operations manual and finding it was impossible to operate solo.

Shouting and footfalls sounded from the open door. Reinforcements had arrived.

He gravitated to a pulse whomper. While a shoulder-mounted weapon that packed a wallop, it could get the job done. It emitted a series of disruptive sound waves. If he positioned it correctly, he could use it to propel himself upward. The trick was getting the right pressure. Too much, and it would smash him into the ceiling. He thought of how Kyle's mom used her hose to water her meager collection of medicinal herbs on her small balcony. She took great care in making sure the stream of water was just right. Logan hoped he could be just as surgically precise. He ran through the schematics and limitations with lightning speed. If he did it right, he might incur a cracked rib or two, but what other choice did he have? Already, the guards were making their way amidst the tech. They weren't being quiet about it either. All were announcing their presence and calling out for his surrender.

Ignoring the torso braces and leveraging straps, he lifted the heavy weapon and centered its stock against his chest. He adjusted the output to build progressively and pulled the trigger. Jarringly, he vaulted into the air. He eased the flow threshold back two notches, and his ascent slowed.

Below, two Hunters squawked in surprise and pointed their bows at him. He nudged the output and soared upward, the dizzying speed causing him slight vertigo. He touched his injury, fearing the sudden jolt had caused more blood loss. Nausea rose in his stomach from the motion. *I'll make it up to the inhibitor, but there's no guarantee I'll be conscious enough to destroy it.*

An arrow sailed by, missing him. Another bounced off the side of the whomper. A third penetrated his left leg at the calf. He bit down on his lip and held back his tears.

Finally, he was up in the dome of the tallest spire. Thankfully, there was a narrow catwalk crossing the open area. He landed on it near the center and dropped the weapon onto the metal mesh floor panels.

Halfway across, a hatch in the durilium-lined ceiling was all that stood between him and the inhibitor. Of course, it would have to sit outside of the shielded interior of the Spires. Logan made short work of the lock mechanism and the hatch swung slowly downward.

He awkwardly pulled himself up through the opening, being careful to avoid knocking the rod in his side against the rim of the opening. Spots appeared in his vision from his strained movements.

In front of him was a four-foot-tall silver obelisk with lit circuitry racing along its surface like pulsating tattoos.

The inhibitor.

He spied the shutdown switch but ignored it. Instead, he attempted to manipulate the tech so it would reverse and direct its nullifying effects on itself, effectively burning it out without inducing an explosion. While he might have been able to do the same from the safety of the ground, his rapidly deteriorating mental alertness would've made such an undertaking uncertain of success. Even though his vision was closing in, blackness reaching from the edges with more aggressiveness than just a minute ago, he plied his tech talent with determination.

The glowing lights crisscrossing the obelisk flared and then extinguished. There was a faint pop, and then the device died.

He'd done it. Tech could return to the enclaves.

He smiled and dropped to his knees, suddenly aware of how weak he felt. The tail end of the arrow in his leg snapped against the metal handrail as he slumped to the metal panel and lost consciousness.

Chapter 48
Kyle

The Guardian continued her anguished wailing for a while longer, slowly trailing off with a choke as she slumped to her knees.

The Fixer hadn't just hit the wall. It remained there, utterly stuck, spreading slowly outward as though a great force were slowly squashing it flat. Blood and gore leaked out and dribbled in all directions across the wall, defying the laws of gravity.

Kyle looked away. He knew the inhibitor had caused this, and he resolved to find it. Somehow, the woman was keeping her tethered Forerunners safe by remaining in contact with them. Why was the Swimmer immune, then? Because it was below ground? That seemed unlikely. It was literally yards away, shielded only by a metal grid flooring. Perhaps because it was protected by the water? Possibly. Or, being the so-called source of all magic, maybe it was simply unaffected by the relatively mundane inhibitor. In any case, the other Forerunners had no such protection. They were dead the moment they left her body, repelled by the powerful force and sent to the far east—if there were no walls in the way.

But where was the device?

The awful wailing had ceased. The Guardian was still on her knees, a shapeless mound of humps covered with a black robe.

Kyle turned to resume his climb up the circular steps. The inhibitor had to be up there.

The Guardian lifted her head. "Go on up. Do your worst!" She struggled to her feet and hobbled toward him again, dragging her foot. Her stench wafted up Kyle's nostrils. "I've seen you on the news streams. I know why you're here. But you *will not* prevail. Order must be preserved."

Kyle threw himself onto the junk and began climbing, not caring that everything toppled under him. He took the circular staircase two steps at a time, round and round, and sprang out onto the upper level looking for booby-traps.

The room was the exact same size as the one below but almost completely empty, just a stepladder in the middle of the floor leading to a skylight. The rungs were smothered with cobwebs, the entire floor thick with dust.

Kyle looked around, confused. "Where's the inhibitor?" he muttered. "I don't get it."

He heard moaning from below. Something was going on with the Guardian. Kyle peered down the circular staircase and glimpsed the woman bent double as something alarming happened. Her robe bulged outward from her back, stretching and stretching until it ripped open. Then, impossibly, the distinctive form of a Hunter began to extract itself as though clawing its way out of a shallow grave. Meanwhile, the Weaver that bulged from her shoulder moved and twisted, obviously disturbed by all the movement.

A Weaver, a Creeper, and now a Hunter, Kyle thought in amazement. Three solid-form Forerunners crammed together in the small frame of a tiny elderly lady. How was it possible? They had to be out of sync with each other, but even so . . .

The Hunter pulled itself partway out of her body and rose up behind her, still firmly embedded in her back but now free enough to look around and take control. It thrust its tusks out mere inches above the Guardian's head and gave a triumphant roar.

Kyle backed away from the trapdoor, suddenly worried. He wasn't concerned about a Weaver or a Creeper, but a Hunter was another matter. It knew how to kill.

He headed toward the stepladder, the only object in the room. A stepladder to a skylight. Perhaps a vantage point for the

Guardian so she could look out on the city from time to time? Judging by the coating of undisturbed dust, she hadn't been up here in years. That didn't mean the inhibitor wasn't up here, though. Perhaps it was out on the roof.

He climbed the stepladder, getting smothered in sticky cobwebs. Reaching up to the grime-coated skylight, he fumbled with the latch. It slipped open just as footsteps began stamping up the circular staircase. He pushed the skylight upward. It creaked noisily, and unfiltered daylight flooded in, causing him to blink. The warmth felt good on his face as he climbed higher.

His feet wobbled on the top step of the ladder as he paused with his head and shoulders poking out above the roofline. Four police cruisers hovered nearby, looking down on the front entrance of the building. One began to spin around to face him.

"Where's the inhibitor?" he moaned again, feeling a crushing sense of disappointment. He was going to fail his mission.

A low wall surrounded the large, square roof. Other than a few vent grilles, flues, and water runoff gutters, the space was utterly featureless, surfaced with the usual lightweight roofing slabs and synthetic gravel.

Still no inhibitor.

A hand gripped his ankle. He yelled and kicked hard, and the grip loosened enough for him to pull himself out onto the roof. He rolled and climbed to his feet as the Guardian clambered up the stepladder after him. The Hunter's head appeared first, then the Weaver's and her own, each equally angry. The Hunter roared and reached for Kyle with gnarled, clawed fingers, this time missing his leg and digging into gravel instead.

The police cruiser whined closer and began to descend. Kyle darted around the roof, looking for an escape ladder. He spotted one and ran to it, but when he looked down, he realized the entire lower half had been removed, probably long ago. He was only two stories up; he could climb down and jump. But then what?

He looked back at the Guardian. She was now out on the roof, hobbling toward him with three heads and several arms, a bizarre, twisted creature with black robes fluttering in the downdraft from the police cruiser. Even the cruiser seemed to have balked, pausing as though the pilot was stunned by what he saw.

"Where's the inhibitor?" Kyle shouted over the constant whine.

The Guardian laughed. Her Hunter and Weaver didn't look so amused, but her old, milky-eyed face was creased with toothless mirth. "What did you expect to find here, boy? A big machine? A magical staff or dazzling crystal? Did you really think the inhibitor would be something so ordinary?"

Kyle blinked rapidly as not one but two cruisers swept closer. "Then what?" he said as the Guardian staggered toward him.

He guessed her Hunter was controlling her legs now. Her eyes were so pale that she had to be blind, perhaps seeing through the eyes of the Weaver. Now that the Hunter was out, it was exerting control and itching to kill the intruder. Kyle sensed its fury and felt its burning hunger. It hadn't gotten to hunt in a long, long time.

I don't have a chance against that thing, he thought.

He considered trying to take the Hunter over, but he didn't think it would cave easily even to him. It was too focused on the kill. The Weaver, though . . .

As the cruisers finally touched down and doors hissed open, he reached out to the Weaver. "To me," he said.

The Weaver lurched sideways, separating the gap between its head and the Guardian's. Blind though she appeared to be, she twisted to look as the Weaver tilted at an angle, looking like it was falling in slow motion, tearing open the robe as it went. The Hunter forced the Guardian to take a few more hobbling steps, then reached forward hungrily even as the Weaver toppled farther out of her body.

Cops began running, drawing their weapons and yelling.

"To *me*!" Kyle demanded.

The Weaver seemed to be struggling. It flailed on the ground, its feet still caught up within the Guardian's body, a freakish sight as it tried to pull itself clear of her.

"No!" the Guardian screeched, twisting around. "Don't let go of me! Don't—"

At the precise moment the Weaver pulled its long-toed feet free, something happened that caused Kyle to leap back in horror. As with the Fixer downstairs, an unseen force picked up the Weaver and whisked it across the roof. Rather than slide to a halt on the gravel, it hit the low wall and bounced upward, then continued flying through the air, heading east, spinning all the way. It narrowly missed a neighboring building and flew past on a dead-straight, unwavering trajectory over the city's perimeter Wall toward the wastelands. Kyle watched in amazement as it diminished to a dot and disappeared.

By this time, the Hunter had dragged the Guardian close enough that it could reach for Kyle with its clawed fingers. Her robe, hanging low off one shoulder, revealed a misshapen body where the Weaver had been for so long. Her own human arm, smothered and disused for so long, seemed to have fused to her torso. The scaly, barrel-chested monster was gone. In its place was a pitiful skeleton of an old woman.

But the Hunter now had more room to move. It quickly shifted around, filling out the Guardian's skinny shoulder and causing it to twist and bulge. Backed up against the low wall at the edge of the roof, Kyle had nowhere to go as the Hunter gripped his throat and began to squeeze.

"Stand back!" the cops were yelling. "We've got the boy covered! Stand back!"

They were dancing about, perhaps waiting for a clear shot, somehow afraid to approach and yank the two apart. Kyle couldn't blame them. The Guardian cut a freakish figure.

As the Hunter squeezed Kyle's windpipe, he reached inside with his mind, grappling with the creature's hand and trying to take control. He succeeded to some degree. He would have been dead already otherwise. He fought hard, a battle of wills to keep those vicious Hunter fingers from throttling him. In one-on-one combat with a true Hunter, it would have flung him to the ground and stabbed him with that jutting horn, but this creature hadn't seen the light of day in a long time and was severely crippled inside the woman's feeble body.

"Leave her behind," Kyle gasped. The grip weakened slightly. It was hard to talk out loud, though, so he sent it his thoughts instead. *Come on, you don't need her. Step outside of her body and fight me like a real Hunter, not some coward in an old woman's body.*

His challenge was met with a terrible roar of anger, and the Hunter scrambled to free itself, practically climbing up and out of the woman's back. As it emerged and grew in mass, the woman fell to her hands and knees, driven down by the increased weight. The Hunter continued gripping Kyle's throat while it kicked its way out of the Guardian's back as if shucking off some tired old boots.

As it lifted its second foot out, the same terrible unseen force smacked the Hunter away, sending it east at breathtaking speed. It roared in anguish as it went, but this time, perhaps because of a gust of wind, it hit the corner of the neighboring building and bounced away, spinning wildly, now silent and broken as it soared into the far distance.

The Guardian sobbed at Kyle's feet. Even while she hunched there on hands and knees, tentacles were appearing through some of the gaps in her tattered robe. Kyle tightened his jaw, knowing exactly what would happen if that creature tore itself free . . . but accepting it had to happen anyway.

He'd figured it out. The Guardian hadn't been protecting and maintaining the inhibitor for the last few centuries. She *was* the inhibitor.

Spore deliveries by Yando and his predecessors kept the Forerunners solid. Their long lifespan, coupled with the Swimmer's magic, had allowed her to remain tethered and survive for hundreds of years.

Cops continued shouting, but Kyle ignored them. "Come on out," he said softly, reaching for the Creeper with his mind while bending to lay a hand on the woman's skinny shoulder. The Creeper was weak-minded and malleable, but as he searched its mind, he realized it was ready to go anyway. "Yes, it's time," he agreed softly.

Our old friend in the basement, it said hoarsely. *Free him. Return him to the Wiscuppa.*

"I will," Kyle agreed. Glancing at the approaching white-faced cops as they trained their weapons on him, he added, "I'll come back for him."

They said nothing as they reached out and yanked him away from the Guardian. They threw him roughly onto the synthetic gravel and pressed down while cuffing him tightly, shouting in his ear about being under arrest.

He barely heard a word. All his focus was on the Creeper. "Time to step away," he said softly, and the Creeper seemed to reach for him with its tentacles. Kyle had the sense of an old, old creature in pain, something that wanted to go away and die. It was past its lifespan. The Forerunners lived a long time, literally centuries, but they'd been compelled to share a single physical body with no way to slip away into peaceful death. While one lived, they all had to. The Hunter had been the youngest and strongest, the Weaver a few decades older and somewhat wiser. The Creeper was practically dead already, forced to keep breathing while trapped in the Guardian's body.

Time to go, it whispered eagerly.

As the robe rippled and tore, the Creeper pulled itself free.

The inhibitor spell flung it away.

As Kyle was dragged to his feet, cops surrounded the Guardian. One tentatively approached and leaned over her, but she was unmoving, a small, huddled figure under a pool of dull-black material. So tiny now, so old and frail, with nothing to keep her alive, she succumbed to the natural order of things . . . and died.

Glancing east, Kyle spotted the Creeper in the distance, still shooting through the air.

Then, unlike the Hunter and Weaver earlier, it simply dropped out of the sky.

Kyle sighed. The inhibitor wasn't so much disabled as dead.

Chapter 49
Logan

Logan woke to the sound of a Fixer cooing in his ear. He swatted at it, and the furry creature hopped off the bed and into the arms of the girl sitting beside him. He instantly recognized her strawberry-blond hair and petite nose.

"Nomi," he sighed heavily.

The Fixer sat in her lap, swishing its three tails against her yellow shirt, causing it to bunch up slightly.

Definitely solid and not a spirit.

To further emphasize this, Nomi exhaled, producing an impressive glowing cloud. It drifted upward.

Logan felt his side for the rod. It was no longer there. He pulled back the sheet to see bandages stretched over the injury.

Nomi smiled. "You really got hurt. Took your mom and me almost all afternoon to mend you."

He sat up but quickly slipped back against the pillow, his head swimming.

"You lost a lot of blood, so take it easy." Nomi continued, "Good news, the arrow was much easier to deal with. I bet your leg'll feel like new by tomorrow."

He ran his hand down to the calf and felt a small bandage where the arrow had been embedded. It didn't throb like the other injury. "Where are we?"

The bedroom was far larger than his own. The long, ornate drapes framing the single window told him he was in a home of someone well-to-do. A delicate sculpture of a Glider decorated an alcove next to the window. Logan briefly admired the craft of the Weaver-wrought art. *Very affluent home*, he thought.

She petted her Fixer. "Your injuries were serious. We didn't dare take you far, so you were brought close by, two streets down from the Hallowed Spires. Sovereign Durant's home. Not that he's here."

"What do you mean?" he asked.

His mother entered from the open door to his far left. She carried a tray loaded down with breads and steaming durgle meat. "Your friend, Mr. Torren, arrived shortly after your encounter with the Guardian. The Council met behind closed doors with him for most of the morning, while Nomi and I tended to you. They came for Durant a little before lunch."

"And the sovereign was not happy with you, Logan," Nomi said. "He refused us entry, but your father stood up to him."

"Durant wanted to deny you medical treatment as well. He spouted off how anyone who would bring about the death of the Guardian was an enemy to all." His mother placed the tray on his stomach and helped to prop him up better. Her Fixer hopped off her shoulder and cuddled up next to Nomi's. It was odd to see his mother's spirit playing well with others. It had always been a loner, prickly around other Fixers.

Logan knew the acting sovereign had been in cahoots with the Guardian. "He sent Kiff underground with a bomb attached to him."

His mother grimaced. 'We know. That was perhaps the most damning evidence Abe provided." Her hand touched his forehead as he tore into a large piece of bread. "I'm glad you were able to disable it with your *gifts*." She said the last word with such reverence.

"What about Kiff? I left him in a barn."

His mother smiled. "He's downstairs. He showed up at our doorstep, going on about your intention to take out the Guardian. We raced here to the Hunter Enclave immediately."

Just like Kiff to disobey him. He should've known his little brother wouldn't sit still all day in that barn. "But weren't you being watched? Didn't the sovereign's Hunters nab you when Kiff showed up?"

"They tried, but your father fought back. His Breaker is even fiercer when it's flesh and blood." Nomi shuddered.

"We arrived shortly after you came spilling out of the Hallowed Spires," his mother said. "Kiff saw you go back inside. We came running but were barred from helping until the Hunters got you down from that rickety catwalk. You were a mess. Luckily, Nomi tagged along with us. She was indispensable." She smiled warmly at the younger Fixer.

"I destroyed the inhibitor," Logan said. "Tech can work again." He quickly chewed a piece of durgle meat, then slumped. "And the Guardian, I killed him."

His father walked in, his Breaker separated from his body. The large Forerunner stood abreast of him, both their chests swelled with pride. Behind them, Kiff slipped past and came around to kneel beside Nomi. He petted the closest Fixer, and it playfully whipped its tails at him.

His father said, "You didn't kill the Guardian. He was long gone before you came. He was a shadow clinging to a world that had grown out of sync with our future. Change needed to occur. What happened was necessary and good."

Logan was not used to seeing him so optimistic. "But I—"

His father raised a hand. "Not one more word about it. The Guardian is a thing of the past." He eyed his Breaker with respect. "We must move forward now, Forerunners and humans as one."

The Breaker spoke, his voice a throaty croak. "Bound together by destiny, but neither of us tethered or made to be less than we are." The creature's eyes held both bitter pain and bountiful hope. It amazed Logan to see such depth in a simple Breaker.

His father bowed and took an apologetic tone. "Where are my manners?" He stood up straight and waved at the Breaker. "Logan, this is Alkwoo. He is whole once more."

The Breaker extended his large, solid hand and Logan shook it, fascinated by his scaly skin.

Alkwoo said, “Thank you for opening the Well and tearing down the inhibitors. You have brought long-sought freedom to my people, and we will forever be in yours and Kyle’s debt.”

Kiff said, “Everything’s good, Logan.”

His mother cupped his face in her hands. “It’s amazing to hold tight to you and your brother once again.” She expelled a cloud of bright spores and slipped one hand free to clutch at Kiff’s small hand. “We’re in sync now, yes?”

Logan held off eating and soaked up her presence, deriving pleasure in her supportive touch. It did feel good to be aligned once again. “Everything’s going to be so different.”

Nomi placed her hand atop his own. “Definitely.”

She smiled.

Chapter 50
Kyle

Kyle and Byron spent four hours and twenty-two minutes in a juvenile holding cell according to the robot boy's annoyingly accurate built-in clock. The only visitor was a guard with a tray of bread and water. Byron grumbled once about the long wait, and Kyle immediately said, "If you'd gone home when I told you, you wouldn't have been arrested. So quit complaining."

Nothing more was said on the matter. Despite his gruff remark, Kyle appreciated his brother's loyalty, not to mention his company in this mind-numbingly boring cell.

Then, finally, the solitude ended.

The door to the hallway hissed open. Three heavily armed jail guards walked in first, eyeing Kyle warily as they spread out along the white-painted bars, their boots clicking noisily on the shiny white floor. "You have a visitor," one barked.

Behind the guards, a bearded man with a rather large nose strolled in with his hands behind his back, accompanied by two personal bodyguards, one of them huge. The man in charge, wearing an extremely dapper suit and tie, walked all the way up to the bars and peered through. He gave Byron a curt nod, looked hard at Kyle, then dismissed the three jail guards with a casual gesture.

He waited until they'd left before speaking. "I'm Mayor Trilmott. This feels rather like a conversation I've had before. Perhaps you'll be a little more reasonable than your long-haired wild-boy twin."

"I doubt it," Kyle muttered.

If Trilmott had heard, he pretended he hadn't. "I want to work with you, Master Jaxx. As I told Logan, the public sees you boys as a force for good, and I'd like you by my side as we face the exciting months ahead. Everything is changing." He blew gently as if to prove his point, a faint glow visible even in the brightly lit whitewashed room. "You see that? Spores! I dug up ancient records about such a phenomenon. It's hard to imagine glowing breath was once the norm." He spread his hands and forced a grin. "So what do you say, Master Jaxx? Will you work with me to appease our citizens, to reassure them that all is well, that centuries of darkness and corruption have been lifted and our world is reverting to its natural state?"

Kyle glanced at Byron and raised an eyebrow, then back at Trilmott. "How about letting us go home first? I haven't seen my parents in a week."

The mayor nodded. "Of course, of course. In fact . . ." He looked sideways at the smaller of the bodyguards and gave a nod. The man turned, stomped over to the door, and slapped the pad by the side. The door hissed open.

Outside in the hallway, two people were ushered into view, and Kyle's heart skipped a beat. His parents! Their faces lit up when they saw him. Kyle opened his mouth to call out—but the bodyguard promptly slapped the pad again, and the door hissed shut in their faces.

Trilmott's grin broadened. "They're here to collect you, Kyle. You're free to go."

With that, he stepped over to an adjacent wall and pressed his hand against an electronic pad. It glowed green, and the cage door slid open.

Kyle frowned. "Seriously? That's it? You're letting us go after I killed the Guardian?"

"Of course, my boy! She was insane. Ever since you—pardon me, *Logan*—uncovered the truth about my predecessor and his corrupt power, I've been working hard to restore this city to its former glory. Logan's incredible command of tech raised questions that hadn't been raised in a very long time. His revelations about a parallel land in the east, the fracturing of our world and the previously unexplained wink-outs, phantom creatures that roam the wastelands . . . It all led to the recovery of ancient records and startling news of a three-hundred-year conspiracy to keep our cultures separated."

Like you didn't already know about it, Kyle thought, sneaking a sideways glance at Byron.

The mayor drew himself up straight. "And thanks to my diligent work since taking office, the restoration of our world is underway. The destruction of the infamous Tower, the re-opening of the Well and the spores now filling our atmosphere, the first sightings of a distant civilization as it comes into focus, and most importantly the astonishing emergence of creatures we believed extinct. Not two hours ago, they walked out of the Ruins toward the Wall. Exciting times are ahead, and it's all thanks to me."

Kyle could hardly believe his ears. "All thanks to *you*?"

"Well, and you, of course. Nobody can deny your involvement. You and Logan together uncovered the truth. You're instrumental in what is already being heralded as the New Beginning." He gestured broadly at this as though speaking to a packed audience at the City Hall. "An ancient race returns to the surface and wishes to negotiate a unification for the future! Tech in return for tethering! Peace and cooperation for all!" A moment later, he let his arms fall to his sides. "The question, Kyle, is what *you* want out of this."

"Huh?"

Trilmott leaned closer, his glare hardening. "The spy footage is all over the Hub—you on the roof, exorcising those phantoms and flinging them far and wide. You either murdered a poor, harmless old woman whose only crime was to devote her life to protecting the city . . . or you saved us from an evil witch. I can spin it either way."

Kyle's mouth flapped open and shut a few times. Next to him, Byron clicked and whirred.

"But she was the *inhibitor*," Kyle managed at last. "She was preventing—"

"Details, details!" The mayor waved his hand dismissively. "How about it, Kyle? Would you like to go home a hero? Or are you going to be . . . difficult?"

The warning in his tone was obvious. Kyle studied his cold, calculating eyes. Like the mayor before him, Trilmott was determined to come out on top and look good in public no matter what. The spores, the appearance of Forerunners and Seekers, the realization that so-called techless deadbeats like Kyle might be perfectly adept at tethering instead . . . Mayor Trilmott would find a way to spin everything in his favor with or without Kyle.

"I can't say I'm happy about what's happening, Kyle," the mayor purred, "but if the maglev is going to leave the station, I intend to be driving it, not hanging off the rear end."

And drive it he would, at least for the time being. It probably didn't matter, though. Apparatum was becoming whole again. In the months ahead, people from the city would venture out and explore the landscape. They would take their machines to the enclaves and offer high-end medical equipment and industrial-sized construction machines, not to mention hovercars to zip about the mountains. Perhaps some of Logan's people would come to the city, bringing their recently fleshed-out Forerunners with them and providing natural alternatives for everyday tasks.

It wouldn't all be rosy, but old towns could be rebuilt, new settlements established. The risk of being possessed by dangerous spirit creatures had been eradicated. Instead, the Forerunners offered the hand—or tentacle—of friendship.

Assuming they can forgive the city for what it did, Kyle thought. *Three hundred years trapped underground . . .*

"Well?" Trilmott demanded. "What's it to be, Master Jaxx? Do you want to go home with your parents or not? I can't stand around here all day waiting for you to make up your mind."

"I want to go home," Kyle said.

The mayor seemed to relax. "And in doing so," he said firmly, "you hereby agree to support me in a public manner?"

"Huh?"

The mayor rolled his eyes. "Come, now, you know what I mean. You and Logan are already in the limelight, together with your robot brother here. If you're to remain in that limelight, doing interviews and what-have-you, then there are certain unhappy aspects of this whole affair I'd like you to spin in my favor. Put simply, the better you make me look, the happier you and your family will be. Do you understand?"

"Sure," Kyle said sullenly. *Play along or meet with an unfortunate accident.* "There's just one thing, though."

The mayor looked suspicious. "Spit it out."

"The Swimmer."

After a moment of confusion, Trilmott's said, "The giant fish in the Guardian's basement? What about it?"

"You have to unseal the door and let it escape into the Wiscuppa."

The mayor blinked a few times. "You want that monster loose in the underground rivers?"

"It's not a monster."

After a long moment of staring at the ceiling as though trying to figure out a reason not to agree, the mayor spread his hands and shrugged. "Keeping it locked up won't do me any favors. So yes, fine, I'll do it. Now, no more demands or I'll have you repurposed."

Kyle drew himself up. Repurposing was another thing he wanted to put an end to . . . but perhaps that mission could wait until he was safely back in the public eye.

Despite everything, he was relieved to be free. This new mayor was less than ideal, but Kyle felt he had done his part. It was time for others to step in, perhaps Abe Torren himself. Let *them* run around playing politics.

All Kyle cared about was that he had, against all the odds, escaped the Repurposing Factory over a week ago with very little chance of survival in the Ruins.

And now he was home.

Epilogue

Kiff kicked at the three-foot-tall post, causing the single blue ribbon tied to it to quiver and jump. These posts were obsolete now. A Banisher would no longer be needed to visit this site and imbue it with magic to ward off untethered spirits from entering the Enclaves. What would Mora Vil, a girl in Logan's class who had just been indoctrinated in the ways of the Banishers, do with herself now?

Logan looked out over the expanse of land before them. Dozens of Forerunners raced around, working alongside large construction machines from Apparati. Kiff still got a thrill at seeing the tech moving freely about. While many in his enclave had been issued solar-powered stream screens until more permanent wiring and hook-ups could be installed, their father had opted to wait, claiming it was more important to let others go first. Kiff found their father's enthusiasm for change admirable. Besides, he liked looking over Logan's shoulder at his wrist tablet. It gave them something to bond over.

Their father was down there supervising the reconstruction of the Forerunner city. Kiff watched him direct a group of Breakers to corner two kalibacks who had emerged from a section of ruins that hadn't been torn down yet.

Logan saw this too and said, "Looks like there's still some stragglers."

Kiff stopped kicking at the pole and walked over to stand beside his older brother. "They're relocating them to some unclaimed territory beyond the Glider Enclave."

"Best place for them. I'm sure they'll try to roam about, but Dad says several Hunters and some of our people have plans to build an outpost there and keep tabs on them. Would you rather they wipe them out?" Logan looked at Kiff with apprehension.

His older brother knew he had been attacked by a kaliback at a young age. "No, that would throw things out of balance."

Logan smiled at him.

Kiff said, "It's amazing how quickly all of this is happening."

In just three months, envoys from both the city and enclaves had come and gone several times between Apparati and Apparata, opening trading and an eagerness to share their resources. Reconstruction of the wastelands had begun. A new sovereign had been elected, one more open-minded than Durant, who now faced a hearing in a few weeks to determine if charges would be leveled for his misdeeds. The man had slapped a bomb on him and sent him after Logan. Kiff wanted him to rot in the Pens, but would never say such out loud.

To hear it from Kyle, sweeping changes were also happening in the city. Kyle's home was onboard with unifying the world of Apparatum. Apparata's government, the Hub, was resetting the priorities of that world. A big step in that direction was the joint effort to level the Broken Lands and the Ruins in order to rebuild the Forerunner's city.

In the distance, near the site of the former Tower, tall ornate buildings were taking shape while, nearby, the fungal cannon in the Well regularly spread its spores out into the world.

Kiff looked at a purple fungus growing out of a fertile patch of soil alongside the creek to their left. Hundreds of these new growths littered the enclaves, helping pump into the air the spores that kept the Forerunners intact both mentally and physically.

Nomi emerged from a slight path behind them, carrying a large basket. She held it up. "You boys hungry for some lunch?"

Logan raced over to her and snuck a quick kiss on her cheek. She blushed as she laid out the spread of food. He grabbed a guddle wrap, a new favorite imported from the city. "Where's your Fixer?"

Nomi smiled. "Harva is probably down there assisting in any work site injuries. She checks in with me from time to time." She tapped at her wrist tablet. "And I can get word to her if I have need."

Logan nodded and slurped at his frundle yogurt.

Kiff ate some sliced kappa melon. As he spit out his share of yellow seeds, he said, "When can I try one of those skip packs?"

"Not anytime soon. The council is slowly introducing tech. Baby steps, brother."

Kiff licked his lips. "Of course, I could go find a Glider agreeable to take me up, but it's not the same." It pleased him that he could bond with the Forerunners so easily while Logan could not. True, his older brother was a master of tech, but Kiff knew Logan still felt a little out of place at not being able to work closely with any of the Forerunners like Kyle did regularly. Kiff looked down at the flurry of construction. *I bet Kyle wishes he were down there right now, working his magic.* Kyle had visited them a few times since defeating the Guardians, and the city boy always seemed wistful around the construction sites.

Kiff asked Logan, "Why do you think Kyle wants to come out here and help with the rebuilding so much?"

Nomi answered, "He just wants to make things right with the Forerunners. Being so close with them, I would imagine it weighs on him that they've been stuck underground or in spirit form for so long." She nodded toward Logan. "Much the way your big brother still feels guilty about what happened with the Guardian."

Kiff knew what she was talking about. Twice he had overheard Logan crying in his sleep and mumbling about the Guardian's fate.

Logan stood and walked toward the edge of the clearing to better gaze out at the construction site. He carried a tweeda stalk with him, snatching bites of it as he spoke. "There's a lot I want to forget but can't. And I shouldn't. The Forerunners were forgotten and look how messed up our world got—counterparts, wink-outs, corrupt governments, crazed Guardians." He inhaled slowly. "It's a new world out there, one where new connections and ties can be forged. I don't know about you, but that sits just fine with me."

Nomi walked over to him and slipped her hand into his. Kiff joined them.

They watched the changes being wrought for a long time, long enough to attract the attention of a Breaker that Kiff had noticed milled about near the edges of the construction but never assisted in.

The Breaker thundered up the incline and came to a stop a few feet from Kiff. It still shocked him to see the Forerunners grounded, using their legs to hustle about instead of coasting through the air. Only Gliders did that now.

It was large. Its right jaw tusk was worn down to a nub. From the simple loincloth it wore, Kiff knew it to be a male. When the Forerunners had been spirits, gender had never been noticeable.

The Breaker looked all three of them up and down, settling his gaze on Kiff. His voice rumbled like distant thunder, "I am Reesk. We have met before."

Kiff stiffened, uncertain what the Forerunner meant.

"I was without my wits and resolve then." He extended a thick arm. "May we commune?"

Kiff nodded slowly.

The Breaker drew close and merged with him. It was disrespectful to call it tethering anymore; most labelled it communing or bonding, a clearer indication that the ritual was consensual.

The Breaker said, "I would share with you."

Kiff felt Reesk's memories seep into his own. Their common experience resolved into focus. Kiff gasped. This was the spirit that had tried to overwhelm him, take control of his young body when he had trespassed in the Broken Lands.

Kiff cringed. He experienced Reesk's bestial side, his inability to control his baser instincts as the scene replayed, including Kyle evicting the savage spirit.

Reesk's words came out slow. "I am sorry for what I did. I am not that thing."

Kiff whispered, relaxing a little, "I know."

"I ask for forgiveness."

Kiff nodded and sent the Forerunner pleasant thoughts and assurances rather than utter his acknowledgement.

The Breaker disengaged and once again stood as solid as a rock before him. Reesk bowed slightly and grinned, then tore off down the hill. In minutes, he was back lingering at the edges of the construction site.

Kiff looked at Logan and smiled.

His older brother said, "You think he'll help out down there?"

Kiff said, "Uh-huh. We all have a part to play."

* * *

Byron decided he'd never grow bored watching Kyle and Rissa together. It was constant entertainment, much of it loud and sometimes involving her fists on his bruised arm. But usually it was good-natured. Kyle had somehow developed a way to handle her. She must really like him on some deep level, though she hid it pretty well.

They were on the corner of Walshum and Gruber in the pristine heart of the city center. Shoppers and office workers milled about, faint green puffs venting from their mouths and noses, a sight so common now that everyone took it for granted. A few Forerunners mingled with them too, moving slowly, nodding politely as they navigated the crowds. While the Weavers and Hunters could almost be missed with a casual glance, the occasional Breaker loomed tall, easy to spot. A Creeper darted by, and several people faltered. Nobody had quite gotten used to these insectoid, tentacled creatures.

Rissa had paused to study her mora fish wrap, her blond hair pulled back in a tight ponytail. She grimaced. "Yet again I have to put up with substandard quality. I ask you, does *this*"—she thrust out the wrap for Kyle and Byron to see—"look *anything* like the picture?"

The street vendor's carefully crafted menu images certainly looked more appetizing than the product. Kyle took her by the elbow. "If you want perfection, don't buy from a man on a street corner. Anyway, have you tried it? Mine tastes great."

"I should remind him again who my father is," she muttered.

"How about I get you a name tag so it's clear?" Kyle said. "Rissa Talios, the only daughter of General Talios, liable to pop a vein if everything isn't perfect. Stand clear."

She glared at him. "Watch it, Kyle Jaxx. You should be nicer to me. It's thanks to me that the mayor doesn't repurpose you."

"No, he doesn't repurpose me because the Repurposing Factory has been closed down."

"My father could sneak you in there if I asked."

Kyle waved his own mora fish in her face. "Eat."

The two of them ate, and Byron watched with absolutely no envy. He'd forgotten what food smelled like, what it was like to bite and chew and swallow, to let a meal sit in his stomach for hours while it digested. He shuddered internally, grateful for his clean, serviceable, artificial framework and more processing power than two dozen computers combined.

Rissa had continually tried to intimidate Kyle for the first couple of months they'd hung out, and Kyle had put up with it, secretly telling Byron that being close to her offered a unique relationship with General Talios. "Keep your friends close and your enemies closer," he'd said. "Anyway, she's pretty."

She'd softened a little in the past month. Still not exactly warm and friendly, though. Byron could think of a whole list of other words that described her better, such as terse, outspoken, arrogant, aloof, and unsociable to name a few. But lately, Byron had detected in her the *tiniest* hint of pleasantness. Kyle somehow managed to counter her complaints with a straight face and wear her down until she either exploded—as she would with anyone else—or caved. Sometimes she even reddened as though glimpsing herself from the outside and being marginally ashamed.

"Hey, Jaxx!" a voice shouted.

Byron turned to see a heavyset man striding forward, his breath puffing out voluminous light. He was accompanied by a Breaker; the huge creature trailed him like a personal bodyguard, though he seemed a good deal more respectful to others on the street than the obese man did.

"You're the Jaxx kid," he said, stabbing a fat finger toward Kyle.

"I'm one of them," Kyle said, his mora fish poised in front of his face.

The man shot Byron a glance, then returned his attention to Kyle. "That's how I know it's you. 'Cause of *him*, the weird tin boy."

Rissa puffed up as she often did when other people were rude and obnoxious. "I warn you to be very careful what you—"

"Shut up, girl," the man retorted. He stepped up close to Kyle, who barely flinched despite being half the size. "My son vanished. Winked out. You said there would be no more wink-outs. You and the mayor told everyone wink-outs were a thing of the past."

Byron knew this was a hot topic in the city. He and Kyle had been questioned about the matter by their own parents soon after arriving home. At first, Kyle had been flippant, saying that the dilemma of his repurposing might not have come up at all if Logan had in fact been put to death by Sovereign Lambost in the enclaves. If Kyle had winked out, his dad would have been spared the job of sentencing his own son to death.

The comment had stung like a whip lash, but it had also cleared the air. Byron felt his brother had been itching to say something like that ever since returning home. Despite the initial hugs and tears during their reunion, the atmosphere had thickened at the same rate as the spores in the air. His wink-out retort, though incredibly hurtful, paved the way for some real, heartfelt discussions. After that, the healing had begun.

Today, Kyle was a different person, and it was obvious their mom and dad saw it. They said he'd grown up too early. Though still only fourteen, he was a man now. But while they regretted what had happened after the failed implant and the horrible week that followed, their pride was plain to see every time Kyle went off to meetings with Abe Torren and Mayor Trimlott. Kyle Jaxx, an unofficial diplomat, the voice of the media, the poster boy with two identities, a young hero whom everyone trusted.

Wink-outs had, of course, been high on the agenda. "We said they *would* be a thing of the past after—" Kyle said.

"He vanished!" the man exploded.

Around them, passersby paused. Several had Forerunners with them—a Hunter here, a Skimmer there. None were tethered, because of course tethering was already illegal on city streets thanks to far too many skirmishes by overzealous thugs. In fact, even the word *tethering* had been outlawed in favor of more palatable phrasing.

"Did you actually *see* him wink out?" Rissa demanded, edging closer to Kyle and standing slightly in front of him.

The man scowled. "Didn't need to. I found his clothes three mornings ago, all in a pile outside the house, his schoolbag on the pavement. Haven't seen him since. The wife and I are going out of our minds, and everybody's giving us the runaround, saying it takes time to establish proof of death." He snorted. "Ha! It never used to. When someone winked out, that was that. But now there are delays, procedures, red tape . . ." He stabbed a finger at Kyle again. "Find out. I want to know what happened to his twin. Find out if he died."

Kyle sighed. "Look, I'm sorry about your son, but the last confirmed wink-out was five weeks ago. We're all separated now, not linked anymore. It sounds more like your son might have just . . . you know . . ."

The obese man leaned closer still, his fists balling. "Might have just *what*?"

Byron booted up his registry database and strode forward. "Excuse me, sir? What's your son's name? I can check to see if there's a match."

The man swung around and glared. His eyes were red-rimmed, his cheeks flushed. But he seemed to understand what Byron was talking about. "You can do that? You have access? His name's Taynor Farchild."

Byron accessed the registry. Getting in was easy because Logan had left him with an encrypted backdoor key to much of the data stream.

To his surprise, the missing boy, Taynor, actually did have a confirmed twin over in the enclaves, though he was still alive. If he'd been in an accident, his death would have been reported three days ago when Taynor had apparently winked out.

"Your son's twin is in the system. It says he's alive and well," Byron said carefully.

Rissa snorted. "See, Mr. Farchild? No wink-out. It's much more likely your son decided he'd had enough of you and gone to live in Apparatum like everybody else who's mysteriously disappeared lately. A new start and all that."

"That's one reason there's a registry," Kyle added. "To stop people faking wink-outs as a quick way to start over."

“Yes, so leave us alone,” Rissa finished “Your son really is a ‘far child’ by now. Can’t say I blame him.”

The man roared with anger and drew his fist back. “How *dare* you—”

Behind him, the enormous Breaker grabbed the man’s arm, squeezing tight enough to force his fingers open and the flesh to slowly turn white.

Byron, Kyle, and Rissa hurried away, leaving the fat man and his Breaker to argue in the street and cause a further disturbance.

“Your power gets stronger every day, Kyle,” Rissa said, grinning now.

“That wasn’t me,” Kyle muttered.

She didn’t appear to have heard. “I really thought he was going to punch me in the face.”

“I wish you’d learn a bit of . . .” Kyle frowned. “What’s the word I want, Byron?”

Byron was happy to offer suggestions. “Restraint? Decorum? Diplomacy?”

“Yeah, all of those.”

Rissa shrugged and studied her mora fish wrap again, muttering to herself as they walked.

A Glider sped past overhead, leaving a green contrail while a sleek two-passenger hovercar flew alongside with a dull droning noise. In the street ahead, in a cordoned-off section, two Breakers scooped out great chunks of asphalt with their bare hands, creating a sizeable hole for yellow-helmeted workers to get at a leaking water pipe. At the moment, Forerunners offered their help for free as part of an ongoing exchange program.

At the same time, plenty of ordinary city folk had taken an extended leave and gone to live and work in the wastelands. The city was far from being deserted, but the street traffic was definitely lighter these days, the daily commute marginally quicker. Especially in the poor, rundown outer suburbs. According to a recent voicemail, Uncle Jeremiah had gone too, vacating his dingy home in East Morley and eager to explore the wastelands in his modified, jacked-up road rumbler.

Byron spied a three-foot-high purple fungal growth on the sidewalk, surrounded by an iron fence with the usual sign warning that it was illegal to touch any of these spore-giving mounds. They sprung up in random spots, and only city officials had the authority to scrape them off roads and other inconvenient places. Wherever possible, they were protected and revered. Forerunners were often found pausing to gaze at the mounds with smiles on their faces.

Kyle's wrist tablet chirped. He hadn't had it long, maybe a month. Rissa had bought it for him one day, casually sliding it onto his wrist and saying, "Network's open to all now," and going on to tell how the mayor had, several weeks earlier, made his first remote conference call with the sovereign in the Hunter Capitol. Relations promised to be much easier with basic communication established across the land.

"Logan," Kyle said with a grin as he switched his tablet onto loudspeaker. "What's going on?"

Logan's tinny voice on the other end said, "Oh, this and that. Just got home. Had lunch with Nomi earlier. How are things with Rissa?"

Kyle glanced at Rissa, who arched an eyebrow at him. "Same as usual," he said with a smile. "Cranky and rude. Complaining about her mora fish wrap. Shouting at passersby."

"Tell her hello," Logan said after a pause. "Oh, and Byron? Are you there?"

"I'm here."

"Kiff says he saw you on the giant stream screen in the square yesterday. He leapt up and down yelling 'I know him, I know him!' and made everyone jump out of their skin."

Byron chuckled. He leaned toward the tablet and told Logan all about the heavyset man and his son's so-called wink-out, then went on to mention how the man had nearly smashed

Rissa in the face for being rude. Only Kyle's power over the Breaker had prevented a bloody nose.

Kyle shook his head. "I told you, that wasn't me. I had nothing to do with it."

Rissa looked astonished. "What? What do you mean?"

"Just what I said. I didn't do anything. I didn't need to. Breakers aren't wild animals anymore. They're smart, and they know what's right and wrong. I doubt he'll stick around with Mr. Farchild for much longer."

Rissa batted him on the arm. "So you *didn't* protect me earlier!"

"Shush—I'm trying to talk to Logan."

"Don't tell me to shush. Have you forgotten who I am? My father—"

"Yeah, yeah, General Talios, very powerful and dangerous, repurposing and all that . . ."

She couldn't help smiling as she batted at his arm again. "If you think closing the Repurposing Factory will keep you safe, think again, Kyle Jaxx of the City."

Printed in Great Britain
by Amazon

19273716R00210